The Badge Meets the Camera

An Anthony and McBride Adventure

Jacquelyn A. Harmon

outskirts press

INTRODUCTION

Hello, I thought that I would introduce myself to you. My name is Sarah Leigh Anthony and I work for the government as a federal agent in Washington, D. C. (which agency is of no consequence to my story.) The job that I have is fulfilling and one that I've always wanted. Some may call me beautiful, with my waist-length brown hair and green eyes, but I've never thought of myself as anything more than pretty. I do admit that I have a nice body, kept toned with exercise and eating right when my schedule allows.

I grew up in Washington, the daughter of Barbara and Walter Anthony, and have an older sister named Katherine, Katie for short. Mom has never approved of my career choice and reminds me of that fact quite often these days. She thinks that I should get married, have children and live close to her and Dad. My sister is married to a good man named Daniel Lane. They've been trying unsuccessfully to have children for several years now. Maybe if they had had kids Mom would lay off of me for a while.

My boss is Director Henry Wilson. He considers me one of his best agents and I have the commendations to prove him right. Of course all of his agents are his best. Henry is in his mid fifties, and unlike a lot of other agency directors that I've met, he still likes to get out in the field with us every now and again. His hair seems to have gotten a little, more gray in it lately, but he's still at the top of his game. He's the one who took me under his wing and mentored me when I first joined the agency. He's a great boss to work for.

Two of the agents that I've been working with these past few months are Patricia Covington and Paul Shapiro. Pat is married and has a couple of children. I'm always amazed at how she can keep her family and the job separate. Paul and his wife have a great relationship. They would've liked to have had more children, but it just wasn't in the cards I guess. We've worked a hard couple of months on our last case and with it finally solved we're all looking forward to a well-deserved break.

It's early Friday morning and I found a great national park in Virginia that I plan to get away to for the weekend. A nice long walk among the snow covered trees, and hopefully the headaches of the past few months will melt away. I'm going to relax and I'm not going to let anything get to me. My cell phone will be turned off, and I'm not planning on telling anyone where I'm going to be. If anything comes up it'll just have to wait until I get back on Monday. I'm really looking forward to this break.

CHAPTER 1

As I headed out, the roadsides were white with snow and the sky was a winter gray. The trip took four hours to get to Virginia, where I found a parking lot that led to some hiking trails. I pulled in and parked.

"It must be too cold today for the hikers," I told myself, stepping out of my car. I unlocked the car trunk and locked my weapon and cell phone in the secret safe that I had had installed a couple of years earlier. There wasn't any cell phone service out here anyway, so I didn't need the phone. I looked around me. There wasn't anyone around, so I locked up my Mustang and started out on the trail. I must have walked a mile or so enjoying my surroundings.

What had been a peaceful walk in the woods on a crisp winter day suddenly turned into chaos. The sound of a far-off rumble interrupted my thoughts, and I turned to see what it was. Up on the mountain I spied the wall of snow barreling down toward me. Quickly glancing around, I spotted a couple of trees in the forest that had grown so close together that they appeared almost as one. They gave me a little protection, but with the massive amount of snow, they were still almost uprooted. The weight of the snow knocked the wind out of me. Thank God, though, I wasn't totally buried.

I don't know how long I laid here, but I knew it wouldn't be long before the sun set. I had begun wishing that I'd told someone where I was going to be now. After all, I've worked for the federal government for how many years now, and here I was without my cell phone or any way to contact someone.

The cold was starting to get to me and I thought I heard the faint sound of a man's voice. Was my imagination getting the better of me? The next thing that I knew I was wrapped up in a blanket near a roaring fire. Someone had their arms around my shoulders warming me up. This must be heaven I thought, and then blackness. I must've fallen asleep.

When I awoke it took my brain a little while to remember where I was. As I looked around the room, my gaze landed on the smiling face of the man I had briefly seen earlier.

"How are you feeling?" he asked as he poured a coffee mug full of piping hot chocolate. Before offering it to me he added a dollop of whipped cream.

I held out my hands and gingerly accepted the mug. "Okay, I guess," was my reply. As I slowly sipped the creamy brown liquid, I quietly told my host that my name was Sarah Anthony and that I didn't know who he was.

The handsome man apologized and introduced himself as Connor McBride. Connor was about thirty-five with blonde hair that was cut short. He was sporting a pair of blue jeans, a gray flannel shirt with the sleeves rolled up to his elbows, and gray wool socks. As he poured himself a cup of hot chocolate, I took in my surroundings.

The log cabin was typical, except for the lack of animal trophies adorning the walls. The main living area had a stone fireplace with a fire going in it. Sitting on the mantel were a couple of fossils, a few pinecones in a wooden bowl, and a black-and-white photo of an elderly man and a boy standing beside a huge redwood tree. The roughly cut coffee table in front of the couch that I was on held a couple of photography magazines, an old thirty-five millimeter camera and a book full of famous wildlife photographs. A Navajo rug spanned the floor under the coffee table across to the Adirondack chairs at each end of the couch. A small writing desk and chair sat under the window on my right. Before I could absorb any more, Connor came and sat down on the opposite end of the couch with his hot chocolate and a plate of store-bought cookies. He offered the plate to me and then set them on the coffee table.

We sat there and sipped our chocolate elixir in silence for a while. The firelight danced in his blue eyes as Connor started to speak. "It's a good thing that I saw you on the hiking path earlier today," he commented. "Not many people go hiking alone this time of year."

"How did you find me?" I asked as I took another sip from my mug.

Connor smiled. "I was chopping wood when I heard the rumble. I hadn't seen you come back by so I thought I would follow the trail and check up on you. I lost your tracks a couple of times with all of the snow. I probably would've missed you altogether if I hadn't seen some movement by the last two trees left standing in the avalanches path. You were really lucky finding those two trees," he stated. "That's probably the only thing that saved your life." Connor shook his head slightly and took another sip from his coffee mug.

I was at a loss for words. What do you say to someone who had just saved your life? I don't know if it was from the fire in the fireplace or the hot chocolate, but I was getting drowsy. "I need some air," I said as I stood up.

Connor arose and asked if I was all right.

"I'm just a little too warm," I answered. I dropped the blanket on the couch and preceded my host outside onto the porch.

The chill of the night air was just what I'd needed. The sky was clear and a full moon lit the forest trees like it was Christmastime. The sight took away my breath. How had I lived in the city my entire life and never been aware of the earth's beauty?

As I stood soaking up the night air, Connor startled me a bit when he put the blanket around my shoulders. "We don't want you catching pneumonia," he whispered.

I smiled and shook my head no. Sitting on the railing, I looked into Connor's eyes. Something about this man made me feel safe. We sat there for what seemed like hours, and then the chill started to settle back in. We made our way back inside the cabin and I was given the grand tour.

The cabin was modest in its furnishings and decor. It had a small, cozy kitchen with all of the standard appliances. The bathroom sported an old claw-foot cast-iron tub along with the modern amenities. There were two bedrooms, each decorated in its own style. Connor's room was decorated with Indian artifacts. The guest room had an Old West feel to it, even down to a pair of old spurs hanging on a hook by the door.

Back off from the living room was Connor's dark room and den. This was the perfect hideaway, I thought to myself. The cabin, the woods, the peacefulness, I think I could get used to this.

I must've been smiling, because my host offered me a penny for my thoughts.

My gaze went to him and I answered, "I just haven't been this relaxed in a long time. My job keeps me pretty busy usually and this is the first weekend I've had off in almost three months."

"Nobody should have to work that hard," Connor lamented. "Listen. It's getting pretty late, so why don't you take the spare bedroom for the night?"

"Are you sure you don't mind?" I questioned. "I don't want to be a bother."

"It's no bother at all," he replied.

We got up from the couch and Connor walked me down the hallway. After opening the bedroom door for me, he told me that if I needed anything to just let him know. As he started toward his room, he turned back and said, "Good night."

I returned the sentiment with a smile, entered the bedroom and closed the door. I leaned back against the door for a moment and then opened it back up and went back out into the hall. I didn't want to seem forward, but I really didn't want to sleep in my clothes. I knocked lightly on Connor's door. When his door opened, Connor was standing there with a bare chest.

"Is something wrong?" he asked.

"Could I borrow a pair of pajamas?" I asked sheepishly.

A smile found its way across Connor's face and he said, "Of course." He went to his dresser and returned with a navy-blue pair of flannel pajamas and handed them to me. "I hope they're not too big." He stated.

"Thanks." I smiled as I accepted them. "I'm sure that they'll be just fine. Good night." I told him before turning and going back to my room. How embarrassed was I at that moment. After all, I had just met the man.

The pajamas were a little big, but comfortable. With the quilt and top sheet pulled back, I climbed into bed. I don't think I had ever slept in a more comfortable bed. Exhaustion set in and sleep came easily.

I'm not sure what time it was when the morning sun streaming through the window awakened me. I stretched and sat up in bed. What a difference a good night's sleep makes, I told myself. As I threw back the covers there was a light knock on the door. "Yes?" I asked.

"I put a clean towel in the bathroom for you and was wondering what you would like for breakfast," the masculine voice said through the door.

I opened the bedroom door and told my host good morning. "I don't usually eat breakfast," I told him. "Most of the time I'm running late and don't have a chance to eat."

"No breakfast? You have to eat something. When was the last time you ate?"

I told him that it was around noon yesterday.

"Okay then," he stated." I'm going to make you a little something while you wash up, and I won't take no for an answer."

I started to object, but Connor put his index finger up against my lips and said, "Shhh." He gave me a wink and walked back toward the kitchen.

I smiled to myself and then headed into the bathroom. After washing up and getting dressed, I made my way to the kitchen. Expecting to see eggs and sausage or pancakes, I was surprised. There on the table was a bowl of granola, a glass of milk and a slice of buttered toast.

"I'm sorry," Connor commented as he looked up from placing the strawberry preserves on the table. "I don't have any coffee. Would you like some hot chocolate?"

I smiled at him and nodded. "That would be perfect," I answered. We both sat down at the table and enjoyed each others company.

After eating I helped Connor wash the dishes. We let them air dry and sat down on the couch and talked. I found out that Connor was a freelance wildlife photographer for lots of different magazines. He sometimes traveled abroad, but stayed mainly in the United States and Canada. He wasn't really fond of flying, and the only animals that he shot were done so with his camera.

Connor didn't own a telephone or a computer, although he knew how to use both. When a magazine wanted him to do a shoot, they would send a telegram to his post office box, which he checked every day. Connor didn't have a television set or a radio, but he did have an old record player and a collection of records.

He owned a four-wheel-drive Jeep that was in town. Every day he would hike to town, check his mail, jump into his Jeep and do whatever he needed to do, like buy groceries, use the payphone, etc. What a simple life.

I told Connor about my job as a federal agent in Washington, and the long hours and red tape. Sure, I carried a gun with my job, but luckily I hadn't needed it very often. At times like this, when I could actually get away from work, I tried not to wear it. "It's never very far away though," I added. "My work also takes me away from home sometimes. I'm always in the United States, at least so far anyway."

I have a first-floor apartment in an apartment building in Washington. I do own a TV, but it seldom gets watched. My life is ruled by my work, not leaving me very much time to socialize.

After we talked for a while, Connor asked if I would like to go for a walk. I told him that I would love to see the slide area that the avalanche had left. "I sort of thought that you might," he told me.

As we got our coats, boots, and gloves on, it began lightly snowing. When we stepped out onto the porch I was awestruck. I paused at the steps and stood watching the delicate snowflakes flutter to the earth.

Connor came up beside me and stood. "It takes your breath away, doesn't it?" he whispered.

"Oh, yeah," I smiled. I don't think that I had ever taken time out to stop and enjoy nature's beauty before.

A few minutes passed before we finally started down the trail. As we neared the slide area, Connor pointed toward two trees. "That's where I found you," he announced.

My thoughts went back to yesterday when I'd first seen the wall of snow. How lucky I had been to find shelter behind those two trees. Although they were leaning over at about a fifty-degree angle, they were the only two trees in the slide area that were still standing. The thought of what might've happened sent a chill up my spine. That was the closest I had ever come to dying.

I turned toward Connor. My gaze met his, and I said, "Thank you," in a low voice. Those two words seemed so inadequate for what he had done for me.

Connor touched my hand and gave it a squeeze. "It's okay. It's all over now," he reassured me in his own low voice. He kept a hold of my hand as we walked back through the woods. The snow had stopped, and the birds were chirping away. We stopped for a while and laughed as a couple of squirrels chased one another through the treetops scattering snow on top of us. It was going to be hard leaving this winter haven, I thought, very hard.

Back at the cabin I helped as Connor fixed lunch. It was nothing extravagant, grilled cheese sandwiches and mugs of nice warm tomato soup. After eating, I insisted on doing the dishes by myself. Connor started to say something, but my index finger went to his lips, and I told him, "No argument."

He kissed my finger and replied, "No argument." Then he shook his head and smiled as he finished cleaning off the table.

With the dishes done, Connor showed me his dark room. Rolls of film hung on a clothesline along one side of the room. On the opposite side of the room beautiful photographs of winter wildlife hung above the trays of developing solutions.

"You do really good work, Connor. These are beautiful," I stated. "Are these for a magazine layout?"

"No," Connor replied. "These are just some that I took when I was hiking a couple of weeks ago. Would you like one?"

"Are you sure that you wouldn't mind?" I asked. "They really are beautiful."

"I wouldn't have offered if I minded," he told me. "Really, which one would you like?"

I looked the photographs over carefully and then pointed to the one of a white snowshoe rabbit nibbling on a berry bush. Connor took the picture down from the clothesline and handed it to me. "Good choice." He smiled. "That's one of my favorites too."

Connor finished showing me his dark room and then led me into his den. On his desk were stacks of photographs and telegrams. He grabbed one of the flimsy yellow telegrams and held it up. "This is my next assignment," he stated. "I have to go to Texas and do a layout for *Woodland Friends* magazine"

"When do you have to be there?" I queried.

"On Monday," he replied as he placed the telegram on top of his desk. "Listen . . . I didn't get all of my wood chopped yesterday, and the fire is getting low. I need to head outside and finish it up. I hope you don't think me rude."

"Can I help?" I offered.

"Sure, if you're up to it. I would love to have the company."

As Connor chopped the wood, I stacked it up against the cabin. It wasn't long before I had to remove my coat in the afternoon sun. Connor had already taken off his coat and rolled up his shirt sleeves. In less than an hour we'd gone through almost a quarter of a cord of wood.

"That's enough for today," I heard him state. "After all, I've got to have something to do next weekend."

Connor grabbed an armful of the chopped firewood, and we headed inside. He put the wood down beside the fireplace in the wrought iron holder. After adding one of the logs to the fire he turned around and glanced over at me. "Do you dance?" he asked.

"What?" I stuttered.

"Do you dance?" he repeated as he went over to the record player.

I shook my head no.

"Everybody dances, Sarah. Come here, and I'll show you."

I was hesitant and Connor came over, grabbed my hand, and pulled me up from the couch. As we walked over to the pile of records, Connor McBride smiled. "Let's start with something slow and easy."

I don't know what the music was that he had put on, but I was beginning to sway to it.

"See?" He asked as he turned toward me, "Dancing is just moving to the music. Some people move in fancy steps while others, like us, just move."

He offered me his left hand, and I accepted it. Connor pulled me into him and slipped his right hand into the small of my back. As the music continued we seemed to melt together. With each movement that he made I was right there with him. I felt like we were in an old Fred and Ginger movie. And then I kicked him. I didn't mean to. Connor had turned quickly, and my step was a little off balance. Both of us laughed and kept right on dancing.

When the song was done, Connor removed the record.

"Want to try something a little faster?" he asked as he put the record back in its cardboard sleeve.

"If you're sure that your shins can handle it." I grinned.

"Hmmm," he thought aloud and then laughed. "My sore shins or another dance with a beautiful woman. That's no choice."

The next muscial selection was from the 1950's. It was one that the DJ's called swing, I think. Dancing to that tune was a lot more challenging. At least Connor didn't try to toss me over his back or slide me through his legs like I'd seen in the movies. We were still quite a sight, I'm sure.

When the record ended I threw up my hands in surrender. That was enough. Both of us were out of breath, and we collapsed on the couch. This had been lots of fun, and I really wished that it didn't have to end. My thoughts were interrupted by the voice of my dance partner.

"You're thinking about having to go back to the city, aren't you?"

I looked over at him. "How did you know?" I asked.

"Your face got a somber expression on it all of the sudden," he replied.

I looked away from him. "You were right." I told him. "I've got to be back at work on Monday. I've been having such a good time, though." I added, turning back to face him again.

"Me too," he said with a warm smile. "But today is Saturday, so we're not going to talk about anything sad right now. Have you ever had popcorn cooked over a fire?"

"I don't think so," I answered.

"Good," Connor said as he stood up and pulled me up from the couch. "Come on, and I'll show you how it's done."

In the kitchen Connor had me get the butter and a jar of popcorn out of the refrigerator while he dug out the popper. The popcorn popper was a rectangular tin box at the end of a two-foot-long handle. The lid to the box slid on and had a pattern of holes cut into it. A foot and a half of the handle was covered with wood. The burnt markings toward the popcorn popper told of its use.

Some butter and popcorn were placed in the popper, and as I carried it over to the fireplace, Connor removed the pillows from the couch. He placed them on the floor in front of the fireplace, and we both sat down. We each took turns shaking the popcorn popper over the fire. As the butter melted and the kernels got hot, some of them would pop out of the holes. We both laughed when one of them landed in Connor's lap. When the popping had almost stopped, we took the popcorn into the kitchen and dumped it into a large bowl. While I lightly salted the popcorn, Connor grabbed us a couple of sodas, and we headed to the couch. As we ate popcorn and watched the fire we laughed about our dancing attempts. Both of us made a pact then and there never to dance in public.

We were enjoying each other's company as the fireplace's light slowly began to fade. "I guess I should put another log on the fire," Connor commented as he started to stand up.

"Leave it for a while, please," I told him. "I'd just like to sit here a while longer with you."

Connor sat back down beside me and put his arms around me. I leaned my head back against his shoulder. I couldn't believe how wonderful the day had been, and this was the perfect end to it. We fell asleep like that on the couch.

I was awakened gently just before dawn. As I rubbed the sleep out of my eyes Connor's voice spoke from beside me. "I just wanted to show you one more thing before you go back to the city," he said in a low voice.

He helped me up from the couch, placed a blanket around my shoulders, and then led me out onto the porch. We sat down on a wooden bench that faced toward the east. The sun's radiant beams began to filter down through the trees. The reds and oranges came streaming through the branches and danced across the porch with a brilliancy unmatched by mankind. As we sat there taking in Mother Nature's gift, Connor leaned over and gave my cheek a kiss. I turned and gazed into his sparkling blue eyes. Smiling, I returned the kiss and put my arms around his neck for a quick hug.

"I love it," was all I could utter.

By the time the sun was up into the trees, we had gone back inside and started another fire. I went and washed up first. When Connor headed to the bathroom to take his turn cleaning up, I was determined to fix breakfast for him this time.

When Connor came out into the kitchen he found a bowl of granola, a glass of milk, and a slice of toast waiting on him. He smiled at me. "I usually don't eat breakfast either," he commented.

"I guess that it's a good thing that I didn't fix you very much then." I laughed. We sat and ate in silence. Neither of us wanted to bring up our leaving. When we'd finished eating, the dishes were washed, dried, and put away. The silence was awkward.

"Would you like to go for one last walk with me, Sarah?" Connor asked, breaking the tension.

"I hope this won't be our last walk together," I answered with a smile.

As we walked through the woods holding hands, I couldn't help but remember what had brought the two of us together. Whether it was fate or part of some grand plan,

I was thankful for it. We didn't walk back toward the slide area. Instead Connor led me toward a partially frozen lake. The banks were lined with jagged edges of white ice. We could see one place where an animal had come to drink and had fallen through.

"This is one of my favorite spots to observe wildlife," Connor said, his voice echoing through the woods.

I squeezed his hand. "This is one of my favorite places now too." I smiled at him.

Returning to the cabin we both got ready to go to town. Connor had retrieved his telegram and packed his camera, equipment, and a backpack. The fire in the fireplace was extinguished and the flue closed. Connor did a once around the cabin checking doors and windows. With that done, we headed toward the hiking trail into town. I offered to help carry some of Connor's equipment, but was politely turned down.

The conversation was slow at first. Neither of us wanted to say what needed to be said. As we came within sight of my Mustang, our feelings surfaced.

"Connor," I started. "I wish that I had the words to thank you sufficiently for all that you've done for me."

"You don't owe me anything, Sarah," he told me, stopping in his tracks and setting his gear down. He took my hands in his and stared into my eyes. "You've already thanked me enough by just being who you are. I've had the best time these past couple of days." He paused. "And I wish that it didn't have to end," he quickly added.

I stepped forward and gave Connor a kiss on the lips. "I feel the same way," I whispered with a quiver in my voice as I hugged his neck. His arms slipped around my waist as we embraced one another. This was definitely going to be harder than I had expected, I told myself.

A little while passed before we finally parted. Connor picked up his things and we continued walking.

I had parked my car in the parking lot beside the trail. Connor's Jeep was still another quarter mile into town. I offered him a ride, and thankfully he accepted my invitation. The drive to town was hard. I couldn't stop the tear that rolled down my cheek as I pulled up alongside his forest green Jeep. Connor tenderly wiped my tear away with his thumb and kissed me on that cheek.

"We'll see each other again," he promised. Connor gave me his address, and I gave him one of my business cards, writing my address on back of it. I told him to call me when he got near a telephone. I was definitely not going to forget this man who had touched my soul. I don't think men like this come around very often. We kissed and embraced again, not wanting to let go of each other.

I finally pushed away, telling him that I had a long drive ahead of me. From Virginia to Washington was about a four-hour drive, and now I wished that I had someone with me for it. After retrieving my badge and firearm from the hidden safe in my car trunk, Connor and I looked at one another.

Connor's flight from Virginia to Texas flew out in about three hours, so he had to hustle. One last embrace and we were off on our separate ways. I hoped that the memories of the last two days would stay with me for a long time.

The drive back to D.C. seemed longer to me somehow. I watched the landscape along the roadside go by in a whole different light now. It was hard to believe that I had driven this same route to Virginia.

As I unlocked the door to my apartment, my telephone began to ring. I hurried in the door and grabbed the receiver. "Hello." I told my caller.

"Hi, stranger," came the familiar voice. "You've been

harder than hell to get a hold of these past couple of days. Where to heck have you been?"

"Hello, to you too Tom," I said dryly. "What's so important that you needed me on my only weekend off?"

"Haven't you been reading the papers? All heck has been breaking loose here and Director Wilson is fit to be tied. You'd better get your butt in here ASAP."

"Okay. Okay. Just let me get washed up and changed and I'll be right there," I told Tom before hanging up and heading to the bathroom.

Fifteen minutes later I was back on the road and headed to the agency. If the director was on the warpath, there must be big trouble, I told myself. I wish that I could have had the rest of the day off. My thoughts drifted back to Connor.

I pulled into the agency parking lot, got out, and went into the building. At the desk I showed the guard my identification and handed him my gun before stepping through the metal detector. He nodded to me and handed my weapon back after I was scanned. I put my weapon back in its holster and waited for the elevator. The building was busy for a Sunday afternoon. I rode the elevator up to the third floor and stepped out. There in front of me stood Tom Henson.

Agent Tom Henson was in his mid-fifties and tended to exaggerate things. He'd been with the agency for going on thirty years now, and didn't do much fieldwork anymore. Instead Tom was the mother hen to us. "It's about damn time!" He said as he grabbed me by the arm. "The director's been pacing the floor waiting for you. Where the heck have you been?"

I ignored Tom's question. When we reached Director Wilson's office, Tom opened the door without knocking.

"Here she is, sir," he announced.

Henry mumbled thanks and waved Tom out of his office. When Tom had left Henry turned toward me. "I'm sorry to have to cut your weekend short, Sarah," he stated, "but this thing has gone all the way up to the vice president, and I need my best agent on it." He stated as he handed me a file folder. "Here's everything we've been able to gather so far. Anything you need will be at your disposal on this case. I have half of Washington jumping down my throat Sarah, so the sooner we get this closed, the better. Let's do this fast and thorough, okay?"

"Yes, sir, I'll do my best," I told him before heading out to my desk. As I sat down at my desk I thought to myself, welcome back to the real world, Sarah.

Connor just made his flight out of Roanoke. He had a window seat and thought he had gotten lucky when a small, elderly woman sat down next to him. Boy, was he wrong, that woman told him her life's story all the way to Texas. Connor turned to look out the window. This was exactly why he wasn't fond of flying. His mind drifted back to the wonderful last two days we had spent together. He was thinking how he might just call D.C. when he reached his hotel.

The elderly woman was now tugging on his sleeve to show him pictures of her family. He turned back to her and smiled. Welcome back to the real world, he thought.

The telephone on my desk was ringing when I came back from the snack machine. "Agent Anthony," I stated as I picked up the receiver.

"Thank God you're all right, Sarah." My mother's voice said in my ear. "When agent Henson called looking for you we got worried."

"Everything is fine, Mom. I just didn't have my cell phone with me this weekend," I explained. "Listen, Mom, I'm kind of swamped with work right now. I'll call you back later, okay?"

"Okay, honey. You be careful now. We love you."

"Love you too, Mom. Bye." I hung up the phone. Damn Tom, I cursed. That's all I needed.

Connor's flight landed safely in Dallas with a plane change and a short hop to Lubbock. Once in Lubbock, Texas, Connor caught a cab to his hotel. When he checked in, he was handed a note from the *Woodland Friends* photography editor, Don Jenkins. Mr. Jenkins wanted to meet with Connor on Monday morning at six o'clock in the hotel restaurant. Connor glanced at his watch. It was five p.m. and starting to lightly rain. He shook his head and followed the bellboy up to his room.

The room was like every other hotel room that Connor had ever been in. How glad he was going to be to get out in the field, he told himself. Stuffy hotel rooms were as bad as flying.

Connor laid his camera gear on the bed and tipped the bellboy. After closing the door to his room and locking it, Connor stood and stared out the window. Pleasant thoughts of me once again drifted through his mind.

The file that Director Wilson had handed me was going to take all night to go through. It seems that Senator Kensington from Maryland had been shot on Friday evening. He was now in guarded condition at the Bethesda Naval Hospital. It wasn't the shooting that we were concerned with, though. What brought me in were the accusations being made against the senator. It seems that rumors of misappropriation of funds on the senator's behalf were surfacing. His records had already been reviewed earlier and sat awaiting me. I'm sure glad that I was given carte blanche on this case. Going through these files alone would take forever.

I made notes about things in the senator's file that might come in handy later, and then I got a hold of two other agents to help me in the morning. It was already going on six o'clock in the evening when I stopped by the director's office. I informed him that agents Shapiro and Covington would be helping me with the records tomorrow.

Director Wilson offered his apology again for bringing me in early from my weekend. "I promise to make it up to you when this whole thing is over," he told me.

I gave him a half smile and muttered, "See you tomorrow." As I headed back down the hall toward my desk, Tom fell in step beside me.

"Heck of a case, huh?" He stated.

"It sure is looking that way," I remarked. "Oh, by the way, Tom," I added. "Thanks a lot for worrying my parents."

"Hey, Sarah, nobody knew where you were and you weren't answering your cell phone. What was I supposed to do?" Tom asked, genuinely concerned.

"I guess you need to LoJack me, Tom," I replied, trying to lighten up the mood.

He grinned and said good night as he headed toward the elevator.

I grabbed the Kensington file and put it in my desk drawer and then joined Tom at the elevator. We rode downstairs together in silence. It had been a long day, and I had been back for less than half of it.

All I could think about on my way home was my bed and how tired I was. The long drive from Virginia that morning had left me beat. Tomorrow was going to come way too early, I kept telling myself.

At six o'clock in the morning Connor walked into the hotel restaurant. Don Jenkins walked up to him and introduced himself. After they shook hands they sat down in the near empty restaurant.

Don was an older man, Connor guessed in his early

sixties. He was gray-haired and a little on the heavy side. Don was very personable and seemed to know his job well.

"Mr. McBride," Don started, "what we need are shots of prairie dogs and their burrows and mounds. If you could actually get a picture from inside one of their burrows, that would be even better."

"What kind of time frame are we looking at?" Connor asked.

"Unfortunately Mr. McBride, we need them by next Monday," Mr. Jenkins answered.

After Connor had given his orange juice order to the waitress, he asked what the big rush was.

Don apologized. "We had another photographer lined up, but he broke his leg skiing last month. You probably know him. His name is Hank Fellows. Anyway, he suggested that we get a hold of you." Don continued, "This isn't going to be a problem is it? We have the permission of a farmer who's got a lot of prairie dogs on his property to shoot there."

"I don't see any problem." Connor told the magazine editor. "Give me a couple of hours to rent a vehicle and pick up a few things, and then I'll go visit your farmer."

"Could we meet here Friday to see what you were able to get?" Jenkins inquired.

"Friday evening it is," Connor answered. "We'll meet here around seven o'clock for supper."

Don stuck out his hand and shook Connor's as both men arose. "We really do appreciate this Mr. McBride," Don Jenkins told him.

After Mr. Jenkins had left, the waitress brought Connor his orange juice. He glanced at his watch and wondered if I had left for work yet.

As I stepped into the shower I thought I heard the

telephone ring. Oh, well, the answering machine would get it, I told myself.

"Hi," Connor heard my answering machine say. "Sorry I missed your call. Please leave your name and number and I'll call you back as soon as I can."

Connor smiled at the sound of my voice. "Hi, Sarah," he stated. "I just wanted you to know that I made it to Lubbock already. I'll be gone for a few days into the field, but I'll be back by Friday evening and call you again. Here's the number to my hotel room. I hope you made it home okay. I'm sorry that I missed you. Take care. Bye." After leaving the telephone number to his hotel room, he hung up. Connor thought how stupid his message had sounded. He hoped that the next time he called me I would be at home.

I had jumped out of the shower and gotten dressed. Boy, I was really dreading going into work today. At least Shapiro and Covington were going to be helping me. Maybe I would be able to wrap up this case in just a couple of weeks, I thought as I hurried out the door.

As I pulled into the parking lot at work I thought about the phone ringing when I was in the shower. I hoped that it had been a salesperson. Then I began wishing that I'd checked the answering machine before I'd left. It would have to wait now, I told myself.

Patricia Covington and Paul Shapiro arrived just ahead of me. Pat had been an agent for about six years now. She hadn't done a whole lot of fieldwork, but was good at the paper end of things.

Paul, on the other hand, was an old hand at the agency. He'd been an agent a little longer than I had, and when it came to fieldwork I could definitely trust my back to him. Being a family man, Paul believed in safety above all else, even if the kids were all grown up. They were both good agents.

In the conference room Senator Kensington's records were split up between the three of us. I took the files from 2001 to 2003. Paul had 1998 to 2000, and Pat had 1996 through 1997. At this point we really didn't have anything specific that we were looking for. After poring over the papers for a couple of hours, we decided to take a break and clear our heads. Paul went outside for a cigarette, and Pat headed to the vending machines. I was just about to head out of the conference room door when Tom came by.

"How are things going?" he asked.

"Slowly," I replied. "Hopefully we'll be down to comparing notes by lunch time. There seems to be a lot of excess garbage among Kensington's files though, filtering through all of that is what's taking us so long."

Tom nodded. "I've been there, Sarah."

Hadn't we all, I thought.

Connor had rented a four-wheel-drive Ford pickup and picked up some camping supplies. It would be incredible luck if he could get the photos that Don Jenkins wanted by Friday evening. It's a good thing I came prepared with my telephoto lens, Connor told himself. Once a prairie dog sentry warns the others, a picture would be very hard to get. With this short of notice, getting a picture from inside a burrow would be almost impossible, but he would give it a try.

Thirty miles outside of Lubbock was Bob Sanders's farm. Altogether Bob owned a total of twenty-five hundred acres. Bob was a jolly old man in overalls. His wife Martha was just as friendly and wouldn't let Connor go into the field on an empty stomach.

After eating a large breakfast of eggs, ham, hash browns, grits, and toast, Connor didn't think he would ever eat again. He thanked Martha with a smile, and then he and

Bob started out.

Bob led the way in his old Dodge truck. Those twenty five hundred acres seemed a lot bigger, Connor thought as he followed behind Mr. Sanders. The field had a couple of well worn paths through it from Bob's tractor, but the majority of their trip was still pretty rough. Bob pulled over and stopped about forty minutes away from his farm. As he got out of his truck, Connor pulled alongside him.

"Right over there is a bunch of them prairie dog mounds, Mr. McBride," Bob drawled as he pointed across the field. "Can't do a thing with them fields as long as them range rats are out there. Government don't give a damn neither."

Connor looked where Bob had been pointing. He reached back inside the rented truck and pulled out his binoculars. This was going to be tricky, Connor told himself. He was going to have to go out there and stay as still as he could until the prairie dogs were comfortable with him being around. He hoped that three days and four nights would be enough time to get his photos. Connor put down the binoculars and thanked Bob for letting him use his farm. "I'll stop by before I leave," Connor promised.

Bob shook Connor's hand. "Good luck to you, son." He grinned.

"I think I'm going to need it." Connor smiled back at him.

When Bob Sanders had left, Connor started up his truck and drove a little closer to the mounds. Once he had gotten where he wanted, Connor set up camp. There wouldn't be any campfire and as little light as possible. Connor was glad that he brought along some infrared film too. It might come in handy.

I had been right. It was almost noon by the time we had finished with Kensington's records. We broke for a half-hour lunch before getting back to the conference room. I really hated this part of my job. Reading this many facts and figures was bound to give me a headache. I could almost feel it coming on already. I popped two Tylenol caplets into my mouth and washed them down with my soda before heading back to the conference room. When Paul and Pat got back to the room I asked if everyone was all ready. Both agents nodded.

"Okay, Pat," I began. "Let's hear about nineteen ninety-six through ninety-seven."

Agent Covington read the notes that she'd taken while going through Kensington's files. A couple of things that she read wiggled around in my mind and I jotted them down.

"All in all," Pat offered, "his records for these two years seem to be in order. There was only one discrepancy that I found. It appears that there is a mistake with the drycleaner's contribution. I wasn't able to find out exactly what the problem seemed to be, though." Pat continued. "If it's all right with Paul, I'd like to look through the nineteen ninety-eight records to see if I can put it together."

Paul said, "Sure," and passed the records across the table to her. While Pat began going through them, agent Shapiro gave his report. The records that he had gone through also had a few similar quirks. There had been money given to the senator's campaign, but not all of it was being accounted for correctly. A couple more things began nagging at me and I took note of them.

I thanked both agents for their diligence and reread my notes. Money was coming in all right, but it wasn't making any sense in the way that it was being distributed. My next move would be to subpoena the senator's personal records. I wouldn't have them until tomorrow morning, so I let Covington and Shapiro go back to the cases that they had been working on. I had a date in Director Wilson's office.

After I knocked on the director's office door, I heard his

voice shout, "Come in." I opened the door and stepped inside. Henry looked up from his desk. "What did you find?" he asked, laying down his pen.

I sat down in the chair in front of his desk and answered, "There are a few things in Kensington's records that don't seem to add up. Most of the bookkeeping is accurate, and then all of a sudden it'll be like the person couldn't add or subtract correctly. I definitely think that there's something going on, but I need to subpoena the senator's personal records. Maybe they'll shed some light on this case."

Director Wilson shook his head and sighed. "I had really wanted this to turn out to be nothing," he stated. "Fill out the paperwork and give it to me. I'll have the senator's bank records to you in the morning."

"Yes, sir." I told him as I stood up. "There is still a chance that everything is okay, you know," I added.

"Sure," the director mumbled under his breath as I went out his office door.

I went to my desk and typed out the paperwork for the subpoena. Why did everything have to be in triplicate, I wondered. By the time I had dropped off the papers with Director Wilson, it was going on four in the afternoon. With only an hour of work left, I went back over my notes. Each separate incident in itself wasn't that noteworthy. When I added up the discrepancies, though, almost two million dollars became very noteworthy. Let's just see where the senator's been spending his money, I thought in silence.

Connor sat near his rented truck for most of the day. There had been no movement for the better part of the afternoon, which didn't surprise him. Two large, loud trucks would scatter away any wildlife. Now it was just going to be a waiting game.

As the sun sank lower in the west Texas sky his thoughts

once again turned toward the avalanche and the past weekend. The pinks and oranges around the wispy clouds reminded him of our last morning watching the sunrise. Of course here there weren't many trees for the sun's rays to bounce off from. He found himself wondering what I was doing now.

When I had reached my apartment, I figured that I had better call my mother back. As she picked up the telephone I remembered my answering machine with its red light blinking.

"Hello?" Mom's voice said in my ear.

"Hi, Mom, I just called to see if you and Dad are all right. I'm sorry that it's so late. We've been really busy at the agency lately," I told her.

"That's all right, Sarah. We understand that you have an important job and it keeps you too busy sometimes." She told me with criticism in her every word. "We just got a little worried when agent Henson told us that they couldn't find you."

"I promise, Mom, the next time I go anywhere I'll try to remember to call you on the phone. I was safe the whole time, though. I wasn't even on a case. I swear," I told her to calm her concerns.

"So what's the young man's name?" she asked.

"Whose?" I asked back.

"Sarah, we've known you all of your life. The only time you have ever felt safe was here at home or when you were with that boy Jeremy in college."

Just how she had gotten from my comment about safety to a man I barely know was beyond me. I guess it must be a mother's intuition, so I answered her. "His name is Connor, Mom, and we are just friends."

Then the inquisition began.

"Mom," I interrupted. "I've had a really long day today. I'll tell you all about him this weekend when I come over. Okay?"

"All right, honey," she said. "We'll see you this weekend. You take care now. We love you."

"I love you too, Mom. Give Dad my best. Goodbye."

"Goodbye, dear," Mother said before hanging up.

Connor, I thought as I hung up the receiver. I had been so busy today that I hadn't had time to think about him. I couldn't believe that I hadn't even thought about him once. Glancing at the flashing red light, I pushed the message button on my answering machine. "Hi, Sarah," I heard Connor's voice say. As I listened to his message I jotted down the number to his hotel. Damn! I thought to myself, I wish that I had answered the phone this morning. Now I was going to have to wait until Friday to talk to him. When the message was finished I decided to call the number he had left and leave him a message.

The receptionist at the hotel in Texas informed me that Mr. McBride wasn't in his room and said that she would put a message in his box for him if I wanted. I said that that would be fine. The message I left read: Hi, I just wanted to let you know that I've been thinking about you too. I look forward to hearing from you on Friday. Sarah.

As the stars began dotting the cool night sky, Connor got ready. He would have to guess about where to dig the observation hole. His idea was to dig a hole beside one of the prairie dog tunnels, place some Plexiglas down there, and wait. This kind of photo was going to be a long shot, Connor thought, but well worth it if he could pull it off. With the hole dug, Connor climbed into the bed of his rented pickup truck. He was going to have to get up early if he wanted a chance at a prairie dog tomorrow. He hadn't realized how tired he'd been. Sleep came upon him quickly.

After popping a microwave lasagna into the microwave, I glanced over my notes again. I wished that I could put my finger on the discrepancies in Kensington's records. There was something that kept nagging in the back of my mind. Oh, well, it would have to wait until tomorrow. Right now I needed something to eat and a good night's sleep.

My dreams were filled with memories of the weekend with Connor. They were nice dreams, but didn't afford me much sleep. The alarm clock beside the bed went off and I got up right away. The senator's personal bank records weren't going to wait. I had to figure out that nagging sensation that I felt.

The shower spray was warm and refreshing. If it hadn't been for the thoughts of today's workload, it might've been relaxing. The senator's personal bank records were going to be interesting reading. Nobody likes people going through their personal things, especially people from the government. The subpoena for the senator's personal records wasn't going to be easy to obtain. I sure didn't envy Director Wilson his task of getting the paperwork for them pushed through.

Connor was awake and up before the sun came over the meadows. After a few hours Connor caught something out of the corner of his eye. Slowly he turned and put the binoculars up to his eyes. There, 250 yards away, stood a lone prairie dog sentry. Connor cautiously grabbed his camera with a telephoto lens and snapped off a couple of pictures. He hoped that in a couple of hours there might be more sentries standing up. Another hour went by, when something else caught Connor's attention, a coyote coming down from the foothills. His camera ready, Connor kept it trained on the prairie dog. As the dog heard the coyote's paws on the rocky surface he barked out his warning. The camera was clicking away trying to capture everything on film. Connor hoped that he'd gotten a photo with the coyote in it too. This was Connor's lucky day. Usually his shoots didn't go that well on the first day.

On my desk when I got to work was a note from Director Wilson. He wanted to see me as soon as I got in. Now what, I wondered as I headed down the hall toward his office. I knocked on the director's door twice before being told to come in. He looked up from his desk as I entered the room.

"I'm glad you're here, Anthony," he stated. "Close the door and have a seat." As I did what he said and took a seat, he continued. "The paperwork on Senator Kensington's personal records has been held up. It seems that the powers that be need more evidence before it will be signed." Henry leaned back in his chair and closed his eyes. When he opened them back up he stared straight at me. "That's going to mean a lot of legwork for you, I'm afraid. Interview everyone you need to and try to come up with something concrete that we can take to the judge. Take any agents you need to help you."

"I think I'll be okay for right now," I told him. "If it gets to be too much for me I'll let you know, though."

"Do you have a place to start?" Director Wilson questioned.

"I've got an idea or two," I replied with a nod of my head.

"All right, but be careful and keep me up to date on your progress. I don't think I need to remind you how important this case is."

"No, sir," I told him.

"Good, then go to work," he stated waving me out of his office.

Director Wilson wasn't much older than Tom Henson

was, but he had been with the agency far longer. Henry Wilson had been my mentor when I first came to the agency. He had made director right before Tom came into the picture. Don't let the gray hair fool you, though, Henry could still keep up with the rest of us when it became necessary.

When I reached my desk I thought to myself that it was a good thing I had worn comfortable shoes today. My first stop was going to be the dry-cleaners in Baltimore.

The dry-cleaning store was on the corner of Preston Street and Madison Avenue. The storefront was neat and clothes hangers were painted on the window. Stower's Cleaners the sign out front read. It looked like a small mom-and-pop owned place.

As I pushed the door open a bell tinkled above my head. There were two customers waiting in line for their clothes when I entered. The woman behind the counter looked beat. Behind her were two revolving racks of dry-cleaned clothes. Somewhere behind them, steam arose above the hissing sound of a press. The building was roasting hot inside. When the customers left, I introduced myself and showed the woman my badge.

She got a little defensive and asked what she had done.

I explained that I just had a few questions to ask her and that no, I wasn't from Immigration. That seemed to calm her down somewhat. Continuing, I told her that I was there to ask about their donations in 1996 to Senator Kensington's campaign.

She stopped me in my tracks.

"My husband and I just bought this place two years ago," she stated. "You probably want to talk to Sylvia and Vince D'Angelo. They owned the business before we did."

I wrote down their names and thanked the woman. Stepping out onto the sidewalk, I looked up at the sky. This was beginning to look like I was going to be putting in a lot of overtime.

Pretty much the rest of Connor's morning was shot. The sight of the coyote had run off any prairie dog within a mile around. Connor took a drink of water and munched on a granola bar. At least he'd gotten a few pictures, he thought. Then his mind wandered back to me.

Around midday Connor decided to check on the hole he had dug. Lying on his stomach he inched forward and lifted the tarp covering the hole. He stuck his head underneath it and waited for his eyes to adjust to the darkness. There wasn't anything moving around in the tunnel so Connor backed out. For all he knew, that could have been an abandoned prairie dog tunnel. As he walked back to the truck Connor began to wonder that if Hank had broken his leg last month, why had the magazine waited so long to contact him? He could've had a lot more time to do this photography job. Of course, Connor had never heard of their magazine either, so he guessed maybe they were just getting started up.

The rest of the day was uneventful. A quick rainstorm slid through the area about three o'clock and left behind lots of mud and one of the most beautiful rainbows Connor had ever seen. It was a double rainbow, with one arch over the top of the other, the rainbow on top being a mirror image with its colors the exact opposite of the lower one. Connor snapped a couple of pictures for the heck of it. Maybe Sarah would like them, he thought.

I spent the next four hours interviewing people from the senator's files. Most of them were business owners, but there were a few individuals who'd given to the senator's campaign independently. I ran into about six or so more cases where the owners had recently bought their businesses, and it was starting to look suspicious to me. What are the chances of seven businesses being sold in the past couple of years, all of which had given to the Kensington campaign?

Around one o'clock I went back to the agency. After a quick bite from the snack machine, I went to my computer and began entering all of the names I had questions about into the system, to see if any of them had records. There wasn't even one traffic ticket or accident report, and none of them had ever been arrested. Okay, let's see if I can get addresses for these people from their driver's licenses then. Not one single hit showed up on my computer screen. This was unbelievable! None of these people had a driver's license? Now things were really beginning to set off alarms in my head. I'd better go and update Director Wilson, I told myself. It's starting to look worse for Senator Kensington.

After updating the director on the morning's progress, I started on the rest of my list. The afternoon went about the same as the morning had, and another four businesses were added to the list. I sure wish I knew what their connection was, besides the senator that is.

At 6:30 I headed back to Washington from Maryland. As I drove I wondered if I would be able to find any of these people in the system. What was the phrase that Alice in Wonderland had used? *"Curiouser and curiouser,"* that was it. That summed up just about everything.

Henry had already gone home by the time I'd returned to the agency. I guess it would wait until tomorrow, I told myself. I still didn't have anything concrete toward getting a subpoena anyway. I left myself a note on my desk calendar and then left for my apartment. Maybe I'll pick up some Italian food for supper on my way home, I decided.

Connor sat in the back of his pickup and watched another sunset. He munched on a few pretzels as he made notes on the day's activities. A radio earpiece in his ear, Connor listened to the weather report. It wouldn't be very smart to get caught in a flash flood out here. A good photographer always kept apprised of his surroundings.

The announcer's voice rattled off the temperatures and rain chances for tomorrow and Thursday. It was looking like Connor would have partly cloudy weather for the next couple of days. The temperatures would be in the low seventies with a slight breeze out of the east. Connor continued listening to the old-time country music station. How country music had changed since these songs had been written amazed him. He began to wonder if Patsy Cline or Hank Williams would make it in today's music scene or if they would change with the times. Then a thought hit him. Boy! Wouldn't his father laugh at him. Now who's old-fashioned, he could hear his dad asking with a big grin on his face.

Connor stood up and carefully headed for the canvas-covered hole into the prairie dog tunnel. It would be a long shot, but maybe he could catch something moving. Infrared camera in hand, Connor got down and edged his way into the hole. He laid there for several minutes motionless, before he felt something crawling on his arm. Careful not to make any sudden movement, Connor glanced down. A scorpion had made its way across his arm toward his shirtsleeve. Connor held his breath and remained motionless. The scorpion spotted a small bug and ran from Connor's arm to capture it. With lightning speed Connor retreated back to the safety of the pickup truck. He made a mental note not to do that again. He then laid down looking up toward the heavens as sleep finally came upon him.

As I arose and got ready for work, I glanced at the calendar. It was Wednesday, and that meant two more days until Connor would be back in his hotel. A smile crossed my lips as the memories of Connor McBride came rushing back through my mind.

When I arrived at the agency I saw the note that I had left myself. I was officially back to reality now, I told myself with a shake of my head. The first thing I needed to do was update Director Wilson. I took a deep breath and grabbed my notes. He wasn't going to be a happy camper.

Director Wilson was on the phone when I looked in his open office door. He waved me in as he continued his conversation. I took a seat and reread my notes again.

Henry's voice suddenly got very loud, and I glanced up from my notes just as he slammed down the receiver. He sat down at his desk and swore.

"Tell me that you've got something Sarah," he pleaded.

"Just lots of questions, sir." I replied.

He shook his head as I relayed all of my findings. He stopped and stared as the information began to sink in.

"What the heck is going on?" he asked.

"That's just it. Nothing makes any sense. I still have about forty more people and thirteen businesses to visit, but I'm afraid I'm just going to find more of the same kind of puzzle pieces. The hard part is going to be finding out how the pieces fit together," I answered him.

The director leaned back in his chair and closed his eyes. After a moment, he sat up and glanced at me. "All right, Sarah. Before you go any further down your list, this is what I would like you to do. Re-interview all of the business owners in question and get descriptions of the previous owners. Let's see if we can find some answers that way."

"That sounds good to me," I commented.

Henry nodded and excused me.

As I walked toward my desk, I had a thought and then dismissed it. A sketch artist would be an expensive proposition, and I didn't want it coming out of my paycheck. Besides, I thought again, who knows what the business owners can even remember after two years? Off I headed once again to Baltimore.

Connor's day began on an unusually good note. As the sun started across the West Texas sky, prairie dogs started popping out of their holes. Connor used his telephoto lenses and began snapping pictures. A few of the photographs contained a sentry, an adult and a couple of young pups. Others photos that Connor took were of a field full of sentries standing guard, taken with a wide-angle lens. Mr. Jenkins should be pleased, he thought. After getting a dozen or so shots, Connor put down the cameras. He would try to get some more photos when the scenery changed with either the clouds or the setting sun.

Grabbing a granola bar, he sat down on the tailgate of the truck and stared into the distance. Not even a whisper of a breeze was in the sky. It's going to get warm today he told himself. Thankfully, he thought, he would be back in Lubbock in another day and a half. The memories of the past weekend flooded his thoughts again. He smiled to himself as he began looking forward to calling me on Friday.

The traffic into Baltimore was a killer. Oh, how I hated the bumper-to-bumper commute. Washington was bad enough, but now. . . I just hoped that this case would wrap up quickly. I pulled up in front of Stower's Cleaners and parked. Before getting out of the car I glanced over my notes again. I was anxious to see what the day's interviews would bring me.

Opening the door to the cleaners, I recognized the same woman at the counter. No one else was around at the moment, so maybe the interview would go quickly.

"Hello," I told her, showing my badge and identification again. "I just need a couple more minutes of your time, if that's okay."

The woman nodded.

"Can you tell me the name of the realty agency that you purchased your business through?" I began

"Martin and Beck Realty," She replied. "James Martin was the gentleman that we dealt with. He seemed very nice."

When I asked if she could give me a description of Sylvia and Vince D'Angelo, she told me no. The D'Angelo's had had Mr. Martin handle all of the transactions.

Great, I thought. This meant more legwork for me, as if I needed anymore.

The rest of my interview was short. The woman really couldn't add anything to what I already had, so I thanked her and went out to my car. As I dialed my cell phone for information, I wondered if these same realtors had handled any of the other businesses sales in question. That might be a prudent question to ask Mr. Martin before I did any more interviews. Once I got the address for Martin and Beck Realty, I called back to the agency to let them know where I would be. Tom Henson answered my phone call.

"Okay, Sarah," he replied. "Be careful and watch your back. You don't know what you'll be getting into. I'll run Martin and Beck Realty and call you right back with whatever I find."

I thanked him and headed across town to Moravia Road and the Martin and Beck Realty office. Just as I pulled into the realty parking lot, I got a call from Agent Henson. Nothing unusual had shown up on the computer, but that didn't always mean that everything was honest and above board. It could just mean that they hadn't been caught doing anything illegal yet.

James Martin was in his mid-forties, I guessed. He had thinning sandy-colored hair and he looked like he kept himself in shape.

"Hello, I'm Federal Agent Anthony," I stated, showing him my badge. "Would you mind if I asked you a couple of questions?"

He stuck out his hand and shook mine. "James Martin. Come on into my office." I followed him into the room and had a seat in front of his desk. He sat down across from me and smiled. "Now, what can I do for you?"

"Could you tell me what Mr. and Mrs. Vince D'Angelo look like?" I asked with my pen and notepad ready at hand.

Sylvia was described as being a tall, thin woman with red hair. From a bottle, he'd added. She had a small space between her two front teeth and had a habit of twirling her hair with her finger.

Vince, on the other hand, had dark hair peppered with gray at the temples. He was almost as tall as Sylvia was without her high heels on, I was told. Vince talked with a New England accent and smelled like cigar smoke, James Martin stated. "I'm sorry," Mr. Martin commented. "Any questions regarding the D'Angelo's business transactions will have to be approved by them before I can give out that information."

"I could get a subpoena for that information, you know," I told him.

"Then that's what you'll have to do. I can't give you any further information without their approval," he replied.

"Okay then, how about you call the D'Angelo's and ask them for their permission?" I stated.

"I'd like to, but they're out of town right now, and I don't think that they'll be back until Monday."

"All right, Mr. Martin. Thank you for your cooperation. We'll be in touch," I told him as I stood up to leave. We shook hands, and I handed him one of my business cards. "Call me if you hear from the D'Angelo's."

When I got to my car I called into the agency again. Tom answered the phone on his desk, and I told him what I'd found out. Before starting the paperwork on a subpoena, I told him that I was going to question a couple of other businesses to see if my hunch panned out. Tom reiterated his caution to me and hung up. Before doing anything else right now, I told myself, I had to grab something to eat.

Connor's day seemed longer than usual. He put the radio earpiece in and was once again listening to the weather forecast. There were a few more clouds now, he noticed, as he watched the sky. He picked up his telephoto camera and scanned the area. Scrub brush, sand, and local vegetation dotted the landscape as Connor panned right. A glimpse of something caught his eye. He snapped a couple of photos and then watched. He couldn't see whatever it was now, but kept watching that area. After a while he spotted a cloud of dust on the hillside. It looked like it might be a pickup truck. No big deal, he thought. The glint must have been from the truck's side mirror or something. He snapped off a couple more shots. Connor made a note to tell Mr. Sanders. After all, Connor wasn't sure where the Sanders's property line ended. It could have been a poacher.

After a club sandwich in a nearby restaurant, I headed for the next business on my list. It was a small grocery store on the north end of town. When questioned, the owners gave me the same answers that I had received at the dry cleaners. They had never met the previous owners, the Dwyer's, and had also gone through Martin and Beck Realty. Two more coincidences like this and I would have no problem getting my subpoena.

I visited two more businesses, and lo and behold, Martin and Beck's names popped up again. Okay, I told myself, back to the agency to do some paperwork. Maybe I could get that subpoena and get back to the realty office by the end of the day.

When I had returned to the agency I stopped into Henry's office and updated him. He told me to make sure that the subpoena listed every one of the eleven businesses I had previously questioned.

"We'll worry about the other thirteen businesses if we need to later," he stated.

At my desk I got started on the paperwork. It took a little while to type up all of the businesses names and previous owners for the subpoena, but I wanted to make sure that no one was missed. I had tried to get everything pertinent in on one form. The paperwork done, I passed it on to Director Wilson to get signed. Hopefully it wouldn't take too long. In the meantime, though, I would call the remaining businesses and see which realtors they went through, if for no other reason than to satisfy my own curiosity.

As the evening sun began to set, Connor snapped a few more pictures. Then as stealthily as he could, he headed for the tarp-covered hole. Lying on his stomach he inched under the canvas, camera ready. Nothing! He must've dug into an unused prairie dog tunnel. Connor debated on whether or not to dig another hole. He only had one more day and a half out here, he reasoned. What the heck? It would give him something to do for a while. Now came the hard part, Where to dig.

Just after the sun had set, Connor started out. First he removed the Plexiglas and filled in the first hole. Having done that, he dug another hole near one of the mounds where he'd seen prairie dogs earlier that morning. He would have to be up early in the morning and lay in wait under the tarp. He hoped he could get the interior shot that he wanted.

Connor returned to his pickup and after a small supper laid down to sleep. He always enjoyed staring at the night sky, and tonight was no exception. Lost among the constellations, Connor slept.

I had one phone call left to make when I received the signed subpoena. I would take Paul Shapiro with me to collect the realtor's records. Two sets of eyes would be better than one.

As Paul and I drove into Baltimore, I brought him up to speed on the case. I had made a list of the people and businesses whose records we needed to collect. I hoped that there wouldn't be any trouble obtaining the files. We arrived at the realty office about 4:30 in the afternoon. Mr. Martin was out showing a townhouse to a client, but Mr. Beck was very accommodating. As we began to pull files, Mr. Beck asked if we were going to be long. He would need to call home and let his wife know if he was going to be late. I told him that he might want to call her.

It was almost six o'clock when Paul and I had finished pulling files. Mr. Martin returned to the office around five and told Mr. Beck to go ahead on home, that he would lock up behind us. As we boxed the last file, I informed Mr. Martin that they would be returned as soon as we were through with them. He nodded his understanding and walked us out the door, locking it behind us.

I opened the trunk to my Mustang, and we placed the three boxes of materials inside. As the trunk lid was closed I took note of Martin's car and license plate number. Something about him concerned me. I couldn't put my finger on anything specific; it was just a feeling that I had.

While we were sitting in the rush-hour traffic, I asked Paul about his thoughts on Mr. Beck and Mr. Martin.

"Beck seemed decent enough," Paul commented. "It doesn't seem like he knows what goes on around the office, though. Martin, on the other hand, knows everything that's going on around him."

"I have a weird feeling about Martin," I told Paul. "I can't put my finger on it, but there's something about him that rubs me the wrong way."

"I got that same feeling, Sarah." Agent Shapiro agreed. "He definitely knows more than he's letting on. I would be careful around him if I were you."

It was almost eight o'clock by the time we pulled into the agency parking lot. After we hauled the files upstairs and into the conference room, I thanked Paul for his help. Tomorrow I would get started on them. Tonight I would lock the conference room door and head on home.

When I got back to my apartment the light on my answering machine was flashing. Both messages were from salespeople. They didn't really expect me to call them back did they?

I sat down to a supper of a grilled cheese sandwich and a handful of cheese curls and then topped it off with a Fudgsicle. After washing the dishes I changed clothes and flopped down on the couch. I turned on the television and began flipping through the channels. I stopped on one that was giving the early evening news. Boring! I turned it off. Going over to the radio I tuned in an oldies station and listened as I put a load of clothes in the washing machine. My mind wandered back to my dancing attempt at Connor's cabin. That had been so much fun. I couldn't help but smile to myself. I wondered if we would ever get the chance to try dancing again.

The buzz around the washing machine brought me back from my daydream. As I tossed the clothes into the dryer I began to realize just how tired I was. I threw a fabric softener sheet in on top of the clothes and turned on the clothes dryer. Tomorrow was going to be one heck of a day, I told myself as I headed to bed.

Connor was awake and out lying under the tarp about an hour before sunrise. He realized that if he was lucky enough to get a photo from inside the prairie dogs tunnel, it would probably kill any photo chances later that morning. Oh, well, he reasoned, it wasn't as if he hadn't already taken some pictures. Mr. Jenkins should be pleased with the photos Connor had already taken. Not too bad for the short notice that he had received on this assignment, Connor thought.

About twenty-five minutes before sunrise, Connor heard a rustling sound. Camera poised toward the Plexiglas, he waited. A couple more minutes passed, and then a couple of prairie dog pups shuffled by Connor's viewing glass. They were closely followed by two adults. One, Connor figured was a sentry, and the other probably the mother. As Connor's camera clicked away taking pictures, he was becoming aware of something else. It was starting to drizzle. By the time he'd finished taking pictures in the hole Connor's pant legs were soaked. As soon as he reached his truck the rain had quit. The clouds overhead had rolled into the area and were starting to build up.

Connor McBride popped the radio earpiece in and listened. A freak storm had popped up and flood warnings were out for the surrounding counties. Connor took the break in the weather to put all of his things in the truck as quickly as he could. He hated leaving the tarp and Plexiglas in the hole he'd dug, but the lightning flashes and thunder claps were getting closer. As he headed back down through the field the way he'd come, he saw another pickup coming toward him. It was Bob Sanders. As the two trucks pulled up beside each other, Bob yelled. "Wasn't sure you'd know to pull out now, Mr. McBride, so Martha sent me to fetch ya."

"Well, let's get going, then." Connor yelled back.

Bob Sanders whirled his truck around taking the lead. They were going faster than they probably wanted to, but they had to get out of the field before the storm hit.

I listened to the morning news as I got up and got ready for work. The weatherman was calling for a cool, windy day with just a slight chance of precipitation. That was fine with me, I told myself. I was going to be spending the better part of the day sifting through the boxes of real estate files that we had pulled yesterday.

Tom Henson was waiting for me as the elevator doors opened. "Morning, Tom," I said, stepping into the hallway.

"Morning, Sarah," he responded back as he fell in step alongside me. "Henry thought you might need a little help going through Martin and Beck's real estate files today."

"It sure wouldn't hurt my feelings any if I had some help," I commented. "It might be kind of nice to go home at a decent hour for a change." I smiled. "Who's the lucky agent?" I asked with a glance over at Tom. His smile answered my question. "Pulled the short straw, huh?" I chuckled.

Tom laughed. "Believe it or not, I volunteered. I wanted to sink my teeth into one last case before I retired."

I stopped in my tracks and looked into Tom's eyes. I couldn't even imagine coming into work without seeing him and being hassled about my latest case. "You're going to retire, Tom?" I asked in shock.

He saw my expression and replied, "Not just yet I'm not. I think that I still have a few more years left in me." He continued, "I guess I'm just feeling a little useless around here lately. Maybe working a case will get the old juices flowing again. Are you going to be all right working with me?" He asked.

I felt like hugging him and smacking him at the same time. "Of course it's okay," I answered. "But I'm depending on you to catch everything that I miss."

"No pressure." Agent Henson smiled as we entered the conference room at the end of the hall.

There were only three boxes of real estate files, but they sure looked bigger this morning. I grabbed two notepads and handed Tom one.

"We have to write down names, banks, dates and transaction amounts for each file and anything else that may seem out of place," I told him. "It shouldn't take too long."

Tom nodded and grabbed a box. I felt a little guilty about the way I had just treated him like a rookie. I grabbed another box and dug in. I would make amends with Tom later.

Two hours later we had finished and taken a fifteen-minute break. I think that we were both going a little cross-eyed trying to make sense of the files. I knew some legal jargon, but boy, were these contracts confusing. As we headed back into the conference room again, Tom Henson set down his coffee cup. "Did you understand any of those files?" he asked.

Shaking my head, I replied, "Some of it, but I wonder who to heck drew up those sales contracts."

"Someone that had something to hide I think," Tom muttered to himself. There was something about this case that was tugging at the back of his mind. It was going to drive him crazy if he couldn't figure it out, he told himself.

As we reviewed our notes and put everything up on the dry erase board, we could see the overlapping information.

Although all of the businesses had used the same realty brokers, only about five of them had used the same banks, not the same branches though. Most of the sales had been between May and August of the year 2002. What was the significance of that time frame, we wondered.

"Okay, Tom," I stated. "This is where you're supposed to be catching everything that I missed," I told him with a smile. We both stared at the notes on the board wondering what the common denominator was between them.

Bob Sanders must've had his foot on the floor, Connor thought. The rain was really coming down now and the tractor path was getting very slippery with all of the mud. A couple of times Bob's truck fishtailed in front of him. After almost thirty minutes the farmhouse loomed ahead.

Connor had turned on the radio in the truck when he'd packed up his gear. News on the storm had interrupted the programming on all of the stations. It was being hailed the storm of the year by one of the radio DJs. Already a couple of bridges had been closed and some roads blocked by downed trees.

Martha Sanders was standing on the porch of their farmhouse waiting as they pulled up. Both men made mad dashes up onto the porch. Martha told them that the sheriff had ordered all of them out of the low-lying country.

"I packed up a few provisions, and we'd better get going," she announced.

Mr. Sanders nodded and looked at Connor. "I'm sorry about yer photo shoot, son," he said. "You want to ride with us or try to follow in your truck? Don't want to lose you along the way."

"I yield to your experience," the wildlife photographer replied. "Just let me grab my film and cameras out of the truck."

Once loaded up, the Sanders', their dog "Buddy," and Connor headed for higher ground. What an adventure, Connor thought.

The storm had intensified so much that at thirty miles an hour it felt like they were speeding. Luckily no one else was on the road. As Connor watched Mr. Sanders drive he was amazed at the steadiness of Bob's hands on the steering wheel. A kind of calmness came over Connor to let him know they would be all right.

After what seemed like two hours, Bob's extended-cab, four-wheel-drive pickup pulled into the parking lot of an old Red Roof Inn. The lot was packed with other trucks. Every make and model was parked with their loads either covered with tarps or inside a topper like Bob had.

"Let's make a run for it!" Bob yelled as he and Martha grabbed the door handles. They all jumped out, Buddy too, and made a mad dash for the hotel lobby. Inside, the sheriff was taking down everyone's names. When he got to them he informed Bob, "Everyone seems to be accounted for except the Hardy family just west of your place."

Bob Sanders let him know that they hadn't seen or passed anyone on the road. "If they had skidded off from the road, with all of the rain that's pounding down, we never would've seen them anyway. Heck! We could barely even see the road as we drove here ourselves," Bob commented.

The hotel rooms were all full and a couple of families were camped out in the lobby and dining room. The kitchen was closed for repairs, but no one seemed to care much. Everyone had come prepared to spend at least one night there. It was getting on about three o'clock when a family of five came staggering into the hotel. It was the Hardy family. They had gone into the ditch a little way down the road and decided that they had better walk the rest of the way instead of taking a chance of being swept away by the rushing water. Everyone grabbed blankets and offered them to the soaked family.

As things began to settle back down again, the electricity went out. Connor was in awe at the preparedness of these people. Obviously they had been through this before, he told himself. This community was just one large family all working together. Connor went and stood watching out the front door with the sheriff.

"It shouldn't do too much damage tonight," the sheriff stated. "Tomorrow'll be the worst of it if the water starts rising. Is this your first flood, son?" He questioned.

"Hopefully, my last one too," Connor replied. "I've seen quite a few things in my life so far, but nothing compares to this. Does this happen very often around here?"

The sheriff replied that sometimes during hurricane season they'd get a bad storm, but this one wasn't going to be anywhere near that bad. This was unusual, though, he added.

As Tom Henson and I went back over our notes and rechecked the findings we had listed on the whiteboard, Director Wilson stuck his head in the door. "How are things coming, Tom?" he asked.

"Well, we haven't been able to find the common thread that links them all together, but there's definitely something here," Agent Henson answered. "This seems so familiar," he added almost under his breath.

The director looked over the notes on the board with great interest. After a couple of minutes he turned and headed toward the door. Stopping at the door he turned and stated, "If anyone can make sense of all of this, my money's on the two of you."

When the director had left, I had the idea to add the information that I'd gotten on my interviews to the whiteboard.

I had hoped that it might help. It was just too bad that we didn't have any descriptions of the other business owners. I wondered if questioning James Martin again would do any good, so I asked Tom what he thought about it.

Tom took a deep breath and let it out. "I'll tell you what, Sarah. Let's go over these files again. This time we'll switch, though, and when we're done we'll return them to the realty office. That'll give us a reason to go back and ask a few more questions," he suggested.

That sounded good to me. "Let's go and grab some lunch first, though," I told Tom. "I'm buying."

As we sat in the restaurant waiting for our food the conversation was a little strained. Tom and I had never socialized anywhere outside of the office. I was about to say something when the waitress brought us our orders. After she left, I began again. "I apologize if I offended you earlier today Tom. I didn't mean to treat you like a rookie."

"Don't worry about it, Sarah. I know there's a lot of pressure coming from all sides to close this case." Tom took a bite of his salad and continued. "Besides, it's not like I've been quite this involved in anything like this for a while now. I am kind of like a rookie again."

The rest of the meal went fine and we discussed the case further. When the check came, Tom grabbed it. He wouldn't let me pay for lunch, so I handed him the money for my portion of the bill. At first he wouldn't take it, but I told him that if he didn't, the waitress was going to be getting a very large tip. He conceded, saying that the service hadn't been all that good.

Back in the conference room we exchanged files and pored over them again. By four o'clock we had finished and compared our notes to those already up on the board. For the most part we had each gotten the same information from the real estate files. There were a couple of discrepancies, but we pulled those files and reviewed them a third time. By five o'clock we were both ready to call it a day. Tomorrow we would return the files and ask a few more questions.

CHAPTER 2

The storm was only a drizzle now, but that was enough. The hotel parking lot had a couple of inches of standing water in it. It would take a lot more rain to get into the hotel itself, though.

Connor wandered around the hotel lobby and into the dining room. A few of the families were playing cards or board games. One farmer was reading a book while his wife sat and crocheted. A couple of children from neighboring farms were running around playing tag with one another. As Connor stood taking in the scene, he felt a hand on his shoulder. He turned to look into the face of Martha Sanders.

"We thought you might like a bite to eat." She said, offering him a sandwich and an apple.

"Thank you," Connor told her. "I guess I am a little hungry."

Martha stood beside Connor as he ate. "Mr. McBride," she started to say, "I hope you got all of the pictures that you needed over the last couple of days. Texas is being pretty inhospitable to you right now."

Connor smiled at her. "I think that I have plenty of pictures, Mrs. Sanders. I'm just glad that everyone is safe right now."

Martha nodded. "Well, we laid out a blanket for you in the dining room near us. Try not to stay up all night."

"I'll be there in a bit."

"I hope you play gin, Mr. McBride," she added. "Bob's looking for someone to beat."

"Please call me Connor, and tell your husband that he's on. I think I might be able to give him a run for his money," he said with a wink. Martha Sanders smiled and said that she would pass that information along to Bob.

When she'd turned to leave, Connor thought, what was I thinking? He hadn't played gin in years. As he followed along behind Martha he hoped that he wouldn't disappoint Bob Sanders too much.

A big smile crossed Bob's face when he heard that Connor played gin. When Bob found out that Connor hadn't played in a while he told him that he would go easy on him for the first couple of hands.

"But after that, son," Bob stated, "yer on your own."

The game came back to Connor quickly. Strategies began to emerge that he'd used when he used to play cards with his father and brother. Connor was really giving Bob Sanders a run for his money.

After five or six games Bob spoke up. "For someone that hasn't played in a while, son, you sure picked it back up awful quick. How long's it been since you last played?"

Connor thought back. His parents and brother had died in a car accident almost eleven years ago, so the last time he had played was in the Navy a few years ago. "I guess it's been about three years or so now." he answered.

"Well," Bob admitted, "I haven't had to work this hard to win at a game of cards in I don't know how long. Ain't anybody around here that's much of a challenge anymore."

Connor grinned at the Texas farmer. "I'm just glad that it all came back to me so that I could give you some competition then."

Both men laughed and headed for their bedrolls, saying good night.

It was around two in the morning when my phone rang. Rolling over and glancing at the clock, I wondered who would be calling me at this time of morning. "Yes?" I said sleepily into the receiver.

"I'm really sorry about calling this early," I heard Tom Henson's voice say, "but I couldn't wait. Everything about this case has seemed so familiar to me, and now I know why. Director Wilson and I worked a money laundering case a few years back." Tom took a breath and continued. "This looks like it could be the same thing, Sarah. That case almost drove us nuts, and if I remember correctly, we never could pin it on the mob."

"Then it's still an open case?" I questioned.

"No," came Henson's reply. "When the man we'd been investigating died, so did the case, and before you ask, he died from a heart attack."

I let out a sigh. "Good going Tom," I told him. "If you get into the office before I do, pull that old case file, and I'll meet you in the conference room. It sounds like the director should sit in on this with us too." I paused and then added, "But invite him in on this tomorrow at the office. He might not appreciate the early wake-up call as much as I did."

Tom apologized again and said that he would see me at eight. I hung up the phone and rolled my eyes. This was going to be an interesting day, I told myself.

There was no telling what time agent Henson had gotten into the agency, but there he was in the conference room, orange juice and donuts on the table, along with the old case file. He looked up as I come in the door.

"Morning, Tom," I mumbled with half a smile.

Tom echoed my greeting and apologized again for his two a.m. telephone call.

Director Wilson came into the room.

"Okay, Tom, I got your note. What's the latest that you wanted me to see?" he asked, having a seat beside me at the table.

Tom went over the points and unanswered questions and then handed the director the closed-case file. One look at the file, and the director gasped. "Good lord! You don't think Senator Kensington knows what's going on, do you?"

"I don't know," Tom replied, "but I'll bet that someone in his office does." The three of us sat and went over the old case and the similarities with our current case. The two cases were almost exact in their details. Names, dates, places, etc., were different, but the set up was the same.

"Okay, you two," Director Wilson stated. "No one outside the three of us is to be involved in this case without my say-so. Tom and I couldn't make the mob connections the last time, and I don't want to lose them this time, so don't let anything leak out."

We both nodded in agreement and then discussed where to go from here. It was agreed that Tom and I would return the realtor's files and ask a few more discreet questions. Things appeared like Mr. Martin was knee-deep in this case, but we didn't want to bring him in and tip our hand to the mob just yet.

Henry decided that we should tail James Martin for awhile and see where that took us. Since Shapiro and Covington had already lent a hand at the beginning of the case, they would be our relief on the stakeout. When Tom Henson and I returned the realty files, only Mr. Beck was there. As we stacked the three boxes on top of one another,

I asked Mr. Beck if he could tell us anything about his partner's realty dealings.

"All I can say," Adam Beck began, "is that he seems to do more business than any other realtor I've ever worked with before."

We thanked him and asked for the address where Mr. Martin had gone this morning. When we left the office we went and sat a half block down the street from where Mr. Martin's car was parked. Tom called in and let Director Wilson know where we were. It was about 10:45 in the morning at that time. Shapiro and Covington would relieve us about four o'clock.

Connor had actually slept pretty well last night. Being a wildlife photographer, he was used to sleeping on the ground so a hard floor felt normal to him. At seven a.m. the hotel was bustling already. The flood threat had been lifted and the sheriff's office had given permission for the folks to go back home. Yesterday's storm hadn't dumped as much rain on western Texas as it had threatened to. There was some localized flooding in places, but most of the farms had been spared.

Families were packing up and departing for their homes. The Sanders' were also getting ready. First though, Bob wanted to see if he could pull Rod Hardy's vehicle out of the ditch. Connor tagged along to see if he could be of some help.

Rod Hardy's station wagon was in the ditch, all right. It was fortunate that in his skidding into the ditch the front end of the car had ended up on the roadside of the ditch. His car should be easy to pull out. Bob turned to Connor and asked if he could hook up the tow strap to the front of the station wagon.

Connor replied, "Sure," and got down on one knee as he

wrapped the strap around the front bumper. That finished, he stood back and Bob Sanders inched his pickup truck forward. The strap tightened and the car groaned as it was slowly pulled from the watery ditch.

Once the Hardy's car was up on the road again, all of its doors were opened to let out any water that might have been inside. Rod Hardy sat behind the steering wheel and put the key into the ignition. When the key was turned, the engine hesitated a bit and then caught with a roar. A cheer went up from the Hardy family as Rod pumped Bob's hand with thanks.

Connor released the strap from the truck and the station wagon and was rolling it up when Bob noticed him. "You don't have to do that, Mr. McBride," Bob said as he approached Connor.

"And you don't have to call me Mr. McBride, Mr. Sanders." Connor smiled looking up from his work.

"Okay, Connor," Bob replied.

"That's all right, I'm done with this anyway." Connor told Bob as he handed him the rolled-up tow strap.

"Well..." Bob stated as he put the strap in the back of his truck. "Guess we'd better get Martha and Buddy and head on back to the house. I hope yer pickup truck faired okay."

They headed back to the hotel and picked up Bob's wife and pet before heading to the farmhouse. Along the way Connor saw many a tree downed by the storm. Some places had washed-out spots where the ditches had flooded over and into the fields. All in all, though, the damage wasn't nearly as bad as Connor had seen on television before.

The Sanders farm had gone unscathed by floodwaters. The fields were giant mud pits, but the house and Connor's rental truck were all fine. Martha fixed another big breakfast as Bob and Connor checked everything out. The electricity had just come back on, but the telephone lines were probably going to be down for quite a while longer.

After eating the large breakfast and complimenting Mrs. Sanders on the meal, Connor offered to help do the dishes.

"I wouldn't hear of it, Connor." She smiled. "Besides, you probably need to get back to Lubbock with your pictures."

Connor nodded and extended his hand to Bob Sanders. "I really enjoyed meeting you, Mr. Sanders. I left a tarp and a sheet of Plexiglas out in the field. I can come back when things dry out and get them, if you want.

"Don't worry none about that, son, unless of course you need 'em." Bob smiled.

"No." Connor smiled back. "You can do what you want with them." As Connor put his gear into the cab of his rental, Bob let him know that he was welcome back anytime. McBride thanked Martha and Bob Sanders again and waved as he drove down the road. When he got a mile or so away he turned on the truck radio. An oldies song made him smile as he remembered that tonight was the night that he would call me again. That thought seemed to make the trip back to his hotel go a little quicker.

James Martin had come out of the building at 11:15 a.m. and gotten into his car. Tom and I followed behind him for about a half a block, as Mr. Martin headed back to the realty office. At around noon Martin left and went for lunch at an Italian restaurant about six blocks away. He parked around back and then walked around to the front entrance. Luigi's had been on the radar for a couple of years now as a possible mob hang out. Since Martin hadn't met Tom Henson yet, Tom decided to go inside the restaurant and order us some takeout.

"All right, Tom, but nothing else. We can't afford to tip our hand right now," I reiterated. "And be careful, just because Martin doesn't know you, doesn't mean that everyone else won't either." We had rules about doing what Tom was going to do. These rules were there for the safety of the agents. I really hoped that nothing happened.

Tom walked into Luigi's and spotted Martin at a table with another man that Tom recognized as one of mob leader Dominic DeLuca's henchmen. Glancing at the takeout menu, Tom placed his order. While he waited, Tom looked around the room. The man sitting with Martin was the only one who had triggered Tom's memory. After paying for the food and heading for the door, Tom noticed Martin getting up from his table. He was headed for the back door with DeLuca's goon behind him.

I picked up on Tom's hand signals as he came out of the restaurant door. Quickly I got out of the car and ducked into the alley beside the restaurant. I could hear arguing as I inched my way down the alley. When Tom got alongside me I put my finger up to my lips. From what we were overhearing DeLuca was nervous that we had taken Martin's records. It seems that Martin was to consider this a friendly warning not to say anything, or else.

As James Martin headed to his car, we retreated back down the alley to ours. We followed behind him once again, and Mr. Martin led us back to the realty office. While we watched the office, Tom and I enjoyed the takeout food. Tom had ordered two lasagna dinners with salad and rolls, not the typical cold sandwiches that we usually have on a stakeout. It was messy, but a nice change.

The rest of the day was uneventful. A couple had visited the real-estate office, and shortly thereafter left with Mr. Beck. Mr. Martin had a woman and a couple of men stop in and visit with him. They signed a few papers and left. About four o'clock agents Covington and Shapiro drove up behind us. It was their watch for a while now.

Tom and I headed back to the agency and informed Director Wilson about the conversation that we had over-heard in the alley.

"It looks like the mob's got an inkling of our investigation," Henry told us. "I wonder what they've been telling Martin to say to us. Everything from now on is suspect."

"Tomorrow we'll go to Martin again and thank him for his cooperation. Maybe we can draw something out of him," Tom suggested.

"If Shapiro and Covington follow Mr. Martin to his house for the night, you two can pick him up again at ten tomor-row morning," Director Wilson told us. "But Tom, stay out of sight and watch Sarah's back. The mob could also be watching the realtor."

Around 8:15 Pat and her partner checked in with the agency. Martin had gone home for the night, so Tom Henson and I headed home too.

When Connor reached the hotel he had already dropped his film off at a one-hour photo processing lab. He looked forward to a nice long shower and a light lunch in the hotel restaurant. As Connor retrieved his room key at the desk, a smile crossed his lips as he read the note that the reception-ist handed him. He wondered what time he should call me later. He finally settled on calling me around seven o'clock my time. That would give him time to pick up his photos and put them in a portfolio for Mr. Jenkins and have any crop-ping done that might be needed.

Around five o'clock Texas's time Connor called my apart-ment. Once again my answering machine caught his call. "Hi, Sarah," Connor said to my machine. "I thought I'd take a chance that you were off work already. I've got a meeting with the mag-azine's photo editor in a couple of hours, so I'll call you when we're finished. I hope it won't be too late. Talk to you soon. Bye."

Mr. Jenkins was very pleased with the photographs that Connor had taken. "They couldn't have come out any better than if you'd actually had a whole month," Don told Connor. "I hope that we'll be able to use you again, Mr. McBride," he stated as he shook Connor's hand. "I'm sure the magazine will make it worth your while."

"I enjoyed the challenge," Connor replied.

When the paperwork was signed and the photos and copy of the negatives had been given to Mr. Jenkins, he headed out of the hotel. Connor finished his lemonade, left enough money for the drink and a tip on the table and headed to his room. He had so much that he wanted to tell me.

The light on my answering machine was flashing when I came into the apartment. Darn, I thought, I had missed Connor again. As I listened to his message, I thought back to last weekend. I was definitely going to have to go back to Virginia and see Connor again when this case was over. While I was changing out of my work clothes the phone rang. It was my mother.

"Hello, Sarah," she said in my ear.

"Hi, Mom," I responded. "What's up?"

"I just wanted to remind you about this weekend," she answered.

I started racking my brain. What the heck was this weekend? I had absolutely no idea, so I asked, "What's this weekend?"

"You said that you would tell us all about your new boyfriend," she stated.

"Mom!" I stated, "Connor is just a friend, and yes, I remember. Listen, Mom, I'm on a case and expecting an important call. I'll call you back either tomorrow or on Sunday. I promise."

"Come over for Sunday dinner, and then you can tell us about your friend, Connor," Mom said. "Okay?"

"If I can, I will. Right now, though, I can't make any promises. I'll talk to you later. Give Dad my love. Bye." I hung up the phone dreading the thought of a personal grilling by my mother. Of course I was sure that Mom would make certain that my sister was there too. I love Katie, but she could be worse than Mom with the questions. Kate was four years older than I was and married. Mom and Kate both think that I should get married, settle down and quit my job for something more sedate. Yeah, right! I wouldn't give up my job for anybody.

Connor went up to his room and sat down on the bed. He dialed my number again. After the third ring he heard me say, "Hello."

"You weren't kidding when you told me that you worked long hours," Connor's voice said into the receiver.

I laughed. "If nothing else, I'm honest," I said.

Connor laughed along.

"How are you, Sarah? I saw the most beautiful rainbow in Texas and took a photograph of it for you," Connor told me.

"I'm fine. I've thought a lot about you too, Connor," I answered getting comfortable on the couch. "I just told myself this afternoon that I would have to come back to Virginia for a visit when this case is over."

"A bad one, huh?"

"If only I could tell you about it," I commented. "Your phone call has made my day, though."

"I'm glad I could help," he said with a chuckle.

"How'd you do with the prairie dogs? Was the magazine's photo editor pleased with the pictures you took?"

"The prairie dogs were very cooperative. I took about

four rolls of film for the magazine. Mr. Jenkins was so pleased he said that they might be using me again in the future." Connor answered.

"So what's next for you now?" I inquired anxiously.

"I've got a little break coming up, and then I think I go to Minnesota for a shoot. I haven't got my schedule in front of me, though, so I'm not one hundred percent sure that's where I'll be going," he answered the best he could. "Wherever I'm going I'll be taking you in my thoughts."

I lump caught in my throat and I choked out, "I feel the same way."

Connor and I must've talked for at least two hours. He told me all about the flash flood and the Sanders's, and regaled me with the coyote sighting and the evening stars in the West Texas sky. And all that I could tell him was that I was under piles of paperwork, and that I'd been doing a lot of leg-work the past few days. Nothing was given in specifics, though, and Connor never pushed for details.

It was about midnight when I hung up the phone. My day would start early enough tomorrow, and I needed some sleep. I was going to have pleasant dreams tonight I told myself, and I did.

Connor hung up the phone, and a smile crossed his lips. Why wait until Sarah finishes her case, he thought. I'll go to Washington and surprise her. He'd have to go home and check things out on his calendar, grab a change of clothes, and make the arrangements. He could probably be there by Sunday evening, Connor told himself. He just hoped that I wouldn't think he was being too forward.

Tom and I were parked near the Martin and Beck Realty office by the time James Martin came to work. James's movements were that of a suspicious person, constantly looking over their shoulder. He seemed very jittery this morning and left the shades down in the office until Mr. Beck arrived. As prearranged, I would go into the realty office and thank Mr. Martin again. Tom would stay with the car and monitor our conversation. When I opened the car door to get out, Tom reminded me to watch myself. He said that he had never lost a partner and wasn't going to start now. After promising him that I would be careful, I walked toward the realty office.

I was greeted by Adam Beck as I went through the front door. Mr. Martin heard the greeting and came out of his office. "I hope you found what you were looking for, Agent Anthony," he said.

"Not really," I responded. "But I do have a few more questions that I hope you can help me with."

"Come on into my office," James said leading the way. "I hope that I can answer them for you. Please have a seat," He remarked, waving to the chairs in front of his desk.

I spent the next twenty-five minutes asking James Martin questions that we knew most of the answers to. His responses were less than cooperative, but we had anticipated that. When I asked about descriptions of certain couples who had sold property, Martin was very hesitant in answering. The couples he did say that he remembered were almost the same description as that of Vince and Sylvia D'Angelo. Oh, the hair colors weren't the same, and their accents conveniently changed, but Mr. Martin never changed their estimated heights or weights. I didn't bother to ask if each woman had a gap between her front teeth. Let him think I'm dumb, I thought.

When I was done, I stood up and thanked Mr. Martin again for his cooperation. As we shook hands I told him that I thought I had gotten everything that I needed. He, of course, told me to come back any time.

As I got into the car, Tom piped up. "I was almost ready to come in there after you. Couldn't you have questioned Martin any faster?"

"Tom, we don't want him to let on that we might know something. I had to make it seem like we were spinning our wheels."

"I know, Sarah. I know. It's been a long time since I was out in the field, and waiting has always been the hardest part of the job for me," Tom replied.

We pulled around the block and came back half a block down the street from the realty office. There was nothing to note on Mr. Martin's movements until about 11:30 a.m. Tom and I tailed Martin to a newer house over on Orchard Street. Waiting there for him was an elderly man and a younger well-endowed woman. They all entered the house at 11:35 a.m. and were inside for a good half hour. When the couple emerged from the house at about fifteen minutes after twelve Tom took their pictures. They climbed into a 1999 Chevrolet Cavalier, and we made a note of the license plate number. At 12:45 we still hadn't seen Mr. Martin come out of the house. We called into the agency to see what the director wanted us to do.

Agents Shapiro and Covington were sent out to act as the next-door neighbors. We were to stay put and out of sight. Paul Shapiro pulled the sport-utility vehicle into the empty driveway next-door to the house we were watching. He and Pat looked at Martin's car next door and wandered over there. When they knocked on the door, it opened slightly.

"Hello, Mr. Martin?" Paul asked loudly. "Have you sold the house?"

There was no response.

Cautiously the agents entered the building, drawing

their weapons as they got inside the front door. Slowly they moved forward, sweeping every room with their guns at the ready. It wasn't long before their gaze fell upon James Martin. He was dead.

Connor's flight out of Lubbock and into Dallas had been uneventful. He wished the same could have been said about the flight into Roanoke. Once again his seatmate had been something else. Connor glanced up as the tall gentleman slid into the row of seats and sat beside him. The man sported a pair of horn-rimmed glasses, a very large Stetson hat, a cowboy shirt, and jeans. He also had on a belt buckle that rivaled the ones that the bull riders won at the rodeo. He was definitely quite a sight. As the plane began to taxi toward the runway, the man began to talk. And boy did he talk! This had been his first trip to Texas, and now he had cowboy fever. He was a computer data processing clerk for his family's business and had gone to Dallas for a convention. As the man rattled on and on, Connor turned and looked out the airplane window. Oh, to be anyplace else, he thought.

"Dead?" Director Wilson yelled into the phone. "What do you mean Martin's dead?"

Agent Shapiro was on the other end of the line. "He's dead, sir. When Covington and I came into the house we found him like that. It looks like he's been stabbed at least a dozen times or so."

"Tell me somebody saw something," the director barked back into the receiver.

"Anthony and Henson are still up the block on stakeout. I'll check with them."

"No," Henry replied before Paul could say anything else. "I don't want their cover blown. I'll contact them."

"What should we do?" Shapiro inquired.

"Call 9-1-1 and make a report. Any questions from the

detectives get directed to me and me alone. Understand?" Director Wilson asked him.

"Yes, sir," came the reply.

Tom's cell phone rang twice before he could get it open. It was Director Wilson. Shapiro and Covington had found James Martin stabbed to death inside the house that we had under surveillance. We were to head back to the agency and meet with Director Wilson immediately upon our return. It was starting to hit the fan, Tom murmured to himself.

It was rush hour as we headed back into Washington. As we inched along Tom Henson was silent. "How did we miss this?" he finally asked out loud.

"There's nothing we could have done, Tom," I said with a sideways glance, "so don't go second-guessing our movements. We've got lots of photos of that couple that he met with at the house, and we'll just have to wait and see what the director wants us to do now."

Tom grumbled something under his breath and nodded in agreement. Everything now rested in the director's lap. He would be the one dealing with the local authorities trying to keep things under control. I was just glad that it wasn't my problem.

Connor's flight touched down in Roanoke on schedule. The cowboy wannabe handed Connor his business card and told him to call if he ever needed computer help. Connor smiled politely and shook the gentleman's hand.

Once Connor had collected all of his gear he headed out to the parking lot. He finally began to relax as he started up his Jeep. The Virginia weather was cool but not cold, and the wind on his face felt refreshing. It was about an hour and a half drive back to the little town where Connor would check his mail and usually leave his Jeep.

Connor's post office box yielded another flimsy telegram

and a couple of copies of magazines that his photographs had been featured in. Not too bad for having been gone for the past four days, he thought to himself. The telegram was for a photo shoot that *Wild Wonders* magazine wanted Connor to do in a couple of months in Canada. He appreciated it when the magazines gave him plenty of notice. They needed his answer by the end of next week, so he'd let it go for now and see how things went in Washington. Right now, Connor was eager to get home and relax for awhile. Driving into Washington would take about four hours, so Connor decided to park in the parking lot instead of in town and leave for D.C. early Sunday morning.

The hike back to his cabin brought back a lot of good memories. The trail was serene, covered with a light dusting of new snow. This was going to be a wonderful evening, Connor mused as he walked down the path.

At the agency Henry was waiting for us. We had dropped off the film at the lab on our way upstairs, with instructions for it to be developed as soon as they could get around to it. We told the director what we had done as we approached him. He nodded his approval and waved us into his office. Closing his office door behind us, Henry said "Okay, you two, tell me everything you saw today, and don't leave anything out."

Tom and I read our notes from my visit at the realty office up to the time that we had received the call that Martin was dead. Just as we were finishing up, a knock came on the door. Director Wilson yelled for whoever it was to come in. The lab tech entered, handed me an envelope with the photos and negatives, and left again. I handed the envelope to the director, and he glanced through them, his expression dropping.

"Okay," he began. "Let's run their mugs through the system and see what comes up. We've got to jump on this before the mob can sweep everything under their carpet. I don't want to lose another chance to nail them."

Tom and I nodded in agreement.

Henry waved us out of his office after passing the photos back across the desk to me. As we got to the door, Director Wilson said, "Wait up a minute, Sarah."

I handed Tom the photos and turned back toward Henry.

"Have you noticed anything suspicious lately?" he inquired.

"Sir?" I asked, curiously.

"Well, you've been on this case from the very beginning, and the mob probably has you on its radar. You haven't noticed anyone following you or anything suspicious like that, have you?"

"Not that I can think of," I told him. "I'll definitely keep my eyes open from now on, though."

"You do that, Sarah, and if you spot anything, call in immediately. We don't need any dead heroes," Henry added.

"Don't worry, sir. I have no intention of letting that happen. "

"Okay then. Get out there and get those murdering bastards!" He growled.

When I met back up with Tom Henson he was at his computer scanning the photographs into the database. So far he hadn't gotten any hits. After several minutes had passed and we hadn't found anything, Tom swore. "This can't be a dead end. It just can't. I won't let them slip through our fingers again," he grumbled angrily.

"Listen, Tom," I said. "Let's see whose prints the boys in blue pulled out of the house. Maybe it was another couple that killed Martin."

"All right," Tom replied hesitantly," but I hope they've got something, or I'll go and dust the house myself."

While we waited for the police report on the killing, I ran the license number from the couple's car. It was a rental from the airport. Oh great, I thought, they've probably already left the country by now. I debated on whether or not to tell Tom the bad news. Before I would tell him anything I wanted to check and see if the car had been returned first.

The woman at the car rental agency had been very cooperative. The couple still had the car and had rented it for a week. The woman who had rented it was one Luann White. The gentleman's name wasn't on the paperwork because he wasn't going to be doing any of the driving, she was told. They agreed to fax me over a copy of her driver's license at my request.

As soon as I'd hung up from talking to the rental agency, I told Tom what I had found out. He was relieved that they hadn't left town yet, and we ran Luann White's name through our computers. We found it interesting that according to the DMV, there wasn't any license issued to a Luann White anywhere in the United States. This was definitely sounding more and more like the mob's doing.

At his cabin, Connor started a fire going in the fireplace and unpacked his things. The glow from the fire made him pause as the memories of last weekend washed over him. Connor had never connected like that to anybody before. It was like he and I were destined to have met. The fates are definitely at work here, he thought.

In his dark room, Connor made photographs from a few of the negatives from Texas. He enlarged a couple of them and put them into a portfolio with a couple of photographs he'd taken near the cabin earlier. He couldn't wait to see my face when I looked through the photographs in D.C. After working in his dark room Connor checked his den and the pile of telegrams. He did have to go to Minnesota, but it would be after his trip to Canada, if he decided to go. At least his calendar was clear for his unexpected trip to the capital.

Connor started a load of laundry going and unpacked the few groceries that he had picked up in town. He hadn't bought much, since he wouldn't be staying at the cabin very long. It was nice to cook something over a stove finally, though. Oh, Connor didn't mind eating cold meals on a photo shoot, but it was always nice to get a hot meal that wasn't from a restaurant. He thought about the two breakfasts that Martha Sanders had made. If she could cook breakfast that well, what must her other meals be like, he wondered.

The rest of the evening was occupied with a warm shower, repacking his clothes, and watching the sunset from the cabin porch. Connor loved his life and was thankful that he could spend it surrounded by Mother Nature's beauty. What a change from what he used to do only a few years ago.

When the fax arrived from the rental agency, Tom and I looked it over carefully. Something about her seemed kind of familiar to me, but I couldn't put my finger on it. The police report had also been faxed to the agency. The detectives had pulled almost thirty different fingerprints from the house. Along with all of the real estate agents' business cards left at the house, about ten of the fingerprints were accounted for. Another seven were from upstanding citizens in the community. The remaining thirteen prints were currently unidentified.

As we ran the remaining prints through our computers, Tom and I brought Director Wilson up to speed on what was happening. He was relieved that the rental car was still out too, but didn't like the thought of thirteen fingerprints being unidentified. Since it was probably going to take a while to match the prints up, Henry told us to go home.

"Be here bright and early in the morning" He called be-hind us as we headed out his office door.

All that I could think about on my way home was Luann White. What to heck was it about her? She seemed familiar and yet I don't think that we had ever met before. I hated this. It was going to bother me all night long now. Even as I racked my memory, I was aware of my surroundings. I didn't see anyone tailing me, but if they were good at it I wouldn't. Of course nighttime was a little harder to spot a tail too, but I felt confident that no one was back there.

My apartment was quiet and welcoming. I searched it as soon as I entered, though, sweeping through it with my gun drawn. Nothing out of the ordinary here, I told myself. I relaxed and put my weapon back in its holster. There's no such thing as being too cautious, I thought, as I remem-bered Henry's warning.

I took a lingering shower and then headed to the fridge. What do I want for supper tonight? I asked myself as I glanced through the contents of the refrigerator. A simple omelet and a couple slices of toast sounded pretty good to me. I turned on the radio and began fixing my supper. After eating I washed the few dishes that I had dirtied, turned off the radio, and turned on the television set. On the local PBS station was an old black-and-white movie, so I left it there. It was almost eleven o'clock by the time the movie had ended. I couldn't even tell you what it had been about. All I could think about was Luann White's face. Damn! I wish I could place her.

It was about one a.m. when it finally hit me. Luann White was our Sylvia D'Angelo. Okay, so James Martin hadn't men-tioned anything about her shall we say large chest, but it would put everything in perspective if I was right. I was dy-ing to share my insight with someone. I thought of Tom, but was sure that his wife wouldn't appreciate the early phone call. No way was I going to call Director Wilson at home either. I guess I was just going to have to wait until tomorrow to tell someone.

The rest of my night was restless. I tossed and turned all night long thinking about all of the events that had taken place in the past couple of days, the money laundering connection, the murder of James Martin, and now the possible identity of one of the suspects. Oh, how I longed to be back at Connor's cabin in the woods. Peace and tranquility seemed a long way off at that moment.

It was 7:30 in the morning when I got dressed for work. There was no chance of my not getting to the agency early today, I told myself. There was too much to check out for a Sunday morning. Sunday. Damn! I'll have to remember to call Mom and Dad and let them know that I won't be over for dinner today. I decided to call them before I left the apartment and catch them before they left for church.

Connor had had a good night and took his time fixing breakfast. It was going to be about a four-hour drive to D.C., and with a map it shouldn't be too hard to find my apartment. He thought that he would start out about noon; that way if I was working he shouldn't have very long to wait for me. He could scout out the local restaurants while he waited. After finishing his meager breakfast he did the dishes and then decided to take a walk along the trail. The morning air was brisk and the new snowfall was glimmering in the bright sunlight. The forecast was for some more snow by this evening, but Connor didn't dwell on that. He would be on his way to Washington by this afternoon.

Connor paused at the avalanche slide area. He was still amazed at all of the damage the avalanche had caused and in awe that I had survived it. The trail had been closed down at this point, and in another few weeks the cleanup would begin. Connor would remember this winter and my close call for a long time. He was hoping that maybe something more would come out of our encounter too.

After a while Connor headed back to his cabin. The fire in the fireplace was a dim glow now. No sense stoking it back up, he told himself. Since he was already packed he figured he would just leave a little earlier than he'd planned.

My dad answered the phone when I called. I explained that I had to work and that there was no way to get out of it. He said that he understood and that he would try to smooth things over with my mother. I thanked him and apologized again. Before hanging up we said, "I love you." I really hoped that Mom would understand. She thinks that my work should be strictly for men. "It's just too dangerous for a young woman, or any woman, for that matter," she kept telling me.

When I had finished my phone call I clipped my holster to my belt, grabbed my jacket, and headed for the parking lot. The morning air was cool and crisp this early in the day. The weatherman on the radio said that we might actually get up to around sixty-eight degrees today. As far as I was concerned it could stay like this all year long.

I glanced around the parking lot as I unlocked my car. Nothing out of the ordinary caught my eyes. Maybe I was just getting a little bit paranoid about the case, I told myself. As I left for the agency, though, I kept a keen eye in my rearview mirror. I thought that I might have had a tail for a while, but then it was gone. Surely not even the mob would be stupid enough to try anything here.

After going through security at the agency I pushed the button to the elevator and waited. Tom Henson had joined me by the time the elevator doors opened. As the elevator doors closed I couldn't contain myself any longer. I blurted out my thoughts to Tom about Luann White and Sylvia D'Angelo.

Tom's expression said volumes.

"I can't believe I didn't see that," he commented.

"Well, nothing is positive yet, but it would sure explain a few things if it turns out to be true," I told him.

Tom nodded.

Director Wilson was waiting for us in his office when we arrived. He seemed a little more enthusiastic when I told him about my theory.

"Maybe we can finally pin the mob down on this after all," he said with some conviction.

All but two of the fingerprints from the murder scene had been identified now. The remaining two prints were being run through all of the federal computers and Interpol. We kept our fingers crossed that something would turn up soon. After only a week on this case the powers that be were screaming for results, and Senator Kensington was one of the loudest. I wondered aloud about whether questioning Beck would do any good. He didn't seem like he knew all that went on in the office, so we'd never really asked him very much, an oversight on my part.

Director Wilson leaned back in his chair and stared at the ceiling. A moment later he leaned forward and let out his breath. "Okay. Do it, but be damned careful. There's already been one murder, and you're at the center of this investigation Sarah, you and Tom both. Go. . . and watch your backs."

We both echoed that we would and headed for the door. Tom suggested that we take his car this time. He explained that my car had been used so much that it would be easy to pick out in traffic. After all, we were supposed to be keeping a low profile. That was fine with me. I called Beck's house and asked that he meet us at the realty office.

While driving back into Baltimore, Tom and I didn't talk about much. He had said about watching some program on PBS last night, but I was only half listening. For some reason the tiny hairs on the back of my neck were standing up. A shiver made its way down the upper part of my spine, and I told Tom to stay alert, that I'd been sensing something. He glanced up into the rearview mirror and after a while stated, "I don't see anything, Sarah. Maybe your radar is off today."

"I hope so, Tom," I replied. " usually when I get this feeling though, it's dead on."

Tom glanced over at me and saw the seriousness in my face. "Okay, Sarah. What do we do now?" he asked with worry in his voice.

"Just be ready for anything," I answered.

The conversation in the car dropped back off as we continued to Baltimore. My gaze panned the surrounding traffic is Agent Henson continued checking his rearview mirror.

Adam Beck was waiting for us when we arrived at the realty office. A quick glance around, and we went inside. I apologized for keeping him from his family and told him we would try to make our visit short. I inquired about any and all of James's customers. As Mr. Beck described the only people that he'd seen in the office, I took notes. I could see that this was going to be a bust. From the sound of it, the only people that went to the realty office to meet with Martin were actual buyers. I gave Beck a weak smile and kept writing. When he'd finished giving us everything that he could remember, he asked, "Should I be worried?"

Agent Henson responded to his question. "If you didn't have any knowledge or dealings with the mob, you should be okay."

Beck looked relieved. "I was just wondering," he said. "When I came into the office yesterday for some papers that I'd forgotten, the place looked like someone had rifled through the files."

Tom and I glanced at each other. "Did you call the police?" I asked.

"I sure did," came Mr. Beck's reply. "When the detectives got here we went through everything. The only thing that we could find missing was the petty cash that I kept in my desk. The cops wrote it up as a simple B and E. They figured some kids probably did it."

"Do you remember the names of the detectives?" I hoped.

"Oh, sure," Beck answered as he walked over to his desk. "Here's my copy of the police report," he said, pulling it out of the top drawer of his desk. "And here's one of the detective's business cards." He handed them to Tom.

"Thanks," Tom muttered as he looked over the report and then handed everything to me.

I read the report noting that one of the detectives had been Rick Springer. Rick and I used to be detectives with the Baltimore Police Department before I became a federal agent. Rick was a veteran detective at the Baltimore P.D. and a good cop. I didn't know Detective Martinez.

The report sounded like they'd done their investigation by the book. There was something fishy about it though, and I made a note to call Rick later and get his take on the break-in.

We thanked Mr. Beck and walked out with him. He locked the door behind us, jumped in his car and took off.

Tom and I pulled out into traffic heading back toward D.C. I told Tom about the family inquisition I was missing at my parents' house.

"So who's the mystery man your family wants to find out about?" Tom asked with a quick glance my way.

"Just a man that I met last weekend and that I'd like to get to know better. And that's all I'm going to say," I told him.

Tom laughed. "Don't worry, Sarah, I agree that your life is just that . . . your life."

"I appreciate that Tom." I smiled.

Connor McBride was enjoying the drive to Washington. It had been a while since he had driven his Jeep any distance. It felt good to be driving his own vehicle instead of a rental. While Connor was enjoying his drive along interstate eighty-one, he fell in behind an older car driven by a white-haired woman. He wondered where she would be going by herself on a day like today. Not many older people, it seemed, drove very far by themselves. About three miles past the Raphine exit the woman's car blew a tire. She skillfully pulled it to the side of the road and stopped. Connor slowed down and pulled in behind her putting on his four way flashers. When he got out of his Jeep he was careful not to alarm the woman. She had opened her door and was getting out when he spoke.

"Hello. Would you like some help with your tire?"

The woman smiled sweetly and nodded her head as she replied. "Thank you, I haven't had a flat tire since my husband died fifteen years ago. I thought the tires were still good."

"Sometimes even new tires can blow without any warning," Connor said as he pulled the jack out of his Jeep. He really didn't want to mess with the jack that came with her car.

While Connor loosened the lug nuts on the tire and then jacked the car up, the woman went and opened her trunk. She began pulling everything out of the way so that he would be able to get to the spare tire. After doing that, she introduced herself as Cora Blankenship. She was on her way to her daughter's house to see her new grandbaby. This was grandchild number six for her, she said proudly.

Connor nodded to her and smiled. "It's nice meeting you, Mrs. Blankenship. My name is Connor McBride."

"And where are you headed on such a beautiful day?" Cora asked, keeping the conversation going.

"To surprise a friend of mine," he replied, pulling off the car's tire. As he rolled it to the back of her car he continued. "I'm hoping she'll be able to take a little break when I get there. She's a very busy lady."

Cora smiled as Connor picked the tire up out of her trunk. "I'm sure she'll make time for a nice young man like yourself. My husband was always thoughtful like that too. Those were the days when gentlemen opened doors for women and gas station attendants pumped your gas for you. Sometimes I wonder why we ever got away from that."

Connor returned her smile as he knelt down and slid her spare tire onto the car. Things had seemed so much simpler back then. He thought of stories his grandparents had told him. Everything had seemed so romantic back then. As the last lug nut was tightened, Cora thanked Connor. He placed her bad tire in the trunk with instructions for her to have it fixed first thing Monday morning. She replaced the contents of her car trunk while Connor put the jack back in his Jeep and wiped his hands off on a rag he had.

When Cora had finished reloading her car trunk she grabbed her purse from the front seat and pulled out a twenty-dollar bill.

"Please let me pay you, Mr. McBride." She said trying to hand the bill to him.

Connor placed his hand on top of hers and politely told her, "No thank you." He told her to put the twenty dollars toward fixing the flat, that his payment was her cheerful smile. She slowly returned the money to her purse. Connor opened the driver side door for her and she climbed into her car. As he carefully closed the door she opened the window.

"I hope that your young lady knows what a catch she's getting." Cora smiled at him.

Connor smiled back and replied, "I hope so too." He watched Cora Blankenship drive off and wished his grandparents were still around. Back on the road he was even more eager to get to Washington.

Tom pulled his car into the parking lot back at the agency, and we got out. As we were walking toward the building Tom commented that my radar must've been out of whack. The words had no sooner left his mouth when a rifle bullet hit me in the left shoulder. Its force knocking me to the ground between a couple of cars. Instinctively I drew my gun and looked over at Tom. "Are you okay?" I asked him when the bullet that had hit me was followed by three more shots.

Tom answered yes and asked how badly I was hit.

I surveyed my left shoulder. "Well," I told him, "the left arm's not good for anything right now, and it's bleeding pretty good. I don't think the bullet hit any bones, though. I'm trying not to let the pain get the best of me. but I think it's a losing battle."

Tom handed me his handkerchief, and I pressed it into the blood-soaked wound. God, that hurt! The parking lot had come alive now with the security guards from our building. Their sweep of the area failed to yield anything, and I was escorted into the building. As I waited for the ambulance, Director Wilson hurried downstairs to find out what had happened.

His worried expression scared me. "How are you doing, Anthony?" he asked me, very official like.

"It's a good thing the guy wasn't a very good shot," I quipped. "It's just a hole through my shoulder, sir. It doesn't feel like it hit the bone."

Henry nodded at my assessment and told agents Hart and Maxwell to ride along with me to the hospital and to stay there with me. As the ambulance pulled up outside, Henry asked Tom to come up to his office and give him a report of the morning's activities. Tom glanced over at me, and I gave him a weak smile and a nod as they helped me up on the gurney.

"Hey, Tom," I exclaimed as he turned toward the elevators. He stopped and turned back around. "Don't tell my folks, okay?" I begged him.

"You have my solemn promise on it, Sarah." He smiled. He knew right then that I was going to be all right.

I wished that they would shut off that stupid siren as we headed to the hospital. The throbbing in my shoulder was enough without my head throbbing too. The EMT's had taken my vitals and were in touch with the hospital. A doctor there okayed an intravenous drip to keep me from going into shock from the blood loss. I was feeling somewhat groggy, but the pain was keeping me awake.

Connor's trip the rest of the way into Washington D.C. was uneventful. He found my apartment building okay and waited outside in his Jeep. It was about three o'clock in the afternoon when Connor decided to check the federal building. As the guard let him into the parking lot, he spotted my Mustang. He pulled into the empty space alongside it and got out. Once inside the building, as he waited to go through security, he heard the buzz about an agent getting shot earlier. The back of Connor's neck got a chill as he turned back toward the front door. A hand on his shoulder stopped him.

"Did you need some help?" the guard asked rather gruffly.

"No. No, thank you. I don't think that my friend is here today," Connor answered. The guard looked him up and down twice and then walked away.

As Connor walked to his Jeep he wondered to himself what I had gotten myself into. He checked his map for the nearest hospital.

Once I'd arrived at the hospital I was examined, x-rayed, and prepped for surgery. Agents Hart and Maxwell stood post outside each room that I was wheeled into.

I guess the surgery went okay. I came to in the recovery room with a doozie of a bandage, an IV, and evidently something for the pain. I had guessed that that was why my shoulder wasn't hurting anymore. I glanced around the room. How cold and uninviting it looked at that moment. Then my thoughts turned to my family and Connor. What would they say when they found out? I was sure I would get more sympathy from Connor. This would just be one more weapon in my mother's arsenal against my being an agent.

By five o'clock the staff had put me in a private room. Director Wilson came by to check on me shortly thereafter. The doctors had given him an update on my surgery and the bullet was sent with agent Hart to the lab, the director informed me.

"Tom said that you didn't want your family notified. Have you changed your mind about that any?" Henry questioned.

"No," I answered. "It isn't all over the news, is it?"

"All that the media know is that there was a disturbance downtown today. We're keeping it as quiet as we can, and everyone, including the hospital staff have been told no names are to be leaked."

"Good," I told him as I laid my head back and closed my

eyes. "Maybe my parents won't find out that I was shot then. Make sure that no one answers my phone and tells my folks, okay? Just tell them that I had to go out of town for a case."

"If you're sure that that's what you want, Sarah, I'll take care of it. If you need anything, just let me know," Director Wilson told me. "I have an agent checking everyone that comes through the lobby, and one checking out the hospital workers' ID badges."

"You don't really think that someone would try anything in here, do you? Couldn't this just have been a warning?"

"Maybe, Sarah, but I'm not taking any chances." Henry got up and headed for the door.

"Sir? You said that if I needed anything to ask," I blurted out.

He stopped halfway to the door and turned around.

"How about the police report on the breaking and entering at Martin and Beck Realty?" I asked.

"What? You want to work from your hospital room? No way!" He exclaimed.

"Aww, come on, sir. I know one of the detectives who worked the case. I'll just ask him a few questions, and if nothing pops up on the radar, I'll drop it."

The director glared at me. "You're not going to let this go, are you? If I say no you'll probably just go to someone else to get it for to you, huh?" I gave him a grin and nodded. "Damn you, Anthony," he remarked. He paused to think about my request. "Okay, but only the B and E report. The rest of your case stays with Shapiro and Covington. No arguments!"

"Let Tom stay on it too, sir." I added. "He really wants this one."

"Okay, okay," Henry said as he shook his head. "Are you sure there's nothing else?"

I gave him a weak smile and said, "I'm sure. Thank you for coming by and checking on me. Now I think that I'll take a little nap," I said with a yawn.

"Get better, Sarah," Director Wilson said opening the door to my hospital room.

Connor McBride arrived at the hospital about 5:30 in the afternoon. In the lobby he showed his driver's license to the agent on duty. He was logged in and asked what his business was there.

"A friend of mine had surgery earlier today," Connor told him. He asked innocently what was going on. The agent told Connor to never mind, and that he hoped Connor's friend was okay. Now to find Sarah, he told himself.

Connor went to the nurse's station, and just as he thought, no one named Sarah Anthony was registered. Connor sat down in the lobby and waited. Around 5:40 p.m. he saw an older, distinguished-looking man exit the elevator and talk to the agent checking ID's. "Now all I have to do is wait," Connor thought. Forty-five minutes later, a man came into the hospital, showed a badge to the guard checking ID's, and then headed for the elevators. He had a file folder in his hand, and as he pushed the elevator call button Connor joined him. McBride said hello when the man gave him a nod. "Don't you just hate hospitals?" Connor asked.

"Yep," was the man's reply as the elevator doors opened. There were five people awaiting the elevator, Connor, the agent, two nurses, and an older woman.

"What floors do you need?" asked the agent. The nurses wanted the second floor. The elderly woman wanted four, and Connor replied, "Fifth floor please." The buttons were pushed and the elevator took off.

On the second floor the two nurses got off and a doctor got on. At the third floor we picked up another nurse. On the fourth floor, the doctor, the older woman, and the agent all got off. As Connor held the elevator door open for an orderly, he made a mental note of where the agent went. The elevator doors closed, and the three of them exited on the fifth floor. Connor glanced around and then headed down the hall to the men's room. He figured that he would wait a few minutes before calling for the elevator again. It might look suspicious if he just kept wandering around the halls of the fifth floor.

The door to my hospital room opened, and Paul Shapiro glanced around it. "So," he said. "this is how to go about getting out of work."

I gave Paul a half smile and asked if that was the B and E report on the Martin and Beck Realty that he had in his hand.

"Nice to see you too," he replied, walking toward my hospital bed. Paul continued. "Director Wilson said to tell you that you can have the file for two days only, and whatever you find out comes straight to us. No arguments, either, and that's an order." He handed me the file when he finished his lecture.

"Okay, I've got it. I probably don't even need that much time, but I'll take it. And I promise to call if I find anything important to the case."

Agent Shapiro's demeanor softened, and he asked me if I needed anything else.

"Just a new shoulder," I replied jokingly. We talked for a little while longer about what Tom and I had found out and where the case seemed to be going. Paul promised not to let me down, as he headed for the door.

I told him to watch his back before he exited my room. He promised that he would and gave me a wave, letting the door close behind him.

Connor waited fifteen minutes and then walked back to the elevators. As he pushed the call button and awaited the conveyance, Connor hoped that I hadn't been injured too seriously. We had kind of hit things off and really wanted to see where it would lead. The elevator was empty when it arrived on the fifth floor. As Connor stepped inside, a woman's voice said, "Hold the elevator please." Connor's left hand darted out and held the door open. A middle-aged woman came hurrying toward the elevator. "Thank you," she sputtered as she entered. "Lobby, please."

Connor let the door close and pushed the L button. The elevator lurched a little bit and began its descent. Its passengers stared at the lit floor numbers as it stopped on the fourth floor. Connor stepped out and headed for the nurse's station. As he approached it a young redheaded nurse looked up and smiled at him.

"Hi," she said. "Can I help you?"

Connor returned her smile and asked if the gentleman in the gray suit was still on the floor.

"I'm sorry. You just missed him. Would you like me to see if I can catch him in the lobby?"

"No, that's okay. I'll catch up with him later. Do you know if he got in to see the patient he was looking for?"

"Oh, yes, the young lady is in room four thirteen down the hall. He didn't stay very long, though," the redhead offered.

"I guess I should look in and see if she needs anything else then," Connor remarked with a smile. "Thank you for your help."

The redheaded nurse watched Connor as he walked down the hallway and wondered if he was married.

The door to my hospital room opened quietly, and Connor peeked around it. I was asleep with the file folder on my lap. He looked at the bandage on my shoulder and the IV in my arm. This wasn't exactly the way he had pictured our next meeting to be like. Connor stepped into the room and quietly set a chair next to my bed. Oh, how beautiful I looked sleeping, he told himself. He gently put his hand on mine as he sat and watched me sleep.

I slowly became aware of the warmth on my right hand and turned my head toward it. As my eyes fluttered open I was greeted by Connor's smiling face. I couldn't help but smile back.

"How did you . . . ?" I questioned.

"I thought that I would surprise you with a visit, but it seems the surprise is on me," he said. "How are you feeling?"

"The shoulder's kind of sore, but the meds are keeping the pain tolerable. How did you find me?" I asked.

Connor started telling his story from the time he got home, to changing Cora Blankenship's flat tire, to hearing about the shooting at the agency and then following the gentleman in the gray suit to my room.

I laughed as he told about following Paul Shapiro. "Paul would have a fit if he'd known you were able to follow him to me, but I'm glad that you did. I've missed you this past week Connor." I lightly squeezed his hand. "I'm sorry that it's under these circumstances, though."

"Don't worry, Sarah, I'm here and I'm not going anywhere anytime soon." He carefully squeezed my hand back. "I know that you can't tell me any details, Sarah, but are you still in danger?"

"The director thinks it could have just been a warning to us," I replied. "But everyone here is being checked out just in case." As I moved trying to get a little more comfortable, the file on my lap fell to the floor. Damn, I thought. I hadn't even gotten around to calling Detective Springer.

Connor picked up the file and straightened it up for me. As he handed it to me, he asked if there was anything else that he could do.

"Would you please hand me the telephone over there?" I asked, pointing to the stand beside the bed.

"Sure," Connor replied. After handing the telephone to me he asked, "Do you need me to wait outside?"

"No, that's okay. Rick Springer is a detective with the Baltimore Police Department. I'm just checking up on a breaking and entering case that happened a couple of days ago."

"Detective Springer," Rick said as he answered the ringing phone on his cluttered desk.

"Hi, Rick," I said into the receiver.

"Well, hi, Sarah." Rick smiled to himself. "What's new up on the hill?"

"Nothing I can't handle," I kidded. "I do need to pick your brain for a moment, though."

"Sure thing, Sarah. What do you need from me?"

"Do you have any leads on the B and E at Martin and Beck Realty?" I asked.

"Hang on a sec and let me find the case file." Rick told me as he rummaged through the files on top of his desk. After locating it, he quickly read through it. "Martinez and I thought that something more was missing than the petty cash, but Beck said that was all that was missing. He seemed a little nervous about talking to us at first. I didn't think much of it at the time, though. We talked to a couple of our snitches," Rick continued, "and according to them, word on the street is that nobody went near the place. What's up?"

"That's just what I would like to know. You knew that his partner, James Martin was killed recently, didn't you?"

"We heard about the stabbing but didn't connect him

with the realty office at first. Want me to do some digging for you?"

"I'll let you know, Rick," I answered. "Thanks for the info, though. Maybe when my caseload lightens you, Jan, and I can get together."

"I know Jan would like that," Rick told me. "Stay safe and don't be such a stranger, okay?"

"You too, Rick," I told him before hanging up the phone. That had seemed like a dead end. I was lost in thought when a touch on my hand brought me back to the present. I glanced at Connor and gave him a weak smile.

"Things didn't go the way you were hoping, did they?" he asked quietly.

"If only I could tell you, and now my case has been taken away from me because of this," I said, nodding toward my left shoulder.

The light squeeze on my hand made me turn back toward my visitor. His sympathetic eyes were comforting.

"I know. I know." I smiled at him. "Everything is going to be all right."

"And I'm here to make sure of it" He said warmly. The tone of his voice reassured me that he meant what he said. Things would work out. We talked for a while and then the nurse came and informed us that the visiting hours were over. After she left, Connor stood up and said that he had better go.

"If you're up to it, I would like to come back again tomorrow to see you." He smiled.

"You'd better!" I smiled back.

Before leaving, Connor came close and kissed me on the forehead. "Be good," he whispered, and then he kissed me tenderly on the lips.

My night passed uneventfully. I don't think I got much

sleep, though. The case had been nagging at my brain all night. I wished that I could figure out how all of the pieces went together. Around 8:30 in the morning Tom Henson stopped by my hospital room. He looked haggard and worried.

"Hi, Tom." I said when the door to my room opened.

"How'd you know that it would be me?" he asked.

"Why wouldn't my partner come to visit?" I answered.

The word partner must've picked up Tom's spirits, because he smiled. As he approached the side of my bed he spotted the file folder on the chair. Nodding toward it, he asked, "So did you learn anything new?"

When Tom picked up the file folder and sat down in the chair I answered his question. "I talked to detective Springer yesterday, and he couldn't give me much. He said that Beck seemed to be holding something back, but that just doesn't make any sense. Unless . . . "

"Unless what?" Tom asked, edging closer to the side of my bed.

"Tom," I said with urgency in my voice. "Get the case files when you get back to the office and then call me. I think we might be able to figure this case out after all. And could you pick me up some paper and something to write with? I need to jot a few things down."

"Sure, Sarah," Tom replied. "Give me a couple of minutes, and I'll be right back."

As Tom left for the gift shop, the wheels in my mind were going about ninety miles an hour. Everything was suddenly beginning to fall into place. I would have to check on a couple of things that didn't fit right now, but most of the case was looking clearer to me.

Tom returned a few minutes later carrying a paper bag. "Sorry about the notepad, Sarah, but this was all they had," he said as he handed me the bag.

I laughed as I pulled the notebook out of the bag. The cover had a big, wide-eyed cat on it, and each page of the notebook had the same cat playing with a ball of yarn in the lower right-hand corner. "This will be fine, Tom," I told him.

We talked for a couple more minutes about his family and my family. My mother had called and was told that I was out of town on assignment. Tom asked if I was sure that that was how I wanted to handle them.

"Are you kidding, Tom?!" I exclaimed. "My mother would not only raise hell with me for getting shot, but she would also raise hell with you for not keeping me safe as my partner. Trust me, Tom, that's one can of worms that we really don't want to open," I paused. "No, we'd better leave things just the way they are."

"Okay, Sarah, you know your family. I just thought that you might like some visitors."

"You guys are my family, Tom," I said as I looked into his eyes. They looked so sad today. "I am going to be all right, you know."

"I know. I just keep thinking that it should have been me who got shot."

"Why? Because I'm a woman?" I snapped back at him.

"Maybe, but also because I'm involved in this case just as deeply as you are."

"Don't worry about it, okay?" I tried to console him. "No major harm was done, and with a couple of days of therapy I'll be as good as new. There's nothing you could have done, Tom. Try to forget about it and move on. I'm okay. Really."

Tom glanced up at me and gave me half smile. "Okay, kiddo, I'll try. Let me get to the office now and see if we can get this case solved. I'll call you as soon as I've got the files," he said as he headed for the door. When his hand was on the doorknob he turned back toward me. "Take care, okay?" he said.

I nodded and responded, "Now get going before you're late for work." I finally got a smile out of Tom as he opened the door and left. I opened the notebook and began making notes on the case and coincidences that had popped up. At least I was keeping busy now and not sitting in this hospital bed vegetating from the mind numbing television programs.

Connor had gotten a hotel room just down the street from the hospital. His night's sleep wasn't much better than mine had been, but for different reasons. Connor never slept very well in hotels. They were usually noisy and always had that disinfectant odor about them. And what's with the windows that don't open? Not that he'd probably want to open them, but it's the thought.

A knock came at Connor's door about eight a.m. It was room service with his breakfast. After paying for it and leaving a generous tip, Connor sat down to eat. His breakfast consisted of two strips of bacon, a couple of pancakes, and a glass each of milk and orange juice. These were things that couldn't be goofed up when being cooked, not like eggs could be.

By 8:30 Connor was wondering what to do with his day. He didn't want to spend all of it at the hospital. Surely I would have more visitors coming by than I wanted. He got out the portfolio of pictures that he had brought for me and grabbed the phone book. When he'd found an ad for a frame shop down the street, he decided to walk over there and see what they could do with some of his photographs.

The framing shop was a small place, but with quite a large inventory. Picture frames and mats were hung or stacked by each wall. When Connor entered, a thin man wearing a carpenter's apron greeted him.

"Good morning, sir," he smiled, "What can I do for you today?"

Connor pulled the photos out of the portfolio and replied. "I was wondering what kind of matting you could do for these."

The gentleman glanced at the pictures and commented on how good they were as he headed toward the work area. He placed the photos on the table and grabbed a couple of mat samples. One by one he laid them on top of each picture. A couple of the photos looked great with dark green mats. The photograph of the snow-covered woodlands looked nice with a navy-blue mat. Connor thought over the choices they had come up with for the photographs. He wondered if I even had room in my apartment to hang them. He had better not frame them just yet, he concluded.

"These are the perfect mats, but I'd better wait until my friend lets me know what she'd like to do with the photographs first," Connor told man. "I'm sure I'll be back in the near future."

The gentleman smiled and said, "Come back any time."

Connor extended his hand and thanked him for his kindness. While walking back to hotel Connor thought that it was refreshing to run into a shopkeeper that courteous. If I wanted to have the photographs framed, he would definitely go back to that frame shop to have it done.

Back at the hotel, Connor picked up a newspaper. After dropping the photos off in his room he returned to the lobby, and in between reading a few interesting articles, he watched the people coming and going. The doorman was looking a bit more haggard than he had been when Connor had left earlier. I guess it's a job, Connor thought as he shook his head. He couldn't imagine working in the city or even living here.

By the time Tom had called I had written down quite a few notes. Now to fit all of the puzzle pieces together, I told myself. "Okay, Tom," I said into the receiver, "up until now we've been concentrating on James Martin. What if Beck was the real lead?"

"Wait a minute, though, Sarah. All of the business owners that we talked to told us that they dealt with Mr. Martin. Beck's name wasn't even mentioned once during our investigation."

"You're right," I answered. "But what if Beck gave all of the business sales to Martin? Maybe he told him that he would handle the sales of homes, because he didn't want to do all of the corporate paperwork, or something like that. That would put Martin on the hook and Beck gets the laundering kickback from the mob and goes under our radar."

"So Martin didn't know anything about the money laundering?"

"I don't think so. Okay, Tom, look in the paperwork there. Did Martin finalize the sales of anything but businesses?"

"Give me a sec, Sarah," Tom replied as he flipped through all of the notes and paperwork that we'd gathered. "I can't find anything like that here," Tom said after a minute or two. "I guess that Martin was such a good candidate that we totally overlooked everyone else."

"Well, we can't look at the realty files again, it would tip our hand," I thought about our next move. "I'll tell you what, Tom. Try to get into the county courthouse's computer records and get the sales information for the last three years on every piece of property in the Baltimore/D.C. area. Have Pat Covington help if you need it. She's good with paperwork."

"Okay. Anything else?" Agent Henson queried.

"While you do that I'm going to talk to Detective Springer

again," I answered. "Let's see if we can finally make some sense of this case."

"I'll call you back as soon as I come up with the figures, Sarah."

"Thanks, Tom," I said before hanging up the phone. I dialed the Baltimore Police Department and asked for Detective Rick Springer.

"Springer here," he said.

"Hi, Rick," I said cheerfully.

"Wow! Twice in one week. What did I do to deserve all this attention?"

I chuckled. "I'm calling to take you up on your offer, Rick. I need some digging done on the Martin and Beck B and E case, but I need it done real quiet, Rick, real quiet."

"What's up?"

"I can't get into it right now, but I promise when we get it figured out, I'll let you know."

"That's good enough for me. What would you like to know?" Detective Springer asked, ready to write down what I needed.

"First, ask around about any mob connection to Beck. Then see if you can find out where Beck was when his business partner was being stabbed to death. Don't ask Beck, though," I cautioned.

"Got it. When do you need this?"

"Two days ago," I replied.

"Where can I reach you?" Rick asked.

I hesitated and then told him room 413 at the hospital. "Do me a favor and keep this under your hat, okay? Stuff is starting to hit the fan here, and I don't want anyone else getting hurt."

"It's that bad, huh? No problem, Sarah. I'll get back to you soon as I can."

I thanked Rick before hanging up the telephone receiver. Now it was going to be a waiting game until Tom and Rick called, and I'm not very good at waiting.

Connor finished his newspaper and decided to head to the hospital. Maybe he would stop at the bakery and pick up a couple of pastries. Sweets usually cheer people up. At the bakery Connor picked up two chocolate-covered cream donuts and a couple of cups of hot chocolate to go. After paying the cashier he headed across the street toward the hospital. The mixture of doctors, nurses, and civilians hovering around the entrance seemed heavier today. As Connor got closer to the door an alarm sounded. It was the hospital fire alarm. He was pushed backward by the sudden surge of people quickly exiting the building. When the flux of bodies slowed down, he made his way to the door. A security guard and the agent from the other day were keeping everyone out of the hospital.

Connor stood off to the side and asked if there was a fire. The answer he received was that it was being checked out. Connor wondered if the rest of the hospital doors were also being covered to keep people out. He decided that he would walk around the building and check things out. The east and west entrances had security guards at them as well as agents to keep people out. The emergency entrance was another story though. A security guard was on duty, but as an ambulance came in, the occupants were admitted inside without being checked. He deposited the hot chocolate and donuts in the nearest trash receptacle and walked in through the emergency entrance. Once inside he made his way to the elevators. The alarms had quit sounding now and people were beginning to be let back inside. Connor pushed the up button and waited impatiently for the elevator.

I had been off the phone with Detective Springer for

about thirty-five minutes when the fire alarm went off. My first thought was if this was a distraction to get to me. Okay, maybe I was a little paranoid, but in this business it pays to be sometimes. I wished that they had let me keep my gun in here. I understood why they couldn't, though. A shoot out in a hospital would just end up getting innocent people hurt or killed, but that fact didn't make me feel any less vulnerable.

The door to my room opened and a young red-haired nurse came in quickly and jabbered that it was just a false alarm and not to worry. She turned and hurriedly left to go to the next room. Okay, so I wasn't going to die in a fire, I thought. Why didn't that ease my mind?

Ten minutes later the alarm went quiet. You would have thought if they'd known it was a false alarm that they would've shut the stupid thing off before now, I told myself. I took a deep breath and relaxed.

The door to my hospital room opened again, and Connor's smiling face peered around it. "Hi, Sarah," he greeted.

I let out a sigh of relief and said hello back as he walked toward my bedside.

"Is everything okay?" he asked with a look of concern on his face.

"I'm fine now," I answered as he sat down beside my bed. I squeezed the hand he slipped into mine and smiled.

"Are you sure that you're not in any danger Sarah?" Connor asked quietly. "I came in the emergency room entrance when the alarm was going off and nobody checked me at all. That doesn't make me feel very good knowing that."

"To be honest, the alarm going off had me a little worried too. I'm sure that it was probably just some stupid kid's idea of a prank," I said, trying to convince myself.

Connor changed the subject, and the two of us talked for an hour and a half before the nurse brought in my lunch and asked if I needed another pain pill. I told her not right then and she turned and left the room.

While I ate my bland hospital food, Connor and I continued talking. The conversation finally came around to my family.

"How come none of your family are here with you?" Connor asked.

I stopped eating and told him that they didn't know that I had been shot. As Connor listened, I explained how my mother felt about my job and what torture I would have to endure if she found out.

Connor was sympathetic and silently wished that his family was still around. He missed his mother's cooking and piano lessons. His dad and brother used to go on hunting trips every autumn. Connor never liked to shoot animals, even back then. At least now he was using a camera instead of bullets.

"I'm sorry, Connor," I said interrupting his thoughts. "Here I am rattling on . . . "

"Sarah, you should know by now that you can talk to me about anything, even obsessive family members."

That statement brought a smile to my lips. "How is it that you always know just what to say?"

He smiled and shrugged his shoulders. Both of us felt as though we had known each other all of our lives. Neither of us had ever had such a connection like this before. It was like we were meant to be together.

It was going on about one o'clock in the afternoon when the telephone beside my hospital bed rang. When I picked it up Tom's voice came through the receiver.

"Okay Sarah, have you got your pen and pad ready? It

took some doing, but I think I've got everything you wanted," he stated.

"Hang on a second, Tom, let me get this stand over in front of me." As I was saying this to Tom, Connor took my dinner tray off from the stand and took it over and set it on the chair beside the door. When he turned back toward me, he pointed to himself and then at the door. I shook my head no, letting him know that he didn't have to leave the room because of my phone call. "Okay, Tom, go," I said into the receiver when I was ready.

I wrote as fast as I could. According to what Pat and Tom had dug up, Beck had indeed only dealt with residential properties. Martin had sold a couple of houses about four years ago, but only businesses since.

"Tom. I think we need to look into Beck's finances and see just how much he's putting away. Let's look at Martin's too. If I'm right, Beck should have a pretty good nest egg somewhere."

"You know that'll tip our hand, don't you, Sarah?" Tom commented.

"Yeah, I know," I replied sullenly. "I'll tell you what. Go ahead and start the paperwork, but hold onto it until I get back to you. Maybe Detective Springer can come up with something more to lock things in place."

"Okay, Sarah. I'll bring the director up to speed and get the paperwork rolling. You give us the go-ahead when you're ready."

I thanked Tom and hung up the phone. As I went back and forth from my notes to what I had just gotten from Tom, it all seemed like it should fall into place. There was something a little off, though, and it was starting to drive me crazy. Why couldn't I see it? I was just about ready to put down my notes when the phone rang again. It was Rick Springer.

"Okay, Sarah, this is what I was able to find out," Rick stated. "A snitch of mine says that Beck's been seen from time to time eating with DeLuca, but nothing as to whether or not there's any business between them. As far as his whereabouts when Martin was killed, I think that I found something interesting."

"Tell me this is a good interesting" I told him.

"Oh, I think you'll like it Sarah. A couple of uniforms gave Beck's car a ticket about the time Martin was killed."

"Where?" I asked curiously.

"Just around the block from where Martin's body was found. Sarah, I talked to the two uniforms, and they said there wasn't anything suspicious, Beck's car was just parked too close to the fire hydrant."

"You're right, Rick, that is very interesting. Anything else?"

"Nope. I hope this helped." Rick paused. "Do you want me to keep digging?"

"Thanks, Rick, but I guess we'd better take it from here," I told him to say hi to his wife for me, and we ended our phone call. When I had hung up the receiver, I glanced at Connor. "I guess this is pretty boring for you, huh?"

"Actually, Sarah, it's interesting. Here you are in the hospital after being shot and still working your case. This is what your mother should be seeing. Then she would know how passionate your work is to you," he replied.

My face felt flush. Except for that remark my mother would love him, I thought. She would never accept the career path I had chosen, though.

I guess my silence to Connor's remark worried him. "I didn't mean anything by that, Sarah," he quickly added. "I just meant that if she could see you as I do now, maybe she wouldn't ride you so much. I mean . . . I'm just digging myself in deeper, aren't I?" He remarked.

I laughed. "Connor, my mother would love you, but when it comes to my life she just wants me in a safer job. Don't worry. You didn't say anything wrong. I wish the same thing every now and then. Mom's not likely to change, though, and I'm certainly not giving up the job that I've wanted all my life. So we'll just have to put up with one another the way we are."

The worry on Connor's face softened, and he changed the subject. Talking with him was the best medicine I could have asked for. Our conversations took my mind off from the murder, the mob, and where I was. His voice carried me away to his cabin in the woods and beyond. We must've talked for two or three hours. It was about 3:20 p.m. when I glanced up at the clock. Oh, crap! I had forgotten to call Tom back. "I need to make a quick phone call to the office," I told Connor. "Can you stick around a while longer?"

"Where else would I have to go?" he replied with a smile.

Tom Henson had been sitting by his phone with great anticipation when my call finally came in. "So, what did your detective friend have to say?" he asked.

"Maybe we'd better do this with the director on the line," I told him.

"Hold on a sec, Sarah, and I'll get him," Tom replied before putting me on hold. He hurried down the hallway and quickly knocked on Henry's door. When the director called for him to enter, Tom went inside. "Sarah's on line four, and she would like you to listen in on this too," Tom explained. He pushed line four on the director's phone and then pushed the speaker button. "Go ahead, Sarah. The director's here too."

"Okay. Detective Springer said that Beck has been meeting with mob boss Dominic DeLuca, but they didn't know for sure if they were in bed together. Something interesting came up, though, on the day that Martin was murdered." I paused. "Beck's car was ticketed around the time Martin was killed. The kicker is that it was ticketed around the block from where the murder was committed. Quite a coincidence, huh?" I asked.

"That sounds like enough to bring him back in and ask a few discreet questions," the director mused. "We'll also look into both Martin's and Beck's finances."

Tom added that maybe the Organized Crime Unit would know if Beck's hands were dirty.

"Sounds like a good start, Sarah. Anything else we need to look at?" Henry Wilson asked me.

"I was just thinking that it would be interesting to see where Senator Kensington's investments were. Maybe in real estate purchased from Martin in Beck Realty."

Tom spoke up. "That would be too easy. No way we could get that lucky."

"We'll look around and see what turns up with Kensington, but I wouldn't get my hopes up too high. If Kensington's as smart as he appears to be, it will be pure luck if we found anything incriminating. Don't worry; we'll dig as deep as we can, hopefully without the roof falling down on top of us," the director added.

"Good work, Sarah," Tom added. "You can relax now, and we'll take it from here."

Just as I was about to say something, Director Wilson spoke up. "And yes, we will keep you up-to-date on our progress."

I smiled to myself as I responded with one word. "Thanks." When I'd hung up the phone, a breath of relief passed through my lips.

Connor smiled and said, "I guess you have been busy since you've been back home."

I nodded and replied, "But it's all in somebody else's lap now. I've been officially told to relax and get better. So what are you doing for the next few days?"

"I guess I'm keeping a friend from getting too bored." He smiled. "What do you think about puzzles?"

"Puzzles?" I questioned.

"You know, puzzles. Pictures cut into interlocking pieces that you put together."

"I haven't put a puzzle together since I was a teenager. I used to love putting them together, though. I'm not sure why I ever even stopped. Just too busy, I guess."

"We'll fix that. What else would you like me to pick up for you?"

I thought for a while. "How about a deck of cards?"

"Anything else?" Connor queried.

"I'm really hoping that I won't be in here for that much longer, Connor." I smiled back.

"A couple of puzzles and one deck of cards coming right up." Connor repeated to me. "I'll be back as soon as I can."

As he stood up to leave I grabbed his hand. "Thanks for being here," I choked out.

Connor leaned over the hospital bed and kissed me gently on the lips. Then put his forehead against mine and whispered, "There's no place that I would rather be." He kissed me again and headed for the door. "Be right back," he said as he left my room.

Downstairs in the gift shop, Connor looked around. "I guess I'll have to go someplace else." He thought. He asked the cashier where the closest toy store or Walmart was, and after getting the directions, he was on his way.

Four blocks west from the hospital was a Toys R Us store. When Connor walked through the door a flood of memories washed over him. He saw toys he had played with as a child, games that he and his brother used play. As Connor went up and down the aisles he enjoyed the memories from his childhood. Just past the Barbie aisle was shelf after shelf of puzzles. There were puzzles from Winnie the Pooh, NASCAR, wildlife, and landscapes and everything in between. Some puzzles had only five hundred large pieces, and some of the more sophisticated puzzles had two thousand small pieces. Connor chose a puzzle with nothing but colorful marbles on it and one with an autumn landscape and a covered bridge. Each puzzle had 1,500 pieces to them. He also grabbed a standard deck of playing cards. The last time he had played cards was with Bob Sanders in Texas. Bob and Martha were good people. Maybe someday their paths would cross again, Connor hoped. By the time Connor had returned to the hospital, visiting hours were almost over.

"I'm back," Connor announced as he entered my hospital room. "I'm sorry that it took so long." He crossed over to my bed and pulled the puzzles out of the shopping bag. As he showed me the puzzle full of marbles, I remarked, "Oh boy! You are going to help me put these together, I hope."

"I don't know," Connor said with a gleam in his eye. "It's been a long time since I've put one together too."

"I guess we'd better start with the landscape puzzle then, so we've got a chance of actually finishing it," I told him with a grin.

Connor's laugh lit up the room. I'd almost forgotten about the hole in my shoulder as we fished through the puzzle pieces looking for the flat edges of the sides. Half of the puzzle's edges were put together by the time visiting hours were over. While Connor put the remaining puzzle pieces back into the box, he asked. "What kind of real food would you like me to bring you tomorrow? You name it. Anything you want."

"You do know who you're talking to right?" I asked.

Connor grinned.

" Maybe I'd better make you a list. You know how picky I am." I smiled back.

We both laughed and then Connor kissed me just before heading for the door. He paused with his hand on the door-knob, turned, and told me to get a good night's sleep, that tomorrow he would challenge me to a game of cards.

"You're on," I told him as he waved and went out the door. I smiled. How did I get so lucky to meet someone like this? I asked myself.

Around ten p.m. the doctor came in and checked on me. Doctor Andrew Sloan was his name. Doctor Sloan was a short, thin man in his mid-sixties. On the end of his nose perched a pair of reading glasses that you would swear were going to slide off any second. His hair was gray at the tem-ples and he was starting to get that midlife paunch. After looking over my chart he examined my shoulder. "You're coming along very well, Miss Anthony. We should be able to release you in another day or two, as long as you keep up with your physical therapy," he said kindly.

"It can't be soon enough for me." I smiled. "No offense."

"None taken." Doctor Sloan smiled back. "I just wish all of our patients were as cooperative as you've been."

He told me that even after I was released I would have to take it easy. That thought wasn't very appealing to me; it meant that I would be riding my desk for a month or so. Who knows? I've got a lot of vacation time saved up. Maybe I'll just take the month off, I thought. The nurse came in and changed my bandages, checked my vitals and asked if I needed anything for pain or to go to sleep. My shoulder was throbbing just a little bit from the doctor's exam, but not enough to want to take the medication.

"No, I'm good," I answered. After the nurse had left I surfed the television channels. There wasn't anything on worth watching so I shut it off. I turned out the lights and dozed off, dreaming that Connor and I were up in the mountains and he was taking pictures of the wildlife for me.

Tom Henson was at his desk at seven o'clock this morning. He had no idea why he had come into work this early. It was around eight when an envelope was left at the front desk for Director Wilson. He would be in late today because of an urgent meeting with the mayor.

It was 10:30 in the morning when Tom's phone rang. "Henson," he said into the receiver.

"Tom," the director's voice rang out. "Come into my office at once."

"Yes, sir," Tom replied and hurried down the hall. He knocked three times and opened the director's door.

"Close the door," he was told. "We've got a problem." Henry remarked. As Tom sat down in front of the director's desk the envelope was pushed across toward him. Tom opened it and stared in disbelief. Inside was a Polaroid of me sound asleep in my hospital bed. Along with the photo was a note stating "Drop it, or your agent dies."

"Oh my God!" Tom gasped. "We've got to get Sarah out of there right now."

"I know," the director said as he sat down at his desk. "But then where do we put her? Whoever sent this is obviously well informed, so how do we keep her safe? For that matter you too."

"Me? What do you mean me too?" Tom questioned.

"Well, whoever shot Sarah knows what you look like too."

Tom muttered under his breath. "I knew that this was going to be a bad day."

"What did you say, Tom?" Henry asked.

"Nothing, just talking to myself," he answered.

"I want you to go over to the hospital and stay with Sarah until I can make some arrangements. Take her gun to her too. To hell with the hospital policy. I'll take full responsibility if anything happens." The director continued. "Don't let anyone relieve you unless they give you the password. Okay?"

"Yes, sir," Tom responded. "What's the password going to be?"

"It's going to have to be one that we've never used before. Got any ideas?"

"What about something like, Aunt Em from the Wizard of Oz?" Tom suggested.

"That sounds good to me." Director Wilson nodded. "No place like home and all that stuff. I think she'll like it."

Tom Henson and Henry Wilson ironed out a few more details and decided that no one else would know about the note until they figured out what to do.

At nine o'clock the door to my hospital room opened and Connor's smiling face poked around it. "Are you ready to lose at cards, or do you want to try to finish the puzzle?"

I smiled back at him. "You're just too eager to play cards, Connor. I think that I'll stick with the puzzle for now."

"Chicken." He laughed as he went to get the puzzle out. "How did you sleep last night?" he questioned with concern in his voice.

"Pretty good actually," I answered.

While we searched through the puzzle pieces, I told Connor what the doctor had said about my going home in a day or so, and my physical therapy. I even opened up about how I felt about riding my desk for a month. He was very sympathetic and held my hand in his. "You'll be fine, you know." Connor's voice comforted me.

I stopped looking through the puzzle pieces and looked at him. He had such an uncanny knack of saying the right thing, I thought again. Then he smiled that warm smile of his. I leaned forward, and my lips found his. Connor's right arm carefully wrapped itself around my waist. The kiss was warm, and in a different place and time it could've led to more, but it was just what I needed at that moment.

When we parted, I apologized. Connor's hand lightly brushed my face, and he said that there wasn't anything to apologize for. After a while we began working on the puzzle again. The company was wonderful, but I forgot how boring puzzles were, and I broke down. "Okay, enough of this. Break out the cards, and let's see what you've got," I told him.

He put the puzzle away and opened the deck of cards. After pulling out the jokers and poker rules, Connor began to shuffle them. It was hilarious. The new cards were so slippery that they flew all over the place as he shuffled. We were both laughing so hard we didn't notice the door opening.

Tom Henson stood in the door of my hospital room watching us laugh. He tried to think back to the last time that he'd seen me this happy.

"Oh, hi, Tom," I said when I noticed him standing there.

"It looks like you're feeling better," he said, eyeing Connor.

"I'm sorry, Tom, this is my friend Connor McBride. Connor, this is my current partner, Tom Henson," I said introducing the two of them.

"So this is the mystery man that I haven't heard anything about," Tom said as he shook Connor's hand.

"Excuse me?" Connor asked.

"No offense. It's just that Sarah hasn't told us anything about you."

Connor turned and glanced at me. "You're keeping me all to yourself, huh?" He winked.

I answered him with a smile. "What's up, Tom?" I questioned.

"We need to talk, Sarah." Tom's remark hinting for Connor to leave.

"Go ahead, Sarah. I'll wait outside," Connor remarked as he stood up.

I grabbed his forearm. "Please stay," I told him.

"Are you sure that you can trust him, Sarah?" Tom questioned.

"With my life, Tom," I answered.

Connor sat back down and squeezed my hand.

"Okay." Tom gave in. "Sometime this morning an envelope was delivered to the front desk for Henry. Inside it was a Polaroid of you sleeping and a note." I squeezed Connor's hand as Tom continued. "The note read 'Drop it, or your agent dies.' "

I took a deep breath. "Okay. What do we do now?"

"Well, first, here's your sidearm back." Tom said handing me my gun and holster. "The director says to hell with hospital policy."

"This makes me feel a lot safer," I replied as I checked the gun's cylinder. "Now what?"

"The director's working on it. He doesn't know who to trust right now, and since there was someone here in your room, that means that it could be somebody on the hospital staff or we've got a leak at the agency. Either way, I'm to stay with you until we figure out our next move."

"Is there any immediate danger to Sarah?" Connor asked.

"We don't know for sure. We haven't stopped our investigation, and whoever sent the note will find that out sooner or later, so time is not on our side," Tom grimly answered.

My hospital room got quiet as the day's events sank in. Connor suggested that with the three of us playing cards maybe I would have a better chance of beating him. That comment broke the tension, and I told him that he hadn't even been able to shuffle the cards yet.

"So what are we playing?" Tom asked as Connor dealt the cards.

"I don't know," Connor replied as he looked over at me. "What are we playing?"

"Strip poker, of course," I answered waiting to see Tom's expression.

"I hope you're a good player then, Sarah." Tom smiled at me cunningly. "From the looks of it in your hospital gown, lose one hand, and you're out."

I laughed. "Don't be so sure, Tom. I've got a bandage here that could take me hours to unwrap." We all laughed. I was glad to see Tom and Connor getting along together.

We played gin rummy for the first hand. What a surprise. Connor won. Tom's choice of card games was Spades. We played a couple of practice hands to learn the rules. I won that game and didn't even know what I was doing. I chose Crazy Eights and explained to Tom, that Crazy Eights was kind of like Uno. He caught on quickly, but Connor won that game too.

The young redheaded nurse came in around noon and brought me my lunch.

"If you want to go and get something to eat," Connor told Tom, "I'll stay with Sarah."

"I can't," he replied. "I'm not supposed to leave her side until someone relieves me with the correct password."

"Okay then, what can I pick up for you at the deli around the block?"

"Hey, wait a minute here," I interrupted. "It seems like I was promised real food by someone in this room yesterday."

"Don't look at me." Tom said throwing his hands up in surrender.

"Okay! Okay!" Connor smiled in defeat. "I'm making a run to the deli. Who would like what?"

While I was thinking, I told Tom to go ahead and order. Tom said that he would take a Reuben sandwich with potato salad and a root beer. I ordered a turkey melt with coleslaw on the side and a root beer too. Connor repeated the orders to us and then headed for the door. "Keep her safe" he told Tom before leaving. "I'll be back as soon as I can."

After Connor had left, Tom turned to me. "He seems like a nice guy," he said. "How'd you find him?"

"You're too suspicious, Tom," I told him, and then added how Connor had found me. "Have my parents called again?" I asked.

"Just that once," he answered. "I guess when we told them that you were away on a case they figured you would call when you got back. So, what exactly do you know about Mr. McBride?"

"I can't believe it, Tom. Not you too. Here I thought that my family were the only ones who would drill me about Connor." I rolled my eyes. "I know enough about him to trust him with my life and yours and anybody else's. You're just going to have to trust me on this, Tom."

"Enough said," Tom replied. "I'm just looking out for my partner."

"And I appreciate that, Tom, I really do. Now how about some gin rummy? I think I need the practice." Tom smiled and nodded at my statement.

As Connor waited for our order at the deli, he began formulating a plan in his head. The plan was to keep a certain government agent safe and out of circulation for a while. By the time our order was ready, Connor had figured it all out, but he was going to need help pulling it off. Big help!

Tom and I were on game number eight of our gin rummy marathon when Connor got back.

"What do I owe you?" Tom asked, pulling out his wallet.

"Not a thing," Connor replied. "It's my treat."

"Thanks," Tom told Connor as he took his dinner over to the chair by the window. "The next time lunch is on me."

Connor unpacked the remaining bag on the table across my hospital bed. "What'd you get?" I asked curiously.

"The same thing you did," he answered. "I haven't had any kind of a melt in years, so I thought that I'd try one too."

"I was kind of hoping that we could share," I said as if I was disappointed.

"Want to split mine?" my partner chimed in.

"Yuck!" I answered. "No thanks."

Connor and Tom laughed. "Boy! She sure was quick with that answer." Connor grinned.

"Do you suppose it's my aftershave or the food?" Tom wondered aloud.

"Oh, it's the food Tom. Your aftershave killed my sense of smell a long time ago," I kidded. We all laughed and joked around as we ate. The deli had done a great job with our food. We'll have to go back there again sometime, I told myself.

When we had finished eating and the garbage had been tossed in the wastebasket, we all sat down and talked. Connor hesitantly brought up the plan that he had formulated. It went as follows: first, a meeting would be held with all of the hospital employees on the fourth floor. While that meeting was going on, Connor would sneak me out of the hospital. During the staff meeting the hospital personnel would be told that my room would be off limits; that no one was to go in without an agent present with them. All meals would be brought in, etc. Of course my room would be empty except for a decoy and an agent. Meanwhile, Connor and I would be headed out of town.

"And go where?" Tom asked.

"To my cabin," Connor replied. "No one knows me or where I live."

"Including us," Tom strongly objected. "I don't like this idea one bit."

I started to say something to Tom, but Connor held up his finger to me and continued. "I will give you directions to my place and even the GPS coordinates if you'd like, Agent Henson. Trust me, no one will find Sarah. That I promise you." Connor turned to me and said, "I didn't mean to be rude, Sarah, go ahead."

I smiled at him. "I was just going to tell Tom that I like your plan. The doctor said I could go home in another day or two anyway, so let's do it."

Tom made a call to Director Wilson to get approval. "It sounds like a good plan to me. When do you think we should do it?" The director asked Henson.

"Well, if we do it around three o'clock when the shifts are changing, we should be able to catch all of the fourth-floor hospital staff from both shifts," Tom answered. "That gives us about two hours to set things up."

"And this Connor McBride can be trusted?"

"Anthony says that she trusts him with her life, sir."

"That's good enough for me then. I'll inform the hospital supervisor on the fourth floor one half hour before the meeting. That way hopefully no one has a chance to leave.

I'll also put Shapiro outside Sarah's hospital room to make it look like she's still in there with extra protection. I think we might just pull this off, Tom."

"Yes, sir," he replied. Tom didn't like it one little bit though. He didn't trust Connor yet. Heck, he didn't know Connor yet. Everything rested on the faith that I had in McBride. Tom hoped that I was right.

CHAPTER 3

A gent Shapiro came into the room with a bag for me. Clothes! Thank God. I really hadn't wanted to go to Connor's cabin in my hospital gown. Pat Covington had gone to my locker at the agency and sent my spare set of street clothes with Paul. Only another woman would have thought of that. My attire consisted of a pair of loose-fitting blue jeans, a light blue long-sleeve shirt, socks, and hunting boots. Pat had also picked up my brown corduroy jacket. Ahhh. It felt so good wearing clothes again. It was a little painful putting my arm into my shirtsleeve, but I bit my lip and prayed that I wouldn't open my stitches.

Connor had given Tom the directions and the GPS coordinates to his cabin. He even promised that we would keep in touch every twelve hours by calling a secure phone at the agency. I thought that was going to be a good trick, since Connor didn't have a telephone in his cabin. Oh, well, anything to appease Tom.

At around 2:45 p.m. the hospital staff on the fourth floor began gathering in the visitor's waiting room. Stragglers were rounded up and escorted to the meeting. At three o'clock agent Shapiro gave us the thumbs-up sign, and Connor helped me on with my jacket.

"Are you ready, Sarah?" He asked as he held my hand.

"Let me just grab my gun, and I'm all yours," I replied. I clipped the holstered firearm onto my belt and covered it with my jacket. Glancing around the room I told him, "Okay, I'm ready."

Tom Henson, Connor, and I walked to the stairway. Tom would escort us to the parking garage but not go in. Most people can spot a federal agent by his suit, or so they say. We weren't going to take any chances. At the bottom of the stairway I turned and gave Tom a hug. "You be careful, okay?" I ordered.

"You too, kiddo," he replied.

"Hey, Tom, do me a favor, would you? Go to the hotel just down the street and pick up my things. We don't want anyone getting a hold of the photographs I took near my place. Here's the key. The room has been paid for. On second thought, maybe you should send someone who's not involved with your case, just in case someone follows you from here."

"Sure thing, Mr. McBride," Tom said as he offered his hand to Connor. When Connor grasped it Tom pulled him forward and said in a low voice. "You keep her safe or else."

"Don't worry, Tom. Sarah's going to be as safe as your money would be in Fort Knox. You have my word on it," he promised.

We walked to Connor's Jeep and were off. I told Connor the quickest way out of D.C. and continually looked behind us, but never saw anything suspicious. Connor noticed and said in a reassuring voice, "Relax, Sarah. We've made it out of D.C. Once we get to my cabin, it'll be almost impossible to find us."

"I know," I answered giving him a weak smile.

The drive back to Virginia was a long one, or so it seemed. My shoulder was beginning to throb a little after being on the road for a couple of hours. Connor glanced over and saw me wince as I tried to shift positions. The Jeep slowed down when a mom- and-pop convenience store came into view.

"What are we stopping for?" I asked him.

"I can see the pain in your eyes," Connor explained. "I figured that I would get you a soda so that you can take your pain medication. We've still got a way to go, and it won't do any good for you to be in pain the whole trip." Connor got out of the jeep before I could say a word. He came around to my side of the vehicle and asked if I wanted anything else or if I wanted to come in with him.

The mom-and-pop store was a quiet little shop. Souvenirs, maps, T-shirts, and some snack foods lined the shelves. The refrigerators along the side held milk, soda, orange juice, and bottled water. Another one held several brands of beer, and a small glass-topped freezer near the checkout was filled with ice cream novelties. While I used the restroom Connor walked around the store.

The woman behind the counter struck up a conversation with Connor, smiling. It seems that her husband died a while back and she kept the store open for something to do. Her three boys had moved away one to Indiana, one to California and the youngest to New Jersey and had lives of their own now. They did still call once or twice a year and sent family photos at Christmas time, though, she told him.

Connor gave her information about us that was vague at best. His parents and only brother were dead, and no we weren't married. When the woman asked where we were headed, Connor answered, "Ohio." She never asked our names and never offered hers, so our cover was still intact.

When I emerged from the restroom Connor asked me what I'd like to drink. I picked up an orange soda, and Connor grabbed two bottles of water. As an afterthought, I also grabbed a package of chocolate-covered graham crackers. Connor paid the woman and said he hoped she had a good day. Once outside he helped me into the Jeep and made sure that I took one of my pain pills before we got started again.

Back in Washington, Tom had Agent Maxwell get Connor's things from his hotel room. When he got back with Connor's belongings, Tom couldn't help but go through them in the conference room. He didn't know what he would find, but he didn't trust McBride yet. There wasn't anything out of the ordinary among Connor's things some clothes, toiletries, and an envelope of beautiful landscape photographs were all that the duffle bag-style backpack held.

Okay, Tom thought, Sarah's going to kill me when she finds out, but I'm going to run Connor McBride through the system. He had to find something that would put his mind at ease about me being with him. He locked Connor's things in one of the lockers and went to his desk. Tom glanced around the office and then typed Connor's name into the computer. It didn't take long for Connor's biography to pop up on the screen. Connor Angus McBride was born March 25, 1969, to Beverly and Thomas McBride in Larson, Montana. As Tom skimmed down the pages, his eyes lit on Connor's military history. Connor had spent ten years as a Navy SEAL and had earned several commendations. He was honorably discharged three years ago. His Navy files were encoded "Top Secret" and couldn't be opened without special clearance. Tom quickly closed the screen and deleted what he had found from his computer. He had found out what he'd been looking for. Tom was sure that I was in good hands now. As he began going through the case file, he wondered if I knew about Connor's background.

It was clear that we wouldn't be able to get to Connor's

cabin before dark. We had passed two traffic accidents and had to slow down for the gawkers to see everything. With three quarters of the trip behind us, Connor decided to stop for the night. I agreed and said that a nice hot meal would hit the spot. Connor looked across at me after pulling into the Swanson Family Inn parking lot. "How's the shoulder holding up?" he asked quietly.

"The pain is down to a mild throb now," I replied. The drive had been tiring and the painkillers had given me a bit of a buzz.

"Let's get checked in, and then we'll get something to eat," Connor told me as he helped me out of the Jeep. "I'll get two adjoining rooms if possible, okay?"

"Just get one room with two queen-size beds, Connor. I'd just as soon not be alone, with everything that's happened," I told him. "I promise not to turn into a vampire or anything." I smiled.

He smiled back at me. "Okay, Sarah, if you're sure."

I nodded, and we checked in as Mr. and Mrs. Hank Roberts from Chicago. Connor paid cash for the room so that his credit card couldn't be traced. After getting the room key and directions to our room, we headed out the door. Connor held my hand as we walked back toward the Jeep. "What are you in the mood for?" he asked.

"To tell you the truth, Connor, I'm so tired that I don't think I could eat a thing right now," I replied with a yawn.

"You need to keep up your strength, Sarah. I'll tell you what. Let's pick something up and bring it back here. Okay?"

"All right I guess," I told him.

"Hold on just a little bit longer," Connor coaxed as he helped me into the Jeep again.

The closest place for takeout food was a Long John Silver's restaurant. I ordered chicken, fries, hush puppies, and coleslaw. Connor ordered the fish, fries, hush puppies and coleslaw. An orange soda for both of us topped off our order. We were back in our hotel room in about fifteen minutes. We watched the television while we ate our meal. Connor saw me picking at my food and said that if I was really that tired, to go ahead and lie down.

"I'm sorry, Connor. I just can't keep my eyes open any longer," I told him apologetically.

Connor stood and helped me up. "Don't apologize, Sarah. It's okay," he said as he pulled back the blanket and top sheet on one of the beds. "I'm sorry I don't have any pajamas for you to change into," he smiled.

I touched his cheek with my hand and told him that I was glad that he had come to Washington to visit. He kissed my palm and said he was glad that he had come too. I sat on the side of the bed and carefully unlaced my boot. After removing my socks I swung my feet around and laid back, exhausted.

Connor placed my handgun on the nightstand between the beds and covered me up.

"Sweet dreams," he whispered before kissing me lightly on the forehead.

"Good night," I said and was asleep within just a few minutes.

Connor turned down the lights and the sound on the television. He was planning our next move so that our trail wouldn't be as easy to follow. After about an hour or so, Connor called the secure phone number that Tom had given him. Not recognizing the person on the other end of the line, Connor just left the message, "All is well so far, kiddo."

Connor's eyelids began to feel heavy too. He hadn't realized how taxing things had been on him, and now things were starting to catch up. He removed his boots and socks and laid down on the empty bed. Sleep came quickly, but didn't last long. Noise from the cars in the parking lot woke him up around one a.m. Connor was able to go back to sleep around two o'clock, and this time he didn't awaken until about eight.

I rolled over and a thin beam of light hit me in the face. Damn! Was it daylight already? I turned back over, and pain shot through my shoulder. A muffled cry escaped my bit lip.

Connor had been in the bathroom washing the sleep out of his eyes when he heard me. Hurrying out to my bedside he asked if I was all right. I gave him a weak smile and told him that I had just forgotten that I had been wounded.

"It sounds like you had a pretty good dream last night then," he said cheerfully.

"Yeah, and then I woke up to the real world." I yawned.

"I'm sorry about that. How do you feel about some breakfast this morning? You didn't eat very much last night."

"I think I could eat something," I replied. "I wish I could take a shower first, though."

"Go ahead, Sarah," Connor told me. "I'll wait outside."

"I'm not supposed to get my wound wet, so I guess I'll have to settle for a washcloth and a towel," I responded to Connor's offer. "You don't have to leave. I'll close the bathroom door."

"Are you sure?" he asked.

"I'm sure," I answered. "Why don't you see if you can get a weather report on the television set?" I asked before closing the bathroom door behind me. I had a little trouble unbuttoning my shirt and pulling it off of my shoulders. This was going to be fun, I thought. The water was warm and felt good against my skin. This was the only bathing I had done since I'd been shot. The nurses did it for me in the hospital.

In the other room I could hear the channels changing

on the television set. I hoped that the weather was going to cooperate for the rest of our trip. The walk through the woods to Connor's cabin would be hard enough without any rain. I carefully dried myself off and pulled on my shirt. I wondered how long it would be before the twinges of pain were gone for good. Not soon enough for me, I told myself. Unbuttoning my shirt had been a lot easier than buttoning it up was going to be. I got two buttons buttoned, but it had taken me almost three minutes to do it. I was going to need help.

"Connor," I called loud enough for him to hear me. "A little help, please."

The bathroom door slowly opened and Connor asked, "Did you need something Sarah?"

"Yes, I do please," I answered. "I need help with a couple of buttons. Would you mind?"

The door opened wider and an embarrassed Connor slowly stepped inside. "Are you sure?" he asked.

"Of course, silly." I smiled. "I could probably do them up myself, but I don't think that we have that much time to spare. Once my arm gets loosened up some, I'll do much better."

Connor stepped forward and carefully began buttoning the remaining buttons on my shirt. He looked up into my eyes and asked if I was ready. We left the inn after having a nice breakfast in the dining room. Everything tasted good to me. Connor had been right; I was hungry. Both of us were full and ready to hit the road.

"What's the weatherman say for today, or didn't you find a weather report?" I asked on the way to the Jeep.

"Clear skies for most of the day, Sarah. We should get to the cabin just after noon," Connor commented.

"That sounds good to me," I replied as I climbed into the Jeep with Connor's help.

Tom Henson's car pulled into the almost-empty parking lot. What am I doing here so damn early? he thought. "Worrying about Sarah will be the death of me" he said to himself as he shook his head. Once inside, Tom went straight to the call center. Agent Samuelson was manning the phones.

"Did anyone check in on the secure line last night?" Tom queried.

"Somebody called, but all they said was that all was well so far, kiddo. I think that someone had the wrong number," Samuelson said. "I don't know of anyone with the code name kiddo."

Tom thanked him and headed up to his office. Well, Connor had been good to his word and checked in. It was smart of him to pick up on his calling me kiddo. No one would ever figure out who that was. As he passed the director's office, Tom noticed a light coming from underneath the door. He knocked.

"Come in," Director Wilson's voice told him.

"Good morning, sir. I guess that neither of us got much sleep last night," he commented.

"Did Mr. McBride check in last night?"

"Yes, sir. The code name he used was kiddo."

Director Wilson stared at Tom. "Kiddo?"

"That's what I called Sarah before they left, sir. I guess McBride picked up on it."

"Have you had a chance to check out Mr. McBride yet, Tom?" Henry asked.

"Yep, last night. It appears Sarah is in good hands," he remarked.

"I agree, Tom." The director stood up and peered out the window. "We're going to need to keep his identity a complete secret. Okay, Tom?" He turned toward Henson.

"Nobody but you and I will know who's with Anthony. And I do mean nobody." He turned back toward the window. "I haven't lost an agent in eight years, and she's not going to be the first."

"Yes, sir." Agent Henson agreed.

Back at his desk there was a file folder waiting for Henson. It was labeled Kensington Finances. Okay, he told himself. Let's see if Senator Kensington had property holdings purchased through the Martin and Beck Realty office. Just as Tom had thought, there wasn't anything to tie Kensington and the realty office together. Tom called the head of the Organized Crime Unit next. He inquired as to whether Beck was mob connected or not. They said that they would have to review their files and they would call him right back. As Henson hung up the phone he wondered how Adam Beck would react when they hauled him in for questioning. He had struck Tom is one cool cookie. Maybe Beck's being parked around the corner during Martin's murder wasn't a coincidence.

Just before we got into town, Connor pulled into a gas station and called the secure phone line again. When it was picked up Connor asked for agent Henson. The secure call was being patched through to Tom's desk.

"Henson," Tom said into the receiver.

"All continues to be well, kiddo," Connor said into the phone.

"Have you reached your destination?" Tom asked.

"Affirmative," Connor answered. "Will report in again in twelve."

"Good luck," Henson told him before hanging up. Even secure lines have ways of sometimes being compromised, so the shorter the conversation the better. Tom left his desk to report to Director Wilson.

Connor hung up the phone and walked back to the Jeep.

"So is Poppa Bear happy?" I asked Connor as he got in.

Connor chuckled. "He didn't say, but he asked if we had arrived safely."

"That sounds like Tom, always the chatterbox," I said in fun. We both laughed.

After stopping into the local store, Connor and I went by the post office. He checked his mailbox but didn't pull anything out of it. If someone did come looking for us, it would look like he hadn't been there for quite a while. We drove to the parking lot, where I had parked the weekend of the avalanche.

"We'll take the groceries to the cabin, and then I'll come back and hide my Jeep," he announced. "Are you up to the walk?"

"Just try to stop me," I told him as I started to get out of the Jeep.

"Hold on a minute, speedy. It's a good mile hike, so let's pace ourselves, okay?" Connor asked as he came around to help me out.

"I'll be careful. I promise." I covered my handgun with my jacket and Connor carried the two bags of groceries that we had picked up at the store. The walk was relaxing. New greenery was popping up all through the forest. Looking at the scenery made me forget all about my shoulder wound. Everything looked so different and new without all of the snow on top of them. I had almost forgotten why I was back here again, but the gun in my jacket reminded me.

We turned off from the trail, and in a short time were at Connor's cabin. As I stood on the porch looking around, Connor set the bags on the bench and unlocked the front door. "Welcome home," he said as he pushed the door open.

I turned and smiled at him. It seemed like ages ago since I had first been here. The wonderful memories of that visit were still sharp in my mind.

"Are you coming in, or are you going to stand there day-dreaming forever?"

Connor's voice snapped me back to the present. "It just seems like a lifetime ago since I was here last. So much has happened . . . " My voice trailed off as I stepped inside the cabin.

The refrigerated foods were put away and the windows opened to air the cabin out. I carefully sat down on the couch, leaned back, and closed my eyes. This felt so good.

"Are you doing okay, Sarah?" the male voice asked from behind me.

I opened my eyes, tilted back my head, and replied, "Yep."

"Are you going to be okay here while I go and get rid of the Jeep?"

"What are you going to do with it?" I asked.

"I've got a friend of mine who will keep it under wraps for me for a while."

"Won't he ask questions?" I wondered aloud.

"We go back quite a ways. Wade is one of the good guys. He'll keep it hidden, no questions asked, for as long as I need," Connor answered. "Are you going to be okay?" he asked again.

"Of course I will. Be careful, and don't be gone too long, okay?"

"I'll be back as soon as I can. You know where everything is, so help yourself." He leaned over the back of the couch and kissed me lightly on the forehead. "I'll be right back," he said again before heading for the door.

The telephone on Tom Henson's desk rang. It was the head of the organized crime unit, Jackson Stone. Unfortunately Stone didn't have any concrete proof about Beck being in bed with DeLuca. Beck had already been dubbed someone of interest to the unit, though. Yes, they had been seen eating together on at least five separate occasions, but there were no other meetings that they knew about. Both Beck and DeLuca were still currently under investigation. Jackson asked Tom what he was specifically looking at Beck for, besides the mob link.

"Money laundering and possibly the murder of his business partner," Tom answered.

Stone whistled into the receiver. "We'll keep an eye on him for you and do a little digging into his business partner's connections. I'll keep you informed if we find anything."

Tom thanked him and said that he looked forward to hearing from him. As Tom hung up the phone, he wondered how Beck had flown under the radar for so long.

It was around 2:10 in the afternoon when the information arrived on Martin and Beck's finances. Looking through the file it looked like Martin was clean. Mr. Beck, on the other hand had a couple of questionable transactions in his folder. Tom would have to sit down with a calculator and a pad of paper to figure them out.

I carefully put the rest of the groceries away and then went out and sat on the porch bench. I leaned my head back, closed my eyes, and listened to the forest. While I sat there I heard three different kinds of birds chattering away in the treetops. Something scurried across the woodland floor and up into a tree. I figured that it had to have been a squirrel. Oh, how peaceful it was out here. I opened my eyes, and there at the bottom of the stairs sat a rabbit. He munched away at the grass and paid no attention to me. I felt like I was in the middle of some nature show on PBS, except this was better.

Connor had gotten into his Jeep and driven to his friend Wade Hood's place a couple of miles outside of town. Wade had served with Connor in the SEALS, and they had been good friends for years. As Connor's Jeep pulled into Wade's yard, a big mixed- breed dog came running out barking. Connor put the vehicle in park and jumped out. "Come on Trooper," he called out to the dog. Trooper almost knocked Connor down when he jumped on him. "What's the matter, boy? Did you miss me?" He was answered with a flurry of tongue licks.

Wade stepped around the side of the house to see what all the commotion was about. "Connor?" he asked. "Man! How long has it been?" The two friends shook hands.

"Only about a month or three." Connor smiled.

"To what do I owe the visit?" Wade asked, clapping Connor on the back as they walked up to the front porch of his house. They had just gotten seated in a couple of wicker chairs when the front door opened. "Look who came around for a visit, Janet," Wade said to the redhead in the doorway.

"Connor? How long has it been?" Connor and Wade laughed as Connor stood up and gave her a hug.

"Too long, I know," he answered.

"Have you got time to stay for supper?" Janet Hood asked him with a smile.

"Unfortunately not today, Jan. I can only stay for a minute or two. Maybe next time," he added.

"I'll hold you to that now," she said, shaking her finger at him. "How about a cup of hot chocolate?"

"Thanks, Jan, that sounds great."

"I'll be right back." She said disappearing into the house.

As Connor sat back down Wade looked at him curiously. "What's up, Cap'n?"

"I need a favor L.T.," Connor replied.

"What kind of trouble are you in?" Wade asked with concern.

"Hopefully nothing I can't handle," came the reply as Janet emerged with two coffee cups.

"Thanks, honey," Wade said, kissing her on the cheek.

"Yell if you need anything else. I've got to finish up my sociology paper for college."

"So you're finally going for your master's, huh?" Connor smiled.

"Yeah" she replied. "You know it was a lot easier when I got my bachelor's degree. Now I spend all of my time studying and working on my thesis."

"College is hell, honey," Wade said with a grin.

His wife rolled her eyes and shook her head as she went back inside.

"What do you need me to do?" Wade asked, turning his attention back to his friend.

"Would you mind keeping my Jeep under wraps for me for a while?" Connor asked sipping his drink.

"Sure, no problem Cap'n. Is there anything else you need?"

"I could use a ride back to my place," Connor said, finishing his drink.

"Just let me tell Janet where we'll be, and then we'll head on out."

Wade took Connor's cup and disappeared into the house. He emerged a couple minutes later with his pickup truck keys in hand and his baseball cap on. "Janet says to tell you not to be a stranger," he told Connor before parking Connor's Jeep behind the garage and throwing a tarp over it.

As the two men drove back toward town, Connor lightly

touched on the highlights of what had happened. Wade let out a whistle. "You think they'll come looking for the agent?" he asked with a sideways glance.

"I don't think so, but I'm going to be as careful as I can. If they can't find my Jeep, that'll be a big help."

"No problem. I'll tell Janet that you weren't at the house today. She'll know to keep your visit a secret."

"I appreciate it Wade," Connor said to his friend. "And everything else is just between the two of us."

"All I know is that you wanted me to watch your Jeep. I figured you were going out of town on a photo shoot," Wade said with a wink.

When they reached the parking lot, Connor got out and shook his friend's hand. "I'll be in touch if all hell breaks loose Lieutenant," he remarked.

"You sure that that satellite phone still works? When was the last time that you used it?"

"I check it once a month or whenever I'm home. We'll be okay."

"You'd better be," Wade told Connor before he started down the trail. "Janet's expecting you for dinner sometime soon."

Connor waved over his shoulder. He hadn't walked very far when he heard Wade's truck drive away.

Tom Henson had pulled out all of the questionable financial transactions. The conference room was the quietest place at the agency, so Tom grabbed pen, paper, files, and a calculator and headed there. He was just getting started when Director Wilson poked his head into the room.

"So here you are," he said, entering the room. "I thought you might have left early."

"I wish," Agent Henson told him. "I just needed a quiet space to do some calculating. A few of Beck's financial transactions don't add up right, so I thought I'd see if I could find the discrepancies." He paused. "I've got to admit, though, a degree in higher mathematics would come in handy right about now."

Henry pulled up a chair across from Tom. He picked up the telephone and told the front desk that he would be out for a while. After hanging the receiver up he turned toward Tom again. "Okay, let's see what you've got."

I went inside after a while and sat down on the couch. Glancing through the magazines on the coffee table I came across an article that had Connor's photographs with it. The article was on beaver dams and the good and bad that they did to the environment. It was really an interesting article. Before I had met Connor, I would have never read an article like this, although I might've watched it on PBS if there wasn't anything else on TV that I wanted to watch. A little while passed by and I had read all of the articles that had sounded interesting to me, so I began looking through Connor's record collection. I found a couple of records that I recognized and put one on to play. As the music filled the room I sat down on the couch and closed my eyes. I smiled as I remembered our dancing attempts.

Music touched Connor's ears as he came up the cabin steps. A memory of better times washed over him, and he quietly opened the cabin door and closed it behind him. As he walked into the living room the record was just ending. I started to get up to change the record when I caught some movement from the corner of my eye. I drew my gun and whirled around. I pointed the gun down quickly. "Don't do that to me," I said to Connor's smiling face. "I could have killed you."

"You're too good an agent to do that, Sarah." he

commented. "But I am glad to see that your reflexes are still intact. How's the shoulder coming along?"

"It's loosened up a little bit, but I'm still getting a twinge every now and then. How did things go with your friend Wade?"

"Just, fine. He's going to keep the Jeep hidden as long as we need him to." Connor walked over to the record player and lifted the needle off from the record. After returning it to its cover, he asked, "Was there another record that you would like to listen to?"

"Whatever you would like to play is fine with me," I said as I placed my handgun on the coffee table in front of me.

"What do you think?" Connor turned and smiled, his blue eyes twinkling. "Feel up to some dance lessons?"

I laughed in response. "You do remember what happened the last time, don't you? Have you completely healed yet?"

"My limp isn't quite as noticeable anymore, so I guess I'm safe." he replied smiling.

"I'd better take a rain check for now. Maybe in a couple of days when my shoulder is feeling a little less sore I'll be able give you a run for your money," I kidded.

"I'm going to hold you to that, you know."

"I hope so." I smiled.

Connor put on an old record of the Mills Brothers, I think it was. We sat on the couch, leaned our heads back, and closed our eyes. The music took us away to another place and time, back when we'd first met and before I'd been shot. "A penny for your thoughts," he said softly.

"Believe it or not, I wasn't thinking about anything at all." I turned my head toward him and opened my eyes. "I was just letting the music wash everything away."

"Are you tired?" Connor asked with some concern in his voice.

"A little bit. I could probably doze off pretty easily right here," I said with a yawn.

"Why don't you go ahead and lie down for awhile?" He asked as he stood up to change the record.

"You know what would be nice? How about we just sit and talk and enjoy one another's company."

"That sounds like a plan," Connor replied. He put on and LP with all music then came back and sat beside me on the couch. "What would you like to talk about?"

"Tell me about your friend Wade. I think it's nice to have a good friend that will do anything for you."

"First, I will have to tell you a few things that you don't know about me," Connor began. He proceeded to tell me about his being a Navy SEAL with Wade. He didn't say anything about his missions, and that was okay with me. I was sure that they were top-secret, and most servicemen don't like talking about the war.

"I guess I know why Tom let me leave with you now," I said after some thought. "Tom would have run you through our computers the first chance he had."

"Do you mean that you didn't check me out yourself?" Connor asked in amazement.

"Nope. My instincts told me all that I needed to know about you," I replied, putting my hand in his. "So far they have never let me down."

"And I hope that they never do." Connor replied with a squeeze to my hand.

We talked about everything under the sun. His family, my family, how I got into the agency, and even what the worst jobs were that we had ever held. My worst job was babysitting the Wagner's twins, two baby boys who were never on the same schedule at the same time.

Connor's worst job beat mine hands down. He had a

summer job mucking out the horse barn of the local equestrian club one year. The worst part was all of the neighborhood kids rode there as part of summer camp. He thought he would never live down the nickname they dubbed him, he told me. When I asked what that name was, he changed the subject, and I couldn't blame him.

"What about middle names? Mine is Leigh after my great-grandmother on my father's side of the family.

"Don't laugh," Connor told me. "My middle name is Angus."

"That's a Scottish name, isn't it?" I asked.

"I guess so. My great-grandfather fought in World War II. During one particular scrimmage, his unit fought alongside a British patrol. The story goes that my great-grandfather saved the life of a soldier named Angus McTaggart. A while later in another battle, McTaggart saved my great-grandfather's life. The two men became friends, and when the war ended they made a pact to name their first grandsons by the other's name to honor each other's courage. Well, my grandfather was an only child, and when he and grandma had my father, no way was grandma going to name him Angus. Grandpa and Grandma had three more children, all girls, so when I was born, my dad wanted to honor his grandfather's pact with Angus McTaggart, and that's how I got my middle name."

"Do you know if Mr. McTaggart ever kept his end of the pact?" I asked with curiosity.

"I've no way of knowing. Since it was so long ago and they live in another part of the world, I don't think I'll ever know," Connor answered.

"I think that it's nice that your dad did that for your great grandfather. Did he live long enough to know what your father had done?"

"Great Grandpa died when I was two and a half years old. Dad said he died with a smile knowing what dad had done."

"I'm sorry I didn't get a chance to meet your family. They sound like they were special people."

"My mom and dad would've loved you," Connor whispered looking deep into my eyes. We sat in silence awhile before Connor spoke again. "Are you up to eating something?"

"I've been enjoying myself so much I don't even know what time it is," I said, glancing out the window.

The woods were starting to get a soft glow from the setting sun. Connor saw my expression and asked, "Would you like to go outside and watch the sunset from the porch?"

I nodded and took the hand he offered me. The oranges, pinks, and yellows of the evening sky were dancing through the treetops. I bet that the autumns here were absolutely breathtaking I told myself. As the first stars started to twinkle in the night sky, I began to feel how cool it had gotten. We went back inside, and Connor started a fire.

While the logs crackled in the fireplace we made soup and sandwiches. I couldn't believe that I didn't miss having the radio or TV set on. Washington seemed like a whole other world away.

The director and Tom Henson went over the figures from Beck's files twice. Rubbing his eyes, Tom put down the file in his hand. "I don't think I can do this anymore tonight," he said.

"I know what you mean," Henry Wilson replied, putting down the file that he had been holding. "We can pick this up tomorrow. I sure wish we could wrap this case up."

Agent Henson stood up and walked to the windows. Pulling up the blinds he exposed the setting sun. "Me too," he said, sipping from his coffee cup. A silence fell over the room, and after a couple of minutes Director Wilson stood up and walked over to the window beside Tom. "Still worried about Anthony?" he asked in a low voice.

"Yes," Tom answered. "I know that I shouldn't, but Sarah is almost like a daughter to me."

Henry put his hand on Tom's left shoulder as they stared out the window. "She'll be okay Tom. We have to believe that."

Tom nodded in agreement.

Henry Wilson left for home, leaving Tom staring out the window. Tom would've liked to have stayed for Connor's next call, but that wouldn't be for a couple more hours.

The elevator dinged as it stopped in front of Tom. When the doors opened, he stepped in and pushed the button for the lobby. Only a few agents were left in the building at this time of day. Oh, how frustrating this case has gotten, he thought, and then something hit him like a ton of bricks. You should stop by the hospital so that no one would be suspicious as to why Sarah never had any visitors. He decided to do that tomorrow morning.

After doing the dishes, Connor and I sat back down at the table. "Would you like to play some cards or something?" Connor asked.

"Sure, if you don't mind being beaten again." I smiled back.

"Oh you're really in for at this time, Sarah." he replied as he retrieved a deck of cards from the desk.

"Why? Are the cards marked?" I quipped.

"Very funny," Connor said as he began to shuffle the deck. This deck of cards was well worn and shuffled easily. The blue pattern on the back was faded somewhat and a few of the cards had been bent at one time or another. "What would you like to play?"

I thought for awhile and then answered, "Let's start with something easy, like Crazy Eights and then work our way up to Gin," I suggested.

"You've got it," Connor said before he began dealing the cards.

The two of us played cards and kidded one another for almost three hours. The luck would change from one to the other of us as we played. All told, though, I guess I wasn't the best card player around. To tell the truth, I didn't really think that I was.

The traveling, walking, meal, and card games were catching up with me. The cards were becoming blurry as my eyes got heavy. I rubbed them and commented on how long the day had been.

Connor nodded and put the rubber band back around the deck of cards. "Come on," he told me. "Let's put you to bed. Tomorrow we'll do a few exercises for that shoulder of yours."

I groaned and rolled my eyes. Connor smiled and pulled out my chair for me. Walking back toward the bedrooms I held his hand. Connor flipped on the light to my room and asked me to hold on for a minute. "I'll be right back," he said before disappearing down the hallway and returning with a pair of pajamas for me to wear. "Good night, Sarah." Connor told me with a kiss.

I returned his kiss and his good night wish. "I'll see you in the morning," I whispered.

Connor went back out into the living room and checked the doors and the windows. When he'd finished he looked at his watch. It was just about time to check in with Sarah's office, he reminded himself. He went into his den and pulled open the top drawer of his desk. Inside in the pencil tray was a key to the bottom desk drawer. He hadn't had to use this key since he'd built the cabin. As he turned the key over in his hand, Connor remembered buying the satellite phone locked in the bottom drawer. It had been at Wade's prompting that Connor had finally given in and bought it.

"You can't live like a hermit for the rest of your life," Wade had said to him. Connor didn't think that he was living like a hermit. He got out and traveled and mingled with the human race when it had been necessary. Connor snapped back into the present and unlocked the drawer. After making a few adjustments to the phone, he walked outside onto the porch and made his phone call. The message was the same, "All is well, kiddo." Connor placed the phone back in his desk and headed for bed. It had been quite a day, he thought as he lay down. Tomorrow should be less hectic, he hoped.

Tom Henson's alarm clock went off at eight o'clock in the morning. Turning over, he hit the snooze bar. Just a couple of minutes longer, he told himself, just a couple of more minutes. At 8:10 the alarm sounded again. This time Tom shut it off and got out of bed, yawning. After breakfast with his wife, Tom headed to the hospital. "I've got to keep up the charade a little while longer," he told himself.

Agent Shapiro was on duty outside the hospital room again. He nodded as Tom approached. "Anything newsworthy to report?" Tom asked Paul.

"All's quiet here," he replied.

Tom nodded and went inside the hospital room. A female agent by the name of Joyce Patterson was acting as my decoy. "At last, a friendly face." Joyce exclaimed as Tom came in the door.

"How are things going? None of the hospital staff have been in here, have they?" Tom queried.

"The only problem here is the total boredom. When was

Sarah supposed to be released? I can get out of here soon, right?"

"It's only been two days. Surely you can't be that bored," Tom commented.

Ten minutes later Tom said his goodbye and left for the office. Oh how he wished he hadn't stopped by the hospital. Patterson was a good agent when things hit the fan, but inactivity wasn't usually a big part of it.

At the office, Tom rode up in the elevator with Director Wilson. He stopped in again and checked for any messages on the secure line. The same cryptic message as the other night, he was told. He breathed a sigh of relief and headed for the coffee pot. After a cup and a half of coffee, Tom started back to the conference room and Beck's financial records. He shook his head and closed his eyes hoping that the files would disappear. No such luck. He sat at the conference table and again began poring over the files. He had been at it for almost three hours when it all began to fall into place. Tom buzzed the director's office and asked if he would come down for a moment. The urgency in Henson's voice was unmistakable.

Director Wilson opened the conference room door and asked, "What've you got, Tom?"

"Look here," he said pushing the files across the table. "I think I finally found something." Tom Henson was talking fast and laying out how Beck was doing some creative bookkeeping with his finances.

Henry stopped Tom twice by saying, "Whoa. Slow down a bit."

What the financial records showed was that someone was laundering money. It was made to look like Martin did it, but the money told a different story. There was still no way to connect mob boss DeLuca to Beck, but that was just a technicality. Once he was brought in for questioning they might be able to get him to roll over on the mob. It was a long shot, but maybe Beck would want to make a deal. Right now the charges were only felony money laundering. They still couldn't pin Martin's murder on him.

"All right now, Tom," the director stated. "We've got to be smart about this. I don't want anyone else getting shot. Take a team and pick up Beck. Bring him in, secure his office, and I'll get a search warrant for his home and business. Maybe we can find a second set of books."

"Okay. I'll take a couple of sharpshooters too, just in case," Tom replied.

"Nobody. . . and I mean nobody goes without wearing a vest. Hear me?" Director Wilson said pointing a finger at Tom.

"Yes sir," Agent Henson agreed.

"Give me an hour or so to get the search warrants before you do anything. In the meantime, gather your team together." Director Wilson headed back to his office while Tom collected Beck's records. While he did that, he mentally put together his team.

I was up at 7:30 and standing in the cabin looking out the window at the sun coming through the trees. I thought how I could get used to waking up to this on a daily basis. My thoughts were interrupted by a noise in the kitchen. I turned and walked toward it.

"Good morning," Connor cheerfully greeted me. "How would you like breakfast on the porch?"

"That sounds wonderful, but it looks a little nippy outside this morning," I answered.

"Okay, then, how about I start a fire in the fireplace and then make us some pancakes for breakfast?"

"Only if you'll let me help" I chimed in. Before Connor could object, I added, "and I won't take no for an answer."

"In that case Sarah, I would love to have the help." Connor smiled in response.

The fireplace sparked to life as Connor lit the tinder. It didn't take long before he had a fire going. The warmth of the fireplace felt wonderful.

Connor pulled out the pancake mix and let me mix the batter while he got some sausage frying. I think he knew when to give up and not argue with me, but I also knew that he could be just as headstrong. Breakfast was peaceful and relaxing. We talked about what we were going to do with our day. A walk in the woods was the first order of business. I wondered what the hiking trail looked like now that some of the avalanche debris had been cleared away.

We took turns in the bathroom, and then he lent me one of his flannel shirts for the hike. It was a blue and brown plaid shirt with brown patches on the elbows that matched the brown collar, and it was as soft as it could be.

As we walked and held hands, we talked. We talked about nothing and we talked about everything. Our lives were open books. The trail seemed much shorter than when I'd last walked it. I guess it was the company. The slide area had been cleared of debris, but only from the trail. You could still see the path that the avalanche had taken, and then, there in front of us stood my lifesaving trees. I was kind of surprised that they hadn't been taken down. I guess that since the tree's roots weren't exposed they were still a living part of the forest. A squeeze on my hand brought me back into the present. I turned toward Connor and smiled.

"What do you say, Sarah? Do you want to see what's farther down the trail?" Connor smiled back.

"You say that like you've never been any farther down the path yourself," I commented.

"I've hiked all of the trails in this forest at least three

or four times, but it's been awhile. And none of them have been with you."

That settled it. I wasn't ready to go back to the cabin quite yet anyway. "Lead on, McDuff," I said to Connor, laughing. The two of us walked for quite a while. The forest was full of scampering squirrels and chirping birds.

Connor looked around at our surroundings like he'd never seen them before.

"I can't believe how much things have changed out here," he commented.

"Changed how?"

"Well, the weather has eroded away a couple of places where I thought the ground was firm enough to hold the plant life. And over there…" he said, pointing to my right, "used to be a little waterfall. Now it's nothing but a trickle down the slope."

"At least it doesn't seem to have affected the wildlife very much," I remarked as we continued walking.

"I'm not so sure about that. We would have to be out here at either dawn or dusk to see whether or not larger animals like deer have been affected."

"Maybe someday we will," I said in a near whisper.

Connor stopped and smiled at me. "How is it that you know just what to say?"

I put my right hand on the side of his face and kissed the opposite cheek. I knew that he wanted to hug me but was afraid he would hurt me, so I slipped my arm around his waist and laid my head on his shoulder. Connor's arms gently wrapped around me, and he kissed me tenderly on the cheek.

Tom had put together a six-man team of agents to apprehend Beck. Two of the men were sharpshooters, along with two teams of two to cover the realty office's front and rear. Director Wilson, good to his word, had obtained the two search warrants. Agents would secure Beck's business first and then hit his house. After some last-minute instructions to the teams, Tom led the way to Beck's office. The adrenaline was pumping as Tom drove across town. It had been a long time since he'd been a part of anything this big. He hoped that he still had what it took.

The realty office was empty except for the secretary. She called Mr. Beck's attorney when the search warrant was presented to her. The attorney told her that he was on his way and to let the feds search wherever they wanted to. After a half hour of searching the Martin and Beck Realty office, all of the relative files and books were seized into custody. The federal agents had Beck's attorney sign a receipt for all of the materials that they were taking. Tom made a quick call to the director. "No, sir. Beck wasn't here, but all relative materials have been confiscated. We're leaving for his home right now." Henry told Tom to leave someone there just in case Beck returned, but it was already being done.

Beck's two-story house was in a sparsely populated area. It was a typical brick house with shade trees front and back. A white picket fence started at the side of the house and went around the backyard. In the driveway were two vehicles, a Dodge minivan and a BMW sedan. Everyone was deployed and in place when Henson and agent Curtis approached the front door. As Tom raised his hand to knock on the door, it swung open. Tom's hand fell to his gun as Adam Beck stepped forward.

"Good morning, gentlemen." Beck said. "I've been expecting you." He motioned for the two agents to follow him inside. "I just got off from the phone with my lawyer. He said you would probably be coming here. What can I do for you?" He asked from the middle of his living room.

"Mr. Beck, you're under arrest for money laundering," Agent Curtis said before reading Beck his rights and handcuffing him.

Tom held up the search warrant and called in the other agents. "Why don't you make things easy for yourself and tell us where your second set of books are." Curtis stated.

Beck denied any knowledge of what they were talking about. The sharpshooters escorted Beck back to the agency while his house was being searched. Almost an hour had gone by with no luck.

"It has to be here somewhere," Tom muttered to himself.

"We've looked everywhere," young agent Curtis commented.

Tom walked through the house. Dresser drawers were half open with crumpled clothing inside. Closets had been searched, and even the bathrooms had been gone over. Down in the basement was a game room. Not a lot to search down there. There was a pool table, dartboard and bar at one end of the basement. A large screen TV sat against one wall with a leather couch across from it. "There just has to be something here," Tom told himself. As he started up the basement stairs a thought hit him. Tom turned around and went back downstairs. Over in the bar area was a refrigerator. Nothing unusual, but a little voice told Henson to open it. Inside were bottles of imported beers and jars of peanuts. Behind all of that were two thin books full of handwritten figures. Jackpot!

Everything in the house was searched again. Even the smallest containers were opened and checked, from the washer and dryer to the cigar boxes full of Hot Wheels cars in the boys' room. In Beck's wife's box of bath powder, a computer disk was found. Henson couldn't wait to see what information it yielded. Everything of interest that they had found was catalogued and packed up. Even Beck's computers were confiscated.

On the way back to the agency, Tom called Director Wilson and informed him of their discoveries. The director was pleased and awaited Tom's full report when he got back.

"I guess we'd better head back," Connor's voice whispered in my ear.

"What time is it anyways" I asked.

He looked at his wristwatch and replied, "Eleven thirty." I gasped and pushed Connor back. "We're going to be in so much hot water. I bet that Tom's had kittens, not hearing from us for so long now."

"Sarah, relax," Connor said in a calming tone. "I was in touch with them at midnight last night, so we're not late yet."

"But...how?" I asked.

"I have a satellite phone in my desk back at the cabin." Connor paused. "I haven't used it more than one or two times since I've lived out here."

"Why do you use the payphones in town to call clients instead of using your satellite phone then?" I questioned.

"For the exercise, mainly, but I also don't like ringing phones bothering me at all hours of the day and night. Can you understand that?"

I glanced at my surroundings. No, I wouldn't want a telephone breaking up the serenity of the forest either. I nodded and said as much. "Let's go call Tom before we have the Army National Guard banging down your door," I told Connor with a soft kiss to his lips. On the walk back through the woods we talked very little. I wondered what else Connor was keeping from me. The phone wasn't really a big deal to me, I just wished that he had confided in me about it.

Back at the cabin Connor showed me where the key and phone were. "I'm not going to keep anything else from you, Sarah," he said. "And when I'm done with this phone call, I've got something to show you."

The telephone in Washington rang and was patched through to Tom Henson's desk. An out of breath agent stated, "Henson."

"All is well, kiddo," Connor repeated once again into the receiver.

"Is she nearby?" he asked.

Connor handed me the phone and shrugged his shoulders shaking his head that he didn't know what Tom wanted.

"Yes?" I asked the caller.

"We've found Beck's second set of books, and now he's in custody. We can't pin murder charges on him yet, though."

"Now what?"

"Stay put and keep your eyes open," Tom answered. "Call me back in twenty-four," he said just before hanging up.

I handed the phone to Connor and sat down at his desk in thought.

Connor shut the phone off and placed it on top of his desk. "Is everything okay?" he asked with concern in his voice.

I hesitated and then shook my head and replied, "I guess so. It looks like things are hitting the fan back home."

"What'd Tom say that he wanted us to do?"

"He said to stay put and keep our eyes open." I glanced up into Connor's eyes. "Are you sure you want to put up with me for a while longer?"

"For as long as it takes and then some," Connor answered. "Come here for a minute," he said as he held his hand out for me to take.

We walked out of his office and into Connor's darkroom. He turned on the lamp over the developing chemicals and turned toward me. "Do you remember me telling you that I used to be a Navy SEAL?" I nodded. "Well, call me paranoid, I guess, but I like to be prepared." Under the counter was a locked cabinet door. Inside were two rifles, a thirty ought six with a scope and an M1 Garand with a serious-looking scope along with a sixteen-gauge shotgun. Below the gun racks were two handguns, a nine-millimeter handgun and a Ruger 357 six shooter in a holster. There was also plenty of ammunition for each of them.

I let out a whistle. "I'm sure glad that you're on our side," I said smiling.

"I just wanted you to know that it's here if we ever need it," he stated. As he locked the cabinet back up, he added, "And I hope that we never need them."

"I second that," I said as we walked into the living room.

Connor wrote down Wade Hood's phone number and gave it to me. "If anything happens, you can trust Wade with your life. I have." Connor's voice drifted off. He had entrusted his life to Wade on more than one occasion, or rather they had trusted each other with their lives. God, that seemed so long ago, another lifetime in a different part of the world.

"Connor?" I said quietly, touching his forearm. "Are you all right?"

He turned and looked at me. "I am now." He smiled. "How about we get going on those shoulder exercises?"

I moaned and rolled my eyes. "If we have to," I told him.

Beck wasn't cooperating at all. He had called his lawyer and was waiting for him to arrive. The lawyer, of course, had told him not to make any statements.

Agent Ron Carson, the computer specialist, was trying

to hack into Beck's computer. Without Beck's password, it was going to take a while, though.

The second set of books that they had found were being pored over by the auditing department in the conference room. From the looks of it, the mob was purchasing businesses and laundering money through them. Whenever they thought someone was getting too close, they went through Beck to sell the business and purchase another. Beck would then get a huge-kick back for his discretion and silence. Now the agency would have to raid DeLuca's place and obtain his books. This wasn't going to be easy. By now the mob knew that Beck was in the custody of the feds.

Agent Henson knocked on Director Wilson's office door.

"Come on in," the voice replied sharply.

As Tom entered the director's office, Henry glanced across the desk at him and held up his index finger as he concluded his telephone conversation. After replacing the receiver he said to Tom, "Okay, now tell me what's been happening."

The conversation revolved around what was in Beck's second set of books and how the next logical step would be to subpoena mob boss DeLuca's books. What a kettle of fish they had opened up. Henry nodded and told Tom that he would start things rolling. "Make sure Beck stays in our custody. We don't want any accidents happening to him."

"His attorney won't like that very much," Henson commented

"I don't much care what Beck's attorney likes. I want DeLuca, and that's not going to happen if Beck ends up like his buddy Martin."

Tom Henson nodded and headed for the door.

"I'll let you know when the okay comes down for DeLuca," Henry told him.

Tom commented that he would be waiting. Out at his desk he made arrangements to hold Beck in tight security. His attorney had strongly objected, but when DeLuca's name was mentioned, the lawyer backed down. There weren't very many people living around Washington D.C. who hadn't heard of Dominic DeLuca. He'd been headline news on several occasions.

Tomorrow would be crazy, Tom thought. He would have to be sure to wear his vest everywhere. Maybe he would even hit the firing range on his way home tonight. It had been a while since he'd fired his weapon. Better to be safe than sorry, he told himself.

My shoulder was beginning to throb a little, but I bit my lip and kept going. Connor noticed the wince on my face and stopped the therapy.

"You should've said something, Sarah. We don't want to undo everything that we've already made progress on."

I gave a huge sigh of relief. "Thank you," I smiled.

"Are you sure that you're okay? Did I push you too hard?"

"No. Don't worry. If it had gotten too painful for me, you would've known about it." I gave him my best evil grin.

He laughed." Yes ma'am. I believe I would've been informed by you immediately."

I laughed. "And don't you forget it."

Connor gave me a salute, and we both laughed out loud. That made me forget about my shoulder for the time being. I really appreciated his helping me like this. We made a fire in the fireplace and then fixed spaghetti and salad for supper. We talked about our childhoods and what we had wanted to be back then. I had wanted to be an actress on a popular television show. Connor revealed that he had wanted to be a forest ranger.

"Don't laugh. I thought that sitting in a tower overlooking

a grand forest would've been fun, nothing but three hundred and sixty degrees of woodland," he explained.

"Didn't you think about how lonely that would have been?" I asked.

"I've always been kind of a loner, so the thought of being alone wasn't that bad. Who knows? Maybe I would've taken up painting or something to occupy my time up there."

"So what happened?" I asked quietly.

"Oh, I just grew out of it. When I was in my junior year of college I met a newly retired Navy SEAL. After talking to him for awhile I knew what I wanted to do for my country." Connor paused. "What happened to being an actress?"

"It's the same old story. Girl auditions for grade-school play, passes out opening night from fright, gives up acting plans." I smiled. "It's not so bad being in front of people anymore, but for quite a while there it was horrifying. Anyway, my second interest was to be a police officer, so I just stepped that goal up a notch. I was in eighth grade then."

The agents working on Beck's computers did so through the night and into the next day. Beck still hadn't given up the password for the disk that the feds had found in his house.

Director Wilson called a meeting of all of the agents to his office at 10:30. When they had all arrived he began, "I don't think I have to tell you how close we are to getting Dominic DeLuca. From now on everything said or heard about the case is not to be repeated to anyone, not your spouse, not your lover, not even the local law officials." Henry glanced around the room. "DeLuca knows by now that we're gunning for him, so let's be thorough and not make any mistakes. We don't need to give the courts any reason to throw this out. Are there any questions?" He asked glancing around the room again. The agents shook their heads. "Okay, then, from now until further notice, everyone wears their vests. No exceptions! Let's get back to work."

Agent Henson held back as the director's office emptied. When the last agent had walked out the door, Tom closed it behind him.

Director Wilson was standing and looking out the window. His hands were clasped behind his back. "What do you think, Tom? Can we really shut DeLuca down?"

Tom stood in front of the director's desk. "We're going to give it one hell of a shot, Henry."

"I just hope that we can keep the press out of it, at least for the time being." He turned around and faced the older agent. "How's Anthony holding up?"

"She sounds okay. I try to keep the calls as short as I can. McBride seems to be right on top of things, though."

"At least she's safe, then. Has anyone been asking about her?"

"Her family still thinks that she's out of town on a case. Do you want me to have her call them so they don't get too worried about not hearing from her?" Tom asked.

"Let's give it a couple more days and see what happens." The director replied sitting down at his desk. "If we can get DeLuca locked up for good, Sarah can come back."

Henson agreed and went to see if the computer lab boys had gotten into Beck's computer yet.

We had just finished washing the breakfast dishes when someone knocked on the cabin door. The knock was followed by a strange whistle. Connor smiled and told me that it was okay; it was his friend Wade. As Connor opened the door he extended his hand to his friend. "What the heck brings you out this way?" he asked with a smile.

"Janet kicked me out because I was underfoot and distracting her from writing her thesis, so I thought I'd get some exercise," Wade answered.

Connor welcomed him in and did the introductions. As I shook Wade's hand I told him that it was nice to put a face to his name.

Wade glanced at Connor and told me. "Don't believe everything this guy's told you."

"That's too bad. Everything I heard about you was good." I winked at Connor.

Wade smiled at me. "Oh, I like her, Cap'n!" he remarked.

Connor turned the logs in the fireplace and we all sat at the table. He inquired about anyone asking around about us. No one had come snooping around yet anyway, Wade told us. The conversation turned to the weather and world news. After a few minutes I offered to fix something to drink.

"Don't go out of the way for me," Wade told me.

"I wasn't going to." I smiled. "I was just going to heat up some water for hot chocolate."

Connor laughed and Wade joined along. "I would love some hot chocolate, Sarah." he replied. "Thank you."

"Three cups coming right up." I stated. I put the kettle on the stove and got out the coffee cups and hot chocolate mix. When the hot chocolate was finished Connor helped me bring the cups to the table with a plate of store-bought cookies. As we drank and ate, Wade asked how I was getting along with no television or newspaper. I told him that I never used to get the newspaper and that my work didn't usually allow me time to watch very much TV.

"I would go stir crazy if I couldn't have my television," he said. He followed that with, "How about a game or two of cards before I have to get back?"

I shrugged my shoulders carefully when Connor glanced my way. "Why not?" I asked.

Connor went to the small writing desk and retrieved a deck of cards. He handed them to Wade, who gladly started shuffling them.

"Okay, boys and girls, what'll it be? Five Card Stud, jacks are wild, or something a little more tame?"

"It's going to have to be something a little more tame for me," I replied. "I know how to play Crazy Eights, Gin, and I learned how to play Spades in the hospital. I'm afraid that's my limit."

"Well, I've never won a game of Gin against Connor, so how about some Spades?"

The first game was won by Wade. He was so pleased with his win that he kept the scorecard. The game had been to five hundred points and had taken us just over an hour and a half to play, so Wade couldn't stay for another game. As he stood up to go he apologized for having to leave so soon. "It's been a real pleasure to meet you, Sarah." he said as the three of us walked to the door.

"It was nice meeting you too, Wade. I hope to see you again soon," I replied.

Connor and Wade walked out onto the porch while I put the cups in the sink. "Thanks for coming by and checking on us, Lieutenant," Connor stated patting Wade on the shoulder.

Wade turned and looked into Connor's eyes. "I really like Sarah, Connor. The two of you make a good pair," he said in all seriousness. "I hope that things work out for the two of you." As Wade started toward the hiking path he turned back and yelled, "Stay safe." over his shoulder. Connor waved at his good friend.

Tom Henson was at his desk when the phone rang.

"Henson," he said into the receiver. "Oh, hello Mrs. Anthony. How can I help you?" The telephone conversation was short and a little hard to understand through Mrs. Anthony's crying. What Tom was able to pick out was that my sister had been in a horrible car accident and might not pull through. He assured her that he would let me know. She thanked Tom and hung up. Tom walked down the hall to the director's office and knocked twice on the door. He was told to enter, and once inside, Tom told the director about the frantic phone call.

"Can we get word to Sarah now?" Henry Wilson asked looking up at Tom.

"Not until they check in, sir." Agent Henson answered.

"Are we sure that that was Mrs. Anthony?"

"Come to think of it," Tom pondered, "even through the crying I'm not sure that it was Sarah's mother. Let me see where the call came from," he said as he picked up the phone on Henry's desk. The switchboard said that the call came from a payphone in the Mercy General Hospital lobby. To be on the safe side, though, Tom called the Anthony house.

My mother picked up the phone when it rang. "Anthony residence" she said into the receiver.

"Hello, Mrs. Anthony. This is Tom Henson, Sarah's partner."

"What's wrong?" she asked with concern in her voice. My dad heard her question and put down the newspaper that he'd been reading. "It's Sarah's friend from work," she told him.

Agent Henson quickly got her attention back. "It's all right, Mrs. Anthony; there's nothing wrong with Sarah. She's out of town on a case and can't make any personal calls for security reasons, so she asked if I would check in on you for her."

My mother breathed a sigh of relief. "Thank God. We worry about Sarah so much."

"Yes, ma'am," Tom told her.

"Well, you can tell her that we are all doing fine and miss her. Do you know when she'll be back?"

"Her case is taking a bit longer than we had anticipated, but we're hoping to finalize it within the next month or so."

"That long? She is safe, though, right?"

"Oh, yes ma'am. I promise you that Sarah is in no danger." Tom tried to sound reassuring. "Well.., it's been a pleasure talking to you. I'll give your daughter your best when we're in communication again."

My mother thanked him for calling, telling him that he had eased their minds somewhat. Tom promised her that he would keep in touch as the case allowed. They both said good bye, and after hanging up, Mom repeated the phone conversation to my father.

After hanging up the phone Tom looked across the desk at the director. "Someone's trying to find Anthony," he said solemnly.

"Damn! All right, let's put some around-the-clock surveillance on her family members, but I don't want them knowing it. The agents need to be invisible to the family." Henry started making notes. "When the Anthony's are out of the house let's discreetly place some bugs around too."

"Okay, Henry, I'll see to it. What do you want me to tell Sarah when they check in again?"

"Not a thing," the director said, looking up from his desk. "Tell McBride so he'll have a heads-up. We'll leave it to his discretion as to whether or not to tell Anthony."

Tom nodded and replied, "Yes, sir," as he headed for the door.

When the office door had been shut, Henry closed his

eyes and said a quick prayer. All of his agents were like his children. Eight years ago two of his agents had been shot and killed unnecessarily. He had almost quit his job after that had happened. Everything had to be done to prevent this from happening again, he told himself.

"I like Wade," I told Connor when he had come back inside the cabin.

"He can be kind of corny at times." Connor smiled. "But he's always there when I need him, and vice versa."

"That's evident by the respect you two have. I've never let anyone get that close to me . . . until now, that is."

"Why is that, Sarah?" Connor asked as he sat down beside me on the couch.

"I'm not really sure. I guess that I was just trying too hard at my job. With my mother against my job decision in a mainly male dominated career field, I guess I just needed to prove myself. Dating and socializing just got pushed to the back burner."

"No wonder your mother is always after you." He grinned.

I smacked Connors arm with my right hand and smiled. "Thanks a lot!"

He kissed me lightly on the cheek and replied, "Maybe we can do something about that."

"Why Mr. McBride," I teased. "Whatever do you have in mind?" We both laughed and talked some more. After a half hour or so, we decided that I had better do some more shoulder exercises. It was painful and hard to do, but I stuck with it as long as I could. When the pain showed through in my facial expression we would quit for the day. I still seemed to be pushing myself, though.

It had been almost twenty-four hours since Connor had called Washington and Tom Henson was anxious to get his call. The telephone rang on Tom's desk exactly on time. Upon picking it up and saying his name, he heard Connor's code phrase.

"Hello, kiddo," Tom began. "Listen closely. Someone called pretending to be Sarah's mother. She claimed that her daughter Kate had been in a bad accident and was near death. We checked the call, and everything was bogus."

"What you want me to do?" McBride asked.

"We've got surveillance on the family. It'll be up to your discretion what to tell Sarah. We don't want her coming back at any rate. It's too dangerous."

"Gotcha," Connor stated.

"Talk to you again in twenty-four," Henson said, signing off. As he hung up the phone he let out a sigh of relief. He didn't envy Connor's decision whether or not to tell me what and happened here.

Connor turned off his satellite phone and placed it on his desk. Sitting on the corner of his desk he closed his eyes and slowly shook his head. He didn't want to keep anything from me, but he didn't want me to worry, or worse, run back to D.C.

As I walked by Connor's office on my way back to the kitchen, I glanced in. "How'd it go with Tom? Have they gotten Beck to talk yet?"

Connor glanced up at me. "He didn't say."

"What did he say?" I queried.

"For you not to worry about anything."

"Like what?" I prodded.

"Let's go into the living room and talk. It's more comfortable in there." As we walked into the living room and sat down on the couch my mind was racing. "Okay," Connor began as he faced me. "Someone called pretending to be your mother. She tried some sob story about your sister being in an accident and near death." He put his hand on my elbow. "It's okay, Sarah." He continued. "They checked it out and the call was a fake. Someone's just trying to draw you out into the open. The agency is keeping an eye on your family just in case, though."

A lump got caught in my throat. My job had never put my family in danger before. A million thoughts raced through my mind. What should I do? I stared silently at the fire in the fireplace. It was so tranquil here. How could the rest of the world be so chaotic?

A squeeze on my hand brought me back to my surroundings. "Are you okay?" the soft male voice whispered beside me.

"I think so," was all that I could choke out. "You're sure that everyone's okay, right?"

"That's what agent Henson said."

"Then I'll try not to worry... too much anyway." I smiled weakly.

Connor carefully put his arm around me and pulled me close. "I'm sure that everything will be okay," he told me with a kiss to my cheek.

From Connor's lips to God's ears, I told myself. We sat on the couch staring into the fire for quite awhile. My mind was trying to think about something other than back home. I closed my eyes and concentrated on the warmth of the pair of arms around me. I was swept away to when I had met Connor and how beautiful the mountains were. A calmness came over me, and I let the cares of the world fade into the background. There was nothing that I could do anyway, except make things worse by going back. I opened my eyes and turned to face Connor. "It'll be okay," I stated confidently. "I know that Director Wilson and Tom will watch over my family like they were theirs." I stood and pulled Connor to his feet. "Let's go outside and watch the sunset."

The crimson clouds shone through the treetops like a campfire in the woods. It was breathtaking. When the sun had hidden its glow behind the mountains, the temperature dropped quickly. The cold air drove us back inside the cabin, and we decided on mugs of soup and grilled sandwiches for supper. As we ate and talked about anything that popped into our heads, Connor remarked, "Oh, crap!"

"What is it?" I asked.

"I received an inquiry about a photo shoot in Canada in a couple of months, and I need to reply by tomorrow."

"That sounds like fun," I told him.

"I'm going to turn it down this time, Sarah. I've worked for them before, so I know that they'll ask me again sometime," he commented. "Right now, though, you're more important. Besides, I've got a job up in Minnesota in three months, so it's not like I won't be working at all. If you'll excuse me for minute, I'll go send them my apologies."

I nodded and replied, "Of course."

While Connor was busy on the phone to the Canadian magazine editor. he got to thinking. If he had any other photography offers in his mailbox, they would go unanswered. That's not good business to leave them hanging that way, he told himself. He would call Wade and have him check his box, but not remove anything but the telegrams. He would have to go in the evening so that no one would see him.

The telephone at the Hood house rang twice. "Hello," Janet Hood's voice said.

"Hi, Janet," Connor greeted. "Is that lazy husband of yours around?"

She laughed. "Yes, he is. I can't seem to get rid of him." Janet handed Wade the phone and told him that it was

Connor. He gave her a kiss on the cheek and took the telephone out into the living room.

"How are you, Cap'n?" he casually asked while still within Janet's earshot. When he'd gotten a little farther away the tone of his voice changed. "Is everything all right?" he asked.

"There are no problems here, Wade. I just need you to check my mailbox. I can't afford to let my job suffer too much."

"Thank God that's all. You worry me whenever you call." Wade relaxed. "So what do you need me to do?"

Connor told Wade what to do and when he should do it. "If there are any telegrams I would appreciate it if you would bring them by. You only need to check the box once a week; that should give me sufficient time for my replies."

"No problem, but if Janet gets suspicious and thinks that I'm cheating on her, you'll have some explaining to do." Wade and Connor both laughed.

"You've got it, Wade. Thanks."

When Connor returned to the kitchen I had already done the dishes and cleaned off the table. "I thought I would call Wade and have him discreetly check my mailbox. He'll be back out when there's a telegram for me. I had almost forgotten what I did for a living. I've enjoyed our time so much."

As Wade hung up the receiver, Janet asked what Connor had wanted.

"Oh, just to pick up something for him while he's gone," Wade replied. He hated lying to his wife, but with everything that was going on with Connor and me, it was for her own safety. His too.

"Well, I've got to be going to class now. Is Connor going to be gone long? There's a young woman in class that I think would be a good match for him."

Wade rolled his eyes and sighed. "I'm not sure how long he'll be gone, Jan." he replied. "Didn't you learn anything from the last time that you tried to set Connor up?" Wade asked as he walked his wife out to her car.

"Of course, silly. That's why I'm trying to get him together with Shelley. She's nothing like Karen was."

"Okay, honey," he said before kissing his wife goodbye. "Drive safely and have fun in class tonight."

Janet's hand waved out the window as she pulled down the driveway. Wade waved in return and walked back into the house to get his pickup truck keys. He chuckled as he thought about Janet's last blind date for Connor. Karen had been about as interesting as a pet rock. Wade had never repeated to Janet what Connor had said about her matchmaking skills, but Connor didn't look like he was going to need to be fixed up again, Wade smiled.

Wade Hood drove his pickup into town and parked in the post office parking lot. It was about eight o'clock, and after surveying the area, Wade went inside. Connor's box was three boxes to the right and four boxes above Wade's mailbox. He used Connor's spare key and rifled through the handful of magazines and junk mail inside. There was a single telegram in the pile. Wade pulled it out and pushed the rest of the mail back into Connor's box.

Just as Wade was locking Connor's box, another vehicle pulled into the parking lot. Wade quickly opened his own box and looked inside. He guessed that Janet hadn't been by to pick up their mail earlier that day. As the older gentleman came into the post office, Wade pulled his bills out of his mailbox. He would have rather had junk mail than bills any old day, he said under his breath. When Wade walked past the gentleman, he recognized him as Donald West. Don lived up the road a way toward the next town. He'd raised four children almost by himself. Don's wife had passed away after the fourth child had been born. The kids were all grown and moved away now.

"Hi, Don," Wade greeted the man on his way out.

Mr. West just nodded in response.

"See you around," Wade said as the post office door started to close behind him. Wade felt sorry for the gentleman. It had to have been hard raising four kids, working, and keeping a household running.

No one followed Wade home, not that Wade head expected anyone to. So far no one knew that Connor and I were up here, at least not yet. Wade knew that no secret could be kept forever, especially in Washington, D. C.

After Connor and I had eaten breakfast the next day and done the dishes, I suggested a brisk walk through the forest for some exercise.

Connor agreed. "Just let me grab my camera."

I pulled on my borrowed flannel shirt, and out of habit clipped my gun unto the belt around my waist. I hesitated a moment, debating on whether or not I should carry a firearm. Connor came out of his darkroom and asked if I was ready to go. I unclipped my holster and laid the gun on Connor's desk. "I am now," I answered with a smile.

Once we were on the hiking trail I picked up the pace. The cool morning air felt so invigorating that I didn't even feel any pain in my shoulder this morning. I didn't have a care in the world. After twenty minutes into our walk Connor slowed down and pointed to my left. There in the distance was a doe grooming her newborn fawn. Connor pointed his camera, focused, and snapped the shot. "Want to take a look?" he asked quietly as he held out his camera to me.

"You bet," I said, carefully taking the camera in my hands. "What do I do?" I asked.

"Look through the viewfinder and then turn the lens until the deer are clear."

Looking through Connor's camera was like being right up beside the pair. I could almost count the speckles on the fawn's back.

"Oh, wow!" I exclaimed in a low voice. As I handed the camera back to Connor I asked, "Is this how all of your wildlife shoots go, or can you get physically closer to them?"

Connor put the lens cap back on and smiled. "It depends on the animal. Most close-up shots that you see though are done with a telephoto lens."

"That's amazing. And you get paid to take pictures like that?"

"Oh, trust me, all of the photographs aren't anywhere near as easy as this. Sometimes I've got to physically get down into the mud to get the shot that the client wants. It's not as glamorous as it may seem."

"I guess both of our jobs are like that," I kidded Connor, and he laughed.

Slowly we picked up our walking pace again. I had never been in this part of the forest before. I could hear the light trickle of a stream and the rustle of dead leaves as a squirrel scampered across the forest floor. It was so quiet and peaceful out here. It was about ten o'clock when Connor suggested that we head back.

"Is it that late? I feel like I could walk all day long."

"Maybe the next time we'll bring along a backpack with a blanket and a picnic lunch," Connor commented glancing, ahead at the trail. "There's a great spot ahead with a small waterfall that you would enjoy. Right now, though, we really need to start back."

"Okay. Okay," I said, turning around to face him. "At least I got to see past the slide area."

CHAPTER 4

Tom Henson got to his desk around 8:30. He had sent Margaret out of town to visit her sister in Akron, Ohio, just to be on the safe side. When she had questioned Tom about it, he had told her that he would be on assignment for the next week or so and didn't want her to sit home alone while he was away. Tom's wife was looking forward to a visit with her sister. She had wished that Tom could have joined her though.

The telephone on Tom's desk rang. It was the director asking him to come to his office. Tom hung up the receiver and headed down the hallway. Henry's office door was open, awaiting him. Tom knocked on the door jamb and stepped inside.

"Close the door behind you, Tom," Henry Wilson told him.

Tom complied and took a seat in front of Henry's desk. There was silence for a brief moment as Director Wilson gathered his thoughts. "I had a hard time sleeping last night, Tom," he said. "This case is going to be the death of me." Tom nodded his head in agreement. Henry Wilson stood and looked out the window. There was another pause before he continued. "Beck still isn't talking, and I'm afraid that something will happen to him, the longer this gets drawn out. Lord knows we can't protect him inside the prison system."

"Maybe that's what Beck needs to hear," Tom mused.

"Hell, I bet that Beck thinks that as long as he keeps his mouth shut, he's safe. The boys are going over the books you found right now. I'm sure that'll be enough for an indictment, but it won't be for his business partner's murder." Director Wilson sat at his desk and interlaced his fingers. "You said that Beck's car was ticketed near where Martin was killed, right?"

"That's what Anthony's detective friend said."

"Go back to that neighborhood and canvass it again. Somebody must've seen something. With all the blood at the scene, you would have thought that it would have been all over the murderer. They checked Beck's car for forensic evidence, didn't they?"

"Yes, sir." Henson nodded. "There weren't any hairs, drops of blood, saliva or anything found. The whole vehicle was combed from top to bottom."

"Where's the smoking gun like in the movies?" Henry mumbled under his breath. He glanced over at Tom and told him to go canvass the neighborhood and report back to him when he finished.

"Yes sir," Tom stated simply. He returned to his desk and got out the notes on where Beck's car had been ticketed. Looking at a street map of the surrounding area, Tom planned out his canvass area. This was going to take him a while, he thought. After donning his bulletproof vest, he left for Baltimore. He was thankful that the weather was still cool. The vests got hot and heavy in the summertime. After sitting in the backed-up morning traffic, Tom finally pulled up near where the police had ticketed Beck's car. He would start down the street and work his way around the block. He was equipped with a police arrest photo of Beck and a photo of the deceased James Martin.

Going from house to house was tedious work. At about

half of them, no one was at home. The rest of the people had either been watching their children or the television set. One older gentleman said that he had noticed Beck's car when he went out to get his newspaper at 8:30. Tom thanked him and jotted the information down. That gave them a timeline to work with, at least. The rest of that street was a bust.

As agent Henson worked his way around the block, he came across a couple of people who thought they might've seen one of the men, but they couldn't be sure. Another bust. When Tom had finished working his way to the house where Martin had been murdered things began to pick up a little. Across the street and three houses down was a house with a landscaping company manicuring their front hedge. His inquiries at the house were met with a negative response. He figured that he might as well ask the landscapers questions, as long as they were there. Bingo! Things were beginning to look up.

The landscapers had been on the other street on the morning of the murder. At first they didn't think anything about the man in a jogging suit cutting across the backyard next to where they'd been working. Kids had done it so often that there was a path worn in the grass. When they spotted the man running back through, though, his jogging suit was gone and he was in shorts and a golf shirt. The man called Luis said that he had commented about that to the other crew members. After looking at the photographs, most of the men weren't exactly sure that Beck might have been the man they saw. Tom jotted down their names and the descriptions of the man's jogging suit, shorts, and shirt. He thanked them before he finished canvassing the rest of the houses.

Back at his car, Tom got in and sat for a while resting his

sore feet. It was going to be an interesting meeting with the director when he got back to the office, he told himself. First, though, he would stop and get some lunch somewhere.

As we approached the cabin, Connor and I both spotted the silhouette on the front porch at the same time. Connor motioned for me to go wide to the right and he would go wide to the left. I nodded and carefully began making my way around to the side of the cabin. Connor was really good at this stuff. I glanced over twice, and he was nowhere in sight.

Connor quickly and silently wove in and out through the trees. His having lived here for so long gave him an advantage. When he'd worked his way around the side of the cabin, he paused and looked for me. There I was, directly across from him on the other side of the cabin. A small wave to me, and Connor gave me the signal to stay put. He'd begun inching his way along the side of the cabin when he stopped and smiled. He would know that profile anywhere. It was Wade. Connor couldn't help himself. He backed up and carefully knelt down and picked up a pinecone. He inched back toward Wade quietly and then tossed the pinecone into Wade's lap.

Wade jumped up like someone had set his pants on fire. "Damn!" he exclaimed, looking around.

Connor walked toward his friend with a big grin on his face. "Hello, Wade." He smiled. "Been waiting long?"

"Where the heck did you come from?" Wade asked.

"Oh, Sarah and I just thought that we would check out our visitor before we showed ourselves."

"Sarah's around here somewhere too?" Wade asked, glancing around again.

"Hi, Wade," I remarked stepping out from behind an oak tree.

"I must be getting old," he said shaking his head. "I never heard a thing."

"That was the object, Lieutenant."

"I know, but I didn't even hear Sarah coming, and she's not a SEAL."

Connor and I laughed, and Wade joined in after a while. "Come on inside and tell me what's going on," Connor said, clapping his hand on Wade's shoulder. Once inside, Wade handed Connor the telegram that he'd gotten out of Connor's mailbox.

"Are you sure that that's all you wanted? Your box was pretty full of stuff," Wade stated.

"That's a good thing, Wade. With so much stuff in my mailbox, no one will be able to tell if anything has been removed. This way it still looks like I'm out of town."

"Gotcha," Wade said as he looked over at us. "So, are you two up to few more games of cards?" A sinister smile crossed his face, and we broke out laughing.

"I hope that's not your poker face," I commented.

"Nope," Connor replied over his shoulder on his way to get the deck of cards from his desk. "That one's even funnier."

"You're just jealous. Admit it, you wish you could play cards as well as I do," Wade fired back jokingly.

"That's it, all right. I'm just jealous."

We all laughed again. While we played Spades it seemed like we had all been lifelong pals. I learned about Wade and Connor's childhoods, and they learned about mine. I had forgotten all about chaos back in Washington until...

"Sarah, we're in trouble now," Connor remarked, glancing at his watch. "We forgot to check in with agent Henson."

"I'm sure he'll never let you forget that, either. Or me, for that matter." I stated, smiling.

Connor hurried to his office and came back with the satellite phone in his hand. "Be with you in a sec, Wade. I've got to check in with Sarah's partner."

The switchboard agent said that Henson was out on a case and asked if Connor wanted to leave a message or if someone else could help him. Connor told him to hang on a minute and put his hand over the receiver. Turning to me he asked, "Tom's not in right now. Anyone else you want to talk to?"

"Ask for Director Wilson. Maybe there's been more news on my parents," I told him.

Our phone call was put through to the director's office. "Wilson," Henry's voice said into the telephone.

"All is well, kiddo." Connor told the voice on the line. "I have a message for you" he commented as he handed me the phone.

"How are my parents doing, sir?" I asked.

"We have them under surveillance and everything's been quiet. How are you holding up?"

"Okay so far. The not knowing is driving me a little crazy, though."

"I wish I could give you something more, but we're doing all we can to wrap things up as quickly and as airtight as we possibly can," Director Wilson said. "Hang in there, okay?"

"Yes, sir," I replied before handing the phone back to Connor.

"We'll check in again in another twenty-four." Connor said into the phone.

"Acknowledged, kiddo," Henry replied.

Connor hung up the satellite phone and came back to the table. After he had picked up his cards he said, "Well, at least we're not in trouble with Tom." He winked as he glanced my way.

"Okay you two. Can we get back to the game now, please?"

Connor and I laughed. "What's the matter, Lieutenant? Can't wait any longer to lose this hand?"

"In your dreams, Cap'n." Wade sneered back. We had finished the first game and were getting ready to start another one when Connor asked Wade where his wife thought that he was this time.

"Oh, crap! I've got to go." Wade glanced at his watch. "You guys are going to be the reason for my divorce," He remarked.

"What did you tell Janet that you were going to do when you left the house?"

"I said that I had to run an errand for you, old buddy. She's not going to believe that it took me three hours to do your errand, though."

"I'll tell you what you do," I interjected. "Let the air out of your spare tire and tell her you had a flat. Dirty it up some if you need to, to make it look used. That might buy you a little more time."

Wade and Connor looked at each other and then at me.

"What?" I exclaimed. "Okay, so I used that excuse to get out of a family dinner one time. But it worked."

"Well, I know that it'll work for me too." Wade chuckled. "I don't have a jack in the truck either, so I would've had to borrow one. I like the way you think, Sarah."

"Thank you," I replied with a smile.

We walked Wade out onto the porch and said goodbye. As Wade walked away from the cabin, Connor turned toward me. "Is there anything else about you that I should be worried about?"

"Who... me?" I asked as innocently as I could.

Connor shook his head and smiled. "I can tell that I'm

going to have to keep my eyes on you." That wouldn't be a bad thing, as far as I was concerned, and I smiled back at him.

Tom got back to the office around 1:30. He had stopped at the local deli and had a turkey sandwich and a Coke before heading back to the agency. He knocked three times on Director Wilson's door, and the director's voice told him to come in. Tom opened the door, closing it behind him. When he turned around he saw agent Maxwell standing in front of Henry's desk.

"Oh, I'm sorry. I didn't know that you were busy," he said. "I'll come back."

"Stay, Tom. We're done here," Wilson replied. He walked Maxwell to the door and closed it behind him.

"Problem?" Tom asked.

"I hope not" the director said as he motioned Tom to sit down from behind his desk. "How did the canvass go?"

Tom took out his notepad. "A couple of people said they might have seen Beck, but couldn't be positive."

"So it was a waste of time?"

"Not entirely. I found a landscaping crew that had worked in that area the day of the murder."

"There wasn't any mention of them in the original canvass of the neighborhood."

"I know. I think they had probably moved on to their next job before things had gotten organized and the door-to-door begun."

"Or," Henry interrupted. "this is a setup." Neither man said anything for awhile. "What all did they tell you, Tom?"

Tom regaled the director with what the landscaping crew had told him. Henry leaned back in his chair with his eyes closed in thought. After a while he leaned forward and put his hand on the telephone. "Okay, here's what we'll do.

We'll never find the jogging suit. It's probably been in the dump for the better part of the week, so let's get another warrant for his house, car, business, and whatever else we can think of and see if we can find those shorts and shirt. If we do, we'll have forensics check them over."

"Sounds good. Hopefully they haven't been disposed of too," Tom agreed.

The search warrant took about an hour to get approved. Director Wilson told Tom to take another agent with him this time. That was just about the last thing that Tom wanted to do, but he followed orders. Paul Shapiro went along to help search the Beck properties.

The work was tedious and each time they had asked Mrs. Beck a question, her answers would come back surly. She wasn't to be believed or trusted. The two agents searched every nook and cranny of the Beck house, from the basement to the attic and then some. Everything. Every container, no matter how small, was opened and checked out thoroughly. No luck. Agents Henson and Shapiro thanked Mrs. Beck for her cooperation and headed for Beck's office.

"That was a big waste of two hours that I'll never get back," Paul remarked in the car. "And the wife... she was shooting daggers at us with her eyes the whole time."

"I know," Tom told him. "You just can't let it get to you, Paul. Lord knows in all of my years with the agency I've had to bite my tongue many a time, even though I felt like smacking the person." Agent Shapiro turned toward the window and smiled to himself. It was nice to know that Tom was just as human as the rest of us, he thought.

At the real estate office they presented their search warrant to the secretary that was there cleaning out her desk. She looked it over and stated, "Help yourself." File cabinet after file cabinet was opened. Every vent and every drawer was searched, to no avail.

Tom turned to the secretary and said, "Excuse me, miss, but I need to search the box you've been packing."

"Knock yourself out," she said, pushing the box across the desk to him. After looking through the stuff, Tom thanked her and apologized for the inconvenience.

"No sweat," the woman replied. "I hope you put Beck away for a long time."

"Why do you say that?" Shapiro asked with curiosity.

She pulled out a pack of cigarettes and lit one up. "I never did like Mr. Beck. See, Mr. Martin was really nice to me, and Mr. Beck stayed in his office and barked out orders when he wanted something done." She took a drag on her cigarette. "You know, Mr. Martin was the only one doing any real work here. Mr. Beck took credit for everyone else's work, though." She took another puff from her cigarette. "It's too bad the wrong man was killed."

Agents Henson and Shapiro glanced at each other and thanked her again. It takes all kinds, Tom thought to himself.

Beck's car had already been impounded, so the two agents headed for the garage. Agent Rogers was in charge of the impound lot. Beck's car had already been searched and nothing out of the ordinary had been found.

"What about any clothing?" Tom asked.

"We found what looked like a pile of rags, but it turned out to be an old shirt covered with dirt and grease."

"Are you sure that's all it was? No bloodstains, maybe?" Agent Henson asked.

Rogers shrugged his shoulders and said, "Don't know. We just assumed it was a regular car rag. You know, for wiping your hands on after working on your car."

Paul Shapiro chimed in. "Do you still have it?"

"Of course. It's over there in that red pail of rags. Hang on, and I'll get it for you." Rogers walked over to the pail and began pulling out rags. The third one he pulled out was a partial shirt. "This is it." Tom held the rag by his thumb and index finger. "Thanks" he muttered.

They took what was left of the shirt to the forensics lab. Gary Reed was the technician on duty in the lab. He looked at the rag in Tom Henson's hand and said, "You've got to be kidding." Tom shook his head and held out the rag for him to take. Gary grabbed a pair of disposable latex gloves and put them on. He carefully took the rag from Tom and asked, "What are we looking for in this mess, gentlemen? The kind of lubricant they used on their vehicle?"

Paul interrupted his fuming partner. "Very funny, Gary. You should tell that to the director."

"Okay. Okay. What do you want? Blood? Semen? Maybe drug content?"

"How about you just tell us everything that's on that rag, okay?" Tom angrily answered. "And try not to take all day with it." Tom turned and walked toward the laboratory door.

When he'd gone out, Gary looked at Paul and asked, "What's his problem?"

"Oh, nothing much. The main suspect in his latest case was murdered, and then his partner was shot. That's all," Paul answered. "Do you need anything else?"

Gary Reed felt about three inches tall as he shook his head and started analyzing the rag in his hand. It was going to take a while to find out everything that the rag had been exposed to, so Shapiro followed Henson back upstairs.

Connor supervised my shoulder therapy as I did my exercises. The shoulder was coming along pretty good. My range of motion still wasn't one hundred percent, but it was a vast improvement over two days ago. I hadn't had to take a pain pill since our drive to Virginia. I was glad that I didn't need them anymore. I hated the way that they made me feel all dopey and tired. I guess that's what they were supposed to do, though.

"Good, Sarah. How about ten more repetitions?" Connor asked breaking my train of thought.

"Has anyone ever told you that you're a slave driver?" I kidded as I did my reps.

"Yep," he answered. "Wade will be the first to testify to that. But hey! He lived through it."

"The question is, though, will I?"

"You've already made more progress than most people would've by now. I'm impressed, Sarah," Connor said with warmth in his voice. I finished the exercises and rubbed my shoulder lightly. "Got a kink?" he asked, coming up behind me and putting his hands on my shoulders. His touch was so light that I thought I would melt.

"Keep that up, and you'll put me to sleep," I told him.

"Okay, I'll quit."

I turned around and kissed him. "Thanks, coach." I smiled.

"Anytime." Connor smiled. "What would you like for supper?"

I thought about it for a couple of seconds and then asked if he had the fixings to make burritos. Connor had everything but the tortillas and the salsa. I told him that if he had a cookbook that I would make some tortillas. He had a cookbook, all right, but the only recipes inside were for Irish dishes. We compromised and made sloppy Joes instead.

Once supper was over we went outside to watch the sunset beyond the trees. I didn't think that I would ever get used to seeing this view. The magic just carried me away into my own little world. We sat on the porch until the sky grew dark and peppered with stars. A cold breeze blew through and chased us inside to the warmth of a roaring fire.

"How about some popcorn?" Connor asked.

"Sure, then we'll try to put that puzzle with the marbles on it together. It'll be a real challenge," I remarked.

"I have to tell you that that puzzle was just bought as a joke. You don't have to put it together."

"I don't plan on putting it together alone, you know," I retorted. "You have to help."

"That'll teach me," Connor said with a smile.

We popped the popcorn and set the bowl on the edge of the table, and dumped out the puzzle pieces. It sure seemed like there were more than fifteen hundred pieces there. The outside edge didn't take very long to put together. The rest of the puzzle pieces we put into piles of the same color, which actually helped a bit. Connor and I talked and laughed and had a good time putting the puzzle together. We had gotten down to the last hole, and there weren't any pieces left on the table.

"It looks like you got shorted," I told him.

"Nope," he replied with a big grin on his face. Pulling the last puzzle piece out of his pocket, he placed it in the empty hole. "I always did this to my brother. He hated it."

"I can't say as I blame him." I smiled back.

"Okay, I'll make a pact with you right now to never keep the last puzzle piece again."

"You're not going to make me spit in my hand and then do some crazy handshake, are you?" I asked him, suspiciously.

"Not unless you want to." He laughed. We spent the rest of the night looking through the magazines on Connor's coffee table and talking about taking pictures. He really was a talented photographer, I told myself.

Tom Henson called down to the lab around six o'clock. A few of the results on the rag had come in, but no DNA results. He told them that he would check back in the morning for the entire report instead of listening to only part of it. By the time he came in tomorrow, there should be a printed report on his desk from the lab techs anyway, he thought.

Director Wilson was still in his office when Tom Henson stopped by. His door was open, and the director was reading through a pile of papers on his desk. Tom knocked on the door jamb. When Henry looked up from his work, Tom remarked. "Are the workdays getting longer, or are we just getting older?"

Henry leaned back in his chair and replied. "Unfortunately it's a little bit of both, Tom. Are you clocking out for the day?"

"Yep. Tomorrow morning the forensics should be back on the rag from Beck's car."

"Good," The director said as he leaned forward in his chair. "I'll be awful damn glad when this case is over. It's starting to give me an ulcer."

"At least we don't have to cover the hospital anymore. Patterson says that since she left the hospital, or rather Anthony did, there's been no problem. Somehow I think it leaked out that Sarah wasn't there anymore."

"That would explain the phone call the other day. When they didn't find Anthony in the hospital, they made their phone call trying to ferret her out." Silence fell across the room. "I hate to think this, Tom, but we might have a leak."

"Do you really think that's a possibility?" Tom asked.

"Right now nothing can be dismissed. We need to make sure that there isn't anything around that can lead someone to Anthony. You haven't said anything about her to anyone, have you?" Henry asked.

"Of course not. I haven't even mentioned McBride's name in front of anyone but you."

"What did you do with the information he gave you as to their whereabouts?"

"It's locked in my desk drawer," Tom replied.

Henry told Tom to go and make sure that it was still there. Tom's desk was still locked and the GPS coordinates to Connor's cabin were still inside. He pulled the piece of paper out of his drawer and put it into his wallet. As he walked back to Henry's office, Tom tried to decide whether the contents in his drawer had been moved around. He just wasn't sure. "Get a hold of yourself," he told himself silently. "We don't need to push the panic button unnecessarily." When he walked into Henry's office, Tom stated. "It was still locked in my desk drawer, sir. I folded it and put it into my wallet for safekeeping."

"You're sure everything's okay? Nothing was suspicious or out of place, right?"

"As far as I can tell . . ." Tom paused. "nothing was moved in the drawer."

"Let's hope not, for both of their sakes," Director Wilson replied.

Tom Henson tossed and turned in bed all night long. The thought that someone might've gotten Connor's information was killing him. How could he not remember what his drawer looked like inside? When the alarm clock beside his bed began ringing, Tom rolled over and shut it off. He wanted to call in, take the day off, and try to get some more sleep. He got up, though, and got ready for work. Maybe today would be the day that something broke loose and helped them close the case. Tom sincerely hoped so, anyway.

Once in the office Tom found the copy of the forensic evidence results from Beck's rag on his desk. Hurriedly he opened it. Tom scanned down the list of greases, oils, dirt, and such. "I must've missed it," he thought. Slowly he read back down the page. Nothing, no DNA of any kind, according to the report, was on the rag. Tom crumpled the report in his left hand. "Damn!" he exclaimed, shaking his head. With the crumpled report in hand Tom headed down the hallway toward the director's office.

Agent Henson's facial expression and the crumpled paper in his hand said everything. Henry Wilson motioned Tom to have a seat. "All right, let's regroup and see where to go from here. There's got to be something we've missed somewhere."

Tom Henson shook his head and smoothed out the paper in his hand. "I don't know what it could be. We've followed up on every single lead that we had, thoroughly. Maybe we should tell Beck what's been going on and how he's being set up to take the fall for Martin's murder. I'm willing to bet that some evidence will miraculously turn up sooner or later. Maybe he'll cooperate if we offer him the witness protection program."

"We've got to do something." The director paused. "Go ahead and see what you can get out of Beck, but do it by the book. Make sure that you don't give his lawyer any reason to throw the case out."

"I'll do my best."

"Oh, and Tom, I want to be in the observation room when you talk to Beck. Maybe I can catch something that you might've missed. A second set of eyes, if you will."

"Yes, sir," Tom replied. "I'll let you know when I get things set up."

I had had a restful nights sleep last night. We'd stayed up talking until almost two a.m. Each day seemed to bring us closer together. I would have to be careful and stay focused on the danger of the case back in D.C. Maybe when it was over... my thoughts drifted away.

A knock on my door brought me back. "Hey, sleepyhead, are you up yet?" I heard Connor's voice say. "It's almost ten thirty already."

"I'm coming," I answered as I headed toward his voice. "Good morning," I said opening the door to my room. "What are the plans for today?"

"First breakfast and then some shoulder exercises. After that it will depend on you."

"How about another dance lesson, if I'm not too sore?"

"We'll see. First things first, though. What would you like for breakfast?"

I smiled and replied, "Whatever you would like."

Connor smiled back. "One of these days, Sarah, I'm going to get smart and quit asking." He turned around and started toward the kitchen.

"Hey, Connor," I called to him. He stopped and turned back around. "How about we skip breakfast, do the exercises, and then go on that picnic? It's only a little while before noon anyway."

Connor glanced at his watch and thought for a couple of minutes. "Okay, on one condition."

"Great! I'll get dressed," I told him turning back toward my room.

"Don't you want to know the condition?" Connor asked.

"Later," I said closing the bedroom door. Nothing Connor could come up with could be that bad, I told myself.

Connor had lent me a couple of T-shirts, a couple of flannel shirts, and a couple pair of socks the day before. I put on a T-shirt and pants and went out into the living room. A whistle left Connor's lips. "My clothes look better on you than they do on me." He smiled.

"Why thank you, sir," I acknowledged.

We began the exercises with a warm-up and then we got into the painful part. I groaned in response to his coaching.

The telephone on Director Wilson's desk rang twice. "Wilson," he said into the receiver.

Tom Henson was on the other end of the line. "We're all ready down here, sir," he told the director.

"I'm on my way. Give me five, and then you can start."

"You've got it," Tom said before hanging up. Within three minutes Henry Wilson was behind the one-way mirror made of shatterproof glass watching Henson interrogate Adam Beck. At first Tom went back over some basic questions like his name, address, and occupation, and then he was asked how long he had known James Martin.

Martin and Beck had partnered up about six years ago after meeting one another at a real estate seminar in Philadelphia. Both had been working for other agencies and decided to go in together and start a realty agency of their own. After a few more questions like that Henson asked him how he had met Dominic DeLuca.

"Who?" Beck asked.

"You were observed on several occasions having lunch with him. Are you going to sit there and try to tell us that you didn't know who you were eating with all those times?"

Beck's lawyer whispered back and forth, and then Beck answered, "Mr. DeLuca and I knew one another in high school."

How convenient, Director Wilson thought to himself.

Tom Henson kept asking questions about any kind of business partnership that Beck had with DeLuca. His lawyer would whisper something to him after each question and then Beck would clam up. Almost an hour went by, and they weren't getting anywhere.

"Do you know that you're being set up for James Martin's murder?" The question had finally been asked by agent Henson.

"I didn't kill anybody." Beck answered, shushing up his lawyer. "And you're not going to pin his murder on me."

"Why were you parked around the block from where Martin was killed during the time he was killed then?"

"What?" Mr. Beck's lawyer tried to calm him down. Beck looked at him and said, "What the heck's going on here? I was never near where Jim died."

"The parking ticket that you got says otherwise." Tom showed him a copy of the citation.

"I swear to you, I never got a parking ticket."

"Mr. Beck, do you own a green jogging suit with a black-and-white stripe down the sides?"

"Are you kidding? Do I look like I jog? What's this all about?" Beck asked, getting a little hostile.

Tom Henson continued. "What about a blue pair of shorts and a yellow golf shirt?"

"Sure, I do. My wife took them to the cleaners last week when I got barbecue sauce on them at a cookout we had at the house. What's that got to do with anything?"

"I'll ask the questions, Mr. Beck," Agent Henson told the man. "Can anyone verify this so-called barbecue?"

"I can give you my guest list." The lawyer whispered into Beck's ear again. Beck stopped him and said, "I'm not going down for something I didn't do. I admit to embezzling from the company and even being a front for money laundering for DeLuca. But I'm not going down for murder. You're fired!"

The lawyer tried talking to his client, but Beck responded by telling him to get out. Reluctantly the lawyer gathered his things and was escorted out of the building by two agents.

"You may have just signed your death sentence. Your so-called lawyer is on DeLuca's payroll. Didn't you ever wonder how you could afford a high-priced mouthpiece like him?" Henson asked, putting the facts on the table. "Here's what we have on you. You're in bed with the mob. Money-laundering alone is a major felony, and murder brings a death penalty most of the time in this state. DeLuca has lots of friends in the pen, so your lifespan doesn't look very good for you. He's made you a patsy, Mr. Beck."

Adam Beck put his head in his hands and thought about what to do. "If I tell you everything I know can we make some kind of a deal?"

"That depends on what you've got and if we can prove it. The state prosecutor would be the one who could offer you the witness protection program. I'm sure that that would be contingent upon getting DeLuca," Tom stated.

"Okay. Dominic planned the whole money-laundering scam to clean the drug money he was collecting. I overlooked it for the cut I was getting, but I don't know who killed Jim. He wasn't privy to the books."

"I think maybe Martin's death was a warning for you to keep your mouth shut. Who else had access to your car on the day of the murder?"

Beck thought for a moment. "My wife went to the store for clothes that day."

"How long was she gone?" Agent Henson questioned.

"I guess about two hours or so. I thought it kind of odd that she didn't come back with anything after being gone so long. Not that she always buys something, though."

"Do you think that she might be having an affair with someone?" Tom delicately asked.

"She would never cheat on me. I give her everything she wants."

"I had to ask. If she was banging Mr. DeLuca, that would explain why he wants you out of the picture."

"She would never cheat on me. We take our marriage vows very seriously." Beck said standing up and planting his hands on the table.

"Okay, Mr. Beck. Calm down. What is the name of the cleaners your wife uses?"

"It's the one on Courtney Street called, "Don't Press Us.""

Tom asked him if his dry cleaning was usually delivered or if he picked it up. Beck replied that the cleaning usually came back in three days, but he didn't know if they'd been delivered yet.

"We searched your house, and we didn't find the clothes anywhere. We'll send someone to the cleaners and see if the clothes were picked up," Agent Henson told him. "How well does your wife know DeLuca?"

"As far as I know she just knows him from the dinner parties we were invited to at his mansion. Why? You don't think she would set me up, do you?"

"We don't know. If she is in bed with DeLuca he might be able to talk her into just about anything."

"The slut!" Beck yelled, throwing the chair across the room. Two agents came running into the room and restrained him.

"I just have one last question, Mr. Beck. Can you think of anyone else who would want you dead?"

"No one that I can think of. Nope. Nobody." Beck asked what was going to happen to him next.

"You'll be kept here in solitary confinement for your own safety," Tom replied.

When Beck had been taken away and returned to his cell, Director Wilson called Tom into the observation room.

"If we believe Beck's story, it sounds like his wife might've been in on the whole thing. What do we know about the wife?" Henry asked.

"Not much. No wants or warrants out on her. She and Beck have been married for about eight years. Looking at the secret set of books we found, maybe it was a woman's writing in them. It was kind of neat for a man," Agent Henson said, looking over his notes.

"So if she knew what was going on, maybe DeLuca recruited her when he got wind of something. Who knows? Maybe Martin was finally catching on to what was going on and wanted his cut. What's Beck's wife look like?"

"Mrs. Beck is an olive-skinned woman with shoulder-length hair. She doesn't like authority figures; I can tell you that. She was shooting arrows into Shapiro and me with her eyes the entire time we were searching the house." Tom paused. "I don't know how or if she knows DeLuca though."

"Let's look into her background and see what pops up. Did the lab find Mrs. Beck's fingerprints in his car?"

Tom thumbed through the file in his hand. "The prints were from Beck, his wife, the valet at Luigi's restaurant, and a mechanic at the dealership where he took it to get it fixed. There were a couple of smaller prints that we figured were his sons."

"Were hers found on the steering wheel?" the director asked, leaning back against the one-way mirror.

"Yes. Mr. and Mrs. Beck's were both found on the steering wheel, door, and shift knob."

"Hmmm . . . interesting," Henry said deep in thought. "Look into Mrs. Beck's comings and goings and keep me posted."

"Yes, sir." Tom answered as the director headed for the door. It was going to be tricky keeping Beck alive now. Tom was sure that the lawyer had already informed Dominic

DeLuca about Beck's cooperation with us. Agent Henson headed for his desk and began making phone calls. First he called his friend Jackson Stone again. He hadn't asked Stone about DeLuca and Beck's wife. Maybe the Organized Crime Unit had seen the two of them together. With DeLuca still under investigation, maybe he met with Shirley Beck to set everything up. Tom should be so lucky.

My shoulder was getting a lot more loosened up. The pain was almost gone, with the exception of the occasional twinge that I got when putting my arm behind my back. "You're doing great, Sarah," Connor cheered. "Just another few reps, and you're done for the day."

I finished and collapsed into one of the Adirondack chairs.

"Is everything okay?" Connor asked, coming up beside me. He began lightly massaging my shoulders. "Your muscles are a lot looser today; that's a good sign. I'll tell you what. Why don't you hit the showers and get changed, and I'll get that picnic lunch started." He paused. "That is if you're up to it."

"Give me ten minutes, and I'll be ready to go," I said, slowly standing up. As I headed for the bathroom I stopped and turned around. "Are you sure you don't want help with the lunch?"

"Get out of here and take your shower. I've got everything under control," Connor replied.

While I was in the shower Connor made two turkey and Swiss cheese sandwiches with lettuce and tomatoes. He also put in the basket a thermos of hot chocolate, some pretzels, and a couple of apples, along with plates, cups, napkins and silverware. Just as I was coming out of the bedroom I saw Connor pick up his camera and set it beside the basket. An old Indian blanket was draped over the top of the basket.

Connor noticed that I had my firearm with me and asked. "Are we expecting trouble?"

"No, but Wade's visit yesterday caught us off guard and I don't plan on letting that happen again."

"I understand," Connor said with a quick glance at his watch. "I guess we had better check in before we get started."

We both went into Connor's den, and he dialed the satellite phone. The agent on the secure line put Connor through to Henson's desk. After four rings a female voice answered. "Tom Henson's desk, Agent Covington speaking."

"Sorry, wrong number," Connor said into the receiver before hanging up.

"What happened?" I asked, sitting on the edge of his desk.

"I was put through to Tom's desk, but someone else answered his phone."

"Did they say who they were?"

"An Agent Covington. It sounded like a woman. Do you know her?"

"Her name's Patricia Covington. She helped me at the beginning of this case," I answered.

"Well, I would rather we kept our contact between Tom or Director Wilson. We'll bring the phone with us and try again a little while later."

"You'll get no objections from me." I smiled getting up from the edge of Connor's desk .

The hike through the woods was beautiful. There was a nip in the air that made everything smell fresh and clean. We weren't on the trail or going toward the slide area. Connor was right; he seemed to know these woods like the back of his hand.

It was then that I heard the trickle of a waterfall. Just

beyond a couple of trees and some dormant blackberry bushes was the prettiest little waterfall I had ever seen.

"What do you think? Was I right?" Connor asked as he began to lay the blanket out on the cold ground.

"It's beautiful," I replied scanning my surroundings.

"Hungry?"

"Famished," I replied.

Connor motioned for me to have a seat and began unpacking our lunch. "It isn't anything special, just sandwiches, pretzels, apples, and hot chocolate."

"That's fine with me. I wasn't in the mood for champagne and caviar anyway." I smiled.

"I hope you never are," Connor quipped, "because I don't even have any of that stuff at home."

We enjoyed each other's company as we ate our picnic lunch. The sun had chased away the chill in the air and was dancing across the waterfall. I could just imagine how this area would look all green in the summertime. Oh, man, I thought. We've been having such a good time that we had forgotten to call Tom again. I looked up at Connor, and it was if he had read my mind. "Tom," we said at the same time.

Connor dialed the secure line again and asked for Tom Henson. The call was once again put through to his desk, and this time Tom picked up the phone.

"Agent Henson," he said into the receiver.

"All is well, kiddo," Connor stated.

"Things are moving well here. Can't go into details, though."

"Internal problems?"

"Uncertain," Agent Henson replied.

"Will call again in twenty-four."

"Affirmative. Out." was all Tom said before hanging up.

Connor turned off the phone and laid it on the blanket

beside him. That hadn't been a very good exchange, he told himself.

"A penny for your thoughts." I interrupted.

"Mine are worth two." He smiled at me. "But for you they're free. Tom implied that the agency might have a leak. He also said that things are moving along well."

I sat absorbing what Connor had just told me. I couldn't believe that anyone I knew would sell out to the mob. Doesn't loyalty mean anything anymore? If his suspicions were true, I hoped that it wasn't anyone that I knew personally. I guess it might be true that everyone has their price. I wondered how much a life was worth.

"A dime for your thoughts." Connor offered.

"What?" I asked, snapping back to the real world.

"I said a dime for your thoughts."

"A dime? How long was I gone? Inflation must have really gone up," I kidded. "I was just thinking about all of the agents that I know and wondered what the price for a human life went for today."

"Don't be so morbid, Sarah. Tom didn't say there was a leak, just that there's a possibility of one." Connor knelt in front of me and lifted my chin with his hand. "Are you okay?"

"Only when I'm around you," I said with a half smile.

"Are you ready to go back now?"

I nodded and helped him pack up our picnic leftovers. As we started to leave, I glanced around for one more look. How had I let our serenity be invaded by the outside world? There wasn't anything that I could do about it from here anyway. I told myself that I was being foolish and fell in step beside Connor.

Director Wilson had been making a few phone calls of his own. The first one was downstairs. He had the building put on alert. Everyone was to be checked twice, and no one was allowed inside the building without a badge. No exceptions.

The director's second call was to the Internal Affairs office. He wanted to know if anyone was currently under investigation for any reason. The only thing being investigated was a sexual harassment allegation against one of the field agents. So far they hadn't found any evidence to back up the allegation though.

Henry's third call was made to Tom Henson's desk. He was asked to come into the director's office immediately. Tom complied. He knocked twice and opened the door.

"Come on in and close the door, Tom." Once he'd done that Henry asked if he had heard from kiddo.

"Yes, sir. I've been assured that all is well ," Tom told him.

Director Wilson pushed a note across the desk toward Tom and kept talking. The note read "Not sure office is bug free. No mention of Anthony or McBride until further notice." Tom glanced up and nodded his understanding to the director. Henry turned the note over for Tom. On the back it asked Tom to get the team to quietly sweep his office and the rest of the third floor. Tom nodded again and then said aloud, "I agree sir."

"I thought you might." Director Wilson said. "Now let's get out there and make things safer for the citizens of Washington."

"I'm on it," Tom said, going to the door. When he reached it he turned and looked at Henry Wilson. Henry nodded to him, and Tom gave a quick nod back before leaving his office. Henry shredded his note as soon as Tom left.

The best time to sweep for the listening devices without anyone becoming suspicious was after five o'clock. Only a handful of people were in the building then. Henson got a hold of the security team and informed them there was a possible breach of information being leaked from the building. Specifics weren't needed for the team to get started on the job. Every man on the security team had a handheld device that would detect any radio waves out of the ordinary. Discreetly the team started on the ground floor and worked their way upstairs. It was about four o'clock in the afternoon then. Director Wilson was in his office all afternoon, so even if there was a bug in there, they wouldn't be able to remove it before the team reached the third floor.

A sweep of the entire building yielded nothing. At least no one had overheard the director and Henson's conversations about Connor and me.

We had been back at the cabin for a couple of hours when Connor said, "Okay, Sarah. The time has come."

"For what?" I asked.

"I told you this morning that we would skip breakfast, do your exercises, and go on a picnic on one condition. At the time you didn't want to hear the condition, though. Well, now's the time to pay up."

"Aw, come on, I'm wounded, remember?" I teased.

Connor laughed. "Wounded? You're still more dangerous than most women. Besides, you don't even know what the condition is."

"Okay then, give me your worst."

"And you said you couldn't act," he said to me, shaking his head. "My condition was that we do the other puzzle tonight. I had a lot of fun time last night doing the marble puzzle, but we never got to finish the other one in the hospital."

"I had a good time too, but I have a condition of my own," I told him.

"And what's that, Sarah?" He asked.

"That instead of popcorn tonight we whip up a batch of brownies."

"I can live with that," Connor said, offering me his hand to shake on it. As I slipped my hand into his, he pulled me into him. "Don't forget our dance later," he whispered before giving my forehead a kiss. He followed it with one to my lips, which I gladly returned. I put my arms around his shoulders, and his arm slipped around my waist. This felt so right. When we parted, we headed into the kitchen to make the brownies. A box mix made things easy, and while the treats were baking we started on the puzzle.

The edge of the puzzle had been put together in my hospital room and was still intact inside the box. As Connor and I worked the puzzle and talked, I slipped a puzzle piece into my pocket. I would have the last piece this time. We took a break from the puzzle when the brownies got done. Sitting on couch with brownies and ice-cold milk was wonderful.

"So who's your telegram from?" I wondered aloud.

"I'd almost forgotten about it," Connor said as he went and retrieved it from the top of his desk. When he returned, he opened the envelope and read it. Passing it to me he asked what I was doing in about four months. The telegram was asking if Connor was free to do a shoot in four months. A magazine called *American Wildlife* wanted him to take photographs of grizzlies in Yosemite National Park. "What do you say, Sarah? Want to go on a photo shoot to the Rockies with me?"

"Won't that be kind of dangerous?" I questioned.

"That depends on how you look at it. If a grizzly charges, all I have to do is outrun you, not the bear." He smiled, his eyes twinkling.

I punched him in the arm. "Very funny," I remarked. "Seriously though, Connor, isn't that dangerous?"

"Not if you know what you're doing and follow the park

guidelines. You know, like no food in the tents and stuff like that. Haven't you ever been camping?"

"Our family went when I was about eight, but I haven't been since then," I answered.

"Not even summer camp?"

"Nope."

Connor whistled. "You've got to get out more, Sarah. When all of this gets settled, you and I are going to go camping one weekend."

"That sounds like fun." I paused to take another sip of my milk. "All right. Let's get that puzzle finished," I said, standing up.

"You've got it," Connor followed along, stopping to put the glasses in the sink.

We put the puzzle together, each working on a specific piece of the landscape. When we had gotten down toward the end, we could see that it was going to be a piece or two short. Nope. One piece of the puzzle was missing.

Connor checked the box and the floor under the table. "I guess the joke's on us this time. It looks like this puzzle was boxed without that one piece."

"Are you sure you didn't slip it into your pocket?" I asked.

"I swear I didn't do it this time," he replied.

I reached into my pocket and pulled out the missing puzzle piece. "Then I guess I did," I exclaimed, snapping the puzzle piece into its place.

"Okay, you. You're going to have to dance for your punishment."

"Are you sure that you aren't going to be the one being punished? I mean, with the way I dance..." I smiled.

"Okay, smartie." Connor pulled me out of my chair and led me to the living room. "What'll it be? Fast or slow?" he asked, looking through the LPs.

"Let's start slow and then see how it goes," I answered.

"Slow it is, then." he echoed, continuing his search of the records. When he'd found what he'd been searching for, Connor turned on the record player and placed the needle down near the middle of the record. The music that began playing was kind of bluesy. With my right hand gently held by Connor's left and my left hand placed on his shoulder, his right hand touching the small of my back, we began to move. At first I was looking down at his feet. "Sarah," he whispered. "Just look into my face and let the music move your feet."

By the time that song had ended we were moving in unison. Connor took that record off and put another one on. "This one's a bit faster," he announced.

I remembered hearing that song on the radio once. This one wasn't one that you held each other close for, at least not for all of it. Once again I was able to keep up with the dance steps while Connor led. When the song had finished he asked me how the shoulder was holding up. "Do you need a break?"

"It's doing pretty good so far. Let's try one more."

"If you're sure," he replied. "What's your pleasure?"

"Oh, let's do another slow one. I was really getting the hang of that kind of dancing." I didn't dare say that it was because his arm felt so good around me.

As the music played we melted into one another's arms. It felt good to just relax and let go of all the worries in the outside world. Who would believe that all it took was a slow song and a great guy.

Henry Wilson thanked the security team as they finished their sweep for bugs. "Okay, Tom." he addressed agent Henson. "The only thing left that could endanger Anthony is someone finding the GPS coordinates from McBride. You're sure they're safe, right?"

"I've got them right here in my wallet," Tom answered. "I haven't heard back from Stone yet as to whether DeLuca and Mrs. Beck are playing house together or not. I'll call him again in the morning."

"Good work. I wonder if we should put a tail on Shirley Beck." The director said tapping his fingertips together as he sat with his elbows on his desk. There was silence as the two men contemplated the situation. "Are Shapiro and Covington still here?"

"I think so, sir."

Henry picked up his phone and called agent Shapiro's desk.

"Shapiro," Paul said into the receiver.

"Grab Covington and come to my office," Director Wilson told him.

"Yes, sir," Paul Shapiro replaced the telephone receiver and told Pat Covington that their presence was requested down the hall.

Agent Henson had the door already open when Covington and Shapiro got there. "Go on in," Tom told them.

The director motioned them toward chairs in front of his desk. The two agents complied as Tom closed the door behind them. Henry paced back and forth behind his desk. "I've come to a conclusion, people," he said, stopping behind his chair. "I don't know if she's involved in this case or not, but I want twenty-four-hour surveillance on her just in case."

"Who, Mrs. Beck?" Paul Shapiro asked.

"Exactly, and whatever you do, don't let her spot you. I know that you've already put in eight hours today, so I'll have someone relieve you around eleven." He paused. "Wear your vests, and don't assume that Mrs. Beck isn't dangerous. Any questions?"

"No, sir." Covington and Shapiro answered in unison.

"Then get out there," they were told.

At eleven o'clock agents Maxwell and Patterson relieved Shapiro and Covington.

"Anything we should know?" Patterson asked them.

"Everything's been quiet so far" Paul answered.

"Go get some sleep," Maxwell told them. "We'll take over now."

Agent Covington and Shapiro headed back to the parking lot at the agency to retrieve their own cars. They stopped by the director's office to check in, but he had finally gone home. The past couple of days it seemed as if he'd been living there.

Agent Henson pulled into the agency parking lot around 7:45 a.m. By the time he got to his desk it was eight o'clock. He hoped that Jackson Stone was in his office already.

"Stone here," Jackson said picking up the ringing telephone on his desk.

"Hi, Jackson," Tom greeted. "Tell me you found out something on Shirley Beck."

"The surveillance team on DeLuca had seen Mrs. Beck with him on several occasions. Each time it was in a public place. You know, nothing intimate." Stone continued. "The only piece of conversation that we overheard was about Beck's not knowing about her using his car. That doesn't mean anything to us. Does it do anything for you?"

"It could," Tom told him. "When was that conversation overheard?"

"Let me check the paperwork." There was a pause while Jackson looked through his team's notes.

The silence was killing Tom.

"Here it is. My team overheard her say that a week ago yesterday. I hope that helps."

"Me too, Jackson. Thanks for the info."

"Anytime, Tom. Good luck on your case," Stone told him.

Tom hung up the telephone and pulled out his calendar. Martin had been murdered a week and two days ago. A week from yesterday would be the day after Martin's murder. It could just be a coincidence, but he would question Beck again about any other times that his vehicle might've been borrowed by his wife. Tom didn't believe in coincidences, though.

Director Wilson agreed with agent Henson's assessment of the new information about Shirley Beck. They would follow up by questioning Beck to double check their facts. Was this case finally going to be solved? Each man wondered.

As the sun's rays began pouring into the cabin in the woods, Connor and I had already been up for a couple of hours. We were on a hike to the stream to watch the animal's drink. I hoped that our visit to the stream would be fruitful. Connor and I had been seated among a couple of blueberry bushes. A slight breeze was in our faces and there was a nip in the air. As we sat there quietly, an opossum walked by and didn't stop to drink. He just kept going as if he had some place to be. A deer and a fawn came to the stream followed by a couple of playful raccoons. It was funny watching the raccoons wash their paws and jump back and forth across the stream. In the treetops above us three squirrels played a game of follow the leader. We sat there for about an hour and a half before starting back to Connor's cabin. Once inside, the fireplace was lit and its warmth filled the cabin. This was going to be a great day I told myself.

"Sarah," Connor's voice said, breaking the silence, "what would you like to do today?"

"I don't know," I answered. "Right now I'm exhausted

from getting up so early for our hike. I could almost close my eyes and go to sleep right now."

"Go ahead and take a nap then," he replied. "I'll wake you in a couple of hours, and we'll do some exercises for your shoulder."

"You talked me into it," I said rising from the couch. "Only two hours, though."

"You've got it; two hours." he echoed. "Pleasant dreams."

Two hours later a knock came on my bedroom door. "Okay, Sarah. It's been two hours. Up and at em."

"Are you sure that it's been two hours?" I asked jokingly. "It seemed like only about ten minutes."

"I guess your two hours aren't as long as mine are then," he commented through the door. "Are you about ready to exercise?"

"Give me a sec, and then you can torture me all you want," I told him. "Do you have any orange juice left? I need something to drink before we get started."

"If I don't, I know I've got some apple juice somewhere. Will that do?"

"That'll be fine," I answered pulling on my clothes. "I'll be right out."

After a slice of toast and a glass of orange juice I started the exercises to strengthen my left shoulder. It was quickly getting back to normal. As long as I didn't need to hold anything over my head, I was good. That limitation would go away with time, I hoped.

"How does it feel?" Connor asked as he lightly rubbed my shoulder.

"It's almost back to being as good as new." I smiled.

"That's great, Sarah. Now you'll just have to maintain this regime so that your shoulder doesn't lock up on you."

"Yes, sir," I replied with a salute.

"Okay, recruit," Connor shot back. "Let's do a mile, double time."

I looked at him seriously. "You're kidding, right?" I asked.

"Maybe about the double-time part, but a mile jog would do us both good. Besides, where else can you go jogging with scenery like this?" Connor said nodding toward the window.

"Okay, you're on," I said, carefully pulling my hair back into a ponytail. We walked out of the cabin and made our way to the hiking trail. "How will we know when we've gone a mile?" I asked.

"Well, if we go to the split in the trail where the signs are, that's just about a half mile, so to the fork and back would be a mile."

"We're not racing, are we?" I asked Connor.

"Of course not. It'll just be a slow jog to the signs and back. I promise." Connor added. "Ready?" I nodded. "Okay let's, go."

The two of us jogged along slowly at first. Taking in our surroundings was wonderful at that pace. When we reached the split signs, we both took a breather. Connor asked how I was holding up.

"Pretty good," I replied. "Are we ready to head back now?"

"I sure am," he said as he took off running. The pace was picked up quite a bit more now. I was determined to keep up, though. The two of us jogged side by side all the way back. I wasn't concentrating as much on my surroundings on the trail now. We fell into a rhythm, and it was almost as if we weren't even running. We slowed down as we neared the turnoff to Connor's cabin. By the time we'd reached it we had slowed down to a quick walking step.

My heart rate was up, and it felt good. "You were right,"

I stated on our walk back toward the cabin. "I feel so awake and alive now. It's amazing what a brisk run does for the body." When we had reached the cabin, I told Connor thank you, that it was just what I had needed.

"Anytime," he replied with a smile.

We sat on the porch bench for a while until our heart rates returned to normal. "Connor," I began. "Is there something that I'm keeping you from?"

"What do you mean?" he asked.

"I mean, you had a routine around here before I came around didn't you?"

Connor answered my question by putting his hand on mine and saying, "Kind of, but it wasn't anything etched in stone. Why?"

"I don't know, I just feel like I'm keeping you from something."

"Sarah," Connor began. "If you weren't here, all that I would be doing is walking to town to check my mailbox and maybe picking up a few groceries while I was there. Every now and then I would swing by and visit with Wade and his wife, except when I'm on an assignment for some magazine or something. Nothing I do around here matters very much if it doesn't get done today. Okay? Don't worry about anything. Just sit back and enjoy your time away from the rat race."

Agents Covington and Shapiro checked in with Director Wilson before relieving Patterson and Maxwell. The director was pleased to hear that their surveillance shift had been uneventful, but warned them to stay on their toes just the same.

Agent Henson had made the arrangements to question Beck this morning at ten o'clock. He stuck his head into the director's office and asked Henry if he would like to question Adam himself.

"That's okay, Tom," Director Wilson replied. "You know what needs to be asked. I don't know if his new lawyer will let him answer any questions without wanting to make a deal, though."

"We'll see," Tom remarked. "It can't hurt to ask him, anyway."

"Good luck, and keep me posted when you're finished."

Beck's lawyer tried hard to cut a deal for his client's co-operation, but Beck stopped him short. "It seems to me that I can only help my case by answering their questions," he told his mouthpiece. "Go ahead. What do you want to know about Shirley?"

"Did she usually borrow your car?" Agent Henson asked.

"Naw, she has her own car. She only borrows mine when hers is in the shop. And then she'd only have it long enough to get her errands done," Adam Beck replied.

"Did she always ask to borrow your car first or just take the keys?"

"Usually she'd tell me, but there were a couple of times I went out to the garage and it was gone. I assumed that Shirley took it; it was always back later that day."

"What about the day Martin was murdered? Where was your car then?"

"It was in the parking lot of our realty office. That female agent Anthony I think she said her name was, was there that morning."

"And you didn't go anywhere after Martin left to show the house?" Tom asked.

"Not until four thirty, when I headed home," Beck replied.

"Does your wife have a key to your car, or does she have to borrow yours when she wants to use it?"

"Shirley's got her own set of keys."

"So she could've taken the car out of the office parking lot without you knowing about it?"

"Sure. I guess so, but her car was running just fine. Why would she need to borrow mine?" Adam Beck questioned.

"Maybe to set you up for Martin's murder. Were the two of you having any marital problems?"

This kind of questioning went on for about forty-five minutes. For somebody who laundered money for the mob, Beck acted like a dummy. Nobody could be that naïve.

When Tom finished his questions, he reported into Henry Wilson's office. Just as Tom was about to tell the director what he had gotten out of Beck, agents Maxwell and Patterson checked in from their surveillance on Mrs. Beck. There hadn't been any activity until seven a.m. when she drove her son to school. After dropping her son off she did some grocery shopping. She only talked with the cashier and bag boy. Returning to her residence, she unpacked the minivan and was still in the house when Shapiro and Covington relieved them.

"Good work, you two. Go ahead on home now, and get some sleep," he told the two agents. They both nodded and headed for the door. As Tom closed the door behind the two agents, he began to tell Henry what Adam Beck had told him.

"So we aren't any better off than we were before, are we?"

Tom looked down at the floor and answered, "It doesn't look like it, sir."

"Damn!" The director swore.

Both men sat quietly thinking. The question that they pondered was where they went from there.

There was a knock on the director's office door. "Come," Henry stated.

Agent Patterson opened the door and looked into the room.

"Was there something else?" Henry asked.

"I'm not sure, sir." Joyce began. The director motioned her to one of the chairs in front of his desk. As the three of them sat down, Henry asked Joyce what the problem was.

"I'm not really sure if it's anything, but I thought that you should know."

"Know what?"

"While agent Maxwell and I were on surveillance at the Beck residence, he began asking questions. At first they seemed innocent enough, but then they began getting a little more urgent sounding."

"Questions about what?" Agent Henson asked.

Joyce turned to Tom and replied. "Agent Anthony."

Tom and Henry exchanged glances. "What exactly did he want to know?" the director questioned as he leaned forward in his chair.

"Like I said, at first it was just a comment about Sarah getting shot. Then the questions started. Ben, er . . . Agent Maxwell asked if I had heard where Sarah was or who she was with."

"What did you tell him?" Agent Henson asked, shifting in his chair.

"I couldn't tell him very much. All I said was that a handsome young man escorted her out of the hospital. I don't know who he is. I assumed he was an agent from one of our other offices."

"Then what did Maxwell say?" Henry asked as he began taking notes.

"Well, he said that he'd had to clean out someone's hotel room for agent Henson and wondered what the big deal was.

"Anything else?" The director questioned.

"Not really. I just thought he seemed awfully interested in where Agent Anthony went from the hospital. I told him I was just a decoy for her, and I didn't have a need to know about anything else." Agent Patterson ended her tale with, "I hope I'm doing the right thing. Ben just seemed overly interested in Sarah's whereabouts."

"Have you said anything to anyone else about this?" the director asked.

"No, sir," Joyce replied.

"Let's all keep this under our hats for now. I'm sure Maxwell was probably just concerned for Anthony's safety."

"Yes, sir," Agent Patterson agreed.

"Thank you for bringing this to our attention, Joyce. You'd better go home and get some rest now." Agent Patterson said her goodbyes and headed out of Henry's office, closing the door behind her.

"I don't like the sound of that," Tom remarked.

"Me either," Wilson answered. "What was in McBride's hotel room? Anything with his name on it?"

"I went through his things, and I didn't find anything with so much as an initial on it. Let me check something, though."

Tom stood up and picked up the phone book. When he'd found the telephone number to the hotel where Connor had stayed, he dialed it. Henson asked the woman at the desk what the gentleman's name was who had stayed there the previous Sunday through Tuesday. The woman checked out her computer and gave Tom two answers. One was a Mr. Brock from Virginia City, Nevada, and the other was a Mr. Scottish from Ohio.

Agent Henson thanked the woman and placed the receiver back in the cradle. "Well, it looks like McBride used an alias at the hotel. That's the good news. I'm going to go through his stuff from the hotel again, though, just to make sure there's nothing to link him to Anthony."

"Get back to me as quickly as you can, Tom," Henry ordered. "I don't want them sitting ducks out there."

"No, sir." Tom walked to the door and opened it. "I'll be back in a minute."

Down the hallway agent Henson unlocked the locker that held Connor's things. Taking the box into the conference room, he dumped its contents onto the table. After he checked each item, he placed it back into the box. The last thing left on the table was an envelope containing landscape photographs. They were pretty good, Tom thought as he flipped through them. "Nothing," Tom said aloud. He took the box back and locked it up.

Back in the director's office Tom read off what had been in McBride's hotel room. When Tom brought up the photographs, Henry interrupted him.

"What were the photographs of?" he asked.

"There were a couple of plain landscapes and a few photos with animals in them. Nothing with any distinguishing landmarks in them, though."

Director Wilson leaned back in his chair and closed his eyes. They were missing something, he told himself. With his eyes still closed the director asked, "Are there any surveillance cameras in the hospital or parking garage?"

"I think that there are. Want me to go and get the ones from Anthony's hospital stay?"

Henry Wilson opened his eyes and looked straight at Tom. "I think that we should cover all of our bases. You go retrieve the hospitals videos and bring them to me. Hopefully no one has thought of this."

"I'm on my way," Tom exclaimed, heading for the door.

"Watch yourself, Tom," the director warned.

Yesterday's jog through the woods had been invigorating. The rest of the day was spent reading magazines and listening to the record player. We had checked in and left the message, "All is well, kiddo." Evidently Tom was out of the office. We would try again around noon today.

I had fixed a light breakfast of french toast and bacon this morning while Connor took his shower. I guess that it wasn't as light as I thought, because I didn't want to do my exercises afterwards.

"See?" my host remarked. "Breakfast is okay if it's light."

"You couldn't have said something before I cooked that?" I asked with a smile.

"I'll tell you what, Sarah. How about we go for a little jog and then start on your exercises. Maybe the run will wake you up," Connor suggested smiling.

"Oh, sure, you just want to see if you can beat me again," I said with a wink. Connor told me that he would slow things down so that I didn't feel so abused. "You're on." I yelled as I grabbed my hiking boots. "You should be glad that I don't have my sneakers with me."

When we reached the hiking trail I asked if we were going to do the same as we had done before, going to the fork in back. "Sure," Connor replied. "On the count of three... one, two, th . . ."

Before he got out the word three, I took off running. The forest was cool and damp this morning, and it didn't take long for Connor to catch up with me. He stayed right alongside me and never tried to pull ahead. At the fork in the trail we took a five-minute break. Instead of jogging back to the cabin, we walked and held hands.

"What are you thinking about?" Connor asked with a sideways glance at me.

"Nothing, really. I'm just soaking in the beautiful scenery," I replied looking over at him.

"It is pretty amazing, isn't it?"

"It's going to be hard to have to go home." I stated as I stopped walking. "I've really been enjoying myself." I smiled. "Torture and all."

"Let's not think about that right now. Let's just deal with whatever each day brings and handle them one day at a time."

"You're right. Why worry about tomorrow when we have today to finish first?"

We continued on to Connor's cabin. Once again the walk had rejuvenated me. Exercising my shoulder muscles went by fast and almost painlessly. When I got finished, it was around noon. "I guess that we had better check in with Tom," I suggested.

"I guess so," he replied. "Let me grab the phone." Connor returned from his den with the satellite phone in hand. We sat at the table and Connor dialed the secure line.

"Williams here, may I help you?" The voice on the other end asked.

"Henson, please," Connor answered.

"He is away from the office right now. Can someone else help you?"

Connor placed his hand over the receiver and said that Tom was out of his office. "Should we talk to someone else or just leave the code words again?" I thought about it and had Connor ask for Director Wilson again.

"Please hold a minute, and I'll put you through," Williams stated.

"Director Wilson here," the director said into his telephone.

"All is well here, kiddo." Connor announced into the phone."

"Things changing here, kiddo," Henry said into the receiver. "Leak possible. Your whereabouts could be compromised. Check again in six."

The satellite phone in Connor's hand went dead as the director hung up. He turned the phone off and put it away.

"What's the matter?" I asked him, placing my hand on his arm.

"The director says that they might have a leak there, and they're not sure if our whereabouts have been compromised or not. I'm to call back again in six hours."

I didn't say word. It was a little hard to digest everything that the director had told Connor. One of the agents? A leak? Who could it be? A million things were running through my mind. Connor squeezed my hand and I looked over at him. How was it that just looking into this man's eyes could make me feel like everything would be okay? "How do you do that?" I asked him.

"Do what?" he asked warmly.

"Make me feel like everything will be fine." I smiled.

Connor shrugged his shoulders. "I don't know. Maybe the trust that we share with one another is comforting." He paused. "Or maybe we have a need to believe everything will be okay to protect our sanity." He grinned, his blue eyes twinkling.

"It's probably a combination of both of those things." I squeezed his hand lightly and smiled.

"Okay, let's get started. We're going to need to put together a few things in case we need to bug out," he told me with a kiss to my cheek.

"Just tell me what you want me to do," I said, kissing him back.

"If you would gather a couple days' worth of food together, you know, things that don't need to be heated or refrigerated, I'll grab a couple of guns and some ammo."

When I finished putting the supplies on the table, I asked what else I could do.

"Go into my room and get a couple days' worth of clothing for both of us. In my closet are two backpacks. Just dump them out if there's anything in them."

"Okay," I answered before going to Connor's room. I felt uneasy going through his things, but did what I had been asked to do. I set the two backpacks and the clothes on the table alongside the food.

Connor came into the kitchen with his .357 holstered on his hip. In his hand he held the M1 Garand and two boxes of ammunition. He put them on the table and went back for some ammunition for my .357 revolver. When Connor returned he also had his satellite phone. We each began packing up one of the backpacks. Half of the food went into each pack; the same with the clothing and ammunition. Connor went into the bathroom and retrieved his first-aid kit. Also packed were some rope, a pocketknife, matches, signal mirror, binoculars, and two flashlights with extra batteries for each. Two thermal blankets were also added to the backpacks.

Connor and I stood back and looked over the packs. "Can you think of anything we're missing?" Connor asked.

"Short a roll of toilet paper, I can't think of anything else." I grinned.

Connor laughed. "We can't forget a roll of toilet paper. There aren't a lot of new leaves out on the plants yet." When a roll had been added to each pack, Connor put them by the back door. On top of one of the backpacks he placed the satellite phone and his GPS map finder.

"Were you ever a Boy Scout?" I asked. "I know their motto is Be Prepared, and you sure are."

"Sure was. I made Eagle Scout with three palms. All of

the merit badges that I earned helped me when I was pre-
paring for the SEALS."

"Really? I never got much out of Girl Scouts," I told him.
"All I remember about scouts was trying to sell those stupid
cookies."

Connor laughed. "I haven't seen a Girl Scout cookie in
the years. Didn't you go camping or hiking or something like
that?"

"Are you kidding? If my troop had done any of that stuff
I probably would've stayed in longer."

"How long were you in?" he asked.

"Oh, about a month or two," came my answer. I glanced
over at him, and he was trying hard not to laugh out loud.
After a couple of seconds he couldn't hold it in any longer.

"A month or two?" Connor was laughing so hard that
he had tears in his eyes. His laughter was contagious, and I
laughed along with him. It felt good to relieve some of the
tension of our current situation. We both collapsed on the
couch wiping tears from our faces.

CHAPTER 5

Around 1:30 p.m. Tom Henson returned from the hospital with a box of videotapes. He took them straight to Henry's office, and once inside set up the television and the VCR. The first tape showed me being wheeled into the emergency room and then into surgery. After recovery I was put into my own room. The surveillance cameras only covered the hallways, but they showed everyone who entered my hospital room.

The first day there was Director Wilson, Agent Shapiro, McBride, and a nurse every now and then that entered my room. Tom made a comment about how quickly Connor had shown up at the hospital.

On my second day in the hospital the video showed Tom coming in to visit me first. The redheaded nurse came in after him, and then Connor. The hospital nurses were in and out all of the time, checking on me. Doctor Andrew Sloan entered my room around ten o'clock that night followed by the redheaded nurse.

The next video wasn't in order chronologically. There was a gap of about thirty minutes. That was the night someone had gotten in and photographed me. Someone had obviously edited out that part of the video.

On the third day in the hospital Connor came by first. Tom Henson entered my hospital room next. Connor left shortly after that and returned with sandwiches for lunch.

The redheaded nurse also returned, and later on, Agent Shapiro stopped by with my clothes.

The videos from the parking garage were less than informative. The stairwell was poorly lit as was the garage itself. Tom could make out about half of Connor's license plate number as he drove in and out of the shadows in the parking garage. Believe it or not, that was good news. This meant that whoever had edited the video from the hospital hallway hadn't thought to get the VHS tapes of the parking garage. Or had they, and then left them for the agency to wonder about?

"I've seen enough" Henry Wilson said as he stood up. Walking to the window he continued. "I've got McBride calling back in another," he glanced at his watch. "Three hours and I don't know what to tell him," he said as he stood staring out the window.

"They need to be warned so that they can be prepared, just in case." Tom Henson sat down and clasped his hands in front of him. "Should we bring Maxwell in and question him?"

Henry thought for a moment. "I'll tell you what we're going to do." The director turned around and grabbed the back of his chair. "We've got three hours, so we're going to have to work fast. Pull all the phone records from Maxwell's home phone, cell phone, and even his desk here. Let's see who he's been talking with. While you're doing that, I'll put traces on his phones. Okay, let's get on it."

After we stop laughing, Connor asked. "What would you like to do now? Are you up to doing some more exercises?"

I rolled my eyes. "Is that all you ever think about?" I asked, glancing at him out of the corner of my eyes.

"Okay, Sarah, What would you like to do?" he asked sweetly.

"How about we just talk for a while?" I answered.

"About what?" Connor asked, shifting around on the couch so that he could face me.

"That photograph on the mantel," I began. "Who are they?"

Connor arose and took the picture off from the mantel. He came back and sat beside me again. "This is my grandfather and my dad when he was about five years old. Dad said it was taken on a trip out west in front of a big redwood tree."

"It's a great picture." I smiled. "Do you take after your mother or your father?" I asked.

"I guess my dad. Mom was fair-skinned and sunburned easily. My brother Sean took after our mother." He paused. "I wish that I'd had more time with them." Connor got quiet.

I leaned forward and gave him a hug. "I'm sorry I brought up such sad memories, Connor," I apologized.

"It's okay. It's just that..." He stopped mid-sentence and put his finger up to his lips. Whispering, he said, "There's someone outside on the porch. Sarah, carefully go through the kitchen, and I'll go over by my den. We'll meet at the back door and get our firearms."

I nodded and quietly went through the kitchen. Connor got up and walked over by his den and to the backpacks sitting by the back door. As I clipped on my gun there came a knock on the front door. Connor unholstered his gun, nodded at me, and quickly swung the door open.

Wade Hood's eyes opened wide when he saw the two guns pointed at his heart. "Don't shoot!" He gasped.

We quickly pointed our weapons down and then put them back into their holsters.

"Sorry, Wade." Connor apologized. "Come on in."

Wade stepped inside the door and closed it behind him.

"What the heck's going on?" He asked glancing at both of us.

"Come on in and have a seat, and we'll explain." Connor stated. Sitting at the kitchen table we regaled Wade with the latest news from Washington.

He let out a low whistle.

"How can I help?" Wade asked looking at me.

"I don't want anybody else involved in this mess, Wade. It's bad enough that I've gotten Connor involved in it," I told Connor's friend.

"Now wait a minute, Sarah. If you'll remember correctly, I volunteered to get involved," Connor interjected. "And I'm not sorry that I did, either." He reached across the table and put his hand on mine.

I nodded and gave him a weak smile.

"Yeah, yeah. So what can I do to help?" Wade asked again.

"Wait a minute, Wade. First I'd like to know what brought you out here." Connor said turning to face his friend.

"Oh, well, you got another telegram, and I was hoping for a rematch from our last card game, but that's not important now."

"Wait a minute everybody," I loudly interrupted. "Nobody's going to do anything until we hear back from Director Wilson in a couple more hours."

Connor and Wade looked at each other and acknowledged that I was right. While Wade gave Connor his telegram, I went and got the deck of cards out. "What are we playing, boys?" I asked as I shuffled the deck.

"Gin," They answered in unison.

As I dealt the cards Connor asked where Janet Hood was.

"She's taken a day off from college to visit her father.

Her brother Dan called down from Ohio and said that he wasn't doing very well."

"What's wrong?" I questioned.

"Well, he's had a lot of medical problems, and the death of Janet's mother five months ago hasn't helped matters much." Wade paused. "You know how some couples are so close that when one dies the other usually follows a short time later? Well, I think that's going to be the case with Jan's dad."

"That's too bad," I commented. "I hope it all works out okay."

"Ditto," Connor remarked. "Let me know if Janet or you need anything, and let her know that I'm thinking about her."

"I will. Oh, I should warn you, Connor, Janet's found the perfect girl for you this time." Connor gave a sigh and rolled his eyes. "Jan says her name is Shelley and that she isn't anything like Karen."

"Nobody else could ever be like Karen, Wade," Connor replied, setting down a trio of cards on the table. "How'd things go when you got home after your last visit?"

"You'll be pleased to hear that Sarah's plan worked like a charm. Janet never suspected a thing. Gin!" Wade smiled, laying down his cards. "If you two aren't going to be more of a challenge, I'm going to have to quit coming out here."

I looked over Connor and we both replied, "Awww" and then laughed.

It was almost time for McBride to check back in as Tom Henson ran down the hall to Director Wilson's office. He opened the office door, stepped inside, and closed the door behind him. In his possession was a stack of printouts of phone calls made from all of Maxwell's phones. After eliminating the phone calls to the agency, Maxwell's home, the local pizza place, and pharmacy from the list, only about nine phone numbers remained unknown.

As Tom read the numbers out loud, Director Wilson typed in a search for them on his computer. Two of the nine phone calls had been made to an airline counter. Henry and Tom figured that Maxwell had either checked to see if Sarah and a guest had flown somewhere or he was planning a trip for himself. Tom used the director's phone and called the number. Ben Maxwell had asked about Anthony, but had also booked a flight to Miami on the 10:35p.m. flight on Tuesday. Damn, Tom swore. Today is Tuesday.

The computer print out had also listed all of the incoming phone calls. It wasn't too big a surprise to see that Maxwell had received numerous calls from Luigi's Restaurant, DeLuca's favorite hangout.

"Okay," The director told Tom. "Grab a couple of agents and go pick up Maxwell. Tell everyone to be cautious. Remember, he's got a gun and knows how to use it. We need him alive, but if he doesn't give you a choice, you know what to do."

"Yes, sir," Tom replied before heading out the door. He grabbed the first two agents that he saw. Agent Williams had just finished half of his shift answering the secured line. Agent Robles was fairly new to the agency in D.C., having transferred in from Iowa because he wanted more action. Both were good men and crack shots on the firing range. After making sure that everyone had on their vests, he told them who they were going to be picking up.

"Remember," Tom told them. "Right now Ben Maxwell is just wanted for questioning. Is that understood?" The two agents nodded. "Okay then, let's get going."

As six o'clock p.m. approached, Connor made a comment to Wade about it starting to get late and how the forest gets dark fast when the sun sets.

"After what you told me, I thought that I might spend the night just in case," Wade said, discarding a three of clubs.

"Won't Janet check in with you tonight to let you know how her father's doing?" I asked.

"I could call her first, but if she can't reach me at the house, she'll call my cell."

"And what exactly would you tell her if her call actually got through?" Connor asked, following that question with the word, "Gin!"

"Damn." Wade exclaimed as he threw his cards on the table. While I collected the cards and began to shuffle them, Wade answered his friend's question. "I don't know. I could tell her that you just got back from the photo shoot and we're going to spend some guy time together."

I couldn't help but chuckle. Connor joined in with me after a few seconds.

"What?" Wade asked. "Think you can do any better?"

"Wade," I began, "Janet's father may not make it, from what you've said, so you're going to tell her that you and Connor are going to have a boys' night out? How do you think she'll take that?"

Wade sighed and replied, "She'd probably be mad about it." He picked up the cards that I'd dealt and sorted them. "So what do I tell her, then?"

"Nothing," Connor replied. "Wade, go home so that you can be there for your wife. I promise that if we need you, we'll call."

Wade glanced from Connor to me and back. "You promise you'll call if you get into any trouble?"

Connor nodded, and Wade looked at me. I pulled his

phone number out of my jeans pocket, showed him, and said, "Cross my heart."

He laid down his cards and stood up. "All right I'll go. I know when I'm not wanted."

We all laughed.

We stood out on the porch watching as Wade headed toward the hiking trail. Connor yelled, "Don't get lost."

Wade Hood turned around and yelled back, "If I thought I'd get lost, I wouldn't be leaving."

Connor and I waved at our friend. When he was out of sight we headed back inside the cabin.

"I guess we'd better check in again," I told the handsome blonde standing beside me. "I sure hope the director is wrong," I said in a whisper.

Connor put his arm around my shoulder and pulled me into him. He kissed me on the cheek and promised that everything would be okay. One look in those beautiful blue eyes of his, and somehow I knew that it would be.

The telephone on Director Wilson's desk rang. "Wilson," he said into it.

"All is well, kiddo," Connor stated.

"Put her on the phone," Henry said to him.

"Sir?" I said into the receiver with a glance at Connor.

"It looks like agent Maxwell might be the leak. We don't know if he's found out your whereabouts though, Henson, Robles, and Williams went to bring him in. Ben has a ten thirty-five flight reserved to Miami. Hopefully they'll catch him before he leaves. He's got a lot of questions to answer."

"What would you like us to do?" I asked.

"Give me another six and call me back," The director answered.

"Kiddo out," I said before hanging up.

"What's the word?" Connor asked me as we went into living room and sat down on the couch.

"It looks like Ben Maxwell might be leaking information to the mob. He's got a flight to Miami scheduled for later tonight." I paused. "The agency's going to bring Ben in and see if he's found out where we are; and if he's passed that information along. Henry said to call him back in six hours."

Connor reached over and held my hands in his. "Tell me what you're thinking, Sarah," he said with concern in his voice.

I gave him a blank stare. "I don't know what to think. This all seems like a bad dream that anytime now I'll wake up from." I closed my eyes and leaned back on the couch. "I just wish this whole mess was over."

"I'll tell you what, Sarah," Connor began. "Let's do something to keep your mind busy so that it doesn't drive you crazy."

My eyes opened and I turned to look at him. "Like what?"

McBride stood up and offered me his hand. "May I have this dance?" he asked quietly. I put my hand in his and told him I would give it a try. He pulled me up and we looked through his record collection. "Fast or slow?" he commented.

"Fast, if you've got your shin guards on." I smiled at him.

He smiled. "Fast it is then." He found a record with a fast beat and started it going. "Try to keep up with me." he challenged.

At first I watched his feet again and tried to follow what he did. Once I got the pattern down, I just looked into his eyes and enjoyed the music. We moved together pretty well. When the record finished, Connor told me that I was getting a little better.

"Thanks to my dance partner." I smiled.

Connor walked over to the record player and asked if I wanted to go again. I told him that my dance card was empty and that I would love to. This time he put on some jazzy music. He took my hand again, and we began to dance. This time we were a little clumsy dancing. We didn't dance as close together, and the steps were a lot more complicated.

"So, Connor," I began, "Who taught you how to dance?"

Without missing a step he answered, "My mother. She taught both me and my brother. "'Proper gentleman,' she would say, 'should know how to dance correctly.'"

"You miss her a lot, don't you?"

"A lot more since you've been around me. You bring out the best in me."

I took a step forward and kissed Connor on the cheek. "Your mother would've been very proud of you," I told him.

He slipped his arms around my waist and hugged me. "Thanks, Sarah," he whispered in my ear, "for everything." The record had ended but we continued our embrace and swayed to the music in our hearts.

Tom Henson and Agents Williams and Robles reached Ben Maxwell's apartment just before seven o'clock p.m. The apartment door was unlocked, and they cautiously entered. It was empty. There were no clothes, no furniture, no dishes, no anything. Tom called Director Wilson.

"It's empty, huh? Well, get yourselves over to the airport and watch for him," Henry Wilson said into the receiver. "I'll see if I can pull some strings and hold the plane until you get there. It's going to take you a while to get to the airport through rush-hour traffic."

"We're on our way," Tom stated just before he hung up.

Director Wilson had been right. It was almost ten o'clock by the time the trio reached the airport. Before exiting his car, Tom told the others to watch themselves. "If you come across any airport security officers, take them along with you. Two sets of eyes are always better than one."

Agents Williams and Robles nodded, and the three of them split up. Tom Henson headed toward the gate. Williams headed for ticketing, and Robles headed toward the baggage claim area. The only place in the airport where you could smoke was outside the baggage claim area in the loading and unloading zones.

Agent Karl Williams found out that Ben Maxwell had already checked himself and his luggage in. He radioed Tom and informed him.

Agent Eric Robles, after looking around the baggage claim area, worked his way up to ticketing. He and Karl searched that floor and continued upstairs.

Tom Henson, on the other hand, had gotten lucky. He spotted Maxwell inside the little Pizza Hut beside Gate A. Tom radioed Eric and Karl about his find. The three agents decided to wait and grab him when he headed for the gate. The area wouldn't be quite as crowded there, in case Ben resisted their invitation to return to the agency with them.

Ben Maxwell gave up peacefully when he saw the three agents approaching. "What's this all about?" he kept asking.

None of the three agents replied, except to say, "The director just wants to ask you a few questions."

Back inside the agency Ben Maxwell was put into an interrogation room. Agent Williams stood guard while Tom Henson went and got Director Wilson. "We've got him downstairs, sir," Tom said, walking into Henry's office.

"Fine," the agency director replied. "He didn't cause any trouble, I hope."

"Nope, he just keeps asking what's going on."

"Well, let's not keep him waiting," the director said standing up and following Tom Henson to the elevators. Once inside, Henry told Tom that Kiddo was going to call back at midnight. "I hate to keep her hanging like this, but we need to know if her whereabouts is common knowledge now," Director Wilson commented.

Down in interrogation the director began by telling agent Maxwell his rights. Ben nodded that he understood them and then asked, "What's this all about?"

"Mob boss Dominic DeLuca and the whereabouts of agent Sarah Anthony," Wilson said, opening the file folder filled with telephone records from Maxwell's phones. For more than a half hour Ben denied any connection with the mob. Henry was getting tired and angry.

"What did you find in the hotel room I asked you to clean out the day Anthony went into hiding?" Tom Henson interjected.

"What? Oh, yeah, there were men's clothes, toiletries, and a manila envelope."

"What was in the envelope?" Director Wilson asked.

"I gave it all to agent Henson," Maxwell replied.

"I didn't ask what you did with it. What was in it?" Henry said, pounding his fist on the table.

"Okay. Okay. The envelope contained a dozen pictures of animals and stuff."

"An even dozen?" Tom asked.

"Yeah, an even dozen." Maxwell sneered back.

Tom excused himself and ran out to the locker where he had locked up McBride's belongings. He pulled out the envelope and counted the photographs inside. There were only nine pictures in the envelope. After locking the locker back up, he grabbed the envelope and hurried back to the interrogation room. Once inside the room, Tom tossed the envelope in front of Maxwell and asked if that was the one that he'd picked up from the hotel room.

Maxwell picked up the envelope and emptied the contents onto the table. "Yep," he said, glancing through the photographs. "That's the envelope."

"How many photographs did you say were inside?" Henson asked.

"About a dozen," Maxwell replied, counting the photographs.

"So what happened to the other three photographs?"

"Okay, so maybe there weren't twelve photographs inside. Big deal."

"Who'd you give them to? DeLuca or one of his henchmen?" Tom demanded.

"I think I want my lawyer now," Ben Maxwell said, folding his arms across his chest.

"Fine. You can have your lawyer, but up to now unless you had something to do with the death of James Martin, you're only looking at evidence tampering. If anything happens to Anthony, though, you'll be on the hook for her murder," Director Wilson stated as he got up to leave.

"All right," Ben said, sweating heavily. "I passed the photos on to DeLuca's number-one man, but I didn't even know where the photographs had been taken. How could I give away McBride's whereabouts?"

"How do you know that Anthony is with McBride? Nobody's mentioned that name," Henry remarked.

"Okay, DeLuca said that if I found out where Anthony was, he would forget my gambling markers. When I found the photographs, I gave the ones with just scenery in them to Frank. He asked for the name of the man who'd helped get Sarah out of town, but I didn't know it. They threatened to break my legs if I didn't find out."

"Go on," Director Wilson told him.

"Well, I asked around the hospital, and one of the nurses said she thought she'd overheard him being called McBride, but she didn't hear a first name."

"Are you the one who took the picture of Anthony in the hospital room?" Agent Henson questioned.

"I was on duty downstairs checking identifications and was approached by Frank Borgetta, DeLuca's number-one man. He had me take the picture on my break, so I shut down the security cameras for about twenty minutes. How did you know?"

"Never mind about that. Then what did you do?" Henry asked.

"I told Frank that the man that helped Anthony was named McBride and gave him the photo I had taken of Sarah. Frank asked for McBride's first name, and I told him that nobody knew. He said that they would be in touch." Maxwell took a break and a sip of water from the glass in front of him.

"When did Deluca get in touch with you again?"

"The other day. He said that I should leave town for a while, so I was going to go to Miami and visit my cousin Denny. He has a charter fishing boat business down there."

Tom and Henry exchanged glances. "What do you know about the murder of James Martin?" Henson asked.

"Only what I've heard around the agency and read in the paper."

"What about Shirley Beck?" Tom prodded.

There was a long pause. "She was with DeLuca a couple of times when I'd met him at the restaurant. Other than that, though, I don't know anything about her."

Director Wilson looked at us wristwatch. It was almost

11:45p.m. He glanced at Maxwell and said, "One last thing. Did DeLuca ever find out where Agent Anthony and McBride are?"

"I don't think they know the exact location, but I got the impression that they knew the general area."

"Keep him locked away. No one is to talk to him unless Henson or I are present." Wilson told the building security head. "No one."

"Yes, sir," the guard replied.

Director Wilson and agent Henson headed for the elevator.

"We're going to have to tell them that DeLuca might know where they are, aren't we?" Tom asked as the elevator doors opened.

When they stepped inside Henry turned to Tom and replied, "We've got no choice. I would like to use Connor's GPS coordinates and go pull them out, but if the mob doesn't know where they are though . . ."

"We'd be leading them right to McBride and Anthony," Tom stated, finishing the director's sentence.

"Exactly." The elevator doors opened and the two men exited on the third floor. "I just hope that McBride is as good as his service records say he is," Henry told Tom as they entered his office.

I had been sitting on the couch with Connor being regaled by his escapades on the photo shoots he'd been on. "I never thought about how hard it would be to photograph wild animals before," I told him.

"That reminds me," Connor exclaimed as he stood and pulled me up from the couch. "I want to show you the photographs I took in Texas while you were back in D.C." he said as he led me to his darkroom and grabbed a handful of negatives. Taking them over to the light box, he placed them down one by one. Handing me a magnifying glass, he said, "Use this."

I was amazed as I looked at the negatives. "How did you get this one? It looks like it's underground," I asked looking up at him.

"It was underground, Sarah. I dug into a prairie dog tunnel and placed a piece of Plexiglas there. I put a canvas tarp over the hole that I'd dug, and after a while, checked underneath it. I really just got lucky getting those shots."

"Well, I think it's fascinating how you do it," I replied.

"I had about a dozen pictures that I brought to D.C. for you, but they were in my hotel room. I'm sure Tom is keeping them safe for me."

"I can't wait to see them when we get back," I told him. "What time is it?"

"Almost midnight. Are you ready to hear what your director is going to say?"

"I think I am" I said as he slipped his hand into mine. At midnight exactly, Connor dialed the secure line to the agency. The agent answering the phone line patched us through to Director Wilson's office.

Henry answered the phone saying, "You're right on time, kiddo."

"What can you tell us sir?" Connor queried.

"Is she listening?"

Connor and I each had an ear up to the satellite phone. "I'm here," I told him.

"Agent Maxwell was the leak. He gave DeLuca's number-one man some of the photos from Connor's hotel room, and he's the one that took the picture of Sarah in the hospital. He overheard the name McBride, but never caught the first name."

Tom continued for the director on the speakerphone.

"McBride, Maxwell says they know the general area where some of your photographs were taken, but no place specifically."

Henry Wilson began again. "I don't want to send a team in to get you until we know for sure that they know where you are, just in case there's another leak. We don't want to tip them off."

"What do you want us to do, sir?" I asked with a sideway glance at Connor.

"Stay out of sight and watch yourselves. If anyone comes calling, notify us ASAP, and we'll be there as fast as we can." He paused. "Sarah, I need to speak to McBride alone now."

"Yes, sir," I replied handing the satellite phone to Connor.

He grabbed my hand and squeezed it. Looking into my eyes he said, "McBride here."

"Keep your eyes open, and if you sense anything, get the hell out of there."

"I'm going to give you a name and a number. If you come and we're not here, Wade will know how to find us." Connor gave them Wade Hood's name and phone number. "Don't worry sir. Wade and I were in the SEALS together. He can be trusted."

"Okay, kiddo," Henry Wilson replied to Connor. "Be in touch in another twelve."

"You've got it. Kiddo out," Connor told him before hanging up.

Director Wilson hung up the receiver and looked at Tom Henson. He was looking tired and pale. "Go home, Tom, and get some sleep," Henry said putting his hand on Tom's shoulder. "McBride and his Navy SEAL friend will keep Anthony safe."

"I'm getting too old for this kind of stuff, Henry," Tom muttered.

"Come on, Tom. I'll walk you out."

After hanging up, Connor put the phone back on top of the backpack.

"What did they say?" I asked quietly.

"Just to keep you safe and to get out of here if I sense anything."

"That's it?"

"That's it," he replied. "Well, I guess we'd better try to get some sleep."

I looked at him in disbelief. "You're kidding right?" I asked.

"Tomorrow is going to come soon enough, Sarah. We've both got to be on top of our games for whatever gets thrown at us," he explained as he sat, holding my hand in his.

"I know that you're right, Connor. I just don't think that I'll be able to sleep."

"I'll tell you what. You go get a nice warm shower, I'll put on some hot chocolate, and then we can talk."

"That sounds nice," I said with a kiss to his cheek. "Okay, but it won't be a long shower." I walked to my room and then into the bathroom. While I was showering Connor began heating the water on the stove. Then he grabbed the satellite phone and took it into the kitchen.

The telephone at the Hood house rang once before Wade answered it. "Hood residence," he stated.

"It's me, Wade," Connor told him. "Listen, I can't talk long. If we have to bug out of here, I'll call you. Meet us at the old mine on the other side of the mountain from us. Do you know where I'm talking about?"

"Yeah. That's where we used to go target shooting, right?"

"Right." Connor replied. "And Wade . . . come armed and ready for anything."

"What about the feds?" Wade questioned.

"By the time I called them and they got here . . . well, let's just say that you're closer. If you hear from a Tom Henson or Director Wilson, you can tell them where to meet us. By then we will have missed our check-in with them at noon."

"You've got it, Cap'n. Anything else?"

"No. Thanks, Wade. Have you heard how Janet's dad is doing?" Connor asked as an afterthought.

"Not good. Jan says she's going to stay another day or two. It looks like he's not going to make it."

"I'm sorry to hear that he's that bad. I'll be in touch."

"Watch your six o'clock, okay?" Wade told his friend before hanging up.

The tea kettle started whistling, and Connor turned off the stove. Good to his word, he had two mugs of hot chocolate waiting when I got out of the shower. As I sipped my cup I asked, "How's Janet's father doing?"

Connor stopped mid sip and looked up at me. "How'd you know?"

I smiled and took another sip of my hot chocolate. "Well, Wade's our backup, right?"

A smile crossed Connor's lips as he nodded. "I guess you could call him that."

"Since you didn't get much of a chance to plan things out when he was here earlier, I figured you would do it while I was out of the room."

"You're a regular Sherlock Holmes. Do you know that?" Connor chuckled.

I smiled back at him. "I don't think that I would go that far. I'm just a little bit more observant than most people sometimes."

"Okay, I concede," my host said as he threw his hands up in the air.

"So, how is her dad doing?" I repeated.

"Wade says that it's not looking very good. Janet's going to stay up there with him for a couple more days."

I yawned and took the last sip of my hot chocolate. Connor noticed and asked if I was ready to get some sleep. "We don't have to contact D.C. until noon. Surely you don't plan on trying to stay up until then, do you?"

"No," I answered sleepily. "But I am going to stay on the couch just in case something happens."

"Sarah, you don't have to worry. I doubt that anyone could find us out here at night. Heck, if you don't know where to look, you can't find us in the daylight." Connor pulled me up from the kitchen table and led me to my bedroom. "If you want, I'll stay with you until you go to sleep."

"You don't have to do that, Connor. I've got my firearm beside the bed. Thanks, though," I told him with a kiss to his lips.

When we parted he said, "Sweet dreams." and closed the door behind him. Connor checked the cabin windows and doors and turned off all of the lights. He settled down on the couch, and in within a half hour he was sleeping lightly.

I had laid in bed for a while unable to sleep. I heard Connor checking the cabin out and figured he'd gone to bed too. After what seemed like an hour staring at the ceiling, I got up to go to the bathroom. When I passed Connor's room his door was open and his bed hadn't been slept in. After I used the bathroom I headed cautiously into the living room. Connor snapped awake and glanced over me. "Sarah? What's wrong?"

"I just couldn't sleep," I told him.

"All right, come on over here." Connor said patting the couch beside him.

As I sat down he pulled the blanket across my lap. I leaned back against him and closed my eyes. The warmth of his body made me feel so safe.

"Do you rescue every damsel in distress that you come across?" I asked in a whisper.

Connor put his mouth next to my ear and whispered, "Only federal agents and older women like Cora Blankenship."

I smiled to myself.

It was eight a.m. when the sun's beam hit me in the eye. Turning my head to avoid it, I saw Connor in the kitchen scrambling eggs. I rubbed my eyes and sat up.

"Good morning, Sarah," his cheerful voice greeted me.

I stood up and stretched. A wince came across my face when my shoulder pinched.

"You okay?"

"It's just a kink. It'll be okay in a couple of minutes," I answered him as I walked into the kitchen. "How long have you been up?"

"A couple of hours or so I guess. Did you want sausage or ham this morning?"

I told Connor that sausage was fine and asked what I could do to help. We both agreed on glasses of milk with breakfast, so I set the table and poured the milk. After breakfast we did the dishes and Connor got a shower. Since I'd had one last night, or rather early this morning, I got dressed and played a game of solitaire at the table.

Henry Wilson grabbed a cup of coffee and headed to work. He hadn't had more than three or four hours of sleep last night. The decision whether or not to go and get me was weighing heavy on his mind. So much could go wrong if he waited, he thought. By the time the director had reached the agency he had made a decision. An extraction team would be put on standby until further notice. Time was going to be of the essence, he reasoned, if they got the call from us.

Agent Henson was already at his desk when Director Wilson got off from the elevator.

"You look like hell, Tom. Did you get any sleep last night?"

Tom glanced up from his desk. "Have you looked in the mirror lately? You don't look that much better you know."

Henry turned around and started toward his office. Over his shoulder he remarked, "You don't have to tell me that."

It was about nine a.m. when Henson knocked on Director Wilson's door. "Come!" Henry called out. Tom opened the door and then closed it behind him.

"What is it?" Wilson asked, glancing up from the pile of paperwork on his desk.

"I thought maybe we should look into Maxwell's banking records. Something last night didn't make sense to me," Tom began.

"Like what, Tom?"

"Like Maxwell said that he was just going to Miami to visit his cousin, yet his apartment was totally cleaned out, furniture and everything. And if he thought enough to disable the hospital security cameras, he had to have known about the ones in the parking garage. Which means..."

"Which means that he probably ran the partial license plate number from McBride's Jeep through the DMV," Director Wilson said, finishing Tom's sentence.

"What you want to do?" Tom asked taking a seat in front of Henry's desk.

Henry stood up and began pacing back and forth in front of the picture window. It was days like this that he wished he wasn't the boss. A couple of minutes passed before he stopped and sat back down. "Let's do it. I'll get you the warrant for Maxwell's bank records, and you can go pick them up. In the meantime I'm going to get an extraction team together in case we need to pick up Anthony and McBride."

"Yes, sir," Agent Henson said, getting up from his seat. "I'm going to go back over the list of telephone numbers and make sure that we didn't miss anything in our haste yesterday."

"I'll get that warrant to you as quick as I can," the director told him.

By ten o'clock Tom had the warrant for Maxwell's bank records and was off to collect them. The extraction team had been set up. Three helicopters were set to head out at a moment's notice, along with six sharpshooters and a half a dozen field agents.

While Tom was out getting Maxwell's bank records, a computer search was being done to see if anyone had checked the DMV records recently. The search revealed that someone had checked on McBride's license plate, but it wasn't done by Maxwell. The license plate search had been requested by agent Patricia Covington. Henry called her into his office. "Did you do a DMV search on a partial license plate number owned by Mr. McBride the other day?"

"Oh, yeah," she answered. "Ben asked if I would do it for him. Was there some kind of a problem?"

"No, no problem. We were just checking on a few things," the director told her. He thanked her for her help, and when she had left his office Henry leaned back in his chair. With his eyes closed, Director Wilson began to piece things together. Everything that Maxwell did was to cover his tracks, Henry thought, clasping his hands behind his head. If he wasn't that deeply involved in this whole mess why would he need to . . . well, the bank records should prove something one way or the other.

By 10:45 Tom Henson had returned with Maxwell's bank records. After he grabbed a cup of coffee he headed down the hall to the director's office with them. Poring over the records was going to be tedious work with all of the balances, debits, etc. After a while it all pretty much looked the same. No, wait! Here was a transfer of funds to an account in the Cayman's. Not much, only a thousand dollars. Tom pointed it out to the director. "Could be that's his retirement account," Tom remarked. "We'll need more than that to go on, though." Farther down the stack of papers was deposit after deposit into the Cayman account. When the deposits were all totaled, the account in the Grand Cayman account held almost three hundred thousand dollars.

"That's the frosting on the cake" Director Wilson exclaimed excitedly. "If Maxwell had that much money, he could've paid off almost any gambling debt he had. All of his excuses won't save him now. There's no way we're going to make any deals with him."

"Shall we go pay agent Maxwell another visit?" Tom asked.

"You bet. Let's get all of this stuff in some kind of order and go see what he's got to say for himself now."

The file compiled on Ben Maxwell had grown measurably. The folder was almost two inches thick with evidence. Agent Henson stood by the door of the interrogation room as Director Wilson sat down across from Ben.

"You're sure that there's nothing else you'd like to tell us?" Henry asked.

"Like what? I've told you everything I know," Maxwell retorted.

"Okay, then, let's start with your trip to Miami. If you were just going for a visit, how come your apartment's been cleaned out?"

"I was going to change apartments when I got back, so I put everything into storage."

"Is that so?" Director Wilson flipped through a couple of pages in the folder and looked over at him. "Well, it says here that Mr. Lyons, your landlord didn't even know you had moved out. What were you going to do, stiff him?"

The sweat beaded up on Maxwell's forehead. "No. I uh... I was going to tell him when I had found another apartment."

Director Wilson looked over at Tom and repeated, "He was going to tell Mr. Lyons after he had found another apartment, even though he had already moved everything out of his apartment."

Tom nodded his head. "Yeah, that makes perfect sense," Tom stated sarcastically.

"Okay, we'll jump past that for now. Item number two. You said that you did what..." Director Wilson glanced at his notes from yesterday. "You did what Frank Borgetta and DeLuca told you to because you had an outstanding gambling marker. Is that right?" He asked looking up from the file in his hands.

"Yeah," Maxwell replied with his arms crossed in front of him..

"How much were you into the mob for?"

"About ten thousand dollars," Ben answered.

"How do you account for the almost three hundred thousand dollars in your account in the Cayman's?"

Ben Maxwell jumped up, knocking his chair over. "That's not mine. This is a setup," he yelled.

"Sit down!" Henry ordered sternly.

Ben Maxwell was red-faced and breathing hard. He looked toward the door and then back at Director Wilson.

"Don't be stupid, son," the director told him. "Sit back down." After a few tense minutes Maxwell picked up his chair and sat down again. Henry poured him a glass of water and pushed it across the table to him. "Here, take a drink and calm down."

Ben pushed the glass away.

"Okay then, let's begin again." The director's voice was low and calm. "How long have you known the DeLuca family?" Maxwell shook his head, leaned back in his chair, and didn't say word. "Okay then, when did you turn the information that you got from running McBride's license plate number over to Borgetta and DeLuca?"

"You can check the records," Ben demanded. "I never ran anything through the DMV."

"We know that you had agent Covington do it for you. Did you really think that we wouldn't find that out?"

Ben folded his arms across his chest and clammed up.

Tom Henson glanced at his watch. It was almost ten minutes before noon. They really needed Maxwell to break so that McBride would have a heads-up, he thought.

I did the therapy exercises for my shoulder twice. With the exception of a small twinge every now and then, I was feeling back to normal. Connor and I played a couple of games of cards and talked small talk. It was killing me not knowing what was going on back in Washington. I didn't know Agent Maxwell very well; I usually stayed pretty much to myself. I began wondering if I had done something to him unknowingly that made him do what he was doing.

"You're doing it again," The handsome man across from me stated, interrupting my thoughts.

"What?" I asked, coming out of my daze.

"I said that you're doing it again," he repeated.

"Doing what?" I questioned.

Connor shook his head and smiled. "You were thinking too much about things, trying to analyze why all this happened to you or what you did to bring this on you," he replied.

I looked into Connor's blue eyes. "How did you do that? Am I that much of an open book?"

Connor smiled. "No. I've just been there before. Someday maybe I'll be able to tell you about it."

I understood what that meant. A lot of men who came back from the service didn't want to talk about it. I was sure that as a Navy SEAL Connor had seen more than his share of unimaginable horrors.

"Okay," I said cheerfully. "That's it. No more talking about Washington. Let's do something fun."

"I'm game. What do you have in mind?"

We both sat there looking at one another and laughed. "Well," I told him. "A staring contest wasn't exactly what I had in mind. Do you have any country music in all of those records? I've always wanted to learn how to line dance."

"That's one dance I never got into," he said as he got up and went into the living room. I got up and followed him.

"You grew up out west, and you never got into country music?" I asked in surprise.

"Oh, I like country music for the most part," he stated as he looked through the stack of records. "It's the dancing to it that I never cared for, and today's country music doesn't even sound much like country music." After a few seconds he exclaimed, "Here it is."

"What?" I asked as I walked over to see what he had in his hands.

"This is one of my parents' favorite records. It's a collection of classic country music hits." Connor took the LP out of the sleeve and put it on the turntable. As the record began turning he put the needle down. The first song that played was *Walking After Midnight* by Patsy Cline. It was kind of awkward to try to dance to that song. The next song wasn't much better. It was *Hey, Good Lookin'* by Hank Williams.

"I guess this kind of country music is only good to listen to," I told Connor, pulling him toward the couch. We sat down and closed our eyes.

Connor saw his parents in their living room listening to this record while his mother sat rocking and knitting and his father read the newspaper. On the floor he and his brother were playing a game of checkers.

When I closed my eyes I saw my sister Kate and me at our grandparents' house sitting on the porch. Grandpa was showing us how to spit watermelon seeds across the yard, and Grandma was snapping beans into a bowl for supper. By the time the record had ended I'd almost fallen asleep.

Connor got up and picked up the needle. "Do you want to hear the other side?" he asked.

"That depends," I told him. "Are you trying to put me to sleep?"

Connor laughed. "You too, huh?" He turned off the record player and put the record back in the pile. "I guess it's about time to check in anyway," he remarked.

"I need to splash some water on my face first and wake up," I told him.

"Go ahead, Sarah. I'll get us both a big glass of lemonade while you're doing that."

The secure line rang, and Connor asked for Tom Henson. He and Director Wilson were unavailable at the moment, he was told. "Would you like to leave a message?" he was asked.

"Tell agent Henson that all is well with kiddo, and will check in again in six." Connor's message stated.

Henry and Tom had been unable to get anything else

out of Ben Maxwell. He was sent back to the lockup as the two agents sat down at the table in interrogation.

"If I didn't know any better, I would swear that some-body got to him," the director said to Tom.

Tom took a deep breath. "Things sure changed around when we broke his alibi apart. What are we going to do now?" He glanced at his watch. "Damn! We missed kiddo's call."

Director Wilson picked up the telephone and called the front desk. "Did a call come in for agent Henson or me?" he asked.

"Agent Henson had a call about five minutes ago. The caller said, 'All was well with kiddo, and would check in again in six.' "

"Thank you," the director said before hanging up. "McBride says all is well. They'll call back at six p.m." Henry got quiet. "I hope they'll be all right until then," he said un-der his breath.

Connor and I ate lunch and were washing dishes when he noticed something outside. He put his finger to his lips and motioned for me to get my firearm. I stayed low and went to the back door. Quietly I put on my holster and checked my handgun. I grabbed Connor's and headed care-fully through the kitchen toward the front of the cabin.

Connor came around the corner squatting low. As he put on his holster he whispered "Someone's outside. All of the birds and animals have gone quiet."

"Do you think it's Wade again?" I whispered back.

"Nope. Remember? I talked to Wade last night and set things up."

"Okay," I whispered again. "Tell me what you want me to do."

"Grab a backpack and follow me out the back door. And

Sarah." he stopped and grabbed my arm. "If anything happens to me, Wade will meet you around the other side of the mountain at an old mine we know. Got it?"

I nodded.

"I'll call Wade as soon as we're outside and away from the cabin. Watch for my signals and stay close to me."

We slipped our backpacks on, and Connor carefully opened the back door. After looking around and listening, he went outside. The woods began about thirty feet from the back of the cabin. Connor ran silently across the open space, and then surveyed the area with his rifle scope. He motioned me to come across.

I felt clumsy with the big backpack on. Once across the yard, though, I felt a little safer. Connor came close and whispered in my ear. "Let's get back in the woods a ways where we can see everything."

I nodded and quietly followed him. We wove in and out among the forest trees until we were a way away but still had a view of almost the entire cabin. He spotted two men armed with pistols cautiously advancing toward the cabin. To the left of our position, Connor made note of another man armed with a rifle. To the right of the two men with pistols was another man armed with a rifle. Connor was still scanning the forest when we heard a noise behind us. I dropped to the ground and drew my revolver. Connor quickly grabbed his rifle and pointed it in the direction of the noise. My heart was about to beat out of my chest.

I held my breath as the noise came closer. A man with a rifle came around from behind a large tree. For a brief moment he was startled when he saw us, but then he raised his gun and shouted, "They're over here!" The man's bullet went wide, but Connor's hit its mark. The man fell over into a pile.

"Come on," Connor said as he grabbed my arm.

The four men behind us were shooting and knocking a lot of bark off from the trees around us, but we kept weaving in and out to elude them. The shooting died down when we got further ahead. We took a quick break, and Connor called Wade.

"Wade, here," he stated answering the ringing telephone.

"Wade, bogies are on our tails. One down, four still in pursuit. Meet us at designated spot ASAP. We should rendezvous in…" Connor glanced at his watch. "About two hours."

"Message received, Cap'n. Watch your six o'clock," Wade ordered.

"Okay, Sarah," Connor said, coming up to me after talking with Wade. "Remember what I told you. There's a compass in your pack. If anything happens or we get separated, head southwest. When you reach the big dead tree, turn to the north. Keep your eyes peeled for Wade. He'll be there before we will."

"What about calling D.C. to let them know what going on?" I asked in a low voice.

"We'll do that when we stop again. Right now we need to keep moving."

The gunfire started up again. This time it seemed like the shooters were just blanketing the forest to see if there was any movement among the trees. We were well in front of them.

Connor sure knew his way around these woods. When we took a break again, we both took a drink of water.

"Are you doing okay?" he asked me.

I nodded. Connor broke out the satellite phone again and called the secure line back in Washington. When someone picked up, Connor asked for Tom Henson.

It was almost two o'clock when the telephone on Tom's desk rang. "Henson," he said into the receiver.

"This is kiddo," Connor said back to Tom. "The cabin was overrun. I killed one man, and four more are pursuing us. We are okay and heading southwest."

"We've got an extraction team standing by. I'll inform the director," Tom said in a shaky voice.

"Call Wade; he'll give you the coordinates to where we'll be meeting him."

"Gotcha kiddo. Keep your heads down." Tom told Connor before he hung up. Agent Henson jumped up from his desk and ran down the hall. He bumped into one of the agents with an arm load of paper and sent it flying on the floor. "Sorry," he said over his shoulder. At the director's office Tom opened the door without knocking and rushed in.

Director Wilson was on the telephone when Tom burst into his office. When he saw the look on Tom's face, he told the caller on the telephone that he would have to call back. He hung up the telephone waiting for Tom to say something.

Tom stood gasping, trying to catch his breath. "McBride and Anthony . . . in trouble." He said between breaths.

"Okay, Tom. Take a deep breath and tell me what they said."

Tom took a couple of big breaths and gained his composure. "McBride just called. He said the cabin was overrun and that he killed one of the men and four more were still following them."

"Take another breath, Tom. What else did he say?" Wilson anxiously asked.

"He said they were headed southwest and that his friend Wade would be able to give us the coordinates to where the three of them will meet up."

"All right, Tom. Call and get the extraction team loaded up. We'll meet them on the helipad in fifteen minutes. I'll call Wade and get the coordinates. Go!"

Agent Henson called the extraction team from the phone on the table in the director's office. When he was finished he went and put his bulletproof vest on.

Henry called the number that Connor had given him for Wade Hood.

"Wade here," he said into his cell phone.

"This is Director Wilson in Washington D.C.," Henry told Wade.

"Yes, sir," Wade said. "I've been expecting your call."

"Can you give me the coordinates to the place you're to meet McBride and Anthony please?" The director asked with pen in hand.

"Hang on a minute and let me pull over," Wade told him. The rustle of the map and the engine noise from Wade's truck made it hard to hear. When Wade had given the director the coordinates, Henry made him repeat them twice to make sure that he had heard them right.

"Our ETA is about three hours. Will you be able to hold out?"

Wade jumped in his truck and started down the road again. "We'll give them hell, sir," he yelled above the noise.

A smile crossed the director's face as he hung up the phone. I just bet you will, he thought. Henry put on his vest and grabbed his gun. Out in the hallway he met up with Tom Henson standing there holding the elevator doors open. "Let's go," Director Wilson said as the two men stepped inside.

On the way down Henry told Tom to go with one of the helicopters to McBride's cabin.

"With a team behind Anthony and McBride, maybe you

can knock off a couple mobsters and give them a better chance."

"Okay, sir. I'll make sure our guys identify themselves so that McBride doesn't take them out."

The doors to the elevator opened. Awaiting there was the leader of the extraction team, Captain Ray Burke. "We are already to go, sir," he told the agency director.

Wilson went over the plan quickly with Burke as they walked out to the waiting helicopters. Ray nodded and motioned for Tom to come with him. As they ran bent over toward the one helicopter Tom's heart began beating faster. The side door opened and Captain Burke hollered some instructions to the pilot over the noise of the whirling blades. As Tom climbed aboard the helicopter, Burke yelled, "Good hunting." to him and closed the side door.

Captain Burke backed up and ran over to the helicopter that Director Wilson had climbed into. Jumping aboard and closing the door, Ray hollered, "Let's go" to the pilot. One by one the helicopters took off and headed westward.

After Connor had packed away the satellite phone, he glanced over at me. "How's the shoulder holding up, Sarah?" he asked in a low voice.

"It's been better," I replied.

Connor came over to me and put his hand in mine. "I'm sorry, but we really need to get moving. Are you ready?"

I gave him a half smile and told him that I would follow him anywhere. He reached over and lifted my face upward and kissed me. "Just let me know if it starts getting to be too much for you, okay?"

I nodded.

Connor looked at me in all seriousness and said, "Promise?"

"I promise, Connor."

"Okay, let's go. We don't want them getting in front of us." Connor and I started weaving our way through the forest again.

The plants and trees were just beginning to get their leaves, which didn't offer very much cover for us in places. There were spots where the bushes were thick, but we kept going. The ground was soft, and we were leaving our footprints behind us for them to follow. Every chance we got we would walk in the rocky areas. There just didn't seem to be any way to shake the men following us.

Wade Hood turned onto the unpaved road that led to the old mine. A little way down, the road was closed off, to keep people out. Wade parked his truck and got out. Reaching across the front seat, he grabbed his holstered .357 caliber revolver and put it on. From behind the truck bench seat Wade pulled out an AR 15 rifle. After slinging it over his shoulder, he grabbed a box of ammunition and two extra clips.

In the back end of Wade's pickup truck was a backpack with water, food, first aid supplies, signal mirror, compass, and a flashlight with extra batteries, along with a few other necessities. Once Wade was loaded up, he started down the gravel road toward the mine. He pushed back his shirt sleeve and looked at his watch. It was 2:35 in the afternoon. From what Connor had said all of us should meet up around four o'clock. Wade figured on setting up in a high spot to watch for us.

Tom Henson's mind was going in several different directions. As the rhythm of the helicopter drummed away, he hoped that everyone got out of the situation safely. He wondered if they were going to have enough to bring in Dominic DeLuca and Frank Borgetta, and then, could they actually get a conviction? What was going to happen if the two mobsters had to be released? Tom looked out the window at the ground passing below him. How insignificant everything looks from here, he thought.

"Are you all right?" One of the team leaders yelled.

Tom turned and looked at the young man. "I'm fine," he yelled back.

"Want a stick of gum? It helps with the noise." The young man yelled again offering Tom a stick of bubblegum.

"Thanks!" Tom yelled back as he accepted the gift.

Director Wilson was thinking along the same lines as Tom was, but it was harder on Henry. He didn't think he would be able to go to another agent's funeral again. These people were the reason he had stayed as long as he had at the agency. Agents like Anthony, Henson, and the others were his family. Henry had never married or had any children, and when he'd become the agency director, everyone under him had become his adopted family.

The mishap from eight years ago flashed through his mind. They had come upon a kidnapping suspect who was holed up in an old barn with his victim. While the team was getting set up to try to talk the suspect out safely, a gung-ho cop thought that he would be a hero. In the end the cop and two agents had been killed. The suspect had been wounded and the kidnap victim had escaped with nothing more than a nick. Henry had sworn then that if it ever happened again, after the agent's funeral he would quit his job.

Director Wilson glanced out the side window. When he turned back Ray Burke yelled, "Everything okay?"

Henry nodded and yelled back, "Can't this thing go any faster?"

Ray leaned forward and said loudly, "It'll only be another hour or so, sir!"

Wilson nodded again. He hoped that we could hold out until the troops arrived.

While jumping a small creek I twisted my left ankle. Connor helped me over to a fallen tree and examined me. "It's not broken, Sarah, but it's going to be sore for a while."

I rubbed my ankle lightly. "Give me a sec, and I'll be ready to go," I said in a low voice.

Connor looked over at me with concern on his face. I placed my hand on his forearm and said, "I'll be all right; I promise."

He gave me a half smile. "Take a drink and relax for a couple of minutes. I'm going to go look around a little."

"Be careful," I said, grabbing his arm.

"I will." Connor promised patting the hand on his arm. "Be right back." With that he headed into the woods with his binoculars and rifle in hand. I poured a little water over my ankle and was tying up my boot laces when Connor returned.

"How are you doing, kiddo?" Connor asked.

"Good as new," I replied.

Connor glanced around. "I'm glad to hear that, because we need to get moving. These guys are being more careful now. They're not talking as loud anymore, and I have a feeling they're trying to get around in front of us. We've gotta go."

I stood up and got my backpack on. Connor did the same thing, and we were off again. "Have we much farther to go?" I inquired, coming up alongside Connor.

"About another hour or so. Wade should already be there by now," Connor stated. We'd walked about a half a mile more when a shot rang out. Connor and I hit the ground. He glanced around and whispered, "Did you see which way that came from?"

I shook my head no, and slowly and cautiously we looked around. "What you want me to do?" I whispered.

"Stay still and let me have a look around." Connor took off his backpack and crawled over into some bushes. I watched as he made his way into a thick patch of trees. From a high spot, Connor gave me hand signals. He wanted me to put his backpack up high enough for someone to see. When they shot at it, he would be able to see where they were and return fire. I slowly picked up Connor's backpack and pushed it slowly up the tree trunk beside me. Nothing happened. After a couple of minutes I began to lower it back down. Bang! The shot took a piece off from the top flap of the backpack. A second shot rang out. That one came from Connor's direction. I started pulling Connor's backpack back toward me when I heard a twig snap. I rolled over, pulling my revolver from its holster. It was Connor. "You scared me," I whispered.

"We've got to go, Sarah. I'm sure I only wounded that one. The others will be coming along anytime now." I passed Connor's backpack over to him. He put it on and carefully stood up. After looking around he offered me his hand. "Ready?" he asked in a low voice.

I nodded and took his hand. We began picking up the pace, but we could still hear them coming up behind us. Connor began slowly angling us through the trees to the west. Out of breath I asked, "Are we close?"

He found a place to stop where we were sheltered somewhat by a small bush. Connor looked at his GPS and then at his watch. Whispering, he answered, "We've got about two more miles to go. Can you make it?"

I took a couple of deep breaths and let them out. I smiled over at Connor. "Only two miles?"

He gave me a wink and asked if I was ready.

I nodded and we started up again. We hadn't gone more

than about five hundred yards when another shot rang out. It found its mark this time. Connor had been hit.

The bullet had hit Connor in the right leg and knocked him to the ground. I pulled him behind a large tree trunk and grabbed his rifle. "How bad is it?" I asked, kneeling down beside him.

"It hit me just above the knee. I'm pretty sure the leg's broken." Another shot rang out. "Get out of here, Sarah." Connor said, looking up. I was gone.

I had hidden behind another tree a couple of yards away. I had an idea where the last shot had come from, so I knelt down and steadied the rifle. After a minute or two I saw the silhouette of a man run out from behind a tree. I pulled the trigger and dropped the man halfway to the next tree. I chambered another round and headed back toward Connor.

I took off Connor's backpack and then my own. Taking out the pocketknife I carefully cut a slit in Connor's jeans where the bullet had entered. Gently I felt the back of his leg, checking for an exit wound. No blood back there; the bullet was still inside him.

Connor laid back on his backpack. "Damn!" he exclaimed through clenched teeth.

"Did I hurt you?" I asked quietly.

"If you did I don't think that I would be able to tell it over the pain from the bullet." He closed his eyes and took a deep breath. Opening them again he gazed at me and asked, "Did you get him, Sarah?"

"Yes, he's dead. Now be quiet and let me take care of your leg," I scolded softly. With supplies from the first aid kit I was able to bandage Connor's leg and temporarily stop the bleeding. He was going to need a hospital though. I gave him a drink of water and a couple aspirin from the kit.

"How's it look, Doc?" He asked giving me a weak smile.

"You're going to need a hospital I'm afraid."

"Sarah," Connor said, "You've got to get to Wade. Don't worry about me; you're the one they want."

A tear rolled down my cheek. "I can't leave you," I told him as I held his hands in mine.

"Sarah, the others will be catching up with us pretty soon. If there's any chance for you to get out of this alive, you've got to go now."

I looked up into the treetops and said a quick prayer. "Okay," I promised. "I'll go, but first I've got to camouflage you somehow." I looked at our surroundings and saw a patch of ferns growing a little way away. I picked up the binoculars and searched behind us. There were two men back quite a way, one of them was helping the other man, who was limping. I carefully cut the ferns and placed them on top of Connor. I worked as carefully as I could, taking the time to make the ferns look as natural as I could get them. Before covering his face I said, "I just keep heading north now, right?"

"Right." He smiled weakly.

I bent over and gave Connor a lingering kiss. "I'll be back as fast as I can with help," I told him.

"Be careful, Sarah," Connor remarked before closing his eyes.

I smiled and promised that I would. After I finished covering him up, I grabbed the rifle and backpack and took off running. I kept the compass in my hand and headed north as fast as I could go.

Wade Hood looked at his watch for the eighteenth time. His watch said that it was 4:32 p.m. They should be coming anytime now, he thought. Taking a sip from his canteen, Wade sat down and watched the woods.

I ran as fast as I could through the forest and never stopped to look behind me, only to catch a moment's breath. The ground was rockier now. Maybe I'm getting close to the old mine, I told myself. I had been heading north for the last half hour or so. Distances in the forest were hard to gauge, and I had no idea how far I'd come. My side was beginning to get sore from all the running and my shoulder was throbbing. I told myself that the next time I slowed to check the compass I would grab a drink of water.

Connor lay as still as he could. The pain in his leg was excruciating, and it felt like it had started bleeding again. A twig snapped behind the tree where he lay. Connor held his breath and listened.

"There are tracks over here," One of the three men reported. "It looks like they must have split up."

"The fed's the one we came here for. If the other one gets in our way, he buys a bullet too."

"Where's Fred?" the wounded man asked.

"He was over there on the right side in front of us. Hey…"

"Shut up, stupid." The first man cussed. "Are you trying to let everybody know where we are?"

"Sorry, I wasn't thinking."

"You two keep going, and I'll cut across and see where Fred went."

"Okay, Tommy," the two men replied.

The two men walked past Connor so close that he could smell their sweat. He thought about bringing up his revolver and shooting them, but he would be a sitting duck for the one called Tommy if he did. Connor had to trust that I would be okay. He closed his eyes and said a prayer.

Tommy McClain cut through the woods toward where Fred had been. As he neared a tall stand of pine trees he saw something. Tommy pointed his pistol at the object and cautiously approached it. "Fred?" He asked in a low voice. "Is that you?" There wasn't any answer. When McClain came around the tree he put his pistol back in its holster. Kneeling down he turned the man's body over. "Damn," McClain cursed.

Fred Borgetta had been shot through the heart. Tommy paused only a minute to gather up Fred's rifle and extra rounds. Before heading back to follow the others he turned toward Fred's dead body and said, "I'll get them for you, Fred. That's a promise." Having said that, he hurried to catch up with the other two men. This job was going to cost DeLuca more than he had offered when they got back, Tommy told himself.

Wade was sitting and scanning the forest when he spotted something. He grabbed his binoculars and scanned the area again. A figure was running erratically through the trees. Carefully Wade made his way down toward the person.

I couldn't run anymore; I had to stop and catch my breath. As I came past the next tree I tripped over a tree root and fell, right into Wade's arms.

"Sarah, are you okay?" He asked, holding me up.

I held up my index finger and took several deep breaths. Wade handed me his canteen and said, "Take it slow and easy."

I took a drink and passed it back to him. After a couple more deep breaths I told Wade, "No time to waste. Connor's been shot."

"How bad is it?" he asked anxiously.

"He needs a hospital, Wade." I replied, a tear running down my cheek. "I stopped the bleeding the best I could, but I don't know if it'll last very long."

Wade pulled out his map of the surrounding area. "Where is he, Sarah?"

"I covered Connor up with ferns about two miles back," I replied, taking off my backpack.

"Stay here and let your boss know where we are," Wade said grabbing his rifle.

"You're not going alone, Wade," I told him. "There are three men behind me. Hopefully they didn't discover Connor's hiding place," I stated." Either way, that's three to one, and I'm going."

"Okay, Sarah. Leave a note for your boss, and let's go."

I hastily wrote a note and left it on top of my back-pack. I shouldered Connor's rifle, checked my revolver, and grabbed the compass. "Ready?" I asked Wade.

"There's just one thing, Sarah," he said. "I need you to do what I say if we run into any trouble, okay? Connor would never forgive me if I let anything happen to you."

"You have my word on it, Wade. Let's go," I told Connor's friend.

"It looks like you're going to have to hike into the co-ordinates you gave us, Mr. Henson," the helicopter pilot yelled above the noise. He pointed down at Connor's cab-in. There was no place to land except the parking lot the hikers used.

Tom nodded his understanding. The pilot swung back around and landed on the back edge of the parking lot away from the cars. As soon as it touched down, the crew was out and scanning the area with guns at the ready. Lieutenant Moody organized the men and headed out. "Agent Henson," he said, walking over to Tom. "We'll take the lead, and when it's secure, we'll let you up front. Okay?"

Tom nodded and answered, "You know best in these matters."

The extraction team with Henson double-timed it to Connor's cabin. They searched the cabin and surrounding area. Behind the cabin they found the man Connor had killed. The trees told the tale of the shootings that had taken place.

"Spread out and stay alert," Moody told his men.

As Wade and I were carefully making our way back toward Connor, we heard two helicopters fly overhead. "That'll be your D.C. buddies," Wade said in a low voice. I nodded and stopped in my tracks. I dropped to one knee and Wade did the same.

"Do you hear that?" I whispered.

Wade listened intently. "What is that? Somebody moaning?" he asked softly.

"That's probably the guy Connor shot in the leg. It must be getting too much for him to be hobbling around the forest," I said in a low voice. "One of his buddies has been helping him. It's anyone's guess where the third guy is, though."

Wade Hood pulled out his binoculars and looked around. He didn't see anything out of the ordinary. "Let me lead, Sarah," he whispered. "Keep your eyes open."

I nodded that I understood.

Slowly Wade and I began weaving our way through the trees. The moaning was a little louder now, and coming from our right. We stopped and looked around again. I tapped Wade on the shoulder and pointed toward a stand of bushes. "Something's over there, Wade," I said softly, "behind those bushes."

Wade trained his binoculars on the spot I had shown him. After a moment or two he finally saw them. One man was on the ground and the other trying to pull him up to his feet. Wade handed the binoculars to me. "Stay here and keep watch for a minute," he said. Wade slowly made his way closer to the two men. Crouching behind a large bush, Wade listened.

"Come on, damn it!" one man said to the other. "Tommy will kill us himself if we don't find that fed and take care of her."

"My leg feels like it's going to fall off," the man on the ground complained. "Just let me rest another minute longer."

"Just quit that damn moaning. Do you want everyone to know where we are?" he asked in a low whisper.

As Wade was making his way back toward me I caught something out of the corner of my eye. I dropped to the ground just as a bullet shattered the bark on the tree beside me. I scampered around the tree, avoiding the next four rounds that followed.

Wade stopped when he heard the first shot. He hoped that I was okay, but didn't come back toward me. That shot would alert the other two men, and it wouldn't do to be caught in a crossfire. He worked his way back toward the two men.

Director Wilson's helicopter along with the other landed near Wades' truck.

"Okay, men," Captain Burke told his team. "We've got a federal agent and two civilians out there. Don't get itchy and shoot the wrong people." He turned to Director Wilson. "Anything else you would like to add?"

Henry faced the team of men. "I'm hoping we'll be able to bring at least one of the mobsters back alive, but your safety and the safety of the three people out there comes first." He ended by saying two simple words. "Good luck."

The extraction team and Director Wilson came upon my backpack and note. Captain Burke divided the men and started toward the woods when the first gunshot echoed. "All right, men, spread out and keep in touch," Burke ordered.

After the fifth bullet landed, I pulled Connor's rifle up to my shoulder and carefully got down on one knee. I was going to need something for this guy to shoot at so that I could see where he was, I told myself. I put the rifle down and untied my boots. I carefully tossed one of my boots into the bushes four feet away from where I was hidden. The gunmen took the bait and fired into the bushes. From around the opposite side of the tree I saw where the man was firing from. I got set and tossed my other boot into the bushes. When the gunmen shot at it, I returned his fire. The tree bark splintered in his face and caused him to drop his rifle. I pulled the bolt back, ejected the brass, and shoved another bullet into the chamber in record speed. My second shot hit the man in the stomach. He fell to the ground and began moaning. I chambered another round and stayed where I was, listening carefully in Wade's direction.

The two men near Wade heard the shooting and dropped to the cover of the bushes. "Sounds like Tommy found the fed," the man said in a low voice to his wounded friend.

"Reckon he needs help? What if that fed joined back up with her friend from the cabin?" the wounded man questioned quietly.

"You stay here. You'll only slow me down and probably get us both killed. I'll go wide and see if Tommy needs help."

The wounded man nodded his approval and sat with his back against a tree. "Nobody's gonna get the drop on me."

Wade looked the situation over and followed the man who was going to go and help Tommy. He would come back for the wounded man later.

The men with Tom Henson heard the gunfire quite a way off. The echoes through the forest made it impossible to know just how far away they were. Moody estimated at least two miles and the team quickened its pace.

The man Wade was following was swinging wide around where I was. Their movement caught my eye, and I picked up Wades' binoculars. Wade motioned for me to stay put. I hoped he knew what he was doing and said a quick prayer.

Tommy McClain's moaning was getting a lot louder to the man as he got closer. "Tommy, is that you?" the man asked in a low voice.

"That damn fed shot me. Did you get her?" McClain asked hoarsely.

"Where is she?" The man asked looking at his surroundings.

"She's over near that clump of bushes, dammit. Get her!"

The man raised his rifle, and before he could fire off a shot, the end of a rifle barrel was pressed into his back. "Back up slowly," Wade whispered to the man." As he started to back up, Wade told the man to pass the rifle back to him carefully. After he had complied, Wade had the man hand over his pistol too.

I watched the transaction between the man and Wade through the rifle scope. Behind them a hunched over figure rose up with a weapon in hand. I took aim and fired, dropping the man again. Wade whirled around and saw the man slump back to the ground. Turning back to the man he'd captured, Wade said, "Too bad about your friend. Guess he didn't know when to quit."

Wade Hood took off his backpack and bound the man securely to a tree. "Don't go anywhere," he told the man. He picked up all of the two men's weapons and came back to where I was waiting. "Okay, Sarah, by my count there's just one left to deal with," Wade told me. "That one shouldn't give me too much trouble. He's wounded in the leg and will probably surrender to get medical treatment."

"All right Wade, I'll come and cover your back," I stated firmly.

"No, Sarah," he said shaking his head. "Go find Connor and let him know that it's over."

"Sorry, Wade, I can't do that," I replied. "If I let anything happen to you, Connor will never forgive me."

Connor's friend laughed. "Okay, come on. Once we've got this guy, though, off you go. Deal?"

"Deal," I replied pulling my boots on.

Wade was right. The wounded man gave up without incident. While Wade searched him and tied him up securely, I took off through the woods. Things were starting to look more familiar when I looked around. The chipped-off bark made it easier to spot the tree where I'd left Connor. Approaching the pile of ferns, I said aloud, "Connor, it's over. Wade's tying up the last one now."

The pile of ferns moved, and I pulled them off Connor. His leg had begun bleeding through the bandage.

"Are you okay, Sarah?" he asked hoarsely.

"I think I'm supposed to ask you that question." I smiled at him. "I'm fine. How's the leg doing?"

"It's killing me," Connor said lying back and closing his eyes.

"Hey, buddy," Wade said, making Connor open his eyes back up. "Are you ready to get out of here, or are you enjoying your little siesta?"

"I would love to get out of here," he replied.

Taking great care, Wade and I helped Connor up on his feet. With an arm around each of our shoulders, we began our slow trek through the woods toward Wade's truck. Connor clenched his teeth and closed his eyes as he hopped between us. When we arrived at the spot where Wade had left the two men, we were suddenly surrounded.

"It's okay, gentlemen," I told the extraction team. "I'm Agent Anthony."

From my left I heard a familiar voice say, "Lower your guns. She's the one we've been looking for." As Director Wilson came through the trees he asked if I was all right.

"Yes sir, I'm fine. Connor's been hurt pretty bad, though."

Captain Burke motioned for a couple of men to check Connor out. Wade and I relinquished our hold on our friend and watched as the extraction team medic examined him.

"What's the situation, Sarah?" the director asked coming up beside me.

"Five men approached the cabin back there. Connor killed one, and the man that he wounded is over there tied up."

"We found him and his two buddies already. What about the fifth man?"

"I killed him back a ways. He's off to the left of our tracks."

Burke nodded at a couple of men and they took off through the woods. A little while later one of them returned and confirmed my story. I turned toward Director Wilson and said. "I'm sorry sir, This is Connor's friend, Wade Hood."

Henry shook Wade's hand. "It sure looks like you gave them hell, son."

Wade smiled and stated, "I didn't do a thing. Sarah here held her own. We could've used her in the SEALS."

When the medic finished with Connor he spoke to Captain Burke. Burke came over to us and said, "McBride's going to need a hospital soon if we're going to save his leg."

"Let's go, then," the agency director stated.

A stretcher was brought in from one of the helicopters,

and Connor was carried out of the woods. At the landing site Connor was placed in one of the helicopters. I told the director that I was going to go to the hospital with him. Henry nodded his approval and said he would be in touch.

As the copter's big blades wound up, I asked where they were going to take Connor. "Roanoke is the closest hospital," the medic replied.

I waved Wade over and yelled, "We're going to the hospital in Roanoke."

Wade yelled back that he would be there as soon as he could.

I nodded and waved as they closed the door. I sat beside Connor and held his hand. He gave it a squeeze and looked up at me.

"I'm sorry." I mouthed the words. My eyes started to fill up with tears. I wasn't sure how long I could hold them back.

Connor motioned me to come closer. When I bent over him, he softly said, "It's not your fault Sarah. I'm just glad that you're all right."

I kissed him and told him everything was going to be all right. Hadn't he told me that same exact thing less than two weeks ago? I asked myself.

Tom Henson and the other extraction team had caught up with Director Wilson just after we lifted off.

"Is everything okay?" Tom asked the director as he watched the helicopter take off.

"Anthony's fine. McBride took one in the leg and is on his way to the hospital now. Did you come across the man that McBride got near his cabin?"

"Yeah. You'll never guess who it was, though."

"Don't tell me it was DeLuca himself. I don't think I could take the good news," Henry commented.

"Nope, but it was his right-hand man, Frank Borgetta."

"You don't say." Henry Wilson thought for a moment. "I bet the two men we've got won't be all that happy to report back to DeLuca. Maybe we can get them to turn on him." Things were starting to look up, he thought.

Wade's voice interrupted Henry's thoughts. "If you don't need me for anything right now, I'm going to head to the hospital."

Director Wilson shook Wade's hand and replied, "We'll get your statement at the hospital later. Thanks for your help, son."

Wade smiled and said that he would see him later at the hospital then. Picking up his backpack and rifle, he headed for his truck.

"Wait a minute, Wade," Director Wilson said as he hurried after him. "I'm going to need to keep your weapons for a ballistics match. Don't worry; you'll get them back." Wade shook his head. "As soon as our investigation here is over, you and McBride will both have your firearms returned."

"I'm going to hold you to that Director Wilson," Wade stated as he emptied the weapons and surrendered them to Henry. "See you at the hospital," Wade said as he continued walking to his pickup truck. When he got to it he threw the backpack into the back end and started the engine. As he headed back toward the road, Wade thought that this had been more excitement than he'd had in a while. He was glad, though, that Janet didn't know what had been going on.

Speaking of Janet, Wade got out his cell phone and called his wife. "Hey, babe," Wade said into the receiver. "How's your dad doing?"

"Not any better, I'm afraid," his wife answered.

Wade could tell by the quiver in her voice that she'd been crying. "Jan, do you want me to come up there?"

"There's no sense in doing that, Wade. I'll be home the day after tomorrow," Janet told him, trying to be strong.

"Are you sure, hon?"

"Yeah, Wade, I'll be home soon." She smiled weakly.

"If you're absolutely sure, then I'm on my way to Roanoke for a while. Connor got hurt, so I'm going to visit him in the hospital for the next day or two. I'll be back by the time you get home though, Jan." Wade told her.

"What happened?"

"He hurt his leg, I guess," Wade answered.

"Well, tell him I said to get better soon. I love you, Wade."

"Love you too, honey. Take care, and I'll call you tomorrow." Wade hung up. He was torn between going to Ohio and being there for his wife or going to the hospital to visit Connor. Why is it that nothing in life can be simple, he asked himself.

CHAPTER 6

When the helicopter landed on the hospital helipad, a bunch of nurses and doctors greeted us. They wheeled Connor into the hospital and straight into an examining room. When I started to go in a nurse grabbed my arm and told me I couldn't. She took me to the admitting desk and had me fill out forms for Connor. I filled the forms out the best that I could. Insurance information and family's medical histories were left blank. I handed them back to the nurse and asked how Connor was doing.

"The doctor will be out to talk to you soon as he's finished with his examination, miss," the nurse told me.

Waiting around was not something I did well. I flipped through a couple magazines and had no idea what they were about; my mind was on other things. It had been twenty minutes before I was finally told anything.

Doctor William Reynolds finally came out and spoke with me. "Mr. McBride's wound is going to require immediate surgery. It looks as though the bullet may have nicked an artery. We'll know more when we get inside and remove the bullet."

"Can I see him?" I asked.

"Only for a moment. We've got to get him into surgery. He's being prepped right now, so he might not know who you are."

Doctor Reynolds walked me into the examining room. "Be brief," he told me.

I went to Connor's side and took his right hand in mine and held it up to the side of my face. Connor looked up at me sleepily and gave me a weak smile. I kissed him on the cheek and said, "I'll be right here waiting for you when you get back from surgery, so do as the doctor says." I kissed him again, and then they wheeled him out.

"If you'd like to do something, miss," Doctor Reynolds suggested, "you could give blood downstairs." I nodded as Connor was wheeled into the operating room. I said a prayer that he would be okay and that the surgeon's hands would be steady and then headed downstairs. I hated giving blood, but I would make an exception this time.

After I'd given blood, I went back upstairs to the waiting room. The minutes ticked away slowly on the clock on the wall. It had already been more than an hour as I paced up and down the hallway. I glanced up when I heard Wade's voice call my name. I put my arms around his neck when he reached me, and he put his arms around my waist, telling me that everything was going to be all right.

I sniffled and let go of him. "I know," I said. "It's just that Connor's been in surgery a long time." We walked over to a bench and sat down.

"Tell me everything that the doctor said," Wade told me as he held my hands in his.

I repeated what Doctor Reynolds had told me and showed him the Band-Aid on my arm telling him how I'd given blood.

"Okay," Wade began. "If the artery was nicked that would take a while to fix, not to mention removing the bullet and repairing any muscle or tendon damage that might have happened."

"You're not helping, Wade," I told him.

"Sorry. What I'm trying to say is that all of those things take time to fix right the first time." I squeezed his hands and thanked him for being there.

"Come on, Sarah, let's go downstairs, and you can watch them drill for blood."

I smiled and told him no thanks, that I wanted to wait for the doctor.

Wade understood and said he would be back as quickly as possible, that he was going to go and donate blood too.

The waiting was unbearable. Just as the elevator doors opened with Wade inside, I spotted Doctor Reynolds coming down the hall toward me. He took off his surgical cap and ran his hand through his hair. His surgical clothes were soaked with sweat, and he looked tired. Wade hurried to my side as I asked how Connor's surgery had gone.

"The bullet took a piece out of Mr. McBride's artery before lodging itself in the bone. We repaired the artery and removed the bullet. We also did a little work reattaching the muscle to the kneecap." Doctor Reynolds paused. "Mr. McBride is going to have to take it easy and let that bone fully heal."

"So everything's okay, Doc?" Wade asked before I could.

"If he follows the instructions that we give him, in about five months he should be as good as new."

"Thank you, doctor," I said with a breath of relief. "Can we see him now?"

"Give him about twenty minutes to come out of the anesthesia, and then you can go in. He's in room two sixteen down the hall. I'll be back to check on him in another hour."

"Thanks again Doc." Wade told Doctor Reynolds as he headed back toward the operating room. Wade glanced over at me. "How ya doing kiddo?" he asked.

"A lot better than I was a minute ago," I replied sitting back down on the bench.

Wade Hood joined me. Neither of us said a word for the first couple of minutes. Finally Wade broke the silence. "What's the matter?"

I shook my head and replied, "Nothing."

"Does Connor let you get away with that?" he asked.

I glanced up at Wade and asked, "What?"

"Your, 'nothing's wrong' attitude. I can tell that something's on your mind. Want to share it with someone?"

"I'm just feeling guilty, I guess," I told Wade as I looked down at the floor.

"Guilty about what? Connor's being shot?" Wade questioned as he slid his hand into mine.

"Of course. It was me they were after not him. He got shot because of my job," I said with tears in my eyes.

"Whoa, Sarah," Wade said, stopping me. "Connor would've done the same thing again no matter what your job was. You didn't drag him into this situation, did you? No. Connor wanted to be involved of his own free will. Just like I did. Nobody made me join in on the adventure. A good friend asked for my help, and I was happy to do it. That's just how we are," Wade stated. "Call us crazy; we like to help people in need."

"And I do appreciate it. Really I do, but . . . "

Wade interrupted me. "No buts, Sarah. Just look at it this way. No one was killed that didn't deserve it, and the doctor says that Connor will be as good as new in a few months. After all, isn't that the most important thing?"

"I think you just gave me the lecture that Connor would've given me." I gave Wade's hand a squeeze. "Thanks, Wade."

"Don't mention it . . . to anyone. I've got my reputation to protect," he said with a wink and a smile.

"Your secret's safe with me." I smiled back.

We sat on the bench in the hospital waiting room and talked for a few more minutes. I asked about Janet's father, and Wade said how he had debated on whether to go to Ohio or visit with Connor. He said Janet would be back on Friday and understood about his coming to Roanoke to visit Connor.

"What did you tell her about Connor?" I queried.

"I told her that Connor had hurt his leg. I'm going to keep the part about how he hurt it to myself."

"What did she say?"

"To tell Connor to get better soon. You'll probably get to meet her in a couple of days or so. I won't be able to keep her away from here."

"What do you think, Wade? Will I pass her inspection?"

Wade laughed. "I think she'll like you a lot. Maybe not your job, but I think the two of you will become good friends."

A nurse came toward us and said that we could visit Mr. McBride now. Wade and I followed her down the hallway to Connor's room. "He's still a little sleepy, but he's going to be just fine," the nurse told us.

I slowly opened the door to Connor's room. It took me back a bit when I saw the IV in Connor's arm and all of the monitors hooked up. Wade put his hands carefully on my shoulders from behind me and whispered, "Be strong." I nodded and took a deep breath. Walking over to Connor's bed, I took a seat beside him, and carefully held his hand in mine.

Connor's eyes fluttered open and he turned his head toward me.

"Hi, sleepyhead," I smiled. "How are you feeling?"

He closed his eyes and swallowed hard. Turning back

toward me he said in a low voice, "I've been better." He gave my hand a squeeze. "How are you doing, Sarah?"

"I'm holding my own," I told him.

"What about me?" Wade asked from the other side of Connor's hospital bed. "Doesn't anybody want to know how I am?"

Connor gave Wade a weak smile. "Okay, Wade. How are you doing?"

"Well, just fine. Thank you for asking," Wade Hood said with a bow.

I chuckled, and Connor gave me a wink. "Don't let this guy corrupt you, Sarah."

"Who me?" Wade asked, pointing to himself.

Connor couldn't help but give a weak laugh. "So what did the doctor say?" he asked.

"It's going to be a boy," Wade answered with a big grin on his face.

"As long as he doesn't look like you." Connor smiled at his friend.

"Why? What's wrong with me?" Wade laughed.

"Seriously, you two. What's the prognosis?" Connor asked, looking over at me.

"Well, no dancing for quite a while. Doctor Reynolds said that you should make a complete recovery within about five or six months. That is, if you follow his orders to the T," I told him.

"That's good to hear," he said closing his eyes and taking a deep breath.

"Hey, buddy, you get a little rest, and I'm going to take Sarah out and get her something to eat."

"I'm not hungry," I told him.

"Sarah, please go with Wade. I know how long it's been since you ate last. Humor me, okay?" Connor pleaded.

"Okay, but we won't be gone long," I said standing up with Connor's hand still in mine.

"I'll be right here when you get back." He smiled.

I leaned over and kissed him on the forehead. "You'd better be" I said before kissing him on the lips.

Wade and I went to a little Italian restaurant not too far down the street from the hospital. While we waited for our orders we talked about what had happened in the forest. "I want to thank you for saving my life today," Wade began. "I was stupid to think that the guy with the gunshot was incapacitated. That was a rookie mistake."

"No problem, Wade." I stated as our salads arrived. When the waiter had left I added. "I'd do that for any of my partners."

"Well . . ." Wade took a bite of his salad. "I for one am very glad that you were there."

"Did Director Wilson say anything to you before you left?" I asked.

"Well, I overheard one of the agents say that the dead man at the cabin was somebody's right-hand man. Director Wilson will be stopping by the hospital sometime to get our statements, and he kept my weapons."

"Don't worry, Wade. I'll make sure that you get them all back when the investigation is over. Anything else?"

"Nope," Wade said as the waiter set his lasagna in front of him. When my lasagna had been placed in front of me and the waiter had left, Wade asked, "How'd you learn to shoot so well, Sarah?"

I pushed my lasagna around on the plate. "I don't know. It's just something that comes easy for me. I was top of the class when we got to the rifle range during training. I even beat the instructor a couple of times."

"Please eat something, Sarah. When was the last time you ate?" Wade asked.

I thought for a while. "Around noon."

"Running the seven miles from the cabin to the mine and then some took a lot out of your system, Sarah. At least eat a couple of bites to make me happy."

I took a bite of lasagna and tore off a piece of garlic bread. The food wasn't too bad and the company was great, but I couldn't get my mind off Connor.

"You really like Connor a lot, don't you?" Wade asked, catching me off guard.

"Am I that transparent?" I questioned.

"A blind man could see that there's something special between the two of you." Wade laughed. "And I'm happy for both of you, wherever it leads."

I ate a couple more bites of my meal and pushed my plate away. "I've had enough," I told him.

"Any way I can tempt you with a piece of chocolate pie or something?"

"No, but go ahead if you'd like some," I commented.

"I'll get mine to go, and then we'll get back to the hospital." Wade smiled, and I thanked him.

It was after seven o'clock when Wade and I got back to the hospital. When we opened the door to Connor's room we got a surprise. Director Wilson and Tom Henson were there. They glanced toward the door when we entered.

"Look, Sarah, company came by to see all of us," Connor stated.

"Hi, Sarah," Tom said, coming over to me. "How's the shoulder coming along?"

"Really good, Tom. Thanks for asking," I replied, rotating my shoulder in a circle. "See?"

Director Wilson addressed Wade. "Would you mind giving us your statement now, Mr. Hood?"

"Sure, but I didn't do very much," Wade told Henry.

"That's all right. We're just trying to piece together all of the events as they unfolded in the woods. Let's see if we can find an empty room somewhere." The three men stepped out into the hallway. After talking with one of the nurses they proceeded down the hall to the waiting room for the families of surgical patients. This time of night no surgeries were being performed, so the waiting room was empty.

I walked over beside Connor's bed and sat down. "How'd things go with Tom and Director Wilson?" I asked as I poured him a cup of water.

"Well, they both think an awful lot of you." Connor accepted the plastic cup and took a small sip. Handing it back to me, he continued. "It seems that a lot happened that I don't know anything about." He smiled over at me. "And all this time I thought that I was protecting you."

"You'll never know just how much you did for me, Connor." I told him. "How are you feeling? Are you in any pain?"

"I'm fine, Sarah. You don't have to worry about me."

"Maybe not, but I'm going to anyway." I smiled at him.

Ten minutes later Wade opened the door to Connor's hospital room and came in, followed by agent Henson.

"Sarah," Tom remarked. "Could we have a couple minutes of your time now?"

"Sure, Tom," I said standing up. "I'll be right back," I told Connor and Wade.

As Tom and I walked down the hall he asked how I was doing.

"It's been a busy day," I told him.

He nodded and opened the door to the waiting room.

"Come on in, Sarah," Director Wilson told me. Tom and I joined the director at the table in the middle of the room. Couches lined the four walls along with end tables full of outdated magazines.

"I know, you need my statement of what transpired to-day," I said.

"You're right, Sarah, but you also need to remember that this thing still isn't over yet," Henry stated. "We're pretty sure that we'll be able to pin DeLuca with those two thugs' testimonies, so until he's behind bars, you'll need to lay low." Director Wilson said pushing my revolver across the table to me. "The preliminary investigation says that all of the shots fired came from a rifle, except for the ones at the cabin, and they were nine- millimeter, so I'm returning this to you."

I picked up the holstered weapon and clipped it onto my belt. "Okay. Now what?" I asked.

"If you will write up your account of what happened in detail for us, we can get back to D.C. and get things rolling," Henry replied. Tom pushed a notepad and pen across the table to me.

As I began writing, Tom went to the cafeteria to get a couple cups of coffee for himself and Director Wilson. Writing down the day's events was easy for me. After I had filled three notebook pages, though, it struck me how the day had actually gone. What took only a few hours in real time seemed like a year as I wrote my report.

Henry was getting ready to go grab another cup of coffee when I put my pen down. It had taken me five pages to detail the events of the day. While the director read over my statement, I got up and looked out the window. It was about 8:30 in the evening, and the city was dark. It always amazed me at how serene things looked at night.

The director finished reading my report and told me what a fine job I had done on the report as well as in the field. "I guess that's all we're going to need for now. I would assign an agent to stay here with you, but I think you'll be all right. I did inform Mr. McBride and Mr. Hood that things weren't over yet. Oh, McBride and Hood had their handguns returned to them too, just as a precaution."

"Yes, sir," I said to him. "Is there anything else that I need to be aware of?"

"No," Director Wilson answered. "Those two friends of yours are something else, Sarah. Hang onto them. It's not everyday you come across someone who will defend you unconditionally. They're a rare breed."

I smiled. "I know," was all I could say.

"Well then, get back in there with your friends. Check in at noon tomorrow like McBride has been doing, so that we can keep you in the loop."

I told him that I would and walked the two men to the elevator. When the doors opened I wished them a safe trip back to Washington and promised to call them at noon tomorrow.

As the elevator doors closed I began walking back toward Connor's room. The thought that this fight could start back up again gave me an uneasy feeling. If either man that they'd captured talked to DeLuca, it would be just a matter of time before he found us. I stood at Connor's hospital room door and shook my head. No, I told myself, I've got to think positive that this was almost over. If I didn't, I knew that it would consume my every thought. I opened the hospital room door and stepped inside. Connor and Wade glanced over at me. "What?" I asked the two of them.

They looked at one another and then back at me. "Nothing," they replied in unison.

As I walked toward Connor's bed I could see them trying to stifle smiles. "Okay, you two. What's going on?" I asked looking at Connor, and then at Wade. "Come on, do I need to put you in a headlock Wade?"

"Whoa! Why pick on me? It was his idea," Wade said, pointing toward Connor.

I took a step closer to Wade and said, "What was Connor's idea?"

Wade looked over Connor and said. "A little help here, buddy?"

Connor smiled at his friend and shook his head. "You're on your own, Wade."

I continued walking toward Wade until I had him almost pinned in the corner. "What was Connor's idea, Wade?" I asked again about an arm's length away from him.

Connor shook his head when Wade looked toward him for help. "Wade . . ." he said, drawing Wade's name out.

"Sure. It's easy for you to say that. She's not going to kick your butt," Wade told Connor. I took another step, and Wade said, "Okay, I'll tell you. Your partner Henson told us __"

"Wade!" Connor warned him.

"Tom told you what?" I asked Connor's friend.

"Sarah," McBride interrupted. I turned around. "Come over here for a minute, please."

I turned back around and looked at Wade again and then headed for Connor's bedside. I smiled inside at Wade's reactions.

Connor took my hand in his and held it lovingly. "What Tom told us was that today was your birthday. Wade and I were trying to plan a surprise for you."

"That's it? That's the big secret?" I asked, sitting down beside his bed.

He gave my hand a gentle squeeze. "I'm guessing that you're not the surprise party kind of person," he said.

"I know she's not," Wade remarked as he walked over to the bed.

I couldn't help but laugh. "Okay, you two, all is forgiven. Don't do that again though, okay?"

The two men nodded and crossed their hearts. We all laughed.

"Happy birthday," Connor told me.

"Yeah, Sarah, happy birthday," Wade added.

"Thank you. The best thing I could have gotten for my birthday I already have."

"What's that?" Wade asked.

"Two special friends like the two of you. The only thing that would've made it better was if we had all made it through the day unharmed," I replied.

"But Sarah, none of us were seriously injured. That's all that really counts, right? Connor stated.

"Right," I smiled giving his hand a small squeeze.

"Want me to leave you two kids alone?" Wade kidded.

"I wish you would," Connor said, giving me a wink.

"Don't think I didn't see that, Cap'n." Wade grinned, and we all had a good laugh. "Seriously, though. What are we going to do now? I think that one of us should be here with Connor at all times until we hear from Washington."

"I'll tell you what, Wade. Get a hotel room across the street, and I'll take the first shift. When do you want to change places?" I queried.

Wade proposed that we do six-hour shifts. I agreed and asked what Connor thought.

"Six hours sounds okay with me. You do know that I'm armed, though don't you?"

"Yes, but I'm also sure that you'll need to sleep sometime to keep your strength up."

Connor looked at the two of us. "I'm not going to win this argument am I?"

Wade and I shook our heads no.

"I'll be back in six hours to relieve you, Sarah. I'll call with the hotel and room number in case you need them," Wade commented.

I got up and walked Wade to the door. I hugged him and thanked him for everything.

Wade whispered in my ear. "You wouldn't have really hurt me, would you?"

"What do you think?" I replied in a whisper, smiling at him.

"On second thought," he said, "I don't think I want to know. Good night, you two." Wade told us before he went out the door.

Connor asked what Wade had whispered to me. When I told him, he laughed. "Poor Wade." Was all Connor could say. We held hands and talked about the day's events. "You're a good agent, Sarah and a damn good shot. Wade told me that you saved his life. I just hope that Janet doesn't find out about what happened. She and Wade almost got divorced when we were in the SEALS. Janet hated not knowing where Wade was or if he'd be coming home in a flag-draped casket."

"Sometimes I think my mom feels the same way. At every family get-together she tries to get me to quit my job. My father's okay with the job, though. Not having a son, he's proud of me for defending our country in my own way."

"What about your sister Kate?" Connor asked.

"Kate's Kate. She thinks that all there is to life is having children and pleasing a husband," I replied. "I can't wait until you meet them."

Connor chuckled. "Will I need my flak jacket and weapon?"

"No. At first my mother will fall in love with you. She's

very big on being courteous. When she asks what you think of a woman doing the job I do, though, you're going to lose points with her."

"I'm sorry that my family will never get the chance to meet you. My mother loved everyone that put me first in their life, although she did take a while getting used to Wade." We both laughed. "My father was a soft-spoken man who wore his emotions on his sleeves. You knew immediately where you stood with him. I think he would've loved your strength and honesty."

"And your brother?"

Connor paused. "He probably would've tried to take you away from me. Sean tended to date the same kind of girl over and over again. He couldn't figure out how to find the ones who would care for him." Connor laid back and closed his eyes for minute or two.

"Want me to get the nurse?" I asked softly.

"Not right now. The pain medication is starting to wear off, but I'm trying to hold out. I don't want to become dependent on it. I saw too many men get hooked on opiates during my Navy years. It wasn't a pretty sight."

I got up and sat on the side of the bed where Connor's good leg was. Bending down I kissed him.

"What was that for?" He asked.

"I was just collecting on my birthday present." I smiled.

"Come here then," Connor said quietly. "You didn't get all of it." He pulled me to him, and I laid down beside him. With his arm around me and a kiss on the forehead I felt so safe and secure. "I've missed you, Sarah. Between the doctors, nurses, Washington feds, and Wade we've haven't had any time to ourselves." He kissed me softly on the lips. "Happy birthday," he said, kissing me again.

The telephone beside Connor's bed rang. "That's got to

be Wade," I stated. I picked up the receiver and said, "Hi, Wade" into it.

"How'd you know it was me?" He asked.

"Ha, ha," I replied.

"Okay, okay. Here's the info I told you that I would call with. Are you writing this down?" Wade asked.

"Hang on a sec, Wade. Let me find something to write with." I found a pencil and pad in the stand beside Connor's bed. "Okay, Wade, shoot." As Wade told me the telephone number and name of the hotel across the street I jotted them down. That information was followed by his room number. "Got it," I acknowledged when he had finished speaking.

"All right, Sarah, it's almost ten o'clock, so I'll relieve you at four a.m."

"Four a.m." I repeated. "I'll see you then."

"Oh, and Sarah, don't keep Connor awake all night."

"Good night, Wade." I said just before hanging up.

"I bet Wade told you not to keep me awake all night, didn't he?"

"How'd you guess?" I asked with a smile.

"Oh, he'll probably want to keep me up all night talking about you." Connor smiled back.

"I guess you'd better try to get some sleep now then," I told him.

Connor and I talked for about an hour or so before the nurse came in to check on him. She tried to tell me that visiting hours were over and I would have to leave. I showed her my identification and badge and let her know that Connor was under federal protection. The nurse said that it was fine, but Connor needed to sleep so his body could begin healing. When the nurse had finished taking Connor's vitals, she asked him if he needed anything for the pain.

"It's not too bad right now," Connor told her.

"The object is to keep the pain away, Mr. McBride," the nurse told him. "It's easier if we keep the pain under control instead of starting over every time the pain returns, which would mean you'd be in pain longer."

"Just give me a small dose then," he told her.

She went out and fifteen minutes later came back with two syringes. As she pushed the medication into his IV Connor asked what they were. The nurse answered his question when she was finished. "The first one was for pain and the other one was to help you sleep." She turned toward me and told me that Mr. McBride needed his rest before she headed out the door.

"Well, I guess you're going to get the sleep you need," I told the handsome blonde. "Before you nod off, I'll go down to the waiting room and grab a couple of magazines. Will you be all right?" I questioned.

"Sure, Sarah, go ahead and do whatever you need to. I'll be fine."

"I'll be right back," I told Connor after giving him a kiss. I jogged to the waiting room and grabbed five magazines. A couple of them I thought Wade might want to look through when he took over at four. On my way back I stopped and used the women's restroom.

Connor was having a hard time keeping his eyes open when I returned. "Boy those meds are really working," he commented.

"Good," I remarked. "Don't fight them. Let them do what they're supposed to do."

"I don't seem to have a choice," Connor said. "I guess I'll see you more clearly in the morning."

I leaned over and gave him a kiss on the lips. "Good night, sweet prince," I whispered. I stood up and flipped off one of the two light switches and then walked over to the window and looked out at the skyline. It was hard to believe that with everything that had happened today, the world looked peaceful now in the moonlight.

I was reading a magazine article when Wade came in the room at four a.m. I put my finger up to my lips and nodded toward the door.

"Any problems?" Wade asked out in the hall.

"None," I answered. "Were you able to get any sleep?"

"A couple of hours I think." He said with a yawn.

"Well, the nurse gave Connor a pain pill and something so he'd be able to sleep." I glanced down at my watch. "That was around eleven o'clock, so he'll probably continue sleeping until eight o'clock or so. I figure that's about when the next nurse will come in and wake him up to take his vitals."

Wade smiled. "They're good at that." He winked.

"Okay, Wade," I told him. "The watch is all yours now. There are a couple of magazines on the chair for you, if you get bored."

"Here's my room key, Sarah," Wade stated handing me the hotel key. "I got us a double room so we would each have our own bed."

I took the key from him and thanked him. "I'll see you about ten," I told him.

"Ten it is," Wade repeated. "Now go get some sleep." I smiled and told Wade good night.

The hotel room was a nice one. It had two queen beds with a nightstand between them. The bed Wade had slept in was sloppy, so I had no problem guessing which one was mine. I took off my holster and placed it on the nightstand. Untying my boots I decided to take a shower before getting in bed.

The warm water cascading over my skin felt good. As I lathered myself up, I remembered all that we had been through. I thought that it was too bad the day itself couldn't have been washed away like this. Once I'd dried myself off, I slipped between the covers. After setting the alarm clock I turned off the light and laid back. I must've been more tired than I thought, because the next thing I knew the alarm clock was going off.

Wade Hood had looked through all of the magazines by the time the nurse came into the room. He glanced at his watch and smiled. I had been pretty close with my prediction, he told himself. It was almost eight o'clock in the morning.

Director Wilson and Tom Henson had arrived back in D.C. around midnight. "Don't worry about filling out the reports tonight, Tom," Henry told him. "Let's get some shut eye and then get an early jump on things in the morning."

"Are you sure?" Tom asked. "I'm kind of keyed up."

Henry put his hand on Tom's shoulder. "Don't worry. Those two thugs are being held in solitary. They won't be able to pass on any information to anybody until twenty-four hours have passed. By then we should have DeLuca and his henchmen behind bars." He patted Tom's shoulder. "Go home, Tom. Be back here at eight."

The two men went to the parking lot and got into their cars. By 12:45 they were both at home and sound asleep.

"Huh?" Connor replied when the nurse shook him awake.

"I asked how you were feeling this morning, Mr. McBride," she replied, taking his blood pressure.

"What time is it?" he asked, yawning.

"It's about eight o'clock, Cap'n," Wade replied from the other side of Connor's bed.

Connor closed his eyes and laid back on his pillow. After a while he looked toward Wade and said, "Good morning."

"Right back at ya, buddy," Wade replied. "You look a lot better than you did yesterday." he told his friend.

"Whatever they gave me last night kicked my butt. I can still hardly keep my eyes open," Connor commented. The nurse heard his remark and asked if he was allergic to any medications. "Not that I know about," He answered.

The nurse checked his chart and made a notation in it about a possible reaction to the two medications he'd been given. "I'll have the doctor check in on you as soon as he gets in," she told him. "The night nurse probably gave you the wrong dosage, but I'll run a blood test, just in case. I'll be right back."

She returned a few minutes later with a tray containing a syringe, alcohol swab, two test tubes, a Band-Aid, and a length of rubber banding. She put the band around Connor's arm above the elbow and patted his arm. When she found a vein she wiped it with the alcohol swab and gently pushed the needle into the skin. The nurse then placed a tube in the open end of the syringe. As Connor's blood began filling the tube, she released the band around his arm. When the tube was full, the nurse pulled it out and replaced it with the empty one. After filling the second tube she pulled it out and then pulled the needle out of Connor's arm. She kept her thumb over the spot where the needle had been until she could get the Band-Aid on it. Before leaving the room the nurse wrote Connor's name on the tubes. "The doctor will discuss the results with you when he comes in," she remarked.

"When will that be?" Wade questioned.

"Around ten o'clock," she replied as she headed out the door.

"Wade," Connor said, turning toward his friend. "Talk to me. Maybe it will help me stay awake," he said, yawning.

"What do you want me to talk about?" Wade asked.

"I don't care," Connor said, yawning again. "Just talk."

"I'll read you the jokes out of the Reader's Digest," Wade said.

Connor dozed through most of what Wade read. Every now and then Wade's laughter would wake him up, but it didn't last very long. Wade was starting to get a little worried. He checked his watch. Only another hour and a half before the doctor checked in. The waiting was going to drive him crazy.

Agent Henson got into the agency building at eight o'clock on the dot. He hadn't slept very well at all. Upstairs he went straight to Director Wilson's office, and after knocking on the door, Tom went inside.

Henry Wilson looked up from the paperwork on his desk. "Morning, Tom," he told his senior agent. "Did you get any sleep this morning?"

"Not really," Tom replied. "I tossed and turned all night."

"Me too, Tom," Henry stated, "so I decided to come in early and get started on the paperwork."

Agent Henson walked up to the director's desk and sat down in front of it. "What have we learned from the two thugs of DeLuca's?" he asked.

"I'm going to go question them again in an hour or so. Want to come along?"

"You bet," Tom exclaimed. "What's all the paperwork on your desk about?"

"I thought I would get a jump on the arrest warrant for DeLuca and search warrants for his businesses and banking statements," Wilson replied. "I know that it's wishful thinking on my part, but this'll speed things up if DeLuca's lackeys turn on him."

"That sounds good to me," Tom agreed. "While we're

waiting I'll type up McBride's, Hood's, and Anthony's statements for you."

"Thanks, Tom, that'll be a big help."

I had hurriedly dressed and picked up a cup of coffee and a glass of orange juice to go from the hotel restaurant. It was ten minutes before ten when I opened the door to Connor's hospital room. Wade stood up and came toward me as I entered. "I thought you could probably use a cup of coffee," I said, handing it to him. "How's our patient?"

Wade took a sip from the styrofoam cup and then answered me. "We've got a slight problem this morning, Sarah. Whatever they gave Connor last night hasn't worn off yet."

"What do you mean?" I questioned.

"They can't keep Connor awake for more than a couple of minutes at a time. The nurse drew a blood sample, and the doctor should be here anytime now."

I walked over to Connor's bedside and put down my orange juice. Holding his hand in mine I said to him, "Hey, sleepyhead. What's going on?"

Connor's eyelids opened as he turned toward me. "Hi Sarah," he said softly.

"Wade tells me that you can't stay awake. How are you feeling?"

Connor closed his eyes and replied, "My leg feels fine, Sarah. I just can't seem to shake this drowsiness."

"Stay with me, Connor," I whispered.

"I'm trying, Sarah. Believe me."

The door opened, and Doctor Reynolds entered the room reading Connor's chart. He approached Connor's bed and put the chart down by Connor's side. Taking out a little penlight he shined it into each eye, one at a time. After doing that he took hold of Connor's left hand and told him to squeeze his fingers. Doctor Reynolds did the same thing with the hand I had been holding. When he finished he picked up Connor's chart and wrote in it.

"So what's wrong, Doc?" Wade Hood questioned.

"Your friend seems to be having an adverse reaction to the medicine he was given. I'm going to give him something that will neutralize their effects. I'm also making a note Mr. McBride's chart so this won't happen again." When he had finished writing he took the chart and headed for the door. "A nurse will be right in with the medication. Don't worry. Your friend's going to be just fine within a few minutes or so. I'll stop back by when I've finished my rounds." And out the door he went. A minute later the nurse entered with the injection that Doctor Reynolds had prescribed. After she'd administered the shot into his IV she told us that she would be back in awhile to change Connor's bandages.

I stood up and went over to the window. Those feelings of guilt were beginning to creep back up inside me again. I felt a hand on my right shoulder. "Don't go doing that again, Sarah," Connor's friend told me. "It wasn't your fault, and you know it."

I lowered my head and shook it slightly. "That's easy to say, Wade, but hard to make my mind accept."

"Then listen to me." Connor's voice interrupted.

Wade and I returned to Connor's bedside. He reached up and took a hold of my hand, giving it a squeeze. "None of this is your fault. None of it. Understand?"

A tear rolled down my cheek as I nodded in agreement. I reached up and quickly wiped it away. "I'm just glad you're going to be all right," I told him.

"I will be as soon as I get something to drink. My mouth feels like a desert."

"How about a little bit of orange juice?" I asked, picking up my cup.

"Or you could have some of my coffee," Wade offered with a smile.

"Thanks but no thanks, Wade. Orange juice sounds just fine."

I held the cup while Connor took a sip through the straw. "Go easy on it. I don't even know if you're supposed to be having anything to drink," I told him.

"Thanks, Sarah. That was just what I needed." He leaned back and closed his eyes, and then looking up at the ceiling said, "I wonder when I can get out of this place."

I looked at Wade, and we laughed. "Yep," Wade remarked. "He's going to be just fine."

The two men from yesterday's shoot-out were put into separate interrogation rooms. After running their fingerprints, the agency knew that their names were Joseph Thompson and Andrew Chapman. Andrew was the one recovering from McBride's bullet.

Director Wilson and Tom Henson decided to start with Joe, and let Chapman sit for a while nursing the sore leg. Maybe he would be more cooperative after a few hours by himself.

Joseph Thompson was in a defensive posture when Henry and Tom entered the room. Arms crossed and leaning back in his chair, Joe looked like he felt confident.

"Hi, Joe," the director said, sitting down across the table from him. "I'm Director Wilson and this is agent Henson. You don't mind if I call you Joe, do you?"

Joe glanced from one to the other and spit on the floor.

"Now, now, Joe. Let's try to be as pleasant as we can under the circumstances. What can you tell us about Frank Borgetta? We know that he was DeLuca's right-hand man."

Thompson stared into the director's eyes. "Frank who?" He asked raising one eyebrow.

"The man killed when you went to McBride's cabin," Henry replied.

"Oh, him," Thompson remarked. "I didn't know that was his name."

"Yeah, sure you didn't. How come you guys kept going after Frank had been killed? Who was in charge then? You? Maybe Tommy? I don't think Andy had enough smarts to lead you."

Thompson continued to sit silently with his arms across his chest.

"Okay, let's move on to another subject. Your file shows that you've been arrested several times for assault with intent to do bodily harm. This last time cost you seven years in the state pen. The guards said that when you got out, a car matching Frank's picked you up." Henry paused. "Still say you don't know who Frank Borgetta is?"

"Fine. I knew Frankie. That's no crime, you know," Joe said.

"That's true, except that associating with mobsters and carrying a weapon are violations of your parole, so it looks like you're going to finish out the rest of your thirteen years with an attempted murder charge to boot."

Joe turned his head and looked toward the wall to his right.

"Big tough guy, huh? Hey, Tom," the director said to agent Henson, "what do you think will happen to Joe in prison this time?"

"They'll probably make his stay a living hell," Tom guessed.

"They'll give me a medal for trying to off that fed," Joe snapped back at Tom.

"Are you sure about that? Mr. DeLuca doesn't like people that fail him. Sometimes their life expectancy gets shortened unexpectedly."

"If you're trying to scare me, pig, it won't work. I ain't afraid of nobody."

"That's good, Joe, that's real good. I hope you last long enough so that DeLuca can see how brave you were before you disappear." This kind of cat-and-mouse game went on for almost a half an hour. "Well Joe," Henry Wilson told the thug as he glanced at his watch. "I've got to go now. You think about what we've said. If you change your mind, just let us know." Tom opened the door for Henry Wilson, and they went out into the hallway. "I'm hoping that Chapman will be the weak link in the DeLuca chain."

"We can only hope," Tom said with a sigh. Both men decided to get a cup of coffee before talking to Chapman. Henry told Tom that he would meet him in the interrogation room in fifteen minutes. Agent Henson nodded and walked toward his desk.

Director Wilson walked to his office. Sitting down at his desk he picked up the file on Ben Maxwell. He hoped that Ben had said something that would help trip up Andrew Chapman. Henry reread the file twice and couldn't find a thing to help them. Oh, well, he thought, I'll bring the file with me just in case.

Andrew Chapman sat at the table with his forearms on it and his fingers intertwined. He put his hands in his lap as Tom and the director entered the room. Tom stood by the door and the director sat across from Chapman. "How's the leg doing son?" Henry asked.

"It's a lot better," Andrew replied.

"Good, good," Wilson said as he opened Chapman's file. "It says here that you've been arrested four times for petty theft. There weren't any convictions though. Why was that?"

Andrew Chapman shrugged his shoulders. "Guess the cops didn't have enough evidence on me," he remarked.

"Hmmm, that's interesting. The last couple of times you were arrested, Frank Borgetta put up your bail. How do you know Mr. Borgetta?" Henry asked.

Andrew Chapman looked down at his shoes and didn't say a word.

"Well . . ." the director told Tom, "at least he's smart enough not to lie and say he doesn't know Mr. Borgetta." The director questioned Chapman for about forty-five minutes with no success. Henry Wilson was about to give up when a question popped into his head. "Do you know Shirley Beck?" he asked.

"Sure. She's a nice lady."

"How do you know her?" Henry queried.

"She's Mr. DeLuca's girlfriend," Andrew announced.

"But we thought Shirley Beck was a married woman." Tom spoke.

"Sure, but she didn't love the guy any."

"Do you know who killed James Martin?" Henry wondered aloud.

Andrew caught himself and clammed up. Damn, he told himself. He had said too much.

"Okay, Andrew. We're going to send out for lunch before we start up again. Would you like anything?" the director asked the man.

"I can have anything?" Chapman replied.

"Anything within reason." he was told.

"Can I get a hamburger with the works, some fries and a soda?" he asked.

"Sure thing. Any kind of soda?" Henry asked looking over at Tom.

"A Dr Pepper, if I can get one."

Agent Henson had written down the order. "No problem," He told the young man.

Director Wilson stood up and grabbed the files. As he headed toward the door he told Chapman that his food would be brought in as soon as it arrived. When the door was closed behind them, Henry told Tom to meet him in his office after he'd gotten someone to get Chapman's burger and fries.

Awhile later Tom knocked on Director Wilson's office door and was told to enter. Once inside he was asked to join Henry at the round conference table. "Did you hear what Chapman said about Shirley Beck?" Wilson asked with excitement in his voice.

"Sure," Tom answered, sitting down at the table.

"I think I might have Martin's murder figured out." Henry took a deep breath. "Okay, Tom, how's this? Shirley Beck and DeLuca are playing footsie. Mr. Martin finds out and he threatens to tell Beck and gets taken out. Beck gets set up for the murder, and that way DeLuca has Shirley all to himself. He can always find someone else to launder his money."

"So why does DeLuca send someone after Sarah?" Tom asked.

"He probably thought that she had somehow found out. Maybe there's something in Sarah's notes that she doesn't even realize is there. DeLuca couldn't take any chances either way, though."

"Now if we can just prove it," Tom commented.

"When McBride and Anthony check in we'll ask her about her notes. We're getting close, Tom. I can feel it." Wilson exclaimed.

Doctor Reynolds returned to check on Connor about eleven o'clock. After examining him, the doctor gave Connor a clean bill of health, well, almost. Connor was handed a piece of paper with the name of the drug he had had the reaction to. I think that the only one who could read it was the doctor.

"Make sure if you're ever asked that you tell them you're allergic to that drug" the doctor told Connor.

"I will," Connor promised. "When do you think I'll be able to go home?" Connor asked.

"Mr. McBride," the doctor began, "you're going to have to be here at least a week, if your leg comes along like it should."

"A week?" Connor asked, looking at Wade and me.

"At least," Doctor Reynolds reiterated. "Tomorrow we'll start you out slowly on your rehabilitation."

Connor laid back and stared at the ceiling. A week? This was going to drive him absolutely crazy, he told himself.

Doctor Reynolds finished writing in Connor's chart and put the pen in his pocket. "Do you have any questions?" he asked. We all looked at each other and shook our heads. "Very well, then, I will see you in the morning, Mr. McBride."

After he'd left, Connor shook his head. "A whole week? What am I supposed to do for a whole week?"

"Catch up on your soap operas?" Wade kidded.

"You're no help." Connor said rolling his eyes. "Oh, crap!"

"What's the matter?" I asked.

"I'm supposed to go on that shoot in Minnesota in three months. I've got to call them so they've got enough time to find someone else."

"What do you need me to do?" I said with a squeeze to his hand.

"The problem is . . . that the number is in my den on the desk."

"It's almost time to check in with Director Wilson. I'll see if it's all clear to go and pick up a few things," I told him.

"Tell you what, Sarah. If you get the go-ahead, Wade

can drive you back and go with you to the cabin. After that you can pick up my Jeep and drive it back here when you're done. Is that all right with you, Wade?"

"Just as long as Janet doesn't see us driving through town, otherwise I might end up staying at your place when she throws me out."

We all laughed.

When noon came I called the secure line at the agency. The agent that answered the call put me through to Henry's desk.

"Director Wilson," He said into the receiver.

"Kiddo checking in, sir," I stated.

Henry could hardly contain his excitement. "It looks like we may be able to wrap things up here by tomorrow. We're going to need to go through all of your notes first though."

"They're in my desk drawer, sir. Go ahead and break the lock. Do you think that it would be safe to get a few things from the cabin?" I asked.

"You won't be alone, right?"

"No, sir. Wade will escort me."

"Get in and get out quickly, just in case, and call in twenty-four. I hope to have good news."

"Yes, sir, twenty-four," I repeated.

"How's McBride?"

"Itching to go home," I answered smiling at Connor.

"I'd be surprised if he wasn't," Henry said, smiling to himself. "So long, kiddo," he said before hanging up.

I hung up the phone and turned to Connor. "The director said I could go to the cabin if I had an escort. He also said to get right in and back out again."

"Okay, Wade, Sarah's life is in your hands now."

"No pressure, buddy," Wade said in jest.

"What all do you need me to get from the cabin, Connor?" I asked.

"Grab the last couple of telegrams, a couple changes of clothes, and the deck of cards," he replied. "And Sarah, in the bottom desk drawer is a strongbox. Count out three hundred dollars and bring it back with you, please."

"Anything else?" I asked after I had written down his list.

"Wade's got the keys to my Jeep, and if you get my personal effects from admitting, you'll find the keys to the cabin and the strongbox."

"We'd better get going then, Sarah. It's about an hour drive, and then the hike. I'll call the house and leave a message on the machine so Janet will know when I should be back," Wade said. "Give me a sec, okay?" he said before going outside to use his cell phone.

"Are you going to be all right?" I asked Connor as I sat on the edge of his bed.

"I'm awake, I'm armed, and I'll be counting the minutes until you get back." He winked. "Be careful."

"I will. I promise," I replied, crossing my heart with my hand.

"Girl Scout promise?" Connor asked, grinning.

"I'm going to regret having told you that, aren't I?"

Connor sat up and said, "Come here, you."

As I stepped forward Connor took me by the hand. Carefully I sat on the edge of his bed. Connor ran his hand around my waist and pulled me into him. Our lips found each other's as my arms encircled his shoulders.

Wade walked into the room while we were embracing and exclaimed. "Get a room."

We parted, and Connor looked over at his friend. Smiling, Connor remarked. "I've got a room already, Wade. The problem is that it's not private enough."

"You need to take a cold shower." Wade laughed.

I kissed Connor again and told him that we would be back as soon as we could.

"Be careful, you two," Connor said as he shook Wade's hand.

We stopped at the admitting desk on our way out of the hospital to pick up Connor's keys. The woman there didn't want to give them to us without checking with the patient first, so we had to wait for her to verify that we had Connor's permission. That was a pain in the butt, but I was glad that the hospital staff were on their toes.

As Wade and I made our way out of Roanoke, he started up a conversation. "So, young lady, what are your intentions toward my best friend?" Wade chuckled with a sideways glance at me.

"Did my mother put you up to that?" I smiled back at him.

"What's your mother got against Connor?" Wade asked.

"Nothing. She doesn't even know anything about him," I said. "I mentioned his name, and it was the Spanish Inquisition all over again."

"What did you tell her?" He asked glancing over at me.

"That's just it. I haven't told her anything yet. Things started happening around the agency and I had to miss the family get together two Sundays ago. My family doesn't even know that I've been shot."

"How can you do that to them, Sarah? What were they told instead?"

"Agent Henson told them that I was undercover on a case and couldn't contact them for a while," I replied.

Wade shook his head. "I don't know about you, Sarah. How can you keep them in the dark like that?"

"You'd have to understand my mother, Wade. She absolutely hates the career that I've chosen for myself. If she found out that I had been shot she would make my life and Director Wilson's miserable."

"So what do you think she'll think about Connor? I'm assuming that you will introduce them at some point."

I gave Wade a dirty look. "I think my mother will love Connor, right up to the point where she asks him what he thinks about my job."

"Well, what about your dad? Is he still alive?" Wade asked

"My dad always wanted a boy, so he's thrilled that I'm doing something to protect the United States in my own way. He's the one who's always been my cheerleader."

"That must make for interesting family dinners," Wade commented.

"Yep. Dinner with my family is pretty much the same every time. When are you going to get a safer job? When are you going to get married and settle down? Why don't you want to be more like your sister Katie?" I let out a deep sigh. "Oh, yeah, I really look forward to family dinners."

Wade chuckled. "Well, at least when you introduce Connor they'll have something else to talk about."

"I just hope he doesn't run out screaming." I laughed.

Wade and I talked about how Connor and I had met. We talked about Wade's wife Janet and her college studies. He never asked about my job, and I never asked about his time in the SEALS with Connor.

It was around 1:30 when we pulled into the parking lot near the hiking path. There were only two other vehicles in the lot, and they both had empty bicycle racks on top of them. As we headed down the trail nothing much was said. We were too busy surveying our surroundings and listening to the forest. Crime scene tape was across Connor's doorway, so I tore it off.

"Isn't that illegal, Sarah?" Wade asked, looking around.

I laughed. "Just stay with me and you'll be okay." I unlocked the door and cautiously entered the cabin. Taking out my gun I made a sweep of the house. Wade took out his weapon and stood guarding the front entrance.

"It's clear in here, Wade," I told him.

"That's good. Now grab the things Connor wanted and let's get out of here. Remember . . . in and out."

I holstered my weapon and told Wade that I would just be a couple of minutes. The first thing I did was grab the telegrams from the top of Connor's desk. I folded them and put them in my back blue jean pocket. Then I got into Connor's strongbox and counted out three hundred dollars. After locking it back up, I went into Connor's room. I took out an old duffle bag and started putting a couple changes of clothes inside. With that done, I went into the kitchen and got the deck of cards off from the table. I stood just inside the cabin door and looked around.

"Whatcha thinking about, Sarah?" Wade asked from behind me.

I turned around and went out the door, pulling it closed behind me. As I put the key into the lock I said, "It just seems like a lifetime since we were last here. It's amazing how quickly things can happen."

Wade Hood nodded in agreement and grabbed Connor's duffle bag. "Let's go, Sarah. Connor will be worried if you're not back by suppertime."

When we pulled into Wade's yard, a barking mixed-breed dog greeted us. I got out of the truck, and the dog came over to me. As I knelt down to pet him I asked Wade what his name was.

"Trooper." Wade replied. He told me that he would be right back and went to get the keys to Connor's Jeep. He hadn't been gone long when he came out with two glasses of lemonade in his hands. "I don't know about you, but I'm thirsty," He stated, handing me one of the glasses.

"Thanks, Wade," I said taking the glass and drinking it halfway down. "I guess I was thirstier than I thought," I commented.

When we had finished our drinks Wade walked across the yard and uncovered Connor's Jeep. Jumping in, he put the key in the ignition and turned it. The forest green Jeep came alive.

"Well, Sarah, here you go," Wade told me as he got out of the Jeep. "Hang on a sec and I'll grab Connor's bag for you." He jogged across the yard and pulled the duffle bag out of the bed of his pickup truck. Trooper ran and barked alongside Wade as he returned with it to the Jeep. "You've got my number, right?"

"Sure do." I smiled.

"Let me know how things go, okay? Jan and I will probably be over to see Connor in another day or so."

"You've got it, Wade," I told him. After he had put the duffle bag in the Jeep I gave him a hug and told him thanks for everything.

Wade returned my hug. "No more blaming yourself, right?"

"Right," I answered. It was around 2:30 in the afternoon when I drove out of Wade's yard.

Director Wilson had Mrs. Shirley Beck brought in for questioning. She wasn't very happy about it either.

"I appreciate your coming in, Mrs. Beck," Tom Henson told her.

"I didn't know I had a choice," she responded curtly.

Tom ignored her comment and began his questions. "Do you know a man named Dominic DeLuca?" Shirley Beck didn't say a thing. "I must tell you that we have proof that you know him."

"Fine," Mrs. Beck said. "So I know the man."

"Just exactly how well do you know Mr. DeLuca?"

"What exactly are you implying? That we're having an affair?" she screeched.

"I'm not implying anything, Mrs. Beck. I'm just trying to find out how well you know Mr. DeLuca," Tom calmly answered. "For example, do you know what Mr. DeLuca does for a living?"

Shirley Beck calmed down a bit and answered him. "Yeah, I know what he does. Mr. DeLuca owns a restaurant and a couple other businesses, I think."

"Is Mr. Beck a jealous man?" Agent Henson continued.

"I guess about as much as any man is, she replied.

"Has he ever gotten jealous and become violent?"

"Hah! My husband wouldn't even know if I'd been cheating on him. He doesn't pay any attention to me at all."

"Did he know about you and Mr. DeLuca?"

"I just said . . . wait a minute. I never said that Dominic and I were having an affair. You're trying to trick me."

"Well, Mrs. Beck, several people told us that you and Mr. DeLuca were very close friends. I find it hard to believe that all of those people could be lying," Tom said, looking at the file folder in front of him.

"So Dom and I are having an affair. Big deal! People do it all the time. That doesn't mean that my husband knew about us."

"Did Mr. Martin know about the affair?"

"I don't know, maybe," Shirley answered staring at the floor.

Agent Henson looked at his notes. "Did he try to blackmail you to keep that little indiscretion from your husband?"

Mrs. Beck sat silently thinking about how or if she should answer that question.

"Okay, I'll ask you this instead. Did Mr. DeLuca find out that Mr. Martin knew your secret?"

Shirley hesitated. "I guess he could have. He has a lot of people working for him."

"So, Mr. Martin was blackmailing you?" Tom said with interest.

"I didn't pay him anything, though," she exclaimed.

"Did Mr. DeLuca tell you that he would take care of things?" Tom asked.

"Yeah, but I thought he was just going to threaten him. I didn't know Dom was going to kill him."

"Do you know for a fact that Mr. DeLuca had James Martin killed?"

"I don't have any proof, if that's what you mean," she remarked.

"Your husband's car got a parking ticket around the block from where Mr. Martin was murdered, about the same time he was murdered. How did your husband's vehicle get there, Mrs. Beck? Your husband said that he had parked it in the lot at the realty office."

In an almost whisper Shirley Beck replied, "Dominic told me to park it there and take a cab home. I didn't know why."

The questioning continued like this for another forty-five minutes or so. The whole murder plan was corroborated by Mrs. Beck, but with no evidence to it, they couldn't even arrest Mr. DeLuca. Mrs. Beck was kept in protective custody with her son. Tom would check with the taxi company and try to verify that part of Shirley Beck's story.

Director Wilson walked into the interrogation room after Mrs. Beck had been taken out. "Good work, Tom," Henry said, sitting down at the table. "Now all we've got to do is get Chapman to rollover on Mr. DeLuca."

"Were Sarah's notes of any help?" Agent Henson inquired.

"I was waiting to go over them with you, Tom. This late in the game I can't trust them to anybody else."

Tom nodded.

"Come on. I'll buy you a cup of coffee," Henry told his agent.

The drive back to Roanoke was exhilarating. The wind on my face made me remember our drive out to Connor's cabin. I was the one wounded then. It seemed like things were coming around full circle. I pulled into the parking lot at the hospital at 3:47. Picking up Connor's duffle bag, I headed inside. Outside the door to Connor's room I heard his television set going and smiled as I opened the door.

"I am so glad you're back," Connor exclaimed. "I'm starting to lose IQ points with all of the junk on TV."

I smiled. "Is that the only reason you're glad I'm back?"

Connor held out his hand to me. "Not hardly, Sarah." He smiled back. I went over to him and started to hold his hand. "No," Connor said. "I want the deck of cards." He gave me a sly look and winked.

"I can go if you want," I said, turning away from him with a smile on my face.

Connor grabbed my hand. "Oh, no, you don't," he said, pulling me back to him. He placed his hand gently on the side of my face and kissed me softly. "I'm very glad that you're back, Sarah," he said in a whisper.

"I'm glad I'm back too," I said returning his kiss.

The moment was broken when the door opened and a young candy striper came in with her magazine and candy cart. "Oh, excuse me," she said in embarrassment. She looked at the floor and asked if we wanted anything off from her cart.

"Do you have a Baby Ruth by any chance?" Connor asked politely.

The girl looked through her cart. "I have one left, sir. Do you want anything else?"

He looked over at me, and I shook my head and said, "I'm good." Connor smiled at my remark and gave me a wink.

The candy striper handed the candy bar to Connor and told him that if he needed anything else that her name was Bridget. He held up the candy bar and thanked her. Bridget smiled and told Connor that he was welcome anytime. She blushed when she realized what she'd said and hurriedly left Connor's room.

Connor and I glanced at each other and chuckled. "I guess I'm going to have to keep my eyes on Miss Bridget," I remarked.

"Don't worry. She might have a crush on me, but I've already got what makes me happy," Connor replied, pulling me into him. The kiss was tender and sweet, and I felt as if I could hold it forever. Combined with those strong arms around my waist I was in heaven.

When we parted I went to get the cards out of Connor's duffle bag. "Oh, here," I said as I pulled the telegrams out of my back pocket. "I almost forgot them."

Connor unfolded the telegrams and noted the dates on them. "Well, I know that I probably won't be making the shoot in Yosemite in four months, and I think that I'll call about the Minnesota shoot and give them the option to replace me." Connor read the third telegram and shook his head. "I can't believe I never even read this telegram when Wade gave it to me."

"Where do they want you to go?" I asked, curiously.

"Oh, just Australia," he replied sounding bored.

"Australia? When do they want you?"

"In about five months. They want some crocodiles photographed for their reptile magazine."

"Don't tell me you're interested in going. What you know about crocodiles?"

"I know you keep away from the end with the teeth." Connor smiled at me, his eyes twinkling. "Come on, Sarah, how can a crocodile be more dangerous than what we've just been through?"

I didn't say anything.

"Besides, I have no idea what I'll be doing in five months. I'll put off answering this telegram for a month, or until I see how my leg's going to heal."

"I'm sorry." I apologized. "I kind of lost it there. It's just that I've seen the nature channel show on crocodiles and alligators. It just looks so dangerous."

Connor gave my hand a light squeeze. "Don't worry, Sarah. That's a long way off yet." He had already called the Canadian magazine from the cabin, so he got started on the two in his hands. Connor called about the shoot in Yosemite and then made the phone call to the photo editor of the Minnesota magazine. They were very understanding and wished Connor a speedy recovery. When he hung up the telephone, he looked at me and said, "How about some cards?"

I had totally forgotten about the deck of cards in Connor's duffle bag. Bending down to pull the deck out, I told Connor that we would play for his candy bar.

"Okay. I get to pick the game, though." he remarked.

"Wait a minute. Why do you get to choose?" I asked.

"Because it's my candy bar," he said, grinning.

"Not for long," I told Connor as I shuffled the cards. "What's your pleasure?"

"Gin, of course," he quickly replied.

I dealt the cards and Connor began first. After about seven times around I laid down my cards and said, "Gin!"

"Aww, come on. You've never beaten me at gin before. Did you cheat?" Connor commented.

I thought about what he had just said. He was right. I'd

never beaten him at gin before. I collected the cards and looked at his hand.

"You're not supposed to do that," Connor said, trying to snatch them away from me.

"Just how long ago did you have gin?" I asked.

"Would you believe during that last turn I took?"

I looked into those baby blue eyes of his. "Nope." I replied.

"Okay. I had gin the fourth time around."

"Pay up," I told him with my hand out.

"You want my Baby Ruth even though I cheated?" He asked.

"Yep. Hand it over, buddy," I said with a smile.

Connor reached over to the nightstand and got the candy bar. "You're just plain cruel, Sarah," he said.

"Didn't you cheat so that I would win the candy bar?" I asked innocently.

"Well, yeah. I guess so." He handed the Baby Ruth over to me with a pout on his face.

I laughed as I took it from his hand. "Maybe if you're a good boy Bridget will bring you another one tomorrow."

"At least she likes me," he retaliated.

"After that comment I'm not sure that I want to share this with you now," I teased. I broke the candy bar and gave Connor half of it. "I hope you realize that I'm only sharing this with you out of pity," I told him.

"Really? And here I thought it was because you liked me."

"That too," I said as I got up and sat on the bed beside him. "How's your leg really doing?" I asked quietly.

"The medicine is keeping any pain in check, and when the nurse changed my bandage, the knee didn't look too bad."

"How big of a scar will you end up with?"

"Well, it's not a small one, but it's not an overly large one either."

"That's a big help," I remarked shaking my head slightly.

Connor looked into my eyes and said in a gentle voice, "Don't worry. It's going to be fine, I promise." I looked back at him, and he continued, "When have I ever lied to you?"

"Not counting just now when you cheated at gin?" I asked.

"Now wait a minute, I didn't cheat to win, I cheated so that you could win. There's a difference."

"Oh, so there's good lying and bad lying?"

"Of course there is. A good lie is one where nobody gets hurt. Like telling a woman her dress is pretty when you think it's hideous. Nobody gets hurt, and you made her feel good. Now a bad lie is one you tell to intentionally hurt the person. For example, if I told you that Wade said you were ugly, which he didn't. The lie was meant to hurt you and get Wade into trouble too," Connor explained.

"You have way too much time on your hands, Connor." I shook my head and smiled. "I've got to get you a hobby. What do you think of puzzles?"

Connor laughed. "That sounds somehow familiar to me."

I joined in on the laughter.

By my watch it was almost seven o'clock in the evening. A little while earlier a nurse had brought in Connor's supper. His meal consisted of a meat patty with green beans and potato wedges. Dessert was a small bowl of peaches. While Connor ate I took the opportunity to use the bathroom. When I returned we began our marathon of card games. By the time it was ten o'clock, Connor and I had played three games of Gin, two games of Crazy Eights, four games of Go

Fish and a hand of War. I placed my hand over my mouth trying to hide a yawn.

"I saw that, Sarah," Connor said shuffling the cards. "Let's call it quits for the night, okay?"

"Only if you want to," I said, trying to hide another yawn.

"I can tell that you're certainly not tired." Connor chuckled. "Why don't you go back to the hotel and grab some shut eye? I'll be okay here. Remember, I'm not totally alone," he said referring to his handgun.

"I know you're not," I told him. "You've got Bridget." I laughed.

"Don't knock my groupie." He laughed. "Seriously, though, Sarah," Connor said, changing his tone of voice. "Go get some sleep. I really don't want you getting sick on me."

I tried to stifle another yawn. Standing up and stretching, I commented, "Okay, you talked me into it." I leaned over Connor's bed and gave him a kiss, telling him that I would be back early in the morning. "Oh, yeah," I said, glancing at his duffle bag on the floor. "What do you want me to do with this?"

"Take it with you and hang onto it for now. Maybe when I start on my physical therapy I'll be able to wear a pair of jeans. I know that the pant leg will need to be split to accommodate the knee, though."

"No problem, Connor. What do you want me to do with the three hundred dollars?"

"Don't use your credit cards yet, at least not until Henry says everything's okay. Go and buy yourself a couple of changes of clothes and keep the rest for food and such. Wade's name is on the hotel room now, and I'll pay him back when he gets the bill."

I shook my head slowly. "All right, if that's what you want. But I'm happy in the clothes that I'm wearing."

"Okay, just buy one outfit then, and I won't say any more about it."

"Just one, and no more argument, right?" I asked.

"Boy Scout promise," he said, holding up three fingers on his right hand.

I rolled my eyes. "I knew that I hadn't heard the last of that." I told him.

Connor smiled and repeated his wish for me to have a good night. We kissed again, and I started for the door to his room. "You try and get some sleep too."

"All I've got to do is turn on the television and find someone playing golf. That will put me out in no time flat."

I laughed and gave a wave as I went out the door. As I walked across the street to the hotel I thought how nice it would be to get a full night's sleep. I just hoped that I could.

After their coffee, Director Wilson and Tom Henson retrieved my notes and began going over them. Along with my notes were copies of all of the photographs we had taken on stakeout as well as the license plate numbers. Tom took my notes and read through them carefully, so as not to miss anything.

Henry Wilson began going through the pictures and license plate numbers. He'd gone through about a dozen or so when something caught his eye. "Tom." Henry showed him the picture. "When was this one taken?"

Tom glanced quickly through the papers in front of him. "Okay, that picture was taken . . . earlier on the same day that Martin got it."

"Where was this?" the director asked.

"That was in front of the realty office. Well, I'll be damned; Shirley Beck was there that same day."

"Did you ever find out if a taxicab picked up Mrs. Beck that same day?"

Tom looked through his own notes. "I talked to the dispatcher of the Checkered Cab company. Here it is. They had a call for to pickup a fare around the block from were Martin was killed. I didn't get a chance to talk to the cabbie, but I was told the pickup was a woman. The driver dropped her off in front of Luigi's restaurant."

"We still don't have any proof that DeLuca was involved in Martin's murder or the attempt on Anthony's life. If Mrs. Beck got on the witness stand she would probably commit perjury rather than testify against DeLuca," Henry said deep in thought.

"Somehow we've got to get either Chapman or Thompson to rat out DeLuca," Tom stated.

"My bet would be on Chapman. I think he's the weaker of the two," Director Wilson said, tapping the file in front of him.

"Of course we've always got the money laundering charge to fall back on," Tom reminded Henry.

"Yeah, but DeLuca's attorney would have him out on bail within fifteen minutes. No. I want him staying in custody until the verdict is read at his trial."

"What about Frank Borgetta? He was the first one killed in the raid at McBride's. As far as we know, none of the five men involved had ever even seen Anthony before. Maybe we could somehow show that Borgetta was working under DeLuca's orders."

"And that brings us back to Chapman and Thompson," the director commented. "Let's work some more on Chapman and see what slips out." He looked down at his watch and said, "It's going on six o'clock now, Tom. Let's put this on the shelf until first thing in the morning. I'll keep the files locked up tight until then."

"What time tomorrow do you want to get started?"

"Let's give ourselves a little bit of time to catch up on some sleep. How does eight thirty a.m. sound? I'll even bring the coffee and donuts," the director told Tom. After agreeing on the time the two men gathered up all of the photographs, files, and notes on the table. Director Wilson went to his safe and Tom went out to his desk. Once the materials were locked up, Henry Wilson grabbed his jacket and headed out the door. While he waited for the elevator he spied Tom at his desk. He walked over beside Tom and asked if he was ready to go.

"I just thought that I would check my desk and make sure that I had all of my notations on this case. Sometimes they're on napkins or whatever I had handy at the time," Tom replied.

"Do you have them all?"

"I think so now." Tom stood up and grabbed a folder from his desk. "I'll take these with me so you don't have to open your safe back up."

"Are you sure, Tom? It's no big deal to open my safe, you know. I know the combination and everything." The director gave Tom a half smile. "That was meant to be funny, Tom."

"It was. I've just got a lot on my mind trying to figure out how to keep DeLuca behind bars so that Sarah can come back to work."

"Me too, Tom, but you can't let life's problems overtake your life completely. Besides, I don't think that Anthony is suffering very much right now."

As the two men walked toward the elevator, Tom asked Henry what he thought of McBride and Hood. "They're two smart, capable young men, and I think that they probably wreaked havoc as Navy SEALS."

"I think that Sarah found a good man to get involved with. McBride seems to really care for her," Tom added.

"I wonder if maybe someday we could get him to work for us," the director thought out loud.

"I doubt it sir, McBride likes being able to do things on his own time schedule."

"I was just wondering out loud, Tom," Henry said as the elevator doors opened. The two men rode the elevator downstairs and walked out to the parking lot together.

"Wanna grab a bite?" Tom asked. "The house is kind of empty with Margaret out of town."

"Sure, Tom. How about that new Chinese place over near the old firehouse on Stanton?"

"Sounds good to me. I'll meet you there."

The food had been good and the conversation had been welcomed. Tom Henson and Henry Wilson had finished eating and were heading home. It began to lightly rain as the two men reached their cars.

"Drive safely, Tom," the director stated.

"I'll see you in the morning," Tom replied as he started up his car.

It was six in the morning when I got up. I had tossed and turned most of the night. My mind kept going over everything that had taken place in the past couple of days. For most people, that probably would've been a nightmare. For me it was just part of the job. In my mind I had gone over every single detail of the past events. I guess it's just my way of rationalizing my actions. The dreaming settled my mind, but wrecked havoc on my sleep cycle. I got up and turned on the light and the television set. With all of the cable channels available I couldn't believe there wasn't anything good to watch. I settled on the Weather Channel. I hoped that maybe it would put me back to sleep. No such luck. The sun was starting to come up, and I could hear all of the movement and traffic starting to pick up outside.

I walked into the bathroom and turned on the shower. Maybe a cool shower would help me wake up, I thought. It sure didn't look like I was going to be able to go back to sleep again. When I finished my shower, I put on one of Connor's shirts and a pair of blue jeans. As I looked at myself in the mirror I thought about what Connor had wanted me to do with his three hundred dollars. I did need some undergarments and a pair or two of socks. After having a light breakfast, I found out where the nearest Walmart was. I walked back across the street to the hospital parking garage and picked up Connor's Jeep. I hoped that the Walmart was a superstore, that way it would be open this early in the morning.

The traffic wasn't too bad, so I made good time. I lucked out and the store was open already. I picked out a couple of bras, a package of underpants and one of socks. They had a selection of pullover blouses on sale that weren't bad looking, so I grabbed two of them. I picked out two pair of jeans that fit me perfectly and headed to the checkout. The whole total came to less than seventy dollars. I was hanging onto every receipt and intended to reimburse Connor for every cent. Before leaving the store I remembered something and turned around. It didn't take me very long to find what I was looking for. I returned to the cashier once again and then made my way back to the hotel. By the time I'd gotten my clothes changed it was almost eight o'clock. I looked into the mirror and smiled. The blouse and jeans hugged my every curve. I pulled my hair back, clipped on my holster, and put on my jacket. Grabbing the shopping bag, I headed across the street to the hospital.

Connor had had a difficult time getting to sleep too. He'd turned down the new sleeping medicine the doctor had prescribed, but did accept the pain medicine. It had been around two o'clock when Connor turned off the television and the lights. Sleep finally came to visit him. Around eight o'clock the nurse came in and took Connor's vital signs. When she had finished, she changed the bandage on his leg.

"According to your chart, Doctor Reynolds has you starting physical therapy today. Don't worry; today you'll probably just get your leg brace fitted and be shown the exercises that you'll be doing." After discarding the old bandages and washing her hands, the nurse turned toward Connor. "Do you need anything else or have any questions, Mr. McBride?" she asked.

As I opened the door to Connor's room he answered the nurse smiling. "No, thank you. Everything I need just walked in the door."

The nurse looked at me and smiled. She grabbed her tray and Connor's chart and headed for the door. "I'll be right back with your pain medication, Mr. McBride."

"Thank you," I told her as she walked past me.

"You're welcome," she whispered. "I'll be right back."

"Sarah," Connor smiled. "You're a sight for sore eyes this morning."

I walked over and gave him a kiss. "You didn't sleep very well last night, did you?" I asked sitting down beside his bed.

"Do I look that bad?" he asked.

"Not bad, just tired," I replied sweetly.

Connor laid his head back and closed his eyes. "I think it must have been around three or so before I was able to get some sleep. I turned down the new sleeping medication last night, and being awakened at eight this morning to have my vitals taken didn't help much either." He opened his eyes and looked over at me. "Speaking of looking tired, how much sleep did you get last night?"

"Not enough," I answered. "I guess we'll both need a nap later today."

The nurse came back in with the pain medication for Connor. After it had been administered into his IV she left again. I stood up and took off my jacket and placed it on the back of my chair.

"Wow, Sarah!" Connor said, followed by a long whistle.

"You like?" I asked, turning around for him.

"You look great," he replied.

"Good, because I got you a little something too," I commented. "Close your eyes."

Connor laid back and closed his eyes. Reaching into the shopping bag I brought out the item I had almost forgotten at the store. I set it in Connor's lap and told him he could open his eyes again. Connor looked at what I had placed in his lap and laughed. "Oh, you shouldn't have." He laughed.

"I know how much you loved working them with me, so I just had to get you one too," I smiled.

There across Connor's lap was a puzzle. This one was going to take a while to put together. It was a field of grass with a single small cow in the middle of it.

"You are going to help, right?" he asked, eyeing me suspiciously.

"Would I ever abandon you in a time of need?" I asked.

"Never," Connor answered.

"So, what's the word from the doctor?" I asked sitting carefully on the side of Connor's bed.

"Later this morning I'm to be fitted with a leg brace, and then shown what kind of exercises they'll be having me do. The nurse said I probably won't be doing anything too strenuous today, though. I just want to get out of here as soon as possible," he stated.

"What would Bridget say if she heard you talk like that? She might think you want to get away from her." I smiled.

"Come here, you," Connor said pulling me into his arms. After a long kiss and embrace Connor whispered in my ear, "You're all I need, Sarah." I kissed him and whispered back that he was all I needed too.

CHAPTER 7

Director Wilson was good to his word and had coffee and donuts waiting when Tom Henson arrived. On the round table in Wilson's office were all of the files, photographs, and notes on the DeLuca/Beck investigation. Along the wall on the credenza sat a pot of coffee and a half a dozen donuts, along with cups, napkins, cream, and sugar. Henry grabbed a cup of coffee and wrapped a napkin around a jelly donut. Tom followed suit with an old-fashioned cake donut. The two men sat at the table and began planning the day's strategies.

First they would go over all of the file materials, photos, etc., to make sure that nothing was missed. After that they were going to question Andrew Chapman again. Both men were hoping that they would get Chapman to break today. If that happened, they could get those arrest warrants served and put DeLuca in prison where he belonged.

"Maybe by noon when Anthony calls in, we'll be able to give her some good news." Henry hoped.

Tom nodded in response and picked up one of the files. "Well, we've only got three hours to find something useful, so we'd better get started," Tom remarked as he popped the last piece of donut into his mouth.

Before they could get started, the telephone on Director Wilson's desk rang. He picked it up on the second ring. "Director Wilson," he said into the receiver. He nodded a couple of times and said "Uh-huh" a couple of more. When the conversation ended, they got back to the files.

"Anything important?" Tom asked Henry.

"Nope, at least not to this case" he answered.

Fifty minutes later, everything on the table had been re-read and taken note of. Tom yawned and rubbed his eyes. "Let me grab another cup of coffee before we start back up again," he said as he stood up and stretched. Director Wilson stood up and stretched too. Taking his last sip of coffee Henry headed for the coffee pot behind Tom.

"How did you sleep last night? Or did you get any at all?" Henry asked as he poured the coffee.

"Believe it or not, I actually got a few hours," Tom replied. "I guess I was more tired yesterday than I thought I was."

"Me too, Tom," Henry stated. After grabbing another donut the director returned to the table. When Tom had joined him, they made a list on what they had so far.

1. Beck was laundering money for Dominic DeLuca, known mob boss.
2. Beck's partner, James Martin, was murdered. Case still open.
3. Mrs. Beck was having an affair with Dominic DeLuca.
4. Mr. Beck's car was found around the block from Martin's murder.
5. Photos showed Mrs. Beck taking her husband's car from the realty parking lot the day of the murder.
6. Ground maintenance crew members said they saw a man running. Upon seeing photos they agreed it could have been Beck.
7. Ben Maxwell worked with DeLuca's number-one man, Frank Borgetta.

8. Two attempts made on Agent Anthony's life.
9. Andrew Chapman confirms Mrs. Beck's affair.
10. Martin blackmailed Mrs. Beck to keep her cheating a secret.
11. DeLuca knew about the blackmail and told Mrs. Beck he would take care of it.
12. DeLuca had been the one who had Mrs. Beck move her husband's car the day of the murder.

Director Wilson and Tom looked over the list. It was all supposition; they didn't have any proof of their theory unless they could get Chapman to roll over on DeLuca. It was time to question him again, the two men decided.

"Good morning," Henry told Andrew Chapman as he was brought into interrogation. "How was your hamburger yesterday?"

Chapman sat down across from the director. "Not too bad," he answered glancing around the room.

"That's good. Mr. Chapman, we have a slight problem, and I'd like to tell you about it." Director Wilson began telling Chapman their theory about how the recent chain of events happened. "As you can see, though, we don't have any proof to substantiate our theory," Henry said in conclusion.

"So?" Chapman asked.

"This is where you come in. We need your help to bring DeLuca down."

"Are you crazy, man? No way am I squealing on the boss. Do you know what he would do to me if I said anything?"

"Actually, Andrew . . . may I call you Andrew?" Director Wilson asked.

Chapman looked around and then shrugged his shoulders.

"Okay, Andrew it is. Actually you've already helped us

out. You told us about Mrs. Beck and Mr. DeLuca's affair. Do you think that he'll be very happy about that?"

Andrew stared at the floor and didn't say a word.

"What's he going to say about you and Joey botching up the hit on agent Anthony twice now? That doesn't look too good."

"Frankie did the first hit on the lady fed. I didn't have anything to do with it," Andrew retorted.

"Okay, Frankie did the first hit on Anthony. You and Joey are the only two left alive after the second attempt on my agent, though, so who's going to pay now?"

"Yeah, but the boss didn't do anything to Frankie for missing his shot," Andrew countered in a defensive tone.

"That is true, Andrew. Frank was DeLuca's number-one man though. How far down are you? Are you indispensable to him?"

They could almost see the wheels turning in Chapman's mind. After a few minutes he shook his head and asked, "If I tell you what you want to know, what'll happen?"

"We'll make sure you're not put in the same prison with DeLuca." Before Chapman could ask, Henry continued. "Andrew, I'm not going to lie to you. You attempted to kill a federal agent. There's no way you're getting off without some hard time. How much you get depends on you, though."

Andrew Chapman gave it some more thought. "What do you want to know?" he asked.

Agent Henson was on the other side of the one-way mirror ready to turn on the video camera. "This is going to be videotaped, okay, Andrew? When we're finished your statement will be typed up for you to sign. Do you understand?"

Chapman nodded. "Can I talk to my lawyer first?" he asked.

"Would this be one of Mr. DeLuca's lawyers?" the director queried.

Andrew thought about what Director Wilson had just said. He would be dead for sure if DeLuca's lawyer saw him talk to the feds. "Can I talk to another lawyer?"

"Sure you can." The agency director turned around and looked into the mirror. "Tom, have somebody from the public defender's office come in and talk to Mr. Chapman." Henry turned back and faced Andrew. "We'll talk again when your attorney gets here, Mr. Chapman." Director Wilson stood up and walked out of the room.

Tom met him out in the hallway.

"Why'd you do that?" Tom asked.

"He's just a big kid that got into something over his head. I'm not saying he should get off, but maybe the lawyer will see what a good deal the prosecutor has proposed and talk him into helping us."

"And if they don't?"

"I think the thought of what DeLuca will do to him on the outside is a powerful motivator. If not, we can still get DeLuca on the money laundering. Maybe that'll hold him long enough to build a solid murder case against him," Henry explained. "Let's see what happens with Chapman first, though. No need to put the cart before the horse." The two men went to the elevators and waited. It was going on 10:15 a.m. Henry hoped that they would have a signed confession before I called at noon.

Around 9:30 an orderly came into Connor's room with a wheelchair. "Your ride's here." I smiled.

"Mr. McBride, my name is Matt, and I'm here to take you downstairs to rehab." He glanced at the chart in his hand. "It says here that your IV can be removed today. Let me get a nurse to come and remove that before we head downstairs.

I'll be right back," he said before he disappeared out the door.

Two minutes later Matt returned with a nurse. She went over to Connor's IV tube and turned it off. Then she put on a pair of gloves and carefully pulled off the tape holding the IV needle in Connor's arm. When she was done she held a gauze pad over the needle and told Connor that it was going to hurt a little bit when she pulled out the needle. Connor braced himself, as the nurse slowly pulled the needle out. Still holding the gauze pad, she placed the needle on the tray table. Taking a Band-Aid out of her smock pocket, she replaced the gauze pad with it. "There you go," she told Connor.

"Thanks," he told her, rubbing his sore arm.

"Okay. Let's get things rolling," Matt stated. He pulled Connor's blanket and top sheet back. "Can you swing your legs over this side for me?"

"I'll try," Connor answered. Taking a deep breath he slowly swung his legs to the side of the bed.

"Good," Matt told him. "Now I'm going to have you put this bathrobe on and carefully get you into the wheelchair." Connor slipped his arms into the robe and slowly stood up, keeping all of his weight on his left foot. Matt put his arm around Connor's waist and helped him into the wheelchair. After he'd put down the footpads, Matt draped a blanket over Conner's lap.

"How long is this going to take Matt?" I asked.

"You're welcome to come down with us, if you'd like to, miss," he replied.

"I would like that very much." I smiled. Connor held my hand as Matt pushed him toward the elevators.

"How are you doing Mr. McBride?" Matt asked after pushing the elevator button.

"I'm not sure. There's some pulling on my right leg. I don't know how to explain it." Connor told him.

Matt carefully lifted Connor's right leg and locked that side of the wheelchair in a straight-out position. "Is that better?"

"Much," Connor said with a breath of relief.

The elevator doors opened and we got in. When we reached the second floor it seemed like we had walked into a giant labyrinth. When the maze of turns ended, I asked Matt, "Do they have maps of this hospital for visitors? I don't think I could find this place again without one."

"Actually, a map is posted by each nurses' station," Matt answered. "I'll be back to get you when you're done, Mr. McBride. I'll let them know that you're here." With that Matt was gone.

"How are you doing?" I asked, sitting in a chair facing Connor.

"Better now. For awhile there it almost felt like I was going to pull out all of my stitches." He looked into my eyes and saw the tears start to well up. Connor placed his left hand on the side of my face. "Don't worry, Sarah. I'm fine." He smiled.

"You're sure?" I asked, leaning my cheek against his palm.

"I'm positive," he reassured me.

We sat and talked for about twenty minutes until a nurse finally came out looking for Connor. Martha was a large Black nurse who called everyone sweetie. You couldn't help but smile when you were around her.

"Now Connor, sweetie," she said. "this won't hurt any at all. They're just gonna try out braces on your leg until they find one that fits you just right." She had started to push Connor into the room when she stopped and said, "You can come too sweetie. You don't have to wait out here."

I smiled and followed them inside.

A young man came over and shook Connor's hand. "Hello, Mr. McBride, I'm Ryan Taylor, and I'll be your therapist. Today, though we're going to get you fitted with a leg brace."

"Can I ask why?" I said. "Doctor Reynolds said Connor's leg wasn't broken."

"It wasn't, but the bullet lodged itself in the bone, and that weakened it. This brace isn't going to be permanent. It's only meant to help strengthen the leg while it heals."

"I was just wondering," I told him innocently.

"That's okay; you can't learn anything if you don't ask." Ryan smiled. He pushed Connor over beside a raised, padded platform. "We need to get you over here so your legs will be flat on the mat." Ryan looked around and asked another therapist to help with Connor. Gently the two men helped Connor over to the mat.

"Thanks," Ryan told the therapist.

The man gave him a nod and told him, "You're welcome."

"Okay, let's see what we've got." Ryan said as he examined and measured Connor's leg. When he finished, he excused himself.

Carefully I went and sat down beside Connor. He was leaning back with his hands behind him on the mat. I leaned over and whispered in his ear, "Cute legs."

Connor blushed a little bit and whispered back, "Thanks," as Ryan walked back in with a brace in his hands.

"All right," he said. "Let's see how it fits." The brace was made of aluminum and fastened across the front and back with Velcro. On each side of the knee was a hinge. Ryan ever so gently lifted Connor's leg and placed the brace under it. As he began to Velcro straps across the top of Connor's leg, he stopped. "Nope," he stated. "This isn't going to work."

He undid the straps and carefully took it out from under Connor's leg.

"What's the matter?" I asked.

"Don't worry, miss, the first brace usually doesn't fit. In Mr. McBride's case, the strap on this brace would have gone right across the top of his wound. That won't work. No problem, though, we'll just try another one." Ryan took the brace and left again.

Connor leaned toward me and whispered again. "So now that you've seen mine, when do I get to see your legs?"

I laughed. "I don't know if you're up to that yet. I don't want to get blamed for keeping you awake at night."

Connor closed his eyes and put his head back.

"Are you okay?" Ryan asked when he returned with another leg brace.

Connor opened his eyes and looked at me. I sat there smiling and gave him a wink. "I'm fine." Connor answered. "Just having a daydream."

Ryan looked from Connor to me and back again. "Gotcha." He said with a smile on his face. When the right brace was finally found, it was strapped on Connor's leg. "Now I know that it's still sore, but let's see if you can stand up for a second. Miss, if you'll help Mr. McBride from that side, I'll help on this side."

I stood up and held Connor's left arm and he slowly stood up. Ryan grabbed Connor's right arm.

"You've got all of your weight on your left side right now. Can you put any of it on the right leg?" Ryan asked him.

Connor clenched his teeth and tried to put some of his weight on his right leg. His leg began to buckle at the knee, and Ryan caught him.

"Okay. Okay. That's enough for today. Go ahead and sit back down." Ryan nodded to me, and together we helped

Connor back to the mat. "Don't worry. It'll take a little while, but you'll be using that leg in no time."

"What about that pulling sensation I had when the orderly had my right knee bent in the wheelchair?"

"The stretching exercises you will be doing will take care of that," Ryan stated. "With the kind of surgery that you had done on your leg, it may take a little longer to regain the full use of it."

Connor closed his eyes and took a deep breath. "How much longer?" He asked.

"You're in pretty good shape, so it may not take too long. It all depends on how much you want to walk and how much you're willing to push yourself, within limits, of course," Ryan stated. "Let me show you just a few things you can be doing in your room between sessions with me." He showed Connor how to flex and release his ankle. Ryan also had Connor do some small leg lifts from the seated position. "Now remember, only do five repetitions each time. You don't want to undo Doctor Reynolds's work in one day."

"Okay, I've got it, five repetitions. How many times a day do you want me to do them?"

"I think that if you wait four hours between each set that it should be okay. Stop immediately if it begins getting sore, though."

Connor was helped back into his wheelchair and given copies of the exercises that had been approved for Connor to do in his room.

"Do you have any questions?" the physical therapist asked.

Connor glanced at me, and I shook my head no. "How long will my sessions with you last and when do we get started?" Connor asked.

"You've got a good attitude Mr. McBride"

"Connor." Connor interrupted him.

"Connor," Ryan stated. "We'll start tomorrow afternoon at two o'clock. The sessions usually last a half hour, but if we need more time, I'll try to double the sessions."

McBride nodded.

"If you don't mind my asking, Connor. What's the big hurry?"

Connor smiled over at me. "I've got a date to go dancing," he replied.

We waited out in the hall for twelve minutes or so until Matt came to escort Connor back to his room.

"How'd everything go with your therapy today?" Matt asked starting the conversation.

"Just fine, Matt," Connor answered, smiling up at me.

Back in his hospital room, Matt helped Connor back into bed. He asked if there was anything else that Connor needed before he left.

"Not that I know of right now," he told the young man.

"Well, I'll probably see you tomorrow then. You two have a nice afternoon."

"You too, Matt," I said as he left the room.

"I thought he would never leave," Connor said pulling me over to him. "So I've got cute legs, huh?"

"Oh, yeah," I replied kissing him on the lips.

It was almost ten minutes after eleven when we'd returned to Connor's room. I made myself a mental note to remember to check in with the agency at noon.

The legal-aid attorney came into the federal building at almost eleven o'clock. Director Wilson was called downstairs to brief her. Ms. Karen Browning was a young, articulate woman with a pair of glasses perched on the end of her nose. She was wearing a brown two-piece outfit with her black hair pulled back in a ponytail. She thrust out her hand as Director Wilson approached her. "Director Wilson? Ms. Karen Browning from legal aid," she said with an iron grip on the director's hand. "Where's my client?" She proceeded to ask.

"If you will follow me, I'll take you to him." As Ms. Browning followed Henry down the hallway, he continued. "Mr. Chapman is being charged with the attempted murder of a federal agent and a civilian."

"Don't tell me any more. I'll find out from my client any further information that I need," she snapped.

Henry raised an eyebrow at the tone Ms. Browning had just used with him. Now he remembered why he had never gotten married. Director Wilson opened the door to the interrogation room and introduced Andrew to his attorney. "I'll be just down the hall if you need anything," he added.

"That won't be necessary Director Wilson. Thank you," she said as she put her briefcase down on the table.

While Henry went to inform Tom about Ms. Karen Browning, he got to thinking that maybe he had made a mistake in letting Chapman speak to a lawyer, at least to this one.

It was almost noon when Ms. Browning summoned Director Wilson downstairs to interrogation. Henry took his time responding to her. No one was going to order him around like that, he told himself as he waited for the elevator.

"Director Wilson," Ms. Browning said when he walked into the room, "my client and I have been waiting on you for fifteen minutes."

"I do have other responsibilities, you know," Henry stated firmly. "What do you want?"

"My client is ready to talk to you, with one provision."

"Which is...?" Henry asked looking over at Andrew Chapman.

"Mr. Chapman will give you the evidence of Mr. DeLuca's putting the hit out on the federal agent. In return we would like full immunity for his part in the matter."

"Anything else?" the director asked as he stood there with his arms crossed in front of him.

"That's the deal. Take it or leave it," Ms. Browning stated.

"I've got an important phone call coming through in a few minutes. Let me get back to you this afternoon," he said glancing at his watch.

"Fine." Ms. Browning glared. "I expect to hear from you shortly."

Henry Wilson opened the door for her as she got up to leave. Turning to her client she said, "Don't say a word to anyone while I'm gone. If you need to talk, you have my card."

Chapman replied, "Yes, ma'am." When she had left the room, Chapman was escorted back to his cell. Henry went back upstairs to await my phone call at noon.

Connor and I had been enjoying ourselves trying to put together the puzzle that I'd gotten him. The edge and the cow in the middle were easy, the rest of the puzzle would be pounded into place if that was what it took, a frustrated Connor had remarked.

"Okay, let's take a break before I end up picking the puzzle pieces up off from the floor," I suggested.

Connor glanced up at the clock on the wall. "It's good that we quit anyway Sarah. It's about time for you to check in with the agency."

I glanced at my watch and shook my head. "You're right. I'll make it quick so that we can get back to our rousing puzzle." I smiled.

Connor rolled his eyes and lay back on his pillow. "How about a game or two of cards instead?" Connor pleaded.

I laughed. "We'll see how the phone call goes first," I said with a wink.

Director Wilson's telephone was ringing when he ran into his office. "Wilson here," he said into the receiver.

"All is well, kiddo," I said back.

"I was hoping to give you good news, but it won't be today. There's a fly in the ointment named Ms. Karen Browning."

"I've heard about her. She's one tough lady."

"So I'm finding out. How is everything going?" Henry asked.

"It's coming along slowly. The doctor says it'll take four to five months to completely heal."

Director Wilson let out a whistle. "Give McBride my best and call back in another twenty-four."

"Yes, sir. Kiddo out," I stated before hanging up.

"No good news today, huh?" Connor remarked.

"Unfortunately. There's a legal aid attorney named Ms. Karen Browning that's going to give Director Wilson lots of trouble. I'm glad that I'm missing the fireworks."

"And you'd rather be hanging around a hospital instead?" Connor asked.

"Not any hospital, just this one." I smiled as I walked back to the side of his hospital bed. "Oh, and the director sends you his best."

"It's too late. I've already got his best," he said with a wink.

I leaned over and put my arms around his shoulders. "Do you know how much you mean to me, Mr. McBride?" I asked.

"I don't think any more than you mean to me, Sarah." He wrapped his arms around my waist and pulled me into him. "We are good for each other," Connor whispered in my ear.

I whispered back, "I know," and kissed him.

At around 1:30 agent Henson knocked on the director's door and was told to come in. When Tom had closed the door behind him he asked, "How are things with kiddo?"

Henry looked up from the paperwork on his desk. "Anthony's fine, and it looks like McBride is going to be down for five or six months."

"I'm glad for Sarah's sake that Connor didn't get hurt worse than he did," Tom commented.

Henry nodded.

"So what's with Ms. Browning? She's got a couple of people downstairs afraid to be around her."

"She sure has an awful big chip on her shoulder, that's for sure. She wants total immunity for proof that DeLuca ordered Anthony's hit and that he also had Frank Borgetta knock off Martin."

"Is that all?" Tom asked.

"She says it is, but I don't think she's finished yet." Henry turned his chair around facing the window. "Did you find anything else that might help us?"

Tom looked over at Henry and shook his head. "Sorry" he replied. "I know that somewhere out there someone saw something, but they're all afraid to talk."

Director Wilson put his hands on the windowsill and his forehead against the glass. "What do I do, Tom? The state prosecutor won't give in to a deal like Ms. Browning wants. Money-laundering should hold DeLuca for awhile, but then what?" He asked his friend.

Tom stared at the floor and said that he didn't know either.

There was a knock on the director's door so Tom stood up and answered it. In the doorway stood the medical examiner's assistant. In his hands were three plastic bags with

Frank Borgetta, Tommy McLean, and Fred Osteen's personal effects inside. Henson signed for the bags and walked over to the round conference table and set them down.

Director Wilson turned around and asked, "What is it, Tom?"

"Just the personal effects of the three men killed in the woods," Tom replied.

Henry came over to the table and sat down. "Have a seat, Tom. Let's see what's in here."

Henry looked through the contents of the bag marked Frank Borgetta. It contained a ring, watch, knife, wallet, GPS unit, sunglasses, loose change, half a pack of gum, a toothpick, keys, a clip with six rounds still in it, and a small container of pills. The ME's report said that the pills were aspirin. Inside Frank's wallet were all of the usual things, driver's license, money, credit cards, automobile insurance card, and a medical card saying that Borgetta had high blood pressure.

"Nothing here to help us," the director said as he began putting everything back into the bag.

Tom had grabbed Tommy McClain's bag and dumped it out on the table. McClain's bag contained a half pack of cigarettes, two peppermint candies, a Zippo lighter, a ring, an earring stud, gold bracelet, keys, a wallet, pocketknife, some loose change, a small rubber ball, and a handful of bullets for his revolver.

Everything was pushed aside as Henson examined the contents of McClain's wallet. Tommy's wallet contained a driver's license, automobile insurance card, some money, an auto club card, credit cards, a picture of his wife, son and himself, a tip chart, library card and a folded piece of paper with "I love you" written in crayon.

"Well," Tom Henson commented. "At least we know one of them could read."

Henry chuckled and picked up the last bag with Fred Osteen's belongings inside. He took a deep breath as he poured the contents onto the table. Director Wilson started sorting through the stuff in front of him. The bag had contained two pieces of bubblegum, a comb, a wallet, two rings, an earring, sunglasses, some loose change, a switch blade knife, matches, tweezers, and a set of keys. What a pack rat, Henry thought.

Inside Fred's wallet was about what the others had had in them; a driver's license, money, auto insurance card, video rental card, a photo of what looked like his parents, a condom, a paperclip, and an old movie theater ticket stub. As the director was putting everything back inside the wallet, he got looking at Fred's birth date. Fred was just twenty-six years old. Maybe he still lived with his parents, Henry thought.

"Tom," he said as he put everything back in the bag, "I'm going to get warrants to search these men's homes. Take Shapiro and Covington with you, and be careful. Check every nook and cranny for something we can use. By now DeLuca should be wondering where his men are, so wear your vests."

"Yes, sir," Tom replied.

"I should have the warrants ready for you in a half hour or so." Director Wilson lowered his voice. "Let's keep this on the QT in case there's another leak we don't know about, okay?"

"I'll pass that on to Covington and Shapiro too," Tom agreed. "We'll be ready to go whenever you give the word."

"Good man. Now let me get a few phone calls made."

Agent Henson picked up the plastic evidence bags and let Henry know that he would lock them up for him. The director nodded with the telephone receiver in his hand.

It was around 2:30 when I thought about Wade Hood.

Connor and I had been playing cards for about an hour after we had given up putting the puzzle together. As I laid down a three of hearts, I said to Connor, "I guess one of us should call Wade and update him on how you're doing."

Connor picked up my three and said, "Gin."

I put my cards down and shook my head. "No more Gin for me for a while." I told him "I've got to find a game that I can beat you at." I smiled.

"Okay, Sarah, we'll take a break, and I'll call Wade," Connor promised as he collected the playing cards.

"I'm going to go down to the cafeteria and get a soda. Want me to pick you up something?" I asked.

"A root beer would really hit the spot. Thanks."

"Call Wade," I told him as I headed out the door of his hospital room.

"Yes, ma'am." Connor laughed.

The telephone in the Hood house rang four times before a voice said, "Hood residence, Janet speaking."

"Hi, Jan." Connor said into the receiver. "How's your dad doing?"

"Not too good. The doctor says that it could be any day now, so I've said all of my goodbyes already," Janet told him. "How are you doing? Wade said something about you hurting your leg."

"Yeah, I had some knee surgery, and I'll be down for a little while, but I'm doing pretty good."

"I'm glad to hear that. Do you want to talk with Wade?" Janet asked.

"Not if he's still mowing the lawn," Connor replied.

"How'd you know that?"

Connor laughed. "I hear the lawnmower in the background, and I'm pretty sure Trooper hasn't learned that trick yet."

"Okay smartie, hang on, and I'll go get him."

Connor smiled to himself as he heard Janet yell at Wade and the lawnmower go silent. He would just about bet that Wade left Janet a sink full of dishes too.

"Hello?" Wade said into the phone as he wiped the sweat off from his face and neck.

"Janet's finally got you doing some work around there, huh?"

"Hey, Connor, How's the leg doing?" Wade asked.

Connor caught Wade up to date on the leg brace and therapy sessions.

"Sounds painful," Wade told him. "Janet and I were just talking about coming to see you tomorrow, if you're up to it."

"Sure thing, Wade. Sarah and I are starting to get sick of playing cards."

"Is that because you're doing all of the winning?" Wade laughed.

"Well..." Connor joined in the laughter. "Hey Wade, I need you to do me a big favor."

Connor and Wade had finished their conversation and hung up by the time I'd returned from the cafeteria. "Here's your root beer, Mr. McBride," I said handing it to him. I pulled a Baby Ruth out of my back pocket and held it up. "And if you need anything else, just let me know." I smiled.

"Why Bridget, you read my mind." Connor smiled back. "Come here, you."

I went and sat down beside Connor on the bed and handed him the candy bar. "So how is Wade's father-in-law doing?" I asked.

Connor tore open the candy wrapper and held it out to me. I politely told him no thank you. After taking a bite, Connor began. "Janet says that it could be any day now. She says that she's doing okay, but I've known Janet for a while now, and I think that she's holding it all inside."

"I hope that Wade's there when Janet gets that call then. She'll need him more than ever," I told him.

Connor looked at me and smiled. "How is it that you have so much compassion for someone you've never even met?"

I shrugged my shoulders. "It's just the way I was brought up, I guess. Besides, I like Wade and wouldn't wish that kind of pain on anybody."

Connor shook his head and looked at me. "I've never met anyone like you before."

"That's a good thing, right?"

He squeezed my hand and said, "That's a very good thing, Sarah."

I looked across at the handsome gentleman holding my hand. Oh, how this felt so right to me.

"Sarah," the masculine voice said, "where'd you go just now?"

"What?" I asked.

"I was just wondering where you went just now," Connor commented.

I blushed. "I was just thinking about a guy that I know. He has this way of making me feel..."

"Feel what?" Connor asked as he put his arm around my waist.

I leaned back into him and closed my eyes.

"Special," I whispered.

Connor put his other arm around me and whispered, "I think I know that guy." Ever so softly he placed his hand on my face and turned it toward his. A single tear rolled down my cheek and he gently wiped it away. "You are special to me, Sarah," he said, kissing me tenderly on the lips.

I put my hand up and softly touched the side of his face. Who was I kidding? I was in love with this man.

Director Wilson had three search warrants signed within thirty minutes. Henson, Covington, and Shapiro headed to Frank Borgetta's apartment first. The three agents thoroughly searched the apartment. They found Frank's blood pressure medicine in the bathroom medicine cabinet along with the little bit of marijuana in a plastic bag. They even searched the garbage cans inside the house. Being De Luca's number-one man, they didn't expect to find very much evidence lying around. And they weren't wrong.

Tommy McClain's place was second on the list to visit. Mrs. McClain came to the door when Henson knocked. She opened it just a crack and angrily asked, "What do you want?"

"Mrs. McClain? I'm Agent Henson, and we have a search warrant." Tom held up his badge so Mrs. McClain could see it.

She opened the door farther and asked to see the warrant.

Tom handed it to her and put his identification back in his jacket pocket. "As you can see, everything is in order, ma'am," Tom told her.

"Go ahead and search all you want. I haven't seen or heard from Tommy in a couple of days now. Do I need a lawyer or something?" she asked.

"That's up to you Mrs. McClain," Tom replied. "We're only here looking for evidence against your husband."

"What kind of evidence?"

"I'm sorry, but I'm not at liberty to discuss an ongoing case with you."

Mrs. McClain shrugged her shoulders and lit up a cigarette. "No skin off my nose," she stated. "Tommy and I have been heading toward a divorce anyway. This just proves that he's no good when the feds come into my house."

"Yes, ma'am," Tom said, not paying too much attention to Mrs. McClain's ranting. The three agents searched every space that could be searched. Nothing of any importance turned up. The warrant covered any and all buildings on their property, so the team went out to the garage. Every paint can was opened and stirred, every jar of nails and screws was dumped out, and the trash bins examined before they left.

As they walked down the driveway, Paul Shapiro spotted something that made him stop in his tracks. "Hey, Tom," Paul said. "What about the kids' treehouse?"

Agent Henson glanced over to where Paul was pointing. "Good eye, Paul. Go ahead and check it out." Tom Henson and Patricia Covington stood watching as Paul climbed the rope ladder to the treehouse. Behind a loose piece of board Paul found a little locked strongbox. Paul held it up and asked what Tom wanted him to do with it.

"I'll see if Mrs. McClain has a key to it," Henson replied.

Mrs. McClain didn't know anything about the box or where a key to it might be. "Go ahead and break it open, for all I care," she told them.

Agent Henson yelled up to the treehouse and told Paul Shapiro to drop the box out the window. Paul shrugged his shoulders and did his he was told. The box hit the ground with a loud bang, and the door popped open. Inside the box were baseball cards, a couple of Matchbox cars, some state quarters, an old map of Virginia, and a bus schedule.

"It looks like someone has been planning to run away," Pat commented.

Shapiro looked out the window and yelled down to them. "Nothing up here but some kid stuff, Tom."

"Go ahead and come on down then," Tom hollered back.

Paul carefully backed down the rope ladder. Reaching the ground he looked up and exclaimed, "I always wanted one of those when I was a kid."

Tom Henson chuckled to himself. He thought that almost every boy in the world felt that same way at one time or another.

Tom walked up on the front porch again and knocked.

Mrs. McClain opened the door and stared at the three agents. "So did you find what you were looking for?" she asked, blowing cigarette smoke in Tom's face.

"We're done with our search and will be on our way now. I just thought you'd like to know."

As the federal agents headed down the sidewalk, Mrs. McClain yelled, "When you find that bum of a husband of mine, tell him he can pick up his things from the trash."

The agents never looked back or said a word.

In the car on the way to Fred Osteen's place, Paul asked, "You think we should have told Mrs. McClain that her husband is dead?"

"If she doesn't know, then maybe DeLuca doesn't know either. That would be a good thing for us. DeLuca won't have time to destroy any evidence that might be floating around out here," Agent Henson answered.

Paul nodded in agreement.

When the sedan with government plates pulled up in front of Fred Osteen's address, the agents were surprised to find an older house with shutters and a white picket fence. Patricia Covington remarked that Fred must be living with his grandparents. A knock on the front door produced a woman who looked to be about eighty years old or so.

"Yes?" she asked. "May I help you?"

"Ma'am, does Fred Osteen live here?" Tom Henson asked politely.

"Why yes, he does. Won't you come in? Fred's not here right now, though." She said as she led them into the living room. "Oh, I'm sorry. My name is Hannah Black and my husband is James. He's in the backyard puttering in the garden. We're Fred's grandparents."

The three agents smiled and said hello to the woman.

"Mrs. Black," Tom Henson began, "I'm Agent Tom Henson and these are agents Patricia Covington and Paul Shapiro," he said with a nod in their direction.

Hannah Black nodded to them and smiled.

"Mrs. Black, we're federal agents, and we have a warrant to search your property and all of the structures," Tom told her.

Hannah looked from one to the other of them and said, "I don't understand. Is Fred in some kind of trouble?"

Tom wasn't quite sure what to say.

Agent Covington stepped forward and told Mrs. Black, "You see, Mrs. Black, we are investigating a crime and were told that Fred might have had something to do with it. I'm afraid we have to search your house just in case. Do you understand?"

Hannah Black nodded her head. "Fred's a good boy, but he doesn't always hang around with the right people."

"Yes, ma'am." Pat replied. She turned toward Tom and held out her hand for the search warrant. Tom handed it to her. "This is a search warrant, Mrs. Black. My fellow agents are going to look around your house while I explain to you what this says, okay?"

"Go ahead, dear," Hannah said to Pat Covington. "Should I get my husband first?"

"If you would like," she answered.

"Come outside with me, and you can tell both of us together."

While agent Covington sat at the picnic table in the backyard explaining the search warrant to the elderly couple, Henson and Shapiro searched the house.

"Try not to mess things up too bad, okay?" Tom told Paul Shapiro as they pulled on latex gloves.

"This feels like I'm snooping through my grandparents' house," Paul whispered.

"I know," Agent Henson agreed.

When they got to the room that looked like it could be Fred's, Tom and Paul read every scrap of paper and searched everywhere. In the closet Paul found a piece of paper that had a set of numbers on it. He placed it in an evidence bag and handed it to Tom. "Think it's anything?" he asked.

"I'm not sure," Tom answered. They somehow looked familiar. All of the sudden it hit him they were the coordinates to McBride's place. Tom hoped that more than Fred Osteen's and Borgetta's fingerprints were on the paper. They continued to carefully search the room. Agent Henson stood in the middle of the room and thought. Where would a young man hide something from his grandparents? How about under the mattress, Tom wondered. Turning the mattress over, Tom found quite a few things, an issue of Playboy from last year, a stash of marijuana, and a map of the forest in Virginia. When Tom unfolded the map, a piece of paper with the names McBride and Anthony on it fell out. Beneath our names was the message "No one comes back alive!" Oh how Tom hoped that it was written in DeLuca's handwriting. It was carefully put into an evidence bag along with the marijuana and Playboy magazine.

When the house and garage had been completely searched, Tom and Paul rejoined Pat and the Blacks in the backyard.

"Mr. Black, do you own a gun?" Tom asked innocently.

"I used to," the old gentleman said. "Fred told me that it wasn't safe to have around, so he offered to sell it for me."

"Do you know who bought it?"

"I'm not really sure that it was sold," James admitted. "I never saw any money from it if it was sold. That was about, what, Hannah? Four weeks ago?"

"No, I think it was more like six," she replied.

"Well anyway, I haven't seen it since," Mr. Black stated.

"What kind of weapon was it sir?" Agent Shapiro asked, taking notes as they talked.

"It was an old nine-millimeter that I bought some years back from a friend of mine who had been in the war. I've got the serial number written down somewhere, if you'd like it," James Black offered.

"If it's not too much trouble, sir," Tom replied.

"Hannah, do you remember where I put that paper from Kyle Pearson when I bought his gun?"

"I think it's in the roll-top desk in your den, honey."

"Come with me, young man, and I'll get it for you," James said getting up out of the lawn chair.

"Would you youngsters like some lemonade?" Hannah asked.

"That would be nice, thank you," Paul told her. Offering her his hand he helped her up from her lawn chair. "May I help?" he asked.

Hannah smiled and patted him on the arm. "You're such a nice young man."

Pat Covington smiled as she followed them into the kitchen.

It took a little while, but Mr. Black finally found a receipt for the nine-millimeter gun he had purchased thirty years earlier. They both headed to the kitchen and had some lemonade and a cookie or two before the agents left.

"Thank you for your cooperation," Tom told Mr. and Mrs. Black, shaking James's hand.

"You're welcome here anytime," they told the three agents.

The agents waved to the elderly couple as they backed out of the driveway. On the drive back to the agency, Pat Covington remarked, "I'm going to go visit my grandparents this Sunday and tell them how much I love them."

"I know what you mean, Pat. I have this urge to call mine and tell them the same thing," Paul stated.

Tom smiled and kept driving. He just silently hoped he would live to be that old and have his memory intact like Mr. and Mrs. Black.

It was almost 5:30 when they got back to the office. Tom told Covington and Shapiro that they could go on home, that he would brief the director. They told Tom to have a good evening as they checked out and headed their separate ways.

Upstairs, Director Wilson was waiting for Tom's report. He'd seen the three agents pull into the parking lot and then saw Covington and Shapiro leave in their own cars, so when Tom Henson knocked on the director's door, he was invited in.

"What'd you find Tom?" Henry asked.

"Nothing at Borgetta's or McClain's, but look what we found at the Black's residence," Tom replied.

"Black? I thought the third thug's name was Osteen," Wilson questioned.

"Oh, it is," Tom explained. "Fred lived with his grandparents, James and Hannah Black."

"Oh," was all Director Wilson could say.

The two men went over the contents of the evidence bags.

"Good work, Tom," Wilson told agent Henson. "I'll take these to the lab personally and make sure that they don't get lost." He gathered up the evidence bags and told Tom to go home and get some sleep.

"I'll be here bright and early in the morning, and this time the coffee and donuts are on me." Tom smiled at the director.

"You've got it, Tom. I'll see you in the morning."

Connor and I had turned on the television set and began channel surfing. He'd been right; there wasn't anything very good on TV.

"Wait a minute, Sarah," Connor exclaimed. "Back it up a channel or two. That's it, right there." The Nature Channel was airing a show on grizzly bears in the northwestern United States.

"See how beautiful the scenery is out there? Someday I'm going to take you camping out there in the woods."

"Okay, but remember what you said about bears? Well, I'll be the one outrunning you from the charging bear now." I laughed.

"Good point. Maybe we'll go someplace a little tamer." He smiled back.

We watched a program on grizzlies. It was fascinating to me how the cameraman got so close to the giant creatures.

Connor watched my expression as I watched the program. "So what do you think? Want to go with me on a shoot sometime?" he queried.

"If it's not going to be too distracting to you, I would love to go with you on a shoot," I answered back.

"Even to Australia?" he asked.

"Can't you take pictures of koalas or kangaroos or something else in Australia instead of crocodiles?"

Connor laughed. "I'm pretty sure that in biology class those weren't considered reptiles."

I punched him lightly on the arm. "I'll have to get back to you later about Australia. Maybe we could work our way up to crocodiles later on."

"Sure, we've got almost two months before I need to let them know if I'm going to do the shoot. And besides, maybe I won't be one hundred percent by then," Connor said.

"Oh, I've no doubt at all that you will be one hundred percent by then," I replied. "Speaking of being one hundred percent, it's been four hours since you did your leg exercises."

"I'll do them again if you do your shoulder exercises. When was the last time that you did them?" he asked me.

I glanced at the floor and sheepishly answered. "About three days ago."

"Okay, Sarah. Are you ready?" Connor asked.

"If you can do yours I can do mine. Let's go!"

I had forgotten how sore my shoulders could get. Running through the forest with the backpack on, the adrenaline must've blocked out any pain I had. My shoulder exercises reminded me that I wasn't one hundred percent either. I glanced over at Connor. His face showed the pain he was enduring too.

"Remind me again. Why are we doing this to ourselves?" I asked.

Connor paused and laughed. "So that we can get out of here and get on with the rest of our lives," he answered.

"Oh, that." I laughed.

For that thirty seconds both of us forgot about the pain. When Connor was done with his exercises he leaned forward and gently rubbed his leg.

I stopped and came over beside the bed. "Did you over-do it?"

"Just a little bit, I think," he replied.

"You've got to be more careful. I don't want you to pull out your stitches or have to have your leg operated on again."

"Don't worry, Sarah. I'll be okay. I promise."

I glared at him. "Don't you dare say scout's honor or I'm leaving," I warned.

"Who me?" Connor asked. He smiled and said that the subject would never be brought up again. Ever!

"Since you've never lied to me before, except with the stolen puzzle piece and then the game of gin . . . Wait a minute. Why should I believe you?" I asked suspiciously.

"Because I've got cute legs?" Connor laughed.

"That's good enough for me." I laughed along.

At six p.m. the nurse came in again and changed Connor's bandage. When she was finished she asked Connor if he needed anything for pain.

"Just a little something, okay?" he told her. "Half of the regular dose should be enough."

The nurse told him that she would be right back. After a couple of minutes she returned with half of his usual pain prescription, and a small glass of water. "Thanks," Connor told her after swallowing the medication.

"Have a nice evening," The nurse said as she headed out of his room.

"Hey, Sarah," Connor said. "Would you do something for me?"

"Do you need me to get the nurse?" I asked with concern.

"It's nothing like that. Would you mind getting me a washcloth and a towel please? I'd like to wash up a bit."

"Sure thing," I answered. I got the washcloth and

dampened it in warm water. "Want a little soap on it too?" I asked, sticking my head out of the bathroom.

"Just a touch," Connor answered.

When I came out of the bathroom Connor had stripped to the waist. I gave him the cloth and he began washing up and down his arms. "Would you wash my back for me please?" he asked. "Lying on the ground on my back all that time, I feel like I'm growing mold." He handed me the wash-cloth, and I scrubbed his back with it. He did have some dirt on his back that had probably come through his shirt. My putting ferns on top of him I'm sure hadn't help much either.

I handed the washcloth back to him when I had finished. "Know what?" I said to Connor. "I'll bring you in a pair of pajamas tomorrow. They'll be easier on you when you're doing your therapy."

"That would be great. I can't wait to get rid of my hos-pital gown, even if it does show off my legs." He winked at me, and I blushed.

Connor finished washing his chest and neck and hand-ed me the washcloth. I handed him the towel and took the washcloth into the bathroom to rinse it out. When I'd fin-ished rinsing it out, Connor tossed me his towel, and I hung it up for him. In the pile with the washcloths and towels was a clean hospital gown. I grabbed it and asked Connor if he wanted it.

"No thanks, Sarah" he replied. "I'll put the bathrobe on, and when you come in tomorrow, I'll have the pajamas to wear."

I put the hospital gown back then went and sat beside Connor's bed. "What else is on television?" I asked. "I don't know about you, but it's boring around this place."

"Well, thanks," Connor smiled.

"The company isn't what's boring; it's just sitting around the hospital. You could never be boring," I told him.

"I think that Wade would probably challenge you on that statement."

"Compared to Wade, the rest of the world is boring." I grinned.

Connor laughed and agreed with me. "He does make things interesting sometimes, all right."

"How long have you and Wade known each other?" I asked.

Connor leaned back and closed his eyes for a second. "Oh, man, it's gotta be going on fifteen years or so now. We met during my junior year of college. You should've seen Wade back then. He had shoulder-length hair and a goatee." Connor laughed and shook his head. "We've come a long way since then, Wade and I."

"What about Wade and Janet? How did they ever get together?"

"Oh, Janet was working at the campus library when they met. The two of them dated on and off for a while and then things cooled off when we began to talk about going into the military." Connor paused. "When we left for boot camp, Janet told Wade if he came back in one piece that she might wait for him. After five years in the Navy, he and Janet decided to take the plunge and get married. Jan wasn't too thrilled when Wade and I stayed in for another five years, though. I told you how it almost broke up their marriage. Wade and Janet have a more solid marriage now than anyone else I know."

"So what happened with you? Didn't you ever want to get married?" I asked.

"I dated a girl named Paula Newton for a couple of months in college. I thought we were getting pretty serious, but then I heard she'd been seeing someone else off campus. When I confronted her, she admitted it and dumped me. I put all of my efforts into school and the Navy after that." Connor explained. "What about you? Did you ever come close to the altar?"

"My story is almost like yours. I dated a boy named Jeremy Daniels about that same amount of time in college. I thought we were doing pretty good together until I saw Melissa Andrews and Jeremy driving across campus in his car. They were almost in each other's lap, so I figured I would devote myself to my studies and then the job." I stared down at the floor.

"Are we a couple of saps or what?" Connor smiled.

I looked over his smiling face and couldn't help but smile back. "Okay, let's change the subject. It's all in the past now, and someone else occupies my time these days."

"Anyone I know?" Connor asked.

"Oh, I think you know him very well," I replied as I stood up then sat on the edge of Connor's bed.

"Well, it's nice that you finally found someone. I think I met my match too," he commented.

"Anybody I would know?" I asked, smiling.

"Oh, I'm very sure you know her. You even remind me a little of her." Connor leaned forward and kissed me.

The two of us sat and channel surfed for a while and then said our good nights. I needed to go to sleep early so that I could hit the stores before coming back to the hospital tomorrow. I put my arms around Connor's shoulders and held him for some time. When we parted, I asked him if he had a preference in pajamas.

Connor replied, "Anything that won't embarrass you to be around me when I'm wearing them." He smiled.

"Mental note to self," I said aloud. "No pink, no bunnies or duckies or flowers. Anything else?" I winked.

I headed for the motel and a shower. I hated leaving the hospital, but a warm shower and a good night's sleep sounded wonderful.

Director Wilson was already in his office when Tom came in at 7:30 in the morning. Coffee and donuts in hand, Tom asked, "Did you even go home last night?"

Henry took a cup of coffee from Tom and replied, "For a couple of hours maybe. I just couldn't sleep at all, so I showered, dressed, and came back in."

"It'll be a good day when things around here get back to normal," Tom commented as he offered the donuts to Director Wilson.

The director took a peanut-covered donut and said, "Thanks." After a couple of bites and half of his cup of coffee, Henry was a little more awake. Around eight o'clock the phone on Director Wilson's desk rang. Hurriedly he answered it. On the other end was the lab with the report on Fred Osteen's affects. "We'll be right down," Henry said into the receiver. "Come on, Tom. Let's go in see if we've got some good news today."

Downstairs in the forensics lab, Debra Kane greeted the two men.

"Tell me you have something important for us," Henry told her.

Deborah replied, "I've got some good news and some bad. Let's start with the piece of paper with the numbers on it. You said you knew what the numbers were, so we checked it for fingerprints. The only ones we could get from the paperwork were Osteen's and Frank Borgetta's." Deborah continued. "The map had about a half dozen fingerprints on it. The computer matched all of them but two. We're still running them. The ones that we could identify belong to Borgetta, Osteen, Chapman, and Tommy McClain."

"The note that read, 'No one comes back alive' was very interesting." Debra Kane pulled out the evidence bag and pointed to a spot on the note. "See this little dot here?" Tom and the director strained to see it and then nodded. "Well, that is a small drop of blood from one James Martin."

"You don't say," Tom exclaimed as he looked at Henry.

"This piece of paper had three sets of fingerprints on it, that of Borgetta, Osteen, and" she paused. "Dominic DeLuca." Agent Kane stated, holding up the evidence bag.

Director Wilson and Tom Henson were speechless. Could it be that they had finally gotten something solid on the mob boss?

"The nine-millimeter that you got from the crime scene was Mr. Black's. We compared it against bullets retrieved from the trees around the cabin. Mr. DeLuca's fingerprints were also on the gun clip." She paused, letting the information sink in for Henson and Wilson.

"Is that everything?" Henry asked.

"Almost. I saved the best for last," Debra Kane told him. "Our handwriting expert compared the note with the handwriting of Borgetta and Osteen. Neither of them were left-handed though. Mr. DeLuca, however, is. We compared the note with the police report DeLuca signed a couple of years ago. The handwriting expert said that they were a perfect match and would testify to that."

"Anything else?" the director asked.

"That's everything until the other fingerprints can be identified."

"Thanks, Debra. Don't let anything happen to that evidence, okay? I'll have someone pick it up later. Call me if anyone comes to get them without my written permission."

"Yes, sir, I will." She said as she placed the evidence bags in the file cabinet. "Here's a copy of our reports," Debra said, handing Henry the manila file folder.

Back in Director Wilson's office the two men had a lot to do. The federal prosecutor was informed of the evidence and the judge signed an arrest warrant for Dominic DeLuca. Tom put together a team of federal agents to coordinate with the local authorities to bring DeLuca in.

The arrest went down smoothly and without incident. The judge denied bail because of the flight risk involved and the severity of the crimes DeLuca was charged with.

Henry sat in his chair and leaned back with his hands behind his head. He couldn't believe they finally had DeLuca. Agent Henson knocked on the door to Henry's office and then opened it.

"Come on in, Tom. What's up?"

"We've been getting calls from police departments all over the area offering their information and surveillance to us to help get a conviction on DeLuca."

"Put Covington and Shapiro on it while we're gone." Henry Wilson said standing up and grabbing his coat.

"Where are we going?" Tom asked.

"I think a trip to Roanoke is in order," he replied with a smile.

Tom smiled back. "Yes, sir! Just give me a minute to make the arrangements with Covington and Shapiro."

Henry nodded, and Tom left for his desk. Director Wilson made arrangements for a helicopter flight into Roanoke, Virginia. A rental car would be waiting at the airport for the two men. Henry looked at his watch. We should be there by noon, he told himself.

I hadn't been able to get to sleep last night, and at ten o'clock I called Connor's room. He'd been unable to sleep too, and we talked until it was almost two a.m. When I hung up, sleep came a little easier. It was about eight o'clock when I got up. I decided to do my shoulder exercises before I left. My first stop would be to Walmart. I was hoping to be able to find some pajamas there for Connor. If not, there was a department store a little farther down the street from there.

I stopped into the hotel restaurant and got myself a glass of orange juice, a glass of milk and an English muffin for breakfast. I hadn't had much of an appetite since Connor had gotten shot, and today was no exception.

At Walmart I found a pair of cotton pajamas that were blue with white pinstripes on them. I also took the time to look through the games. We had both been bored with the cards and the puzzle, so I thought I would look for something different. I was down the third aisle of toys when I saw it. It was a box with several games inside, checkers, pickup sticks, tiddly winks and jacks. That should keep us busy for a little while, I hoped.

By the time I reached the hospital it was already 9:15. I poked my head into Connor's room. He was lying back with his eyes closed and the television remote in his hand. When the door closed behind me, Connor glanced my way and smiled.

"How are you this morning, Sarah?" Connor asked.

"A little tired like you are, I see." I smiled. "Look at what I brought you. Orange pajamas," I exclaimed as I put my hand into the shopping bag.

"You didn't," he said hopefully.

"Of course not. You would look like a prisoner from a road gang in orange. A handsome prisoner, though," I said with a wink. Pulling the pajamas out of the bag I held them up. "What do you think?"

"You've got good taste. I probably would've chosen the same ones if I had been with you," Connor answered.

I unbuttoned the pajama top and gave it to Connor. It fit him great, not too tight or overly loose. I undid Connor's leg brace, and he pulled the pajama bottoms up. They went over the bandage on his leg, but it was really tight there. I took out the pocketknife that I taken from Connor's backpack in the woods, and ever so carefully I slit the pant leg up past Connor's knee.

Connor laid back and finished pulling the pajama bottoms the rest of the way up. When he finished, he threw the sheet off from across his lap. "It feels good to be wearing pants again," he said looking up at me. "Hey, I know that pocketknife."

I folded the blade and handed it to him. "The last time I used that knife was to put a slit in your blue jeans."

"I remember. You're pretty good in a crisis," Connor said turning the pocketknife over in his hand. He looked at me and handed the knife back. "Here, I want you to keep it. Consider it a memento of our adventure together."

"I'll make you a deal. I'll hang onto it until you're back on your feet again. Okay?"

"We'll see," he answered.

"Now let's see if we can get your brace back on," I told him. Between the two of us we finally got the brace fitted back on Connor's leg. "Does that feel right?" I asked.

"It feels fine, Sarah. Who needs a nurse when you're around?"

I smiled. "Oh, I picked up a little something else for you too," I said bending over and getting the box out of the plastic shopping bag.

Connor looked at the box and laughed. "So, Sarah, which of these games can you beat me at?"

"I don't know," I commented sitting down beside him. "I just figured that with more games I'd have a better chance of beating you."

Connor shook his head. "Okay. Let me get the rules straight. I can't let you win, and I can't win, so what's the point of playing again?"

"To spend quality time with me and keep from being bored silly?" I asked.

Connor smiled and put his arm around me. "What shall we play first?"

"Whatever you want," I told him.

"Right now I'm enjoying holding you like this." And with that he slipped his other arm around me and leaned back in the bed.

"You're going to get us into trouble, you know." I smiled.

"What will they do? Throw me out?"

"No, they'll probably throw me out," I replied.

"Then we'll go together," Connor said as he kissed me on the cheek. We sat there in each other's arms for quite a while talking. It was probably a quarter of ten when we began playing some of the games I'd brought.

Checkers was our first choice. We had to define the rules right from the start. I was brought up where you could jump your own man without being kinged first. Connor was brought up not being allowed to jump your own man until after it was kinged. The first game was played Connor's way and the second was played my way. It was more challenging my way.

Our second game choice was pickup sticks. We laughed and laughed when neither of us could move a single stick without moving another one.

"I guess we found a game that neither one of us is good at," Connor remarked.

"Well, I know you can beat me at jack's," I replied. "I could never get past twos."

"To tell you the truth, Sarah. I have never played jacks in my life. I don't even know how to play."

"Here. I'll show you," I told him.

Connor got the hang of jacks rather quickly. In no time he had cleared out all the jacks with one swipe of his hand.

"Are you sure you've never played jacks before, Connor?" I asked.

"Never" he promised.

"Then you're the luckiest person I've ever met. Okay, let's try the tiddlywinks. Do you know how to play that ?"

"You just flip the thing in the cup." He laughed. "Which is the tiddly, and which is the wink?"

"I know these games are a bit childish, but I'm having fun." I smiled.

Connor's table was too slick for us to flip the tiddlywinks pieces into the cup. We had a good laugh though when they went sliding across the table and off into the other person's lap. When we finally gave up trying to play that game, I put everything away. "We'll donate this to the children's ward," I told Connor.

He thought that it was a great idea, and said to add the puzzle along with it too.

Connor and I did our exercises after the nurse had been in to check his vital signs. We had just finished when Doctor Reynolds came by to examine Connor's leg.

After commenting on how well Connor's leg was healing, Doctor Reynolds asked if he had been doing any of the leg exercises that the therapist had suggested.

"Every chance I get, Doc." Connor replied.

"Any pain when you do them?" the doctor asked, looking up from his chart.

"Not when I do them, but when I'm done the leg's a little sore."

Doctor Reynolds asked Connor to show him where the pain would be. "That's from having the muscle reattached to your kneecap. That muscle just needs to be stretched out so your knee will work properly again. Have you tried putting any weight on the leg yet?"

"Yesterday," Connor told him.

"And how did it go?"

"I about fell on my face."

Doctor Reynolds nodded as he wrote in Connor's chart. "It may be a week or so until you can do that. Hang in there though, Mr. McBride. Your leg will heal with time and exercise. How have you been sleeping?"

"What's that?" Connor asked.

"I see," he said, making more notes in Connor's chart. "I take it that you haven't taken the new sleep medication that I prescribed for you." He glanced up from the chart and looked at Connor.

"I've been kind of leery about taking sleep meds with the pain meds."

"That's perfectly understandable, Mr. McBride. You had an allergic reaction that could have been potentially dangerous. You do need to get some sleep, though, so your body has time to help heal itself. Please reconsider taking the new prescription tonight, okay?"

"I will definitely think about it tonight, Doc," Connor told him.

"Very well then, I'll see you later this evening." Doctor Reynolds stated.

"Thanks for everything," I told Doctor Reynolds as I walked him to the door.

"You look like you could use some sleep yourself," He told me.

I smiled and nodded.

When Doctor Reynolds had left, I turned around to face Connor. "It's almost eleven o'clock. How about I go out and bring us back some real food?" I asked as I walked back to Connor's bedside.

Connor closed his eyes and said, "I can't even imagine real food anymore." He opened his eyes and smiled. "Know what I would love to have at this very moment, Sarah? A big Oreo cookie Blizzard from Dairy Queen."

"Sounds good to me. Is that all? No pizza, sandwich, or hamburger?"

"Nope."

"Okay, if that's what you want, you've got it," I said, grabbing my jacket from the back of the chair. I pulled it on and took a step toward the door.

"There is just one other thing," Connor added.

I turned around. "What's that?" I asked.

Connor curled his index figure in a come-here motion. When I got up beside his bed he pulled me into him. "A goodbye kiss," Connor answered.

"You've got it." I smiled, following it up with a long passionate kiss and embrace. When we finally parted I looked at him. "Now what was I doing?" I asked with a wink and a big smile on my face.

I got back from Dairy Queen at about 11:45. While the two of us enjoyed our Blizzards we watched the Nature Channel on television.

It was just almost one o'clock when the door to Connor's room opened. "Are you decent?" a familiar voice asked.

"Come on in, Wade," Connor replied. "Where's Janet?"

Wade came in, shook Connor's hand, and gave me a hug. "How are you guys holding up?" Wade asked.

"Janet?" Connor asked his friend.

"Oh, she had to stop by the gift shop. She'll be up in a minute. So, how are you guys holding up?" he asked again.

"Pretty good so far, Wade," Connor answered, turning off the television set.

Wade came over beside me. "And how about you, Sarah? Any relapses?"

I shook my head and smiled at him. "Nope. I guess you cured me."

"Okay, you two. What are you talking about?" Connor asked.

Just then the door to his room opened again. "Hi, Connor." The redhead smiled. "How are you feeling?"

Connor smiled back. "Hi, Janet. I'm doing a little better."

She walked over and gave Connor a kiss on the cheek. Handing him a teddy bear with crutches, she said, "I thought you could use some cheering up."

"Any word on your dad?" Connor asked.

Janet shook her head. "Not today."

Connor glanced over at me and said, "Janet Hood, this is a very good friend of mine, Sarah Anthony."

"It's nice to meet you," I told her with a smile.

"How long have you known Connor?" she asked.

"It's been about a month now," I replied glancing at Connor. She looked at the gun on my hip, and I explained to her that I was a federal agent.

Janet pulled a chair up on the other side of Connor's bed. "How did you two meet?" she questioned.

Before I could answer, Connor replied, "I pulled Sarah out of an avalanche slide a few weeks back. We've been friends ever since."

Just as Janet was about to question us further, the door to Connor's room opened again. There stood Director Wilson and Tom Henson. "I'm sorry. I didn't realize you had company," Henry said as the two men turned to go.

"Come on in Director Wilson," Connor stated. "It's okay."
The look on Wade's face was one of horror.

"Director Wilson, Tom Henson, this is Wade Hood's wife Janet. Janet, this is my boss and my partner," I said, standing up.

"It's nice to meet you," Henry told her. "Good seeing you again too, Wade." Turning his attention back to Connor, Henry asked, "How long are you going to have to be in the hospital, son?"

"I'll be in here for at least a week, but I won't be back to my usual routine for four or five months."

Tom whistled. "That's quite a while," he remarked.

"What brings you down here today?" I queried.

"We need to discuss a couple of things with you, Sarah," Tom answered.

"Let's step outside for a bit," I told them. I grabbed my jacket and gave Connor a quick kiss. "Be right back," I said with a wink.

"Sarah?" Wade said in a low voice as I passed him.

I touched his arm and gave him a nod letting him know that it would be all right.

The three of us walked outside and sat on one of the benches along the sidewalk. "What's happened?" I asked with concern in my voice. "Please don't tell me they know where we are."

Director Wilson smiled and replied, "Just the opposite Sarah. Dominic DeLuca was arrested this morning and is being remanded without bail until his trial."

"It's over, Sarah," Tom smiled at me.

"It's really over?" I asked, dumbfounded.

"The federal prosecutor says that he should get a conviction hands down on DeLuca for money laundering, attempted murder of a federal agent, the murder of James

Martin, and anything else he can add to the charges," Director Wilson told me.

"You wouldn't believe it, Sarah. We're getting information and tips about DeLuca from all over the place since his arrest," Tom added excitedly. "By the time DeLuca goes to trial who knows what all he'll be charged with."

I was silent. Henry put his hand on my arm. "Are you okay?"

I shook my head. "I'm just trying to let it all sink in," I replied.

"Well, listen. Stay with McBride for another week and then report to work a week from this Monday. Okay?"

I nodded. "That's fine. I'll be there a week from Monday, sir." I repeated.

Director Wilson and Tom stood up, and I followed suit. "I just thought we would come and give you the good news in person, Sarah," Henry stated.

I threw my arms around Director Wilson's shoulders and gave him a hug. "You couldn't have brought me any better news. Thank you both," I stated before hugging Tom.

"Take care, kiddo." Henry smiled.

"You have a safe trip back." I told them.

As they walked toward their rental car, Tom turned around and said in a loud voice, "Call your parents now."

I waved and promised that I would.

When the car was out of sight I sat back down on the bench. Closing my eyes and taking a deep breath, I said a quick prayer.

"Is everything okay?" Wade's voice asked startling me.

I looked up. "What are you doing out here?" I questioned.

"Connor was concerned and had me come and check on you. Bad news?" he asked, sitting down beside me.

"Great news, Wade." I smiled. "It's over. The mob boss

has been arrested and remanded without bail." I was so happy I hugged Wade. When I let him go, I asked if he and Janet were okay.

"Well, Jan wanted to know how I knew your boss, so Connor told her that we'd met the last time I was here visiting him. I'm just glad they didn't say anything else in front of her. Connor is probably trying to explain to Janet how he got hurt. Of course, she could be grilling him about you too."

"Wade, I think a rescue is in order."

"Yes, ma'am," he replied, jumping up from the bench. He offered me his hand and pulled me up. As we walked back inside the hospital, Wade asked, "Are you sure that you wouldn't like Connor tortured for just a little while longer to make up for the way he's always winning at cards?"

"Tempting as that is, if he ever found out, we'd both be in the doghouse." I laughed.

Connor was being grilled, all right. At first it was about how he had injured his leg. When he had satisfied Janet's questions about that subject, the inquiries came aimed at our relationship. We opened the door to Connor's room and went in. Everything got quiet when we did. I glanced at Wade and smiled. He had evidently been right about Janet's interrogation of Connor.

Wade broke the silence. "Hey, Jan. Can we please go and get something to eat now? I'm starved."

"Oh, Wade," Janet said, "we just got here."

"And Connor's not going anywhere," he interrupted. Wade looked over at his friend. "Would you mind if I took Janet out to eat?"

Connor smiled and shook his head no.

"See? That settles it. Let's go get something to eat, and then we'll come back. Okay?"

"I guess so," Janet replied. "It was nice meeting you, Sarah," Janet said as if she didn't expect me to be there when they got back.

"You too," I told her.

When Wade and Janet had left I took my coat off and placed it on the back of the chair again. I was just about to say something when Wade came bursting back into the room. He ran over to Connor and handed him something out of his pocket. "I almost forgot to give you this." Wade glanced at me and smiled. "See you two later," he said before hurrying back out of the room.

Once Wade had gone I asked Connor what that was all about.

"It was just a little matter that I had asked Wade to take care of for me." Connor patted the bed beside him. As I sat down Connor asked, "What did Henry and Tom want? Don't tell me you've got to go back to D.C. already."

I leaned forward and kissed him. "They came to tell me that the mob boss, Dominic DeLuca was arrested and is being held without bail." I kissed Connor again and this time he pulled me to him.

When we parted Connor asked if that meant I was going to have to go back to Washington now.

I shook my head. "Director Wilson said I didn't need to check back in until a week from Monday, so I'm all yours."

Connor smiled and replied, "I like the sound of that."

"Me too," I agreed with a hug around his neck.

Connor's arms encircled my waist. We sat and talked about the future. He wouldn't be able to walk all of the way back to the cabin for quite a while. Wade and Janet would let him stay with them for a while, but that would be too much of an imposition. Connor didn't want to lose the friendship he had with Wade over something like that.

"So you come to D.C. and stay with me," I told him.

Connor started to say something, but I stopped him with my index finger to his lips. "You can stay with me until you are well enough to go back to the cabin. Then I'll be out to see you every weekend."

Connor kissed my finger and then removed it from his lips. "I would like that, Sarah. Thank you."

I was somewhat surprised. "You know of course that you're going to have to work hard so that Doctor Reynolds will release you in time to go back with me."

"As long as you're here to help, I'll be able to do it," Connor stated.

We turned the television back on to the Nature Channel and watched a show on sea turtles. Halfway through the show Connor turned to me. "Sarah? What did Wade mean earlier when he asked if you had had any relapses?"

I squeezed his hand. "I kept blaming myself for your getting shot. I know, I know. Even though you had told me not to, I did. Wade gave me a talking to, and I haven't gone there since," I replied with my head down.

Connor put his hand under my chin and picked it up so that I was looking at him. "I'm glad Wade did that. Guilt is a powerful emotion and destructive, if you let it get away from you." He kissed me tenderly. "None of this was your fault, Sarah."

"I know," I said, staring into his handsome face.

It was about two o'clock when Wade and Janet came back to the hospital. "How was lunch?" Connor asked.

"There's this nice little Italian place just down the street that was good," Janet answered.

I glanced at Wade, and he winked. That was where we had gone a couple of days ago.

"How are your studies going, Janet?" I asked. "Connor says that you're going for your master's degree."

"I've got four more semesters to go," she replied. "If someone would let me do my homework without interrupting, it would go smoother."

We all looked at Wade.

"What?" he asked. "Can I help it if I'm crazy in love with my wife and want her attention?"

The four of us sat and talked and laughed until Matt came in to get Connor for therapy.

"You guys going to stick around for awhile?" Connor asked as Matt and Wade helped him into the wheelchair.

"Honey," Janet said to Wade, "Why don't you go to therapy with Connor while Sarah and I get better acquainted."

Connor and Wade exchanged glances. This couldn't be very good, they thought to themselves.

"Sure, Jan," Wade replied, giving her a kiss on the cheek. "You girls have fun."

When the men left, Janet turned toward me.

"Something you would like to know, Janet?" I asked.

"Tell me about yourself, Sarah," she replied.

I told her about my family and how I became a federal agent, and then she asked what I thought of Connor. That question was like a dead elephant in the room. You could walk all around it, but sooner or later you'd have to talk about it. "Connor is great. I wish I'd met him years ago," I said. Before Janet could say anything else, I added. "You don't have to worry about him, Janet. I have no intentions of ever hurting him."

"How'd you know I was going to say that?" she asked in surprise.

"Because if I had a good friend like Connor, I would only want the best for him too. He and Wade are two great guys," I told her.

"Wade? I thought you just met him a couple of days ago."

"Connor and I have talked a lot about our friends and family. He told me how he and Wade were in the SEALS together and how much they trust and respect one another. Doesn't that sound like two great guys to you?" I asked.

"You're a very observant, person aren't you, Sarah?"

"I like to think so. In my line of work it helps if I am."

Janet shook her head and said to me "There's something about you, Sarah that . . "

"That what?" I questioned.

"That makes me want to trust you. Connor needs someone like that in his life."

"Don't worry, Janet. I'm not anything like Paula Newton."

Janet's eyes opened wide. "Connor told you about Paula? You two have gotten close," she remarked.

I smiled.

In Connor's therapy session Wade helped him onto the exercise table. "What do you think those two are talking about?" Wade asked his friend.

Connor raised an eyebrow at Wade.

"Oh, yeah, you," he replied. "Think that Janet will run Sarah off?" Wade asked.

"Nope. I just hope your wife is still alive when we back up to the room," Connor kidded Wade.

Ryan told Connor that he could tell that he had been doing his exercises in his room. "Keep improving like this, and maybe by the end of the week we'll have you on crutches," Ryan commented. "You're not overdoing them, are you Connor?"

"No, sir," Connor promised. "I do my five repetitions every four hours, and that's it."

"Good," Ryan told him. "Let's get started on your therapy."

At the end of thirty minutes Ryan had Connor stop. "How are you holding up? Any pain?" he asked his patient.

"Just a little soreness," Connor replied, "but not too bad. Do we have time for another session?"

Ryan checked the schedule on the clipboard in the office. When he came back out he said that he didn't have any more openings today. "But I can put you down for a double session tomorrow, if you want."

Connor told him to go ahead and pencil him in.

"Okay," Ryan said as he wrote on the clipboard. "Well, you're all set for tomorrow. Matt should be here in a while to take you back up to your room."

"Thanks," he told the therapist.

Wade helped Ryan get Connor back into the wheelchair. As they waited in the hall for Matt, Wade asked, "Did you give it to Sarah yet?"

"Not yet," Connor replied. "I thought I would wait until after you and Janet leave. You know . . . set the mood a little."

"It's not like you're giving her an engagement ring, Connor," Wade stated.

"I know, but Sarah's special and I want to make this something that we'll always remember."

Wade clapped Connor on the shoulder. "How come you've never married is beyond me, Cap'n."

Matt finally came, and the three of them headed back upstairs to Connor's room.

Janet and I had had a good chat. I think she finally realized I wasn't a gold digger or some such thing, and that I really cared for Connor. I got the impression that she didn't approve of my job, though. Oh, well, I didn't need her approval anyways. When the door opened I asked how the therapy session went.

Connor replied, "Good," as Matt helped him back into the bed.

"Don't believe it, Sarah," Wade told me. "It went so well that Connor is going to double up on his sessions."

"The sooner I get out of here, the better," Connor remarked.

I joined him on the edge of his bed. "I'm all for that." I smiled.

Connor took my hand and smiled back.

"All right you two," Wade interrupted. "Who's up for some cards?" He turned toward his wife. "Want to play a couple of games, Jan?"

"Sure, why not? It'll be a nice break from all of my class work." She smiled.

I got out Connor's deck of cards and began shuffling them. "So, what are we going to play?" I asked.

"How about a game of Spades? Guys against the girls," Wade suggested.

"I only know how to play three-handed Spades," I remarked.

"That's okay, Sarah. I hate playing Spades," Janet stated. "How about a couple of hands of Gin instead?"

"Gin it is." I said, smiling.

Connor won the first game and Janet won the second. Wade lost the third to Connor by one card.

"I don't think I like this game anymore." Wade pouted. "How can you keep playing this game with Connor, Sarah? Doesn't he win all of the time?"

I glanced at Connor and then to Wade. "Oh, every great now and then I win. As long as I win on my own, and not because someone lets me," I said, looking at Connor. "I don't mind losing too much."

"He cheats so that you'll win?" Janet asked. She looked at her husband. "How come you don't do that for me?"

"Because you win most of the time," Wade exclaimed.

We all laughed. Wade turned the television to the TNN channel and we listened to the country music videos while we played a couple more hands of cards. It was getting on about 4:30 when we took a break from playing cards.

"I'm going to go down to the cafeteria for a soda," I announced. "Anybody want anything?"

"Another root beer would be nice," Connor said.

"Two root beers," I repeated. "How about you guys?" I asked Wade and Janet.

"Wade, why don't you go with her and bring me back a diet Pepsi, okay?"

"Sure thing, honey. Anything else you want?" he asked, getting to his feet.

"No, the soda will do me until supper," Janet replied.

I gave Connor a kiss and told him and Janet that we would be right back.

Wade kissed Janet on the forehead and said the same thing. While we went down to the cafeteria Janet talked with Connor.

"I really like Sarah, Connor," she began. "It sounds like the two of you were made for each other."

Connor smiled. "I've never met anyone like her before, Jan. It's almost like we can read each other's thoughts at times."

"It shows on your face," she told him. "I don't think that I've ever seen you this happy. How serious is it?"

Connor blushed slightly. "Well," he began "that's kind of personal, Janet."

Janet Hood apologized. "I'm sorry if I went too far. The two of you do look good together, though."

Connor grabbed Janet's hand and gave it a squeeze. "I like Sarah a lot, and we're going to take things slow and see what happens. Does that answer your question?"

Wades wife stood up and kissed Connor on the cheek. "I hope things work out for both of you."

Connor smiled and thanked her.

Wade and I talked on our way downstairs to the cafeteria. "I guess Jan didn't get everything out of Connor earlier." Wade smiled.

"Well, Janet gave me the impression that she approved of me," I told him.

"That's a good thing, Sarah. Jan is very critical of people, so if she approves of you, that's big."

"What would've happened if she didn't like me?" I queried.

Wade held open the cafeteria door for me. "If Janet didn't like you, she wouldn't hold back. She would come straight out and tell you so. You two are a lot alike in that respect."

"Actually, Wade," I said as I filled the cup with root beer, "I would never come right out and tell a person something like that. I would just try to avoid being around them as much as possible."

"You're a bigger person than Jan is, then." Wade chuckled.

After getting our drinks we headed back upstairs to Connor's room. "So, what do you think about Connor and me being together?" I asked as we waited for the elevator.

"I think it's great," Wade replied. "It's about time Connor found someone he can share things with."

As the elevator doors opened and we stepped inside, I asked, "Do you think I'm good for him?"

"Sarah, you don't need anyone's approval except Connor's. But yes, I think you're good for him."

"Thanks Wade," I smiled. "You know Connor better than anyone, so that really means a lot to me."

"Don't worry about Janet or anyone else. I think Connor wants you around for a while."

When we returned to Connor's hospital room I handed him his soda. He thanked me, and I told him he was welcome. We sat and talked some more as the TV played country music videos.

It was getting on about 5:30 when Janet glanced at her watch. "We really should be heading back, Wade. I've got a couple of days of schoolwork to make up before Monday."

As the Hoods stood up to leave, I joined them. When Janet finished getting her jacket on, she turned to me. "It was very nice meeting you, Sarah. I hope we'll see you again sometime."

"It was nice meeting you too, Janet," I answered. "I'll keep your dad in my prayers."

Janet came over and gave me a hug. "Bye, Sarah," She said. She gave Connor a hug next. "You take care of yourself, and if you need anything, let us know."

"I will," he promised. "You guys have a safe trip back."

Wade opened the hospital room door and told Connor and me to be good. That was followed by a smile and a wink. We laughed and said goodbye as the door began to close behind them. I went and sat down beside Connor's bed.

"So what'd you think?" Connor asked.

"About what?"

"Janet, of course," he replied.

"She seems really nice, and she's very protective of you."

"I hope she wasn't rude to you," Connor stated.

"Oh, no, it wasn't anything like that. Janet just wanted to make sure that I have your best interests at heart." I paused. "She didn't grill you about me?"

"Of course she did, but I told her that you were exactly what I needed."

"You did?" I smiled.

"Not in those exact words, but I let her know how I feel about you."

I gave Connor's hand a squeeze and smiled at him."What would you like to do now?"

"Hang on a minute," Connor replied. He buzzed out to the nurse's station.

"Do you need help, Mr. McBride?" the nurse asked over the speaker.

"Could I get a wheelchair and go down to the cafeteria for supper?" he asked.

"Let me look at your chart. Hang on a minute." A couple of minutes later the door to Connor's room opened. In came the nurse pushing a wheelchair. "Do you need any help?" she asked.

"No, I've got it, thanks." Connor told her.

"Don't be gone very long. I need to change your bandage at seven," the nurse warned Connor before heading back to the nurse's station.

I pushed the chair over beside the bed and locked the wheels. "How can I help?" I asked.

"Put your arm around my waist, and I'll try to hop over to the chair."

As I put my arm around him he hugged me. "I needed that." Connor smiled. He did a good job getting into the wheelchair without too much pain. Once in the chair, I put the right leg up for him.

"Ready?" I asked.

"As I'll ever be." He smiled.

While we waited for the elevator Connor asked if I knew where the solarium was. I had no idea and told him as much.

"Maybe after supper we'll try to find it. It should be nice and peaceful in there at night," he commented.

"That sounds nice," I said, pushing him into the elevator.

Downstairs in the cafeteria I picked up a tray and silverware for both of us. Connor wheeled himself ahead of me in line.

"What would you like, honey?" the cafeteria worker asked him. Connor asked for the chicken with rice and broccoli and a side of green beans. I opted for the turkey and gravy with mashed potatoes and a side of corn.

"Here you go, sweetie." she said as she handed me each of the plates. Farther down the line I grabbed us both a roll and for dessert pumpkin pie for me and cheesecake for Connor. We both chose a glass of lemonade to drink with our meal.

At a nearby table I unloaded the tray and sat down beside him. "This is a nice change." I smiled.

"I couldn't let you eat alone again, and I really needed to get out of that room. It was getting to me."

"I know only too well what you're going through. When you came to visit me it was tolerable. The nights were the worst, though. Nobody to talk to, nothing worth watching on TV, and when I did go to sleep, they would wake me up when they came to check on me."

"Stop. You're depressing me." Connor smiled.

"I'm sorry." I apologized.

"I'm kidding, Sarah. Besides, I really enjoyed our telephone conversation last night. You make my stay here more bearable," he said, touching my hand.

"Tonight you need to try the new sleep medication, though, Connor," I told him. "Like Doctor Reynolds said, you need sleep for your body to heal."

"What about you?" he asked before taking another bite of his chicken and rice.

"A nice, long, warm shower, and I'll probably be asleep in no time at all tonight," I replied.

Connor closed his eyes and put his fork down.

"Are you okay?" I asked.

He smiled. "I was just thinking about how a nice, long, warm shower would feel right about now."

I blushed when he looked over at me.

"I didn't mean it like that," he exclaimed. "It's just that a shower would feel better than just washing up with a wash-cloth. Heck, a soak in the tub sounds good too."

"I'm glad you got me out of the hospital before I started dreaming about showers and baths. Of course I still have to be careful when I wash up too."

We both laughed. What a strange dinner conversation we were having.

When we had finished our meal, Connor asked me if that had been the first complete meal that I had eaten since he'd been shot. I nodded.

"You've got to take care of yourself, Sarah," he told me.

"I know. Every time I thought about your getting shot, it twisted my stomach into knots. Now that I know for sure that you're going to be all right, maybe I'll be able to eat better."

"I hope so. Well, I guess we'd better head back upstairs and get my bandage changed. Then we'll go exploring," he said with a wink.

When the nurse had finished changing Connor's bandage we asked her where the solarium was. With the directions in hand we started out. Just as we had expected, the solarium was empty. I guess patients only went there for the warmth of the sunshine. I turned all but one row of ceiling lights off, and as we sat and stared up at the sky, I imagined the evening sky from the cabin. It was amazing how close the stars seemed to be there. We could only see the lights from a passing aircraft sitting here in the solarium, but it was peaceful.

"What are you thinking about?" I asked quietly.

"How peaceful and quiet it is in here," he answered.

I smiled at him. "I was just thinking the same thing, that and watching the evening sky filled with stars from your porch."

"Let's see if I can get on the couch without hurting myself too badly," Connor said, locking the wheels of the wheelchair. With my help, Connor made to the couch. He sat with his bad leg stretched out across the cushions.

"How are you doing?" I asked as I pushed his wheelchair off to the side.

"Just fine now, Sarah," he answered. "Look at that," he said pointing into the air.

I came over and sat down beside him. "What?" I asked, looking up.

"See that bright star in the sky? That's really the planet Jupiter."

"Cool! I didn't think that we would be able to see very much, what with all of the streetlights and stuff." We sat in silence for the next few minutes just staring into the heavens.

"Sarah," Connor whispered.

"Yes, Connor?"

He turned and faced me, those blue eyes of his sparkling. "You are very special to me, Sarah. I've never met anyone that I've had a connection with like I do with you." He paused.

"I feel the same way, Connor," I said sliding my hand into his.

"I have something to give you to show you how much you mean to me." Connor took my hand and placed an ID bracelet around my wrist. Engraved on it were a snowflake and the date that we had met.

"I love it," I exclaimed kissing him passionately.

"Belated happy birthday, Sarah," Connor said hugging me back.

"I love you," I whispered to him.

"I love you too, Sarah."

There. It was finally out in the open, and he felt the same way I did.

ACKNOWLEDGMENTS

I'd like to thank my husband for his encouragement and patience for my long hours at the computer keyboard. I love you!

Thanks to Mom, Ann Mitchell, and Doe Gaczewski for being the first to read my stories and their continued support for me to keep writing.

And a big Thank You to Jim and Doe Gaczewski, without whose Wi-Fi hot spot and encouragement this wouldn't have been possible. You are my favorite cheerleaders and have a special place in my heart.

To everyone else who supports me from just hearing the storyline, Thank you.

CPSIA information can be obtained
at www.ICGtesting.com
Printed in the USA
FSHW010925240521
81692FS